Beth and Wyatt are characters you root for from the very first page and the way Cass immerses you into her universe is unmatched! Do yourself a favor and read The Romance Rebuttal immediately.

— Evelyn Leigh

The Romance Rebuttal pulled me into a world of competitive debate and gentle love. Through the smallest of moments, I found myself falling in love with Beth and Wyatt's friendship turned relationship, and in the tiniest ways, they've turned into one of my favorite YA couples.

— Maya @mayasbooksncafe

The Romance Rebuttal

CASS ROUGEAU

THE ROMANCE REBUTTAL

CASS ROUGEAU

Book Cover Design by Cass Rougeau and Canva

Front Artwork by @agusballester (Fiverr)

Font Design by VP Creative Shop

Interior Formatting by Evelyn Leigh

Editing by Emerald Editing LLC

First edition 2025

__To high school Cass__, the debate nerd who met every challenge with an appetite to win. . . and who fought to survive through her darkest days.
Your love is a gift.

Playlist

Rett Madison | Flea Market
Debbii Dawson | Downer
The Neighbourhood | Reflections
Noah Kahan | Northern Attitude
Chaisyln | Make Believe
Boys Go to Jupiter | Lovers Always Lose
Zinadelphia | Love Language
Chappell Roan | California
We The Kings | Check Yes, Juliet
Benson Boone | Pretty Slowly
Paramore | crushcrushcrush
Stacey Ryan | Fall In Love Alone

Dear reader of *The Romance Rebuttal,*

Thank you for picking up this book and giving my YA debut a chance! I intend the story to be read as a coming-of-age, romantic comedy reminiscent of the beloved romance movies of the early aughts. However, the story discusses and addresses the following topics, which may be sensitive to readers:

- grief/the loss of a parent (anticipatory grief, talks of kidney disease/transplants)
- on-page references to anxiety (anxiety attacks, mentions of medication/therapy)
- implied homophobia (past)
- implied bullying (past)
- harassment

If any of these subjects are triggering for you, please proceed with caution. Your mental health matters and prioritizing it comes before any book. If you need to DNF for those reasons, feel free to do so. No hard feelings on my end. Take care, darlings, and please enjoy the read otherwise.

THE RULES OF PARLIMENTARY DEBATE

Parliamentary debate is one of four debate categories recognized by the California High School Speech Association. Unlike the other forms of debate, parliamentary debate topics change every single round, requiring debaters to keep up on current events and maintain an index of offline resources such as news articles, scholarly journals, and op-ed pieces.

A parliamentary round begins when the new resolution is announced and commences with 20 minutes of prep time. During this time, debaters can only communicate amongst their partnerships and use their allotted resources (sans internet access) until prep time ends. The following list describes the order of speakers and their mandated speaking time.

PRIME MINISTER CONSTRUCTIVE SPEECH –
7 MINS
LEADER OF THE OPPOSITION CONSTRUCTIVE
SPEECH – 8 MINS
MEMBER OF THE GOVERNMENT CONSTRUC-
TIVE SPEECH – 8 MINS
MEMBER OF THE OPPOSITION CONSTRUC-
TIVE SPEECH – 8 MINS
LEADER OF THE OPPOSITION REBUTTAL
SPEECH – 4 MINS
PRIME MINISTER REBUTTAL SPEECH – 4 MINS

GLOSSARY

CHSSA: Short for the California High School Speech Association; the governing body for all statewide and local tournaments, including the State Championship

Double-Entered: When a competitor attends a given tournament in both speech and debate; competitors who have double entered are often the busiest, running from round to round with less downtime than their counterparts.

Dramatic Interpretation: A 10-minute, memorized speech where a speaker must perform pieces of a dramatic fictional monologue or a longer work with a cohesive story for the audience. They are judged on their portrayal of the piece, the characters, and other theater-esque elements.

Elimination Rounds: The rounds at a tournament, post-preliminary, where losing the match merits an elimination, such as quarter-finals or semi-finals.

Flow/Flowing: A specific version of tracking arguments on both the affirmation side and the opposition side; debaters take their legal pad and turn it horizontal and have columns for each argument, carrying the arguments that succeeded across with arrows and crossing out those that get defeated or "dropped."

Invitational Tournament: Non-league tournaments at college campuses or more fancy high schools that span over several days. Invitationals are usually open to all competitors, with some minor exceptions.

League: One day tournaments at local high schools in a given regional zone of the state; in order to qualify for the State Tournament, a given student or debate pair must compete at the local level and win a spot at their respective qualifier around March.. League tournaments are only open to those in the league.

Lincoln-Douglas: A debate type where solo debaters argue two topics per season, depending on the month of the tournament; a mix between policy and public forum but solo and focusing on more mastery of a subject yet flexibility to switch subjects mid-season.

Original Advocacy: A 10-minute memorized platform speech where the speaker must address a contemporary societal or political issue, its root causes, and petition Congress with legislation they have written to solve for the problem and its harms. Speakers are judged on their presentation of the issue, efficacy of the solution, and other speaker metrics.

Paradigm: A publicly accessible cheat sheet regarding a judge's preferences or personal likes/dislikes in debate style; these are found on Tabroom and can provide a debater with an advantage heading into a round if studied and applied correctly.

Preliminary Rounds: The first three rounds at a given invitational whose scores often determine who moves onto further competition. Some tournaments only have three rounds, such as league tournaments, so this doesn't always apply.

Program Oral Interpretation: A 10-minute, mostly memorized speech where the speaker must compile a selection of literature, poems, songs, or other spoken media centered around a collective theme. This is one of the few events that allows props—speakers use a binder with pages to signify the transition between speeches. They also can do voices, body language shifts for characters, and other ways to show the changes in their piece.

Point of Information: Questions or a short statement during a speaker's speech by the opposition, often asking for clarification. They must be recognized by the speaker before asking, can't take more than 15 seconds, and will count against a speaker's remaining time.

Point of Order: A challenge used when a given team is suspected of introducing a new argument in rebuttal speeches, which is prohibited. This challenge can be rebutted by the accused but remains strictly for the rebuttal speeches at the end of the round.

Policy Debate: A type of debate where pair debaters argue a single topic for the year, focusing on topic mastery and rehearsed strategy.

Power Matching: The act of pairing teams with similar win-loss records against each other, intending to eliminate one of them from the playing field. This allegedly happens during elimination rounds, starting with quarter finals.

Public Forum Debate: A type of debate where pair debaters argue a new topic every month or so, focusing on breadth of knowledge and researching skills.

SCDL: Short for the Southern California Debate League; the original zone where Wyatt competed at his previous school.

Tabroom: A website for judges and competitors where information such as room assignments, ballot scores, and other pressing announcements about the tournament are posted for all registrants. This website is the holy grail of most modern tournaments unless the organizers prefer to go analog with a wall of paper.

WBFL: Short for Western Bay Forensics League; the home league of Beth and Wyatt as East Shores falls under the regional zoning.

For the full list of events + rules and regulations or answers to any questions, please refer to the CHSSA website at https:// chssa.org/ or feel free to send an email/DM my way!

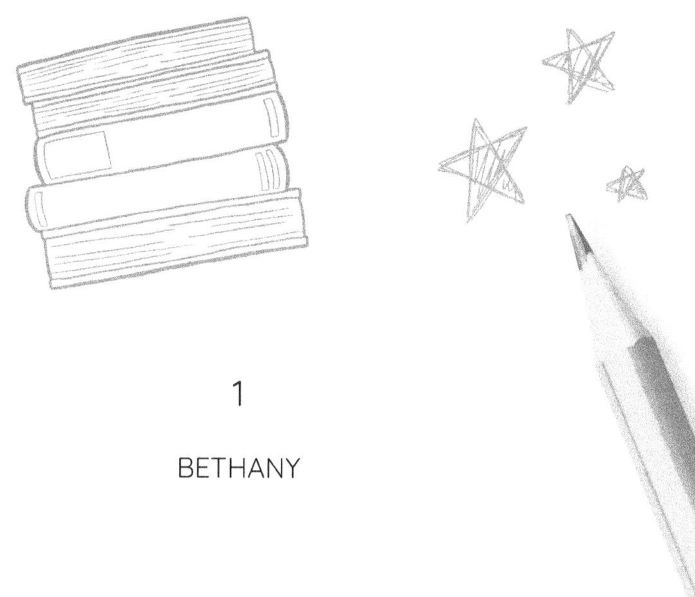

1

BETHANY

August, Week 3

IF THE LAST three years of high school have taught me anything, it should be that being a teenage girl feels like a never-ending example of Murphy's Law. Anything that *can* go wrong *will* go wrong–the living nightmare of a self-proclaimed Type-A personality. And, much to my dismay, my luck appears ready to fall in line with Murphy again because I'm running late. *Majorly.* The California sun overhead promises to boil me alive the second I roll up my car windows, so, as I cruise down the roads that I know better than any concept taught in my pre-calc class last year, a merciful breeze offers some reprieve from the harshness and heat.

I turn the last corner at full speed and pinball off the edge of the curb. "Oh god-!" I yelp when the wheels wobble from the impact of the bounce. Most days, I don't play bumper cars with the unsuspecting sidewalk, but the word of the day might be "unconventional" considering how out-of-alignment life feels. *Please tell me no one saw that.*

The screech of rubber on the hot road as I veer into East Shores High School's parking lot nearly sets a fire in my wake. But I can't slow down or risk something else breaking my momentum. *Not now.* I must've upset some force in the universe if hitting every red light between my house and school, is any indication. But that hardly matters once my front bumper crosses the cracked blue finish line.

What a great start to my tenure as the newly minted Captain of the East Shores' Speech Team. August and Andrea will never let me hear the end of it—I, Little Miss Punctual, arriving late to debate tryouts.

The minute I slide my Toyota Camry Solara into park, my shiny new sneakers hit the cracked asphalt of the student parking lot. The ignition of my car quiets, giving way to the distant cry of birds and shouts coming from inside the campus. With my tote bag and keys dangling from my fingers, I sprint toward the wide-open gate.

On weekends, East Shores' campus remains open for public use by students and the local public; if the popularity of the weekend farmer's market hosted here every Saturday is anything to go by, the grounds get plenty of use outside the student body and faculty. Although I might be a straight-A student, I like my weekends away from campus... no exceptions.

Well, maybe *limited* exceptions, like today.

As I brush past the gates, I spot several other students engaged in extracurricular activities during their pre-semester preparations. *The debate team isn't the only one thinking ahead.* The intermediate dance team gathers by the outdoor lunch tables, taking a five-minute break from practicing choreography. A gaggle of choir kids sit outside one of the classrooms, running vocal scales while someone inside plunks at the piano. In the green of the outdoor amphitheater, the school's JROTC drill team marches down the rows with their show rifles slung over their shoulders. Everyone appears immersed in their little microcosms of campus space...until I sprint past them like a madwoman.

I undoubtedly look like a mess, wide-eyed, chest heaving, and sporting a sloppy half-updo of dark hair held together by a miracle and a frayed scrunchie.

Is it my fault for napping after breakfast, aware I had academic commitments in the afternoon? *Probably.* Yet the half-hour I would've spent freshening up in my shared bathroom was better enjoyed in my bed, sleeping off the lingering jet lag. My mom and I spent the last two weeks in Massachusetts for college visits, including Wellesley College, my dream college since my freshman year.

My hope of moving across the country for college has grown insatiable since the plane touched the tarmac at LAX. Missing Massachusetts, I dream of trading LA's palm trees and constant sunshine for the leaves changing colors and more rainy days in a year than I could count. So long as my senior year proceeds at least halfway according to my plan, I will be in Massachusetts next fall, enjoying a taste of independence and academics that challenge me.

What once was a feverish sprint across campus slows to a standstill when I reach the Hawkins building.

East Shores High inherited its bones from a 1970s community college. Thankfully, the district bought and repurposed it, only keeping the layout from that era. Classes are divided across three main buildings on campus, grouped by their subjects. Hawkins is the keeper of the humanities, Rowe hosts all STEM classes, and any extracurricular activities are found at Fuller.

Similarly, all extracurricular clubs borrow rooms corresponding to their subject group, which means speech and debate meet in Hawkins. Although the sheer overlap of students in both theater and speech and debate should be studied for posterity, debate and theater are like cousins, but sharper-tongued and more inclined to business professional clothes on the debate side.

One sharp, forceful exhale escapes me when I bolt up the stairs to the second floor of Hawkins. I, not the most athletic person on a good day, heave the entire way up the stairs until reaching our usual room. An apology for almost being late settles on the tip of my tongue, but I tug on the door to no avail.

It's *locked.*

Pausing, almost incredulous, I try the door again. It doesn't budge. Heat crawls along the back of my neck while I stare at the locked door and the darkened windows. *Where's everyone? Did I mix up the days? It wouldn't be the first time..* Too focused on the door, I almost miss my tote bag buzzing. *My phone!*

My hand jams into the bag and quickly finds a few unread notifications, none as pressing as the one from Devon, my co-captain of the entire club.

DEV

hey! big turnout today, so we're in the auditorium, starting in 5

please don't tell me you ran to Hawkins

The auditorium is part of Fuller—the building closest to the cafeteria, but sitting all the way on the opposite side of campus. *Fan-freaking-tastic.* Instead of dignifying the texts with a response that my probably red cheeks and disheveled appearance will confirm once I get there, I jog to the auditorium, filing inside behind some stragglers I don't recognize.

On stage, Devon stands with the rest of the Council in a tight half-circle, illuminated in the warm, yellow glow of the stage lights. I step around the cluster of students hovering in the doorway, who search for an open seat between the other newcomers and the returning members.

People greet me when I pass, usually with a "Beth!" or a few cheeky "Ahoy Captain!" from the speech people. Warmth spreads through my chest, soft and fuzzy around the edges, welcoming in a way that feels worlds away from the heat of all the running. I wave once, then bounce up the short staircase tucked into the corner of the stage. Devon spots me first, face breaking into a toothy grin and hickory eyes gleaming. Devon Lowery embodies what I call the "All-American golden boy" archetype; he looms over most people at a casual 6'1" with a bulky, corn-fed frame and fluffy hair the same shade of wheat fields painted golden by the sunset. In another life, he might've found himself parading down the hallways in a varsity jacket instead of his favorite navy blue suit for competition days.

Devon's hands cross over his chest. "Our fearless leader has returned," he says, prompting the heads of the Council to swivel around and seek me out. "How was Massachusetts?"

"Better than I could've imagined. Mom took plenty of notes during every tour so we could cross-reference during application season." Playful groans erupt from the others at my response.

"Meanwhile, August and I joked about setting up a dart board and picking colleges to apply to at random," Andrea Torres, the Parliamentary Representative, crinkles her nose, sending a ripple in the freckles dusting over her face. Her twin brother, another teammate, performs the same move. "I wouldn't be surprised if Beth has a whiteboard with a color-coded ranking of every college in the state."

Rohan and Fallon, the Policy and Lincoln-Douglas representatives, laugh at that. Andrea preens, tossing her silky, chestnut hair over her shoulder, glowing with a momentary flash of pride.

I huff, prepared to retort in my defense, but the click of heels on the nearby stairs stops me. Ms. Goodwin, the team's faculty advisor, glides up the stairs in her signature stiletto pumps—the same ones she wears every day while teaching AP World History and US History. Rumor has it she was a ballerina before becoming a teacher, and no matter what, she always looks absolutely impeccable. It's awe-inspiring, truly.

The rest of the Council and I shuffle to the side, leaving center stage for Ms. Goodwin's welcome speech. I end up next to Devon, who nudges his hip against mine when I start mouthing along with Ms. Goodwin.

Ever since I joined, she's kicked things off the same way. First, she mentions the packet she sent out outlining the distinctions between parliamentary*, public forum*, policy*, and Lincoln-Douglas* debates, and the nearly fifteen recognized speech events that East High competes in. Then, she gauges demographics through several questions to split the crowd for auditions. *Who wants to compete in debate? How about speech? Does anyone want to try both? Who here has previous experience?*

Results tend to vary. Speech tryouts may not draw as many people as debate, but we make it work. And honestly, the speech team's trophy count compared to the rest of the squad pretty much speaks for itself—tight crew, big wins. And *none* of those trophies are cakewalks to win, despite what some disgruntled debaters might sneer.

While Ms. Goodwin crawls through her welcome speech, my thoughts wander away from the auditorium, where the lingering aroma of baby powder and recently dried hardwood floor cleaner grounds everything in a stilted quiet. *I grabbed my binder for performance today, right? I should've grabbed some water before I left the house. Yeah, I'm a hot mess.*

No one will know, as long as I pull myself together before leaving this stage.

"–And for any questions, you can contact Devon and Bethany, our co-captains." The mention of my name, coupled with Devon's hand clamping down on my shoulder, yanks a wave and a smile from me. A smattering of polite applause ripples through the room—mostly from prospective students and a few returners—before the scramble begins, and everyone makes a beeline for the double doors leading to the courtyard outside.

The Council splits in opposite directions, all heading toward our respective coaches. However, I'm the only one with two different coaches. That happens when you're one of the few kids doing speech *and* debate on your team. But, before I can assess where I'm needed first, Coach Kruger falls into step beside me.

Coach K grew up with debate in her blood—raised by two college professors who taught it, and then competing in parliamentary debates throughout high school and college herself. Her trademark tough-love approach isn't exactly gentle, but it's been key to my success. She took a timid girl, petrified of public speaking, and shaped her into a woman whose favorite weapon is her words. So, I know her well... and from the weight of her hawkish, icy blue eyes on my profile, I know we're about to have a conversation I've avoided all summer.

"Beth," Coach K sighs, catching the door. Her manicured, pearl-pink nails gleam in the August sunshine while she holds the door for other students. "Have you decided who will replace Nadia as your partner this year?"

Something bittersweet twines around my tongue, its thorns sinking into my impending denial. Nadia Rossi had been my best friend and debate partner since freshman year, taking me under her wing years ago. She's starting at Stanford University this year. With her departure, Coach K tasked me with finding a new partner by the time tryouts rolled around—*today*.

But no one would come close to the type of magic Nadia and I created. We could finish each other's sentences, and the running gag among our teammates was that she and I secretly developed a telepathic link. Birds of a feather, you know?

Although I know the disapproval waits on the other side of my admission, I shake my head. "No."

"Beth, we talked about this." Coach K's brow furrows downward.

"We did. But none of our returning members and I work better than their existing partnerships. We have four great teams with natural chemistry and years of experience debating with one another. Besides, no one deserves to spend their senior year babysitting a stammering, inexperienced freshman," I retort. If Coach K has a problem with the edge in my voice, she doesn't show it.

"While I understand your concerns, my hands are tied," Coach K strides past the students interested in any other form of debate. Their heads swivel when her voice rises louder than their conversations. Heat stings along the column of my neck under the scrutiny of these strangers. *I earned this scolding.* "You're my best debater, but if you don't secure a partner before the start of the semester, I'll have to drop you to speech-only."

My body jerks to a stop, sticking firm to the courtyard's tiles like someone's chewed-up gum sticks to the bottom of my sneakers. The thought of me not debating at tournaments awakens an almost violent fit of nausea, which lodges itself in my throat. No noise, no clever reply fights past the swelling, burning lump on the verge of breaking through my skin.

Coach K continues without me, even trailing behind her. She gestures to the small gaggle of students, who likely gather for parliamentary tryouts. She spares me no sympathetic glance or a final word to close out our conversation. *Her word is law.* "Alright, I will group you into pairs based on your experience level for today's tryouts."

Her instructions are lost behind the muted buzzing in my ears, even when I spin on my heel and sprint across the courtyard toward the speech kids. The new additions mingle with the returning students, all under Coach Estrada's supervision.

The concern jumps through the thick lenses of Coach E's sparkly blue cat-eye glasses before I reach her side. The stack of scripts resting in her arms offers me something to do to shake off the jittering, sickening ache burrowing into my chest. Without a word, Coach E passes me the scripts, and I, in turn, hand them out to the prospective students. There are five new kids, which seems in line with expectations.

Only when the speech students trickle into one of the nearby classrooms for tryouts does Coach E nudge me. Her sympathetic smile tells me all I need to know—she heard *everything.* Considering my luck today, I'm sure everyone has probably heard.

"Keep your chin up, Beth," Coach E leans in and whispers, doing her best to spare me any more embarrassment. I look into the face of the woman whose heartfelt, nurturing guidance shaped my speech work into something close to art. The smile lines around her eyes and the soft gray streaks in her feathered curls do what her words don't—ease the sting to my pride. "I know you're smart enough to find a solution without my help. However, we can develop a second speech event for you before the semester begins. Speech is always a safe place to land."

"You're the best, Coach E," I murmur, able to push the jitters further down. *Imagine if I had forgotten to take my medication this morning.* She says nothing more, and slips an arm around my shoulder and guides me toward our tryout room. It's a small comfort, but a comfort all the same.

XOXO

"-TELL ME, how does it feel with my teeth in your heart?" A snarl launches off my tongue at the enraptured audience sitting around me. Their wide eyes and parted lips cling to each word, sheathed in honeyed malice, punching all the air out of the room. But, when my fingers snap the black binder closed, life rushes back through the vents and the cracked open door.

Thunderous applause rocks the walls of the borrowed classroom as I take my first bow of the season. Any lingering reservations about the controversial slant of my performance piece this year sink into the distance while the room's reactions wind down into silence.

Coach E rises from her chair, "It goes without saying that Bethany knows how to tell a story. She's our star example of Program Oral Interpretation*. Let's give her one last round of applause before she heads out. As the semester progresses, we'll get an encore performance of *Monstrous: A Parable of Feminine Rage.*"

She waves me off to gather my things, her smile steady and unwavering. Our eyes meet, and with a subtle wink, she sends a quiet jolt of encouragement my way. We both know I can't dodge the parli team forever, and I'm not ready to give up on debate that easily.

I hoist my tote bag onto my shoulder, nodding to the rest of the room, "It's great to see all of you! See you when the semester starts for another award-winning season!"

My back knocks against the door when I push out of the

classroom. Spinning on my heel, I head to the opposite end of the hallway, where one door remains cracked open with a sign taped over the door. Someone wrote *PARLIMENTARY* in sloppy lettering in the unmistakable neon green of a highlighter.

I duck inside and slide into the nearest desk without so much as a squeak of my sneakers or the groan of the plastic desk chairs. The rest of the team sits scattered around the room, including the newcomers, all watching the two new freshmen stammering through their arguments at the podium. Seemingly unaware of my return, Coach K scribbles rapid-fire commentary onto her signature yellow legal pad—that *wretched* thing.

Coach K's usual rule is that latecomers wait outside—no interruptions, no breaking a speaker's focus. But judging by the scene inside, the freshmen are off to the expected, awkward start. My sudden entrance won't throw off much of anything.

Movement in my peripheral–a flash of mint blue, the same shade as last year's team crew neck–turns my attention to Andrea and August, her twin brother and debate partner, scooting a few chairs up.

"Hey," August whispers. He and Andrea are unmistakable as twins; they have the same tawny, sun-kissed skin down to the freckles dotting their cheeks like constellations and are almost the same height. His slate-colored eyes, however, appear a shade darker than his sister's, now giving me a concerned once-over. "You doing okay?"

"I'm fine." He knows—probably everyone does, since Coach K just tore into me about being partnerless. "So, what'd I miss?"

August's mouth twitches, "Besides the usual freshman trainwreck auditions, not much." He glances at Andrea, who's got a glitter gel pen clenched between her teeth while her hand rifles around her backpack.

"Coach K wants you to debate one of the new kids. He's a senior with prior experience," Andrea whispers once she drops the pen onto the desk. "Says his name is Wyatt Keene. I tried to look him up in Tabroom, but he never mentioned the name of his last school." Her thumb points over her shoulder toward a lone figure.

My gaze follows until I see him. This Wyatt guy sits on the opposite side of the room. His legs stretch out from beneath the tiny desk he has squeezed into—not bulky like an athlete, but definitely on the taller side. Dark, textured fringe—either black or deep brown—falls just above his eyes, which from a distance look like warm, woodsy brown. A strong, squared jaw and a long-bridged nose with a slight downturn sharpen his otherwise diamond-shaped face.

If he notices my attention, he doesn't glance away from his notepad while he writes in a diligent, quiet study. *So, he's got some experience?*

"-Ah, Bethany, you're back," Coach K's voice shatters my cursory examination of the new kid, flinging me back into the moment with all the force of a rubber band snapping in half. "You up for a debate?"

Although that sounds like an invitation, it's never a question with Coach K. I nod, reaching into my bag for my phone and notepad. "Of course."

"Great. Today's topic: after the President's State of the Union speech addressed the dangers of putting other nations first, the United States ought to turn to isolationist policies." Several gasps echo around the room as all eyes fall between me and the new guy. "Bethany, you're the affirmative. Wyatt, you're the opposition. I'll give you ten minutes."

No sooner than she stops speaking, two pens click open, and silence falls over the room. *Alright, Wyatt Keene...game on.*

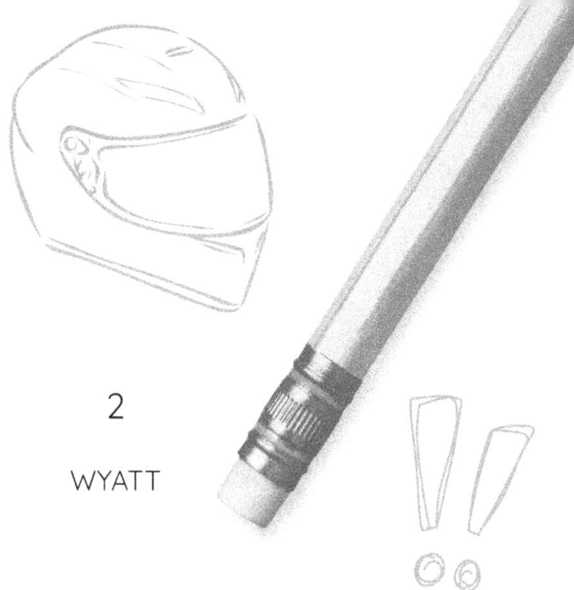

2

WYATT

August, Week 3

LOADED like a fist winding back to throw a punch, the silence might take me out if Bethany Edwards doesn't get to me first.

As soon as Coach Kruger hits the 'start' on her stopwatch, I'm racing to write down every argument bubbling in my head. She might've given me the more defensible position, but any experienced debater can turn an unsavory, unpopular position into a winning argument with the right finesse. Even within seconds of being in the same room, Bethany radiates the calm, assured confidence of a seasoned debater from every pore.

Somewhere between fetching my second pen and calculating potential rebuttals, my eyes land on Beth right in time to see the visible shift in her demeanor. It starts with the twitch of her jaw, muscles pulling taught to cast a shadow over her face. Then, her shoulders hunch forward before she starts writing, feverish and laser-focused. Her pen flies across the page so fast I'm shocked she doesn't tear the ballpoint tip through the flimsy college-ruled paper.

Beside her, the Torres twins exchange looks on the border-line of bewilderment. Or, maybe, that shock becomes amusement when their glances jump toward me, flicking their eyes in a pointed once-over that screams *"good luck, dude"* in flashing, neon font. Either I'm about to escape from this debate by the skin of my teeth, or I'm walking straight into a trap. I'd ask them to convince me that Bethany isn't about to maul me verbally, but I doubt they're miracle workers.

I put my head down and focus on the paper in front of me. *Isolationist policies often result in economic decline or depression, an inevitable outcome. America is committed to supporting our neighbors and allies. Globalism has become a 'boogeyman' for the sake of political interests and talking points.*

Anyone with a grasp of basic economics would likely reach the same conclusions. Yet as my pen drags across the page, smearing ink into the margins and crowding the lines, nothing I write seems to carry the certainty I need to believe I can win. Oh. That's *bad.*

The pen fumbles out of my hand, clattering to the floor. Several heads snap toward me—everyone *except* Bethany's—until I pick up the pen and wave them off. The weight of their attention dwindles fast, considering the ticking clock hanging over my head.

Don't take this too seriously. A small voice rattles above the noise, sounding oddly similar to my dad, when my gaze drifts toward Bethany again. *It's only a tryout. No school would deny a qualified candidate to their program.*

But it is *that* serious. Today marks more than a simple tryout. This is the first impression people at this school will have of me, one on my terms. In any other circumstance, I wouldn't care what people thought of me or whether they had some preconceived idea of who I am. I don't have room to be choosy here.

I need more than common sense to win the argument. I need to drown myself in statistics—so many that I either make myself sick or push Bethany to the brink of strangling me out of sheer annoyance. Granted, the unresolved tension from her blow-up with Coach Kruger in the quad still hangs in the air, ready to ignite like a powder keg at the slightest spark.

My hand shoots into the air while my eyes remain on my messy, harried notes. "Are we allowed to consult outside sources? I have a running index of news and scholarly articles I prep for competition use."

"Yes. As long as you can access it without the internet," When Coach Kruger's head tilts back, the glint in her eyes catches the light. She doesn't hide her piqued curiosity, nor do the Torres twins or any freshmen who tried out already. "It's my philosophy that our team trains under the same conditions as competition."

"It's why we have more trophies than other debate styles." August snorts. He dodges the quiet scowl from Coach Kruger, opting to sneak a high-five from his sister underneath the desk.

"Yeah, all my reserves are offline. I add to them daily." Even when I speak, Beth remains "in the zone." She jots down notes with effortless focus, pausing only to swap pen colors or glance at her phone. *Fair is fair*—if I'm cleared to use sources, Bethany deserves the same.

Coach Kruger waves her hand—a silent agreement to proceed—before she resumes her note-taking on her yellow legal pad. Her permission lessens the tight, squeezing grip looping around my chest, albeit temporarily. But it's long enough for me to grab some articles and relevant op-eds written the day after the State of the Union. You know, for a clearer picture of how poorly the speech was received by the general public.

Time slips through my occupied hands, unnoticed. I almost

forget the world beyond my desk exists—until a sharp phone alarm slices through the heavy silence. *It's time.* No one moves but Bethany and me when Coach Kruger clears her throat and says, "Stop writing. Take your places." She silences the alarm, and the soft screech of chairs and shuffle of footsteps mark our slow walk to the front of the room.

I should've practiced more during the summer. *I've become rusty.*

Then again, I assumed that switching schools might bring an end to my debate career—a reality I only recently bypassed when my mom left the brochure from East Shores' open house on my bed.

As I reach for the desk closest to me, Bethany moves to take the chair. Our hands briefly touch when she grips the back of the chair. I stiffen, "Oh, sorry-"

"You're all good. We usually sit government on the left side, but it doesn't matter for practice," Bethany replies, words audibly overlapping with mine. She releases the chair from her grip and brushes her hair away from her forehead. Up close, I get a clearer view of her face after the glimpses from a distance.

Shiny black hair in a sleek ponytail swishes with every tilt, turn, and movement of her head. All of it is piled high and out of her heart-shaped face, showcasing her narrow, upturned nose and a pair of medium-full pink lips drawn into a resting frown. Her eyes, however, yank me in from the sheer green of them; they hum in the mossy verdant of the forest reflected in a lake's still water. I've seen plenty of green lakes during camping trips with my dad in the foothills of the Sierras.

Grabbing the desk chair, I stumble head-first out of my stupor. But instead of sitting down, I push the chair out and gesture to it. "Take it. I won't deny tradition."

Beth says nothing. She rakes her eyes over me and steps forward to take the chair as intended. Her head dips into a gracious bow, wordless yet so perfectly understood. She settles into her seat while I walk the extra few steps to my desk.

I toss my notebook and a fresh sheet for flowing onto the desk with a soft *thud,* just barely quieter than the unceremonious *thunk* of my landing in the plastic chair. The rustle of paper and pens fills the otherwise silent room. Bethany and I sit taller underneath the metaphorical spotlight, surrounded by our peers and Coach Kruger, who sets up her notepad.

"Alright, you two...I expect a good effort on both ends," Coach Kruger clears her throat and clicks her pen, ready to track every argument or mistake either of us makes. "You each will get five minutes per constructive speech and two for the rebuttal. Start whenever you're ready, Beth."

Beside me, Beth's shoulders bristle. Her hands sift through her materials—notes, flow paper, and several pens. She grabs the edges of the desk as she rises out of her chair, knees bumping against the wood.

Shifting in my seat to face her, I meet her eyes for a split second. The pen in my clammy hand idles, waiting for her opening to thunder out as boldly as she entered the room. But then, Beth angles her body towards mine and leans forward, hand outstretched.

"Good luck," she remarks, voice level yet softer than before. Only when I grasp her hand in a firm shake does a smirk tug the corners of her lips upward. "I won't take it easy on you."

"Wouldn't dream of it." The words jump off my lips before my brain catches up and stops me from sounding like an idiot. However, Beth's eyes *sparkle,* and her lips wobble as if fighting back a smile.

We drop the handshake as Beth returns her attention to Coach Kruger and the rest of the room. This time, her whole body shifts. She gains another inch or two in height from a simple squaring of her shoulders. The amusement she once wore fades into a neutral expression, except for the intense glint circling her dilated pupils. *She looks ready to lunge across the desks.*

"Good afternoon. My name is Bethany Edwards, and I will be the government's first speaker. After the President's speech at the State of the Union, we, the government, contend that the United States should turn to isolationist policies. For this debate, 'ought' suggests a value debate. Therefore, you must award the victory to the side that establishes its argument as the superior view."

Beth's gaze locks on Coach Kruger when she speaks. However, the weight of her words crushes me underneath a brand-new tidal wave of adrenaline. Beth doesn't need to look my way for me to feel every ounce of pressure bearing down on me.

Well, I've never been the type to roll over and take defeat.

XOXO

BETH IS GOOD. And oh, does she know it.

I don't know what I expected when walking onto campus earlier this afternoon. However, nothing would've prepared me for Bethany Edwards or the sweet, cutting smile she levels at me before she shreds one of my arguments into tatters. She wields points of information* with precision, reducing my three years of parliamentary debate experience to nothing.

Every time she lifts her hand, wearing that saccharine grin —like a fox slipping through barbed wire toward a flock of unsuspecting chickens—I know what's coming. A perfectly timed, devastating blow. Even with under a minute left in my speech, Beth's hand flies up at the slightest pause or stutter in my voice.

"America's history and position on the world stage are incompatible with isolationist policies. Our reliance on other nations for pivotal resources and our current economic model cannot be self-sufficient. Furthermore, if we move according to the president's proposed timeline, such a drastic change would make the United States economy crash harder than the 1929 stock market crash. We're already struggling as a country. The last thing families who are barely able to keep their lights on or food on the table should worry about is a recession or economic depression."

No sooner than those words cross my lips, Beth's hand rockets into the air. *Case in point.* "Point of information?"

"I'll accept it," Although I have every right to say no with so little time left in my constructive speech, running from Beth's questions won't make me look better. It's best to face the questions head-on rather than skirt around them. "Go ahead."

"Couldn't you say this is all speculation? Did the President say this would be an immediate change?" Beth asks. Her head cocks to the side, and innocence softens her voice. However, I know a classic intellectual trap when I'm in one.

"He did indeed. His full statement is, and I quote, 'We will immediately retract our financing of failing nations and global initiatives for which we receive no benefit. We are done being bled dry by others. Let them fend for themselves.' Although political speech often falls into hyperbole, his past political record implies his willingness to follow through on ridiculous decisions due to his impulsivity," I reply.

From how little Beth's face shifts, my response doesn't shake her. Or, maybe her unflappable demeanor is a side effect of defending a position she doesn't believe in, playing devil's advocate. It occasionally happens when a debater takes a stance far from their own viewpoint, aiming for an impassioned but ultimately contrived argument to win. Beth's subtle jaw clenching when affirming the president's comments on economic policy tells me she feels on the wrong side of the debate. "May I have a follow-up?" Beth asks.

"Not at this time," Beth's eyes brighten despite my swift denial. *Ah, so she approves.* "Judge, I ask you not to let blind nationalism win over the benefit of the ordinary American citizen. One politician's pride should never be more important than the government serving the people. Our entire system was influenced by Rousseau's social contract, where citizens are what endow power onto the government; therefore, it's in their best interest that the government must abide by."

The beeping of Coach Kruger's phone signals the end of my second constructive speech.* While she resets the timer for my final speech—the rebuttal—Beth and I return to our respective flows to edit what's been dropped and what can be referenced in the final speeches. We're in the final five minutes of the debate now, and I'm on equal footing with Beth.

She's held her ground, but so have I.

Glancing toward her, my shoulders tense when finding her eyes already on me. Beth flicks her gaze in a once-over but drops her attention back to her paper. She mumbles something under her breath. Pink stains her face as she chews on the end of her pen.

"Coach Kruger, are you ready?" Asking that, my voice attracts everyone's attention. Several necks snap away from Beth, and everyone focuses on me again. The entire debate had been a spectacle for our audience, whose heads bounced between Beth and me like an intense tennis match. "For closing speeches?"

"Yes, give me one second. . ." As she fiddles with her phone, the door swings open. Ms. Goodwin steps into the room, not a speck on her jumpsuit or a single strand of bleach blonde hair out of place.

"Sorry to interrupt," Ms. Goodwin's voice wavers when she realizes Beth and I sit at the front of the room. "Coach Kruger, can I speak to you for a second? It won't take too long."

"Sure. Beth and Wyatt, we'll resume with rebuttals when I get back. You all can talk amongst yourselves." Coach Kruger slinks out of her desk to follow Ms. Goodwin outside. Before the door shuts, the room explodes with various overlapping conversations from the spectators.

I, however, see a chance to test the waters. With a tiny scoot of my desk, I lean toward Beth, "You're the scariest opponent I've ever faced."

Beth faces me, a grin stretching across her face to the showing of two perfect dimples in her cheeks. "Thank you! I'm taking that as a compliment...you're not so bad yourself, Keene," she props her elbows on the desk and rests her chin in her hands. "How many years have you been at this?"

"I assume the same as you—three years. I started during my freshman year at Viewbrook Academy. The academy is in the SCDL*. East Shores is in the WBFL*, so different leagues."

"Ah, that's why we haven't encountered one another. I'd recognize you if we'd debated before."

"A woman of many talents," I wiggle my eyebrows at Beth, who snorts and rolls her eyes. But I see the smile she bites back when sinking her teeth into her lower lip. "So, speech and debate? How long have you done both?"

"Since freshman year." Beth scoots her desk a little closer when the volume of the conversations surrounding us rises. A few of her colored pens roll toward the edge of the desk, but my hand snaps out to catch them.

I nod, "So that's why you're the team's captain." Beth has mastered not one but *two* highly competitive events. I read enough of the brochure to count the achievements of the debate team, including which events are the highest scorers. Speech reigns supreme, with parliamentary debate right beneath it. Since Beth competes in both, I assume she has something to do with it.

"That, and a few good performances at local tournaments and invitationals. My last partner and I made it to the quarterfinals of the state tournament. I've got one last year to beat that," Beth says, confidence turning her demeanor bright and airy. Although her voice wavers over the mention of her old partner. *Note to self: leave that topic alone.*

"And you need a partner for that, right? I heard what Coach Kruger said earlier—" I clear my throat. Ripping off the bandage will hurt less than dragging the question out. "—I could be your partner for the season. We're both seniors and experienced in debate. You won't need to hold my hand or drag me along like intellectual dead weight."

Beth pauses, her brow furrowing. I can practically see the gears in her head whirring faster. As silence lapses over our hushed conversation, flecks of brown become more noticeable among the mossy green of her eyes, swirling and shifting with a kaleidoscopic shine. Beth's lips part a few times as if ready to speak, only to snap closed when she re-evaluates.

Eventually, she hums, "You're right. I need a partner, and you want to be on the team. You can hold your own...and probably keep up with me. I'm in."

A laugh rumbles deep from within my chest, the kind that aches in my insides. "Nice to meet you, partner."

Beth bridges the gap between the desks, snatching my hand with hers, "I hope you're ready for me to put you to work. I take debate *very* seriously." A pang of electricity buzzes through our connected fingers when Beth's sharp grin reaches me.

Before I can respond, the door swings open again when Coach Kruger hustles back inside. She claps, "Alright, let's wrap up these speeches. If you're not a returning member of the team or Wyatt Keene, you may leave. If you made the team, you will be emailed in the next few days." Her words spur an exodus of the nervous or bored freshmen from the room, leaving me with Beth and the other veterans.

Coach Kruger waits for the room to clear, turning toward Beth and me. "We'll pick up with Wyatt's leader of the opposition speech. Anything to address before we get started?"

"No, ma'am-"

"Yeah, *one* thing," Beth interjects from her chair. "I hope you accept Wyatt onto the team because he's my new partner."

The response from the room is immediate. Andrea gasps—August elbows her in the ribs to shut up. The rest of the debaters break into a small flurry of whispers. However, Coach Krueger's eyebrows shoot into her hairline. Her steely gaze assesses us for a brief moment. Then, she nods.

"Look at you, Beth. Killing two birds with one stone. Yes, I planned to admit Wyatt to the team already, but you've given me some extra incentive. Is that everything you wanted to share?" Coach Kruger grabs her phone to reset her alarm before she reaches for her legal pad.

"That's everything from me." Beth laces her hands on the desk, borderline preening at the compliment. Coach Kruger nods. She faces me like she hadn't snuffed out the anxious urgency creeping up behind me.

"Two minutes for you, Wyatt. Whenever you're ready." She remarks. Her finger hovers just above the stopwatch, waiting. She's watching me, along with Beth. And now, so is the rest of the room watching, too. Everyone within these four walls has their eyes on me, waiting for my next word.

So, I stand taller and exhale. Then, I speak.

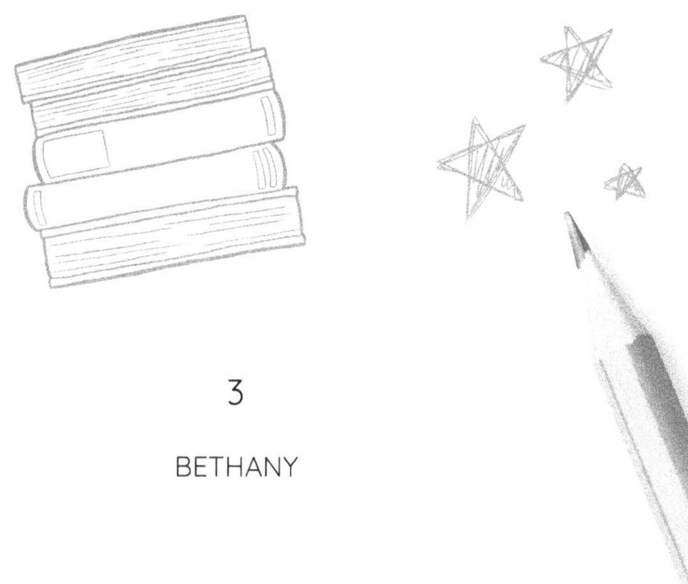

3

BETHANY

August, Week 4

THE FINAL WEEK of summer passes, slipping through my fingers in a combination of Southern California sunshine and the relative peace of my coastal hometown, Searidge Hills. Life moves slower than molasses around "the Hill," which works for some people.

I am *not* one of those people.

Despite the hungering urge to suddenly grow wings and fly away from this coastline for the other side of the country, a slight excitement buzzes under my skin when I step into my first class of the semester: AP Government and Microeconomics. The clock ticks with the ever-present countdown to graduation, to the start of the rest of my life. It got me out of bed this morning when I wanted another hour of sleep.

Conversations crash into one another with all the grace of fender benders, while fellow seniors crowd themselves into their seats by cliques. Friends latch onto one another and cram into clusters. The jocks—and a stoner or two—vie for spots in the back rows while the academically inclined overachievers stake out the front. That's where I aim—a seat just off-center, nearest to the board.

I squeeze through narrow aisles between columns of desks. My bag jostles and nearly slides off my shoulder while I shift the angle of my waddle through the controlled chaos. I bend around the people around me, who move with little regard for their surroundings.

Some people's attention perks up as I pass, eliciting a few greetings in my wake.

"Hey, Beth!"

"Hey, how are you?"

"Love your outfit, Beth!" I wave to the friendly greetings with a quiet "morning!" before cramming my hands into the back pockets of my dark blue, mid-rise jeans. Since my mom scheduled my senior portraits for this afternoon, I picked something comfortable yet cute to wear. I fished a pear-green sweater out from the depths of my closet—it hadn't seen daylight in a while, but the color still made me smile. It even matched the fresh scrunchie I used to tie my hair into a sleek, swishing ponytail.

Miraculously, my hair cooperated this morning, feeling almost like a good omen.

I nearly dump half of my backpack's contents onto the desk for a binder, several glitter pens, and the assigned textbooks. Most of the seniors on the debate team opted for the semester split for government and economics, taught by the football coach, Mr. Maynard. The course fits graduation requirements, and students can earn their shiny A by not falling asleep in class when he goes on a tirade about gas prices and ineffective state government.

Me? I'd prefer the full year to digest the subject material for a dual AP course. But hey, what do I know? I have an unbroken streak of 5s for every AP exam I've sat for.

"Good morning, everyone," The gruff voice of Mr. Alvarez —the instructor for the dual AP course—booms from the doorway. He skirts the outer edge of students with his cross-body knapsack and the egg white-colored Henley he wears. He has a rich, terracotta complexion, with old acne scars carving indents into his cheeks. Shaggy brown hair halos around his forehead in a terrible boy band cut that makes him appear younger than he is. "You have a few more minutes to socialize before we get started. I have a no-gossiping-during-class policy."

The students around me seem to take his comment as seriously as a heart attack, from how the chatter quells, silence ricocheting off every wall. I, however, sink further into my seat. *Thank goodness... people who talk during class sit at the top of my list of pet peeves.*

I like Mr. Alvarez's teaching style, which is best defined by a low tolerance for petty classroom annoyances. I took his AP Seminar course last year and was thoroughly impressed with his classroom management. So, when I saw him on the offerings for AP Government and Economics, I ranked his class as my first choice. Having gotten an A in AP Seminar didn't hurt either.

I sift through my pens until I find a sparkly green one as rich as emeralds and a deep blue to match the American flag. Hesitation almost crosses my mind when my fingers skim over a red instead of a blue. *The last thing my notes need to look like is an explosion of Christmas and glitter gel.* After adding a regular ballpoint to my little stack, I shuffle the remaining pens into my bag.

Everything else falls into perfect sync. I jot down the heading on the first page of my binder, date and all. Each movement flows deliberately in its slowness and ends with a tiny flourish. All those hours practicing calligraphy back in middle school have proven helpful.

As I write, my thoughts drift back to the last week of summer vacation. After a season of laid-back beach days, everything shifted. The Massachusetts trip and debate tryouts kickstarted a new wave of busyness in my life. I hardly had a quiet moment between wrapping up final summer assignments and catching up with fellow debaters at Fresh & Frosted, the favorite cold-treats spot near East Shores.

However, the chaos culminated with an influx of new Instagram followers. I recognized some as students I had met on college tours. Others were the new freshmen who made the speech and debate team. A particular new follower was none other than Wyatt.

Of course, I followed him back. I might've snooped a bit, curious about what I might find.

I'll admit Wyatt's bare-bones social media presence surprised me. Beyond a simple bio and a clear profile photo, his account has ten posts and follows under 200 other pages. His follower count is even smaller. I've never been one to be attached to social media, but Wyatt's the king of being chronically offline.

I'm *still* impressed, honestly.

So lost in my thoughts, it takes a loud 'thump' to the open seat on my left to knock me out of my daze. I almost smack several pens off the desk from how my hand spasms, startled by the suddenness and the movement in my peripheral.

A subtle glimpse of a teal and silvery gray letterman jacket raises an alarm in my brain. *Please don't be who I think it is.*

Like clockwork, the universe decides to laugh in my face as the faceless letterman leans over the arm of his desk. The weight of his presence grinds against any notion of "personal space" when he inches closer to me. "It's Beth, right?"

"You ask that like we haven't been attending the same schools since junior high, Travis," I glare ahead at the shiny whiteboard. I refuse to give Travis Maynard more attention than his massive head can endure.

Beside me, Travis guffaws, like I told a funny joke. Nothing about the sound feels genuine. It's rather hollow and grating against every last nerve in my body. He runs his hand through his crew cut, flattening the cropped, buckwheat-colored hair. With broad shoulders, a perfectly square jaw, and the star power of the high school quarterback, Travis Maynard plays the "golden boy" act all too well.

He might be some girl's dream, but he remains a nightmare to me. Before Nadia graduated to bigger and better things at Stanford, Travis and his little gaggle of mouth-breathing, vapid cronies had given her a hard time since her sophomore year. The school district refused to intervene after endless microaggressions directed toward Nadia's sexuality because the ringleader is the football coach's son and a borderline decent athlete.

So, like a good best friend, I hate the twerp on principle. But even beyond that little detail of Travis's *shining* personality —his inability to use an indoor voice, the cheap department store cologne that barely covers his rancid body odor, and an ego I'm honestly surprised he doesn't trip over daily—there's very little to like for anyone with standards.

Instead of responding to his outburst, I crinkle my brow before returning to my notes. I'll reciprocate the way he would regard me whenever he came to bother Nadia—the silent treatment. But, much to my chagrin, Travis doesn't move from his spot beside me or catch a clue that I'm not interested in speaking to him.

No, the gag-worthy heaps of cologne and fresh morning sweat continue to invade my personal space, punctuated by heavy breaths and heavier staring burning against the side of my face. The assault of his presence frays at what little patience I reserve for 8 AM to 10 AM, so much so that I snap, "Can I help you?"

"Woah! No need to be hostile." Travis remarks while his hands raise in surrender. Yet, the lightness of his tone—the audacity to play dumb—severs me from any tether to a calm, collected response.

"No, there's a need to be hostile. For the last three years, you actively ignored me whenever you harassed Nadia. Why would I willingly speak to you?"

"Is that why you didn't add me back on Instagram?"

Among the influx of new followers, Travis had requested to follow me. I rejected his request, only for him to ask at least four more times afterward. *Man, he genuinely can't take 'no' for an answer.*

"As if it wasn't painfully clear already, I think you're an absolute—" Whatever scathing, unfiltered insult readies itself to fling out of my throat skids to a halt at the sudden quiet in the room around us. I glance up to find Mr. Alvarez hovering between Travis and I's desks—his eyes darting between us.

I'm so in trouble. I shift further into my desk. But Mr. Alvarez's attention focuses on Travis, and the curl of his lip douses whatever jitters start to whisper within my chest.

"Mr. Maynard, I'd advise you not to get too comfortable. I assign seating by last names," says Mr. Alvarez, who stands there with arms across his chest. "I would like to start class." His implication isn't lost on me or Travis, who scrambles from the desk and stumbles when trying to scoop up his backpack.

I reach for my bag to clear my desk. However, Mr. Alvarez puts his hand on the desk, shaking his head, "You'll stay here, Ms. Edwards. Your last name puts you front and center. I hope you're fine with that."

"Yes, sir," I reply.

As Mr. Alvarez passes to rearrange the rest of the class to their proper seating arrangements, I imagine a downright devious smile cracks through whatever scowl's left behind. I manage to quiet a snicker, especially when I see Mr. Alvarez point Travis to a desk toward the back of the room and several rows down. Far from me, where he should be.

Maybe this year can still get off to a good start.

XOXO

REGRET GURGLES in the pit of my gut as I stare at the textbooks scattered across my cluttered desk...*Why did I sign up for three APs in my senior year?* Suddenly, my mom's description of me as a "glutton for punishment" feels a little too loud, blaring over the tenth loop of Phoebe Bridgers's *Stranger in the Alps*.

Then again, I'm getting ahead of the curve, knee-deep in assignments for the rest of the week beyond tonight's home-work and what's due for tomorrow's classes. Things are wonky on a block schedule. Half of the week, I have AP Government/Economics, Calculus, and French 1, while the other days are for AP English Lang, AP Environmental Science, and Ceramics. Deadlines often run parallel to one another, which turns my color-coded, annotated planner into my saving grace.

Phoebe's melancholic, feather-light vocals swirl around the noise-canceling headphones. Melting my bedroom and the rest of the world into the background. It's me and my homework. That is, until "What is Love" interjects at top volume, signaling an incoming text or two from Nadia. We'd set the ringtone back in sophomore year and never changed it.

The sudden blare of the text tone and the subsequent jolt of my body knock my headphones off. They slide down to rest around my neck, buzzing with unrelenting insistence. Over the last few days, Nadia and I have swapped texts about her adventures at Stanford, complete with photographs of her going with her orientation friends to hike at Foothills Nature Preserve. In each one, she looks happier than I've ever seen.

The phone rings from somewhere underneath several textbooks, binders, and handwritten notes from today's lectures after the usual first-day syllabus talk. I shove all these things aside, more rough than I intended, to find it somewhere around the middle. Nadia's messages brighten the otherwise dimmed screen.

QUEEN NADIA

bestie, i'm bored. classes already have me reconsidering bioengineering.

tell me how your first day went! meet any new people? how were debate tryouts this year?

My phone rumbles in my hand as I work on a loving nudge for my best friend to focus on her college homework. This time, the text chime is the default, and Wyatt's name flashes at the top of the screen in a tiny banner. The notification vanishes before I read what he sent, leaving me to finish up with Nadia.

ME

There's been some interesting developments. I'll call you later.

I expect a string of emojis or a follow-up of groaning about making her wait for the juicy gossip, but Nadia knows I always deliver. So, I jump into the other, newer text chain with Wyatt.

WYATT

hey. I finished tonight's news update in the database. Feel free to access and download the folder at your convenience so we have extra copies of everything. https://drive.-google.com/drive/folders/4822dailynewsup-dateaugust29/view?usp=sharing

One of the shiny new perks of being Wyatt's debate part-ner: access to his academic journal and news article database. According to him, he spends two hours a night updating the folder, keeping up with the 24-hour news cycle. If I thought my folder of resources, sorted by topic, was top of the line, Wyatt's system exists light-years ahead of mine. He organizes every-thing by date, further divides them into folders for sources, and even uses an extensive tagging system to sort.

Wyatt laughed when my jaw dropped when I first accessed the database. But he severely underestimates how much I love a robust organizational system. *Bye-bye, anxiety. I have every-thing I need at the press of a button.*

ME

You're a lifesaver. I'll check everything out shortly!

"Shortly" never comes, not when a crisp knock against my bedroom door interrupts my flow. "Beth, dinner's ready. Home-work can wait," my mom remarks from the other side of the thick, wooden door. Although she treads the line of "soft-spoken," I know the difference between asking and insisting on my presence. *It wouldn't be the first time I forgot dinner due to studying.* The floor outside the door creaks under her footsteps.

"Coming!" My hands dip into my lap to move the white and gray cat napping on my thighs, who has been there since I first sat down. Ziti's disgruntled 'mrow' precedes the gentle squeak of her sinking into my bed. She, still sleepy, curls up on the medium gray and cream-colored duvet, purring whenever my fingers trace down her back. "I'll be right back."

The black-and-white flower wallpaper and pops of coral fade into a cider-brown wall that spans the rest of the house. Hardwood stairs announce my presence before I enter the kitchen's doorway, where I find the waiting faces of my family sitting around the dining table.

Busier than a bee, my mom flits between the table and the kitchen counter, carrying dishes for dinner and sides to the table. Her apron of choice, wrapping around her slender frame, matches the rosy lipstick she wears, delicate and pink. The light shades contrast nicely against her sleek, chin-length bob and molten brown eyes. People have called us carbon copies of one another; I can see the resemblance, even with the thirty-year age gap separating us.

At the head of the table, my dad's stocky frame radiates the kind of jolly, warm aura the world should aspire to have. He has a shock of ashy brown hair, which sits long enough to fall into his vibrant jade eyes. He still wears his charcoal gray suit from work, professional down to his shined black Oxford dress shoes. If I look like my mom, then I keep a few of my dad's shining personality traits—mainly his snarky laugh.

Then, Sawyer and Kelsie, my younger siblings, perch on their usual chairs. Despite being two years apart, thirteen and eleven respectively, people frequently mistake the two as twins. For now, they're the same height, but Sawyer is overdue for his overnight growth spurt. Any day now, I'm sure. They both have dark hair, somewhere between mom's and my inky black and dad's ash brown, and brown eyes to match. Sawyer's frame is lankier from hours of swim practice. Handmade bracelets hang off Kelsie's thick forearms, the byproducts of her natural artistic inclination. Each of us has our thing, which seems to slot into a perfect and diversified dynamic for our quintet.

When he notices me, Dad waves me over. "Pumpkin! How was your first day of senior year?" He extends an arm for a hug before I take my seat to his left.

"It was good." I smile as Mom sets the final dish—chicken piccata—on the table. She sits at the opposite end of the table from Dad, clasping her hands together. She lets out a pointed breath and points to the middle.

Her eyes linger on me when she says, "Everyone knows the rule. Phones in the middle." A collective sigh rises from the other occupants of the table, who all begrudgingly reach into their pockets. In the center of the table, the metal bowl of our KitchenAid stand mixer rests upside down, leaving room for us to pile our phones underneath. We have a rule in the Edwards household: meal times as a family require us to unplug. *No work calls, no music, no texting.*

Once everyone's phone is tucked beneath the bowl, Mom reaches for the serving spoon for the mixed greens salad. One by one, we begin to serve ourselves. Even Ziti emerges from her tenth nap of the day and plods into the kitchen to partake in her dinner—a fresh can of chicken pate. Through the scrapes of silverware against plates, conversation flows between everyone else in my family.

Dad discusses the clients he helped at work while Sawyer mumbles about upcoming tryouts for the swim team. Kelsie downright vibrates in her chair when Mom asks about her first day of middle school. I, however, only half-listen to the conversation between bites of chicken and pasta and the running mental tab of my never-ending to-do list.

Yet, the real world sucks me back in when the mixing bowl rattles in the tell-tale vibration of someone's phone going off. *Ooh, someone's in trouble.* Whatever momentary flutter of amusement grazes across my chest splutters to a catastrophic end when "What Is Love" cuts in. *It's me. I'm in trouble.*

Everyone's eyes jump toward me, who probably looks paler than a sheet when Mom sighs. "You know the rules. Pass Dad your phone." She picks up the bowl, revealing my phone vibrating in the middle of the pile.

I hand the phone to Dad, who scrunches his nose apologetically, but the twinkle in his eyes tells a different story. *What a little gossip.* The other significant rule about dinnertime and the no phones policy is that if anyone's phone goes off with a text, it will be read aloud for the rest of the table.

I usually put my phone on silent, but I forgot. Hence, I brace further into my seat, sinking into the cushion. My hands pick at denim while my eyes avoid the rest of the table.

Dad clears his throat dramatically as if he prepares to deliver a Shakespearean monologue instead of reading his teen daughter's texts. "Nadia sent a chain of emojis, hearts mostly— tell her we hope Stanford is going well—" he squints at the screen, and his brow furrows. "—and then Wyatt says—"

"Who's Wyatt?" Mom drops her fork to the clatter of metal. Two truths can coexist: my family is highly involved in my life, and they know the names of all my close friends, *and* I don't have many close friends.

I sigh, "Wyatt is my new debate partner. We're working on our databases for the semester."

"You didn't tell us you found a new debate partner! What's he like? Are you two in the same grade?" Mom gasps, immediately invested.

"Did you choose him, or did Coach Kruger assign him to you? Poor guy." Sawyer snickers. *Twerp.*

"Is he cute?" Kelsie bats her lashes, which elicits several groans from the rest of the table. Leave it to my preteen sister to turn the conversation to boys.

"He's too old for you. Quit it," I gesture for my phone, which Dad hands over without a fuss. "Wyatt's a senior like me. He's got a lot of experience and suggested we become partners since he transferred to East Shores without one. He's organized and good at debate." I switch off the ringer, which signals the end of my willingness to answer questions. Everyone else accepts my answers, but I can't shake their curious glances as dinner proceeds.

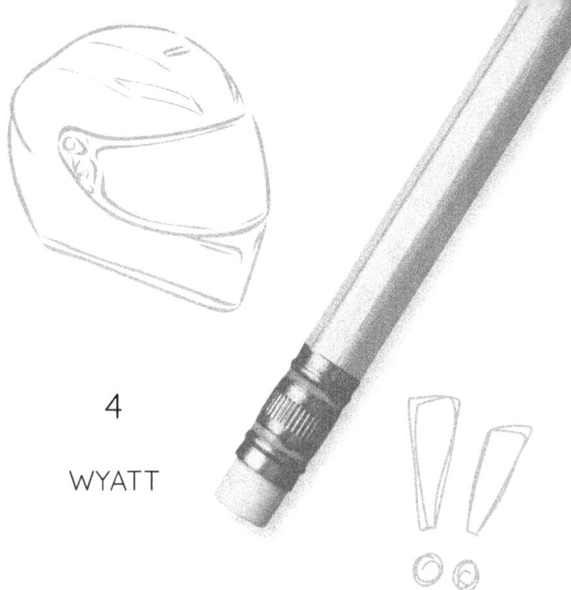

4

WYATT

RIGHT AS CRISPER weather returns to Searidge Hills, the coastal town I now call home, I learn the ins and outs of East Shores's speech and debate team. Back at Viewbrook, the academy classified our team as an on-campus, student-run extracurricular activity rather than a school-funded one, which added a whole new dimension of loopholes to navigate and funding challenges. It also meant that, besides the bi-weekly meetings of the members with our faculty advisor and liaison to the administration, most of our practice happened independently. Any given debater needed the drive to success to propel them to greatness.

Here, at East Shores, however? The school seems to take winning competitions as a matter of personal pride. The team meets twice a week—on Tuesdays for the speech team and Thursdays for the debaters—for several hours instead of the cramped lunch meetings. Attending one practice weekly is mandatory, barring any excused absence or extenuating circumstances. It's nice to be somewhere that invests in its students beyond the athletics department.

So today, a Thursday, I head through the empty halls to our room for practice. Beth sent me all the information around lunchtime, mostly things about where and when we meet and everything else I'd need to know. *She's a good partner, on top of everything.*

Whatever lingering breeze remains from the morning laps against my skin and the loose folds of my favorite leather jacket. The worn brown leather has always been a size too big, but I've always preferred the extra room in the sleeves and around the shoulders. The undone zipper jingles when skimming against the railing as I take two stairs at a time, racing to the second floor of Hawkins for practice.

I spot the propped-open door at the end of the hallway before I hear the incessant, overlapping voices booming through the thin, metal doorframe. Ducking into the classroom —obviously, an English one from the book cover ceiling tiles painted by someone's talented hand, and the Shakespeare posters on the walls—a chorus of "Wyatt's here!" and "You didn't scare him away" greets me.

Beth's head snaps up at that, which adds a slight bounce to the strands falling out of her bun, coiling around her cheeks. The short, puffy sleeves of her ivory blouse crinkle when she waves me over, almost as much as her nose does when Andrea nudges her, commenting on something lost under all the other ongoing conversations. Beth remarks something back and shoos her away, making room for me on the desk beside hers.

"Hey," Beth's posture straightens as I cram myself into the desk. My knees knock into the leg of the chair, followed by a hollow ringing; the throb of pain radiating through my knee, however, aches deep in my marrow. "How did your first week at East Shores go?"

"Besides the 'Are you new?' questions and the first day of icebreakers, it went by faster than I expected," I say while nudging my backpack with the tip of my sneaker. At first, my eyes wait for the tiniest shifts in Beth's expression, but that focus flickers out when I notice the clutter scattered across her desk. Her notebook, pens, laptop, various stacks of paperwork, and a soggy drink container with two tall glasses of an iced drink—not coffee but something else. Tea, maybe?

Beth's eyes follow my gaze—a light dusting of pink flusters her cheeks. "My old debate partner and I had a tradition of grabbing boba from Fresh & Frosted before every practice. I still went, but I totally forgot that it was just me until the barista handed over the usual order of two drinks. I didn't have the heart to ask for a refund."

Like some athletes or theater kids, debaters can be a superstitious bunch. That, or Beth considers herself a creature of habit. Either way, I get it.

"I'll take one off your hands," I say, reaching for the drink carrier. "Which one would you recommend? I'm on the inexperienced side when it comes to boba. I've had it once, maybe twice."

Beth points to the caramel brown drink instead of the purple one, "So, we usually got brown sugar milk tea and taro milk tea with the homemade honey boba. The taro is my preference, but I'll switch-"

Before Beth finishes her sentence, I grab the brown drink. I raise the cup. "Cheers to tradition. I look forward to weekly boba." My words soften the subtle crease in Beth's brows, replacing it with a quiet streak of elation that lights up her eyes, drawing out the warm flecks of brown.

"Cheers." Beth grabs her taro boba, taps the plastic lids of our drinks together, and pops her straw through the flimsy plastic lid. I follow suit, and when she takes a sip, I do, too. The tea is sweet, with a heavy presence of brown sugar and vanilla flavors, and is delightful nonetheless. So distracted by the initial sweetness that I forget about the tapioca pearls until several of them hit the back of my mouth.

The look on my face must be spectacular from the snort escaping Bethany, who slaps her hand over her mouth. Her shoulders shake, and her head lolls, all while she tries not to spit out her drink. Amusement pours off her in palpable waves, even as Ms. Goodwin and Coach Kruger enter the room.

Ms. Goodwin clutches a clipboard in her perfectly manicured hands, scraping along the side with a brain-scratching echo. "Afternoon, everyone. Before I run through the announcements, let me mark everyone here as present." She scribbles something down. "Okay, so we have the season's first tournament next weekend. I know it's a fast turnaround for some of the newbies, but the Lane Rogers Invitational at El Camino College is a chance to dive into debate headfirst. Anyone not already registered can bring me their entry fee of $75 and their signed permission forms by Monday, at the latest, to register."

"Beth, do you intend to go solo? I didn't see you registered for debate yet," Coach Kruger chimes in from her casual lean against the wall by the doorway. Besides me, Beth tenses midsip. Her whole body goes rigid when several pairs of eyes now focus on her.

Before she says a thing, I raise my hand. "If Beth wants to go, I'll be there. I can bring the check to your classroom tomorrow, Ms. Goodwin." All the attention flips onto me, even after Beth nods. This wouldn't be my first invitational tournament anyway, so I have no qualms about flinging myself head-first into the deep end with Beth.

"Sure thing, Wyatt. Find me after practice to get a copy of the permission slip. You can stop by Hawkins during the morning snack break to drop them off with the check. Outside of that, everyone who is not going still needs to fill out their emergency contact forms and other district-mandated paperwork. And Bethany and Andrea, don't forget we have a meeting after practice at five. That's all." Ms. Goodwin punctuates each announcement with a click of her pen. She steps back, and Coach Kruger takes her place in the center of the room.

Coach's fingers point at Beth and me, right past our shoulders. "Alright, since Wyatt and Beth will be joining us at Lane Rogers next weekend, I want them to get some practice in. Andrea and August, are you two ready for a round?"

"Yes, Coach!" The twins chorus, not even a millisecond out of alignment. *It's scary how good they are at that.* The desks behind Beth and me scrape, and papers shuffle as the Torreses relocate to the opposite end of the room. The arrangement of desks in a half-circle puts them directly across from us.

Beth nudges our desks together, leaving no room between us. In a swift sweep, she clears her desk beyond the barest essentials. "We've got this," She says with a wink my way.

"We've got this," I repeat. This will be the first time we work together, rather than against one another. *A true sink-or-swim moment, huh?* Either we're about to make some magic, or our senior year debate careers will be off to a rocky start.

Coach Kruger pulls out her tablet, clearing her throat, "Today's topic: Congress should eliminate the filibuster. Beth and Wyatt, you're on the affirmative. Andrea and August, you'll be the opposition. Please take the full twenty minutes to prepare your arguments, as we'll proceed for the full duration. Also, decide your speaker before we get started."

She starts the timer without another word, prompting both us and the Torreses to get to work. I grab my phone and a fresh stack of paper for our brainstorming.

"Okay, we should get started. Any preference on speaking order?" Beth seizes the reins. Her hands fly across the keyboard of her laptop. Within seconds, she's opened our new database, diving deep into the tagging system.

"Ladies' choice." I adjust her laptop to sit more equally between us.

Beth's lips quirk up in the corners. "Such a gentleman." She hands me a pen in between pulling up various articles about the recent filibuster on the Senate floor.

"And they say chivalry is dead," I snort under my breath, but Beth hears me anyway. Her shoulder jostles into mine, gentle yet knowing. Her smile matches, like a secret we both share, when we resume our scroll through the documents. Somehow, I have a feeling that everything's going to be more than okay with Beth.

XOXO

THE FOLLOWING Saturday arrives without pomp or circumstance. The nerves make their presence known on the ride to school, kicking and screaming over the loop of *American Idiot* pulsing in my helmet. Building in anticipation of the drive to El Camino from Searidge Hills. Despite them, I ride along the sloped roads under overcast September skies, veering into the sparsely occupied parking lot. Students in their suits loiter around a big, yellow school bus right in front of the gymnasium, their numbers dwindling one by one while people board the bus.

With under three minutes to spare, I rev into the nearest open parking spot. I dismount fast once the engine of my motorcycle putters out. The soles of my riding boots crunch over the broken asphalt of the parking lot, joined by the sharp scream of the zipper as I shrug off my favorite riding jacket. I trade it—and my helmet—for a dark blazer pulled from the backpack strapped to my back. Since I wore the crisp white button-down and pressed slacks on the ride, the backpack had more than enough room for the blazer and a pair of dress shoes.

After scraping my fingers through my hair for a quick, effortless fluffing, I join the shrinking line as the last member of the team. I pass Ms. Goodwin at the door, who doesn't lift her gaze off her clipboard to greet me while she checks my name off the list.

"That's everyone!" she announces to the gray-haired bus driver, who chews on his gum with pointed disinterest. I stumble down the narrow aisle, bending around backpacks protruding into the walkway and shoulders leaning over the edge of the crumbling seats. I find a safe harbor toward the back of the bus, sitting next to Beth. She doesn't even stir at my arrival, never taking her eyes off the window or slipping off her headphones. "Alright, I'm only going over the safety briefing once-"

Not even three seconds into Ms. Goodwin's spiel about the rules of off-campus decorum and how we "represent East Shores," two other Parli debaters, Josh Reeves and Zion Marshall, lean over the seat in front of us, eyes wide.

"Wyatt, you ride a motorcycle?" Josh asks while gesticulating toward my bike parked by someone's beat-up sedan.

"Yeah," I shrug. "Is that surprising?"

"A little bit. You're such a quiet guy that most of us wouldn't assume you're the adrenaline junkie type," Zion says, exchanging glances with Josh. "Your parents are cool with it? My mom would have a fit if I even mentioned wanting a *motorcycle.*"

I slouch a little in my seat when the seats around us glance toward me. "My mom took me to my driving lessons for it.

Then again, I used to ride dirt bikes with my dad during family vacations, so I got plenty of practice."

"Lucky."

"What brand is it?" One of the new freshmen to the Parli team, Mai Nguyen, says. Scooching to the edge of her seat across the aisle and one ahead of our row. She pokes her head out. "My older brother is an enthusiast, and I'm trying to learn more."

"It's a 2023 Kawasaki Ninja 400." The audible "oohs" and "ahhs" accompanying my answer sound like a pending interrogation. Except the excitement bursts in a frantic fizzle when Ms. Goodwin claps her hands together, cutting through the chatter.

"Alright, buckle up, and we're heading out!" she announces seconds before the bus pulls away from the curb. With a groan, we roll through the vast, empty parking lot and into the intersection at the onset of a yellow light. Beyond that minor hiccup, the bus marches onward toward El Camino.

As the rest of the team settles into their seats, swapping conversations with their neighbors, I turn to Beth, still in her own world. She bobs her head along to whatever plays in her sage green headphones, tapping the tip of her classic black Converse against the bus's wall.

I tap her shoulder gently so I don't scare her. Beth's head snaps toward me, moving so fast that her headphones fall to rest around her neck. "Hey. I didn't realize you made it."

"I could tell. Whatever you're listening to has you lost in space. It's got me curious, I can't lie," I reply.

Beth's nose scrunches, and her eyes crinkle at the corners, but the expression screams amusement. Her cheek concaves, as if she's chewing on it. I can see the gears spinning in her head before Beth tips her phone screen toward me. The movement awakens the screen, which displays none other than "Lay All

Your Love on Me." However, it's specifically the Mamma Mia movie soundtrack version.

"I didn't take you for a musical theater girl—or are you a secret lover of romantic comedies?" My brows shoot for the sky when Beth snatches her phone back. She taps on the screen, scoffing at my question.

"Who says it can't be both?" she challenges me. "I do have a great appreciation for musical soundtracks. Not to mention Mamma Mia happens to be one of the greatest modern romance movies next to Ten Things I Hate About You and How To Lose a Guy In 10 Days," Beth states matter-of-factly.

"Ah, a true Renaissance woman, then. Do musicals get you hyped up to perform?"

"Sort of. It's more that music gets me out of my head. It improves performance and passes the time. I'll listen to music on the drive and between rounds to keep me level-headed. Besides, I didn't spend the last three years curating a masterful playlist for nothing."

Beth offers me her phone again. This time, however, I get a full glance at her Kiwi playlist.

Wow. Actually, *wow* might be the only word in the English language capable of capturing the sheer chaos and eclectic brilliance of the music Beth manages to string together on a single playlist. From Jeff Buckley to the Glee Cast, classical music to the top hits of the radio now, Beth's music tastes span genres and break barriers. Most of the items I see when I scroll fall into the main categories of pop, musical theater, alternative, or classic rock, but the outliers range across genres.

"Woah, this playlist has a little of everything," I scroll through the playlist for the third time to process the sonic spectrum. *This feels like a glimpse into Beth's mind.* "I see some Wicked, some Britney Spears, a lot of Queen. . ."

Beth's ears flush as red as her cheeks and neck. She

slouches deeper into the seat, arms crossing over her chest, and the jacket of her suit dress crinkling ever so slightly around the lapels. "Queen's one of my favorite bands, right next to ABBA and the Arctic Monkeys," She explains.

"They're one of mine too," I interject, hands rising in surrender. "Honestly, I'd say your selection is perfect, but you're missing one of the best songs on their discography."

"Oh, and what's that?" Beth's brow quirks. She makes no move to take her phone back, so I hit the search bar. Within seconds, the upbeat piano intro of "Good Old-Fashioned Lover Boy" blares from the headphones still around Beth's neck.

"How could I forget about this banger? Maybe you and I should make a new playlist to share—we can't have another oversight like that on my part," Beth laughs. She shimmies her shoulders and sways her head from side to side, devolving into a compact dance on our bench. The more she dances, the more her entire face glows with a grin that reaches from ear to ear.

"Sounds like a plan-" If there was room for a joke there, it stumbles to an ungraceful skid when the bus around us full-on jolts. Thankfully, I buckled in before we left the parking lot, or I would've ended up with my face smashed into the peeling, slightly odorous leather of the bench ahead.

Beside me, Beth gasps. I catch a glimpse of her, bending over my outstretched arm. *I hadn't realized I threw it toward her.* The bus shudders, its metal frame creaking and groaning with a sick cry when Ms. Goodwin snaps to her feet.

"Everyone off the bus now!"

5

BETHANY

September, Week 2

WE'RE *SCREWED*.

In all my years as a debater, I've heard of tournament horror stories. I even earned a few of my own and have witnessed some up close and personal. To this day, I refuse to look at a paper carton of chocolate milk unless I want to relive the time some poor competitor drank an expired carton before his rounds. *It didn't end pretty.*

But today marks a new, unspeakable low. The East Shores speech and debate team crams itself onto the narrow sliver of sidewalk, sinking into the mounds of browning, dry grass and leftover dirt from a long-abandoned road work site. Cars and trucks zoom past us without any regard for the high schoolers stranded on the side of the road, crouching next to a broken-down bus.

Time's been slipping—somewhere under an hour out here, give or take. At some point during our wait for the bus driver to fix the engine, the sun and its heavy-handed heat emerged from behind the overcast skies. *So much for fall weather.* SoCal weather is as fickle as the sea.

Our position on the side of the road leaves us with limited options for shade. With the sun climbing in the east and our bad luck putting us on the right side of the road, the bus doesn't offer much shade. Several debaters use their backpacks as seats while others remain standing despite the cramps bound to form in their legs. I choose the former, squatting on my durable tournament duffle while I clutch my speech binder to my chest. Wyatt, however, chose to stand at my side, free of any complaints. Sometime during our wait for assistance or a fixed engine, he stripped off his blazer and is holding it above our heads to block us from the sun.

Dirt and flecks of rocks shift underneath my black suede pumps, further cementing the regret swirling around my gut. *Of course, this happens on the one day I forget my favorite competition flats.* Despite hiding from the heat behind Wyatt's thick blazer, sweat beads along the back of my neck. Dampness weighs down my hair, curling against my sweat-slick skin, and summons a whole-body itch beneath my skin.

Everything about this sucks.

"Okay, good news!" Ms. Goodwin pops her head from around the front bumper of the bus. Her voice carries over the rush of nearby traffic and the occasional slam of a car horn. "Help is on the way! Since the bus engine can't be fixed roadside, the bus company is sending a couple of smaller buses to transport all of us. Speech kids will get on the first bus because your rounds are posting first. The tournament organizers are aware of our predicament."

An audible groan of relief rises from the team. My relief wells up in my chest, but my dry mouth and the hour-long anxiety stewing within me mutes any sound that wants to arise.

The world becomes a little brighter when Wyatt's blazer drops as he offers his hand to me.

I grasp his fingers. Our mutually sweaty palms slide a little when he yanks me onto my feet. Even when my pumps sink into the dusty gravel of our roadside haven, Wyatt's grip holds me steady until I can keep myself upright.

"Thanks." The raspiness of my voice elicits the tiniest snicker from Wyatt, who reaches into his bag and hands over an unopened bottle of water. I nearly spill some onto our fingers as I rush to accept a drink. "How are your arms holding up?"

Speaking of arms, Wyatt stretches his arms wide and swings them around. "Eh, they'll be alright. I'll consider this as my shoulder workout for the week," he says, flexing like a bodybuilder and grinning. He looks like a dork posing in his pressed button-down and deep green tie, even though his arms have some definition. But Wyatt firmly lands on the lanky side of the fitness spectrum, nicely between noodle arms and definitely juicing.

"You're ridiculous," I roll my eyes at him. However, the gentle reprieve ends when Ms. Goodwin races over the uneven terrain in her heels, undaunted and still somehow effortless.

"Alright! Speech team! We'll have you all go with our chaperone, Noemi, on this first shuttle. She will handle registration, but everyone else head to your rounds. The tournament organizers are aware of our delays." Ms. Goodwin's sharp whistle cuts through any distraction, gathering everyone's attention. "If there's extra room on this ride, we can fit a few more kids to go with Noemi."

She waves the speech team over right as a smaller white and blue bus veers toward the curb. Before I lean down for my backpack, Wyatt has already slung it over his shoulder with his backpack. He doesn't let me ask to take a bag to ease his load or say much of anything. Instead, his hand hovers above the small of my back as I step forward.

The first step wobbles from all the gravel and the thinner stiletto of my heels, but I don't fall. No, I latch onto Wyatt's arm as an anchor. He loops our arms together and escorts me on the short, yet unsteady walk to the line of speech kids piling onto the first bus.

The two of us are at the back of the line, watching seats fill rather quickly. We approach the steps when Mikey, our school's best dramatic interpretation* speaker, raps against their window, eyes wide, "We have two seats left! Get on!"

"Wyatt, you go with them," Ms. Goodwin materializes behind Wyatt and me. I'm ashamed to admit I jump, but Wyatt keeps cool for us and shepherds me onto the bus. We take the last seats at the front, not even buckled in, as the shuttle zooms away from the curb. The sudden movement knocks me into Wyatt's side, who tightens his grip around me while we fumble for the shared seatbelt. *Great.*

"We'll get there in about fifteen minutes," From the middle of the bus, Noemi makes the announcement. She's been with East Shores longer than I have—volunteering as a chaperone and stepping in as our donated judge for every local and invitational tournament we've had. We're in good hands. *Everything is going to be okay, hiccups aside.* "For any newbies, tournaments don't always go smoothly. Once you get used to the unpredictable, things like this don't faze you."

"Um... not to freak anyone out, but round assignments* just dropped," another speech student and our sole Original Advocacy speaker, Deanna, intercedes. She holds her phone above her head and braces as several students scramble toward her or whip out their phones. "They'll wait for us, right?"

"They might proceed ahead and let you move to the back as long as we make it on time," Noemi assures the rest of the bus.

However, those words smack headfirst into the wall of pure adrenaline rushing through me. It roars in my ears, or maybe that's the echoes of my pulse. It rings out, staccato and loud enough to mute the shuttle's engine and any surrounding traffic rattling the windows.

My phone cries out with a text notification from my bag. It's probably my room assignment through Tabroom*. *I should check it. C'mon.*

Sweat from the back of my neck beads in new clusters while more sprout across my neck and forehead. My hands are so slick that I almost drop my phone trying to check the notification.

The text link immediately directs me to the Tabroom website, where I can find my room assignment and placement in the order.

I'm the first speaker. We're running behind, and I'm up first.

The spasm in my chest takes me by surprise—if the jagged exhale punched out of my gut is any indication. Even with the extenuating circumstances, there's a real chance our terrible turn of events might make me miss the round entirely. My room assignment is located in the Communication Building, which is a considerable distance from the nearest parking lot. I've been to El Camino's campus enough times to know where the shuttle will drop us off after riding down Crenshaw Blvd.

The ache squeezes around my throat, tight and insistent. I don't even know if I'm breathing at all.

"Beth!" Wyatt's voice pierces through the chaos rumbling in my head. However, the panic doesn't dispel at his presence or the firm eye contact he forces. When he grasps my hands in his, I realize they're shaking. "Hey. You're hyperventilating, okay? What can I do for you?"

"I—" Breaths sound and feel more like hiccups now that I

can hear everything. In my peripheral vision, the concerned faces of the speech team surrounding us only add more fuel to the embarrassment raging in my chest. "Are we headed to Lot K?"

"Yes." Noemi leans over her seat. "Beth, hon, are you okay?"

"I'm fine. . . Wyatt, I need-" I manage a gulping inhale and sit myself taller, still clawing at Wyatt's hands like a lifeline. "Can you take my backpack? I only need my phone and binder."

"Of course." I pass over my things with shaking fingers, letting go of Wyatt and his steady, grounding touch. The tremors are mild, not enough to deter the rushed plan piecing together in my head. Instead, I slip off my heels and stare at the scenery rolling past the window.

The roads melt into the familiar blue and white buildings of El Camino, and the driver does me the favor of parking as close to the curb as possible. The doors to the shuttle bus fling open, and I'm through them within milliseconds. Stockinged feet touch hot asphalt, yet the sting of early morning heat spurs me to move faster and to keep moving.

In my hands, I clutch my phone, competition binder, and shoes with a vice grip as I sprint further onto campus. College students *and* fellow competitors, easily identifiable by the difference in clothes, walk on the paved pathways winding through campus. Regardless of why they're in my way, everyone veers aside as I rush past.

"Excuse me!" and "Thank you!" fly out of my mouth in record numbers as I weave past clusters of confused, disgruntled, and otherwise inconvenienced students. But I keep my pace. On a better day, I'd enjoy the ten-minute stroll across the campus, soaking in the vibrant color palette of stark, pure white and cobalt blue in eye-catching bright spots compared to the other buildings. Today, however, I've cut that time in half, zooming past labeled buildings like "campus theater" and "Schauerman Library," rushing across paved roads and almost cartoonishly green grass when the students on the road won't move out of the way.

If all else fails, maybe I have a career in track and field to consider.

My pace slows at the quiet throbbing of a muscle cramp in my calves. Yet, nothing burns harder than my lungs, which strain and gasp for air and greedily drink the new breeze picking up around me. I cross into the dense cluster of buildings just past the art gallery. Years of visiting this school like clockwork should mean I know it well, but the details spin out of reach and force me to pause. Time is the one thing I don't have.

Most competitors might be stressed if they were in my shoes. Stress doesn't begin to cover the flood of emotions running through me right now, driven forward by the firm hand of my anxiety. If a situation starts bad, leave it to anxiety to make everything feel ten times worse.

Despite the momentary disorientation, I push forward until I spot the Behavioral Sciences building, standing tall and unmistakable. The rest of my muscle memory comes flooding back at the sight of it. *Communications should be behind it! It's the tricky one.* Nadia used to describe it that way, and the descriptor stuck with me.

Lo and behold, the communication building rolls into view with its ramp leading to the outward-facing classrooms. A small gaggle of students leans against one of the red brick walls and the raised stone wall, carrying binders and running through the motions while facing the walls. *Practicing. Yeah, I'm in the right place.* And if everyone waits outside, the judge must not be here yet.

The thought shifts every stress or lingering thread of anxiety within me to the backseat as rationality takes the wheel in its steady hands. A dry mouth ache scrapes the inside of my throat as rough as sandpaper; water would be nice, but I forgot it with Wyatt. I saunter up the ramp, shoeless and smoothing over my hair. My late arrival and unkempt state earn a few weird looks from the competitors gathered outside the room.

Ignoring them, I glide further down the hallway to stake a small slice of practice space. Late start be damned, I will not let the competition get in my head further than anxiety already has.

XOXO

THE SECOND DAY of competitions tends to crawl by with the deliberate speed of the DMV on a busy afternoon—this year's Lane Rogers tournament isn't an exception to the pattern. The borderline tortuous pace should make up for the chaos of yesterday morning, which blurred time together in a mishmash of crystal-clear memories and gaps where panic took over. Sometimes, I'd blink, and a whole hour would vanish, slipping through my fingers like grains from the sands of time.

Still, I like to think I turned a bad situation into a winning hand. Despite the hellish start and my mad dash across campus, I dominated the first round—and the two after it—beyond from the occasional stammer or stumble.

Running away with nothing lower than second place in the preliminary rounds basically guaranteed me a spot in the elimination rounds*, which required me to spend the remaining half of my weekend sequestered away with dozens of other students in the spacious Marsee Auditorium, wasting away the hours between rounds.

"-Wait, so the judge actually pulled a face? That's so unprofessional." Devon scoffs, and a few rogue gasps from the other debaters sitting in the circle with us on the auditorium's stage join in. A few competing schools commandeered the space but sit a respectful distance away from each other, forming little cliques by school allegiance.

"Yeah. It was noticeable enough that the other team switched tactics mid-debate, dropped* all their other, less successful arguments, and focused their rebuttal speeches on that one point. We reminded the judge that he needs to weigh the arguments on the merits and that the other team didn't have any points that carried* their argument beyond one. He didn't seem to buy it or like us when we approached to thank him." Wyatt sips at his long-cold coffee. He grimaces and shakes his shiny black tumbler like he could reheat his drink through willpower.

When his eyes flit toward me, I shrug, shifting the textbook perched on my lap to the rattle of the colored markers and the transparent sticky notes.

Much like my solo endeavors, Wyatt and I pulled through the preliminary rounds as a team to beat, heading into the quarter-finals with a 2-1 record. For our first tournament as a team, I'd consider this a win. However, it's harder to celebrate when our last round will knock us out of the running.

Inexperienced judges can happen, as can biased judges who can't separate their personal values or be impartial for the sake of fairness. Getting a two-for-one special from an inexperienced judge who rules with their outside biases and can't be bothered to hide their obvious ideological slant *sucks*. Only time will tell if Wyatt and I make it to the semi-finals against all odds.

For now, I pass the time in the pages of my French textbook. Even while double-entered*, hours pass between each back-to-back round, leaving wide-open gaps with nothing better to do than rehearse speeches and chat with your teammates.

I return to the bolded conjugation chart in my French text-book and the grainy photographs of smiling teenagers, probably taken in the '90s. *Yay, grammar. What a thrilling adventure.* The sarcastic thought comes and goes within a blink, but a dull and uncomfortable sensation approaches in its wake. I blink at the page, finding the words and images out of focus more than once. *On second thought, I don't feel so good...*

A band of pain wraps around the circumference of my head, squeezing against my temples. Headache. The taste of chalky dryness weighs down on my tongue until I swallow hard. Laughter from my friends rattles in my ears, but the words are lost, merely noise against the gradual screaming of discomfort. The conversation could've moved on to something new, and I wouldn't know.

Without a word, I get up, discarding my textbook onto the stage floor. Someone will keep an eye on it; no one's fiending to steal a French textbook older than anyone in the entire compe-tition pool. No one calls after me or pesters me with questions. That's probably for the best anyway.

I wander past the rows of red, cushioned chairs, stepping around people, as I approach the doors at the back of the room. The arches of my feet ache into the padded soles of the flats; all the running from yesterday left my body in a wreck. Track isn't for me. I know that now.

I stagger further than the corridor and break into the fresh air of the early afternoon. Sitting on the steps outside the audi-torium, I breathe, full and deliberate, in my slowness, to savor how air burns all the way through. Warmth bears down from overhead, its touch cascading across every inch of exposed skin.

The occasional flicker of conversation floats past whenever students walk by, but those pull me out of the moment.

Conversations accompany footsteps, but they so rarely swerve off the path for the staircase. The sound of someone approaching from behind and waiting irks me; hopefully, they'll pass and leave me alone. *Someone's cranky, wow.* Instead, the scuffle of hard-soled shoes against the smoothed pavement stops right at my side.

There's no need to face the presence when it sits beside me. Wyatt's voice rumbles against the shell of my ear, close without even trying to be, as he asks, "Are you okay?"

"Fine," I grumble. Every inch of my spine screams in relief when I straighten my posture into a semi-acceptable position. My gaze meets Wyatt, who awkwardly crouches his knees to his chest so he can sit beside me on the top step. "My head hurts. That's all."

"Headache, huh?" Wyatt examines me, head cocked to the side while he does. "When's the last time you drank anything? Ate?"

"I finished my water thirty minutes ago, and I haven't eaten anything. I don't like to eat before rounds. I have an anxious stomach. That, along with Cafe Camino, is halfway across campus and closed on weekends. I'd need to find a vending machine or wait for the nearby food trucks to maybe roll by." The admission rolls off my tongue, rather sheepish. I considered texting my mom during her lunch hour to see if she'd take pity on me and drop me off a meal. But the hunger pangs claw and gnaw at me, cutting the time to wait short.

Wyatt hauls his backpack over his shoulder without skipping a beat, revealing a beat-up lunch bag. The worn blue and gray exterior has seen better days, but no obvious holes or tears mean it still works. He opens the bag, and a mini fridge's worth of food nearly tumbles onto the stairs. Unfazed, Wyatt plunges his hand into the bag and grunts, "Any dietary restrictions?"

"No. . ." Next thing I know, Wyatt drops a wrapped sandwich into my hands, stacked high with lettuce, tomato, cheese, and what appears to be turkey—alongside a chocolate chip cookie and some apple chips. "Wyatt."

"Eat. You need food if you're going to replenish your energy and keep your mind sharp. You have speech rounds to win. Besides, what good would I be as a partner if I let you starve?" Wyatt bumps his shoulder into mine while grabbing a small protein box of an egg, string cheese, and some mixed veggies like cucumber and carrots. He cracks the box open and stretches out his legs.

Well, we're on the same page about our chances of advancing. It seems Wyatt's nice enough to care about my speech chances and not just the part of the competition he's involved in.

Wyatt basks in the sun, not waiting for me to accept his lunch before diving into his snack box. Underneath the clear sky, his skin is lavished in a subtle glow, brightening his features in the way only the California sun can.

A sharp, insistent growl of my stomach cements the decision for me, especially at the sight of the full meal in my hands. So, I follow his lead and dig in. We say nothing more—there's no need to—and eat.

As I study Wyatt's leisurely quiet, I can't help but be struck by the calm of his presence. Although we're best friends, Nadia and I took our time adjusting as partners to each other's quirks. And now, I see Wyatt step so seamlessly into my chaos, unbothered by it.

I'm glad we're here. Together.

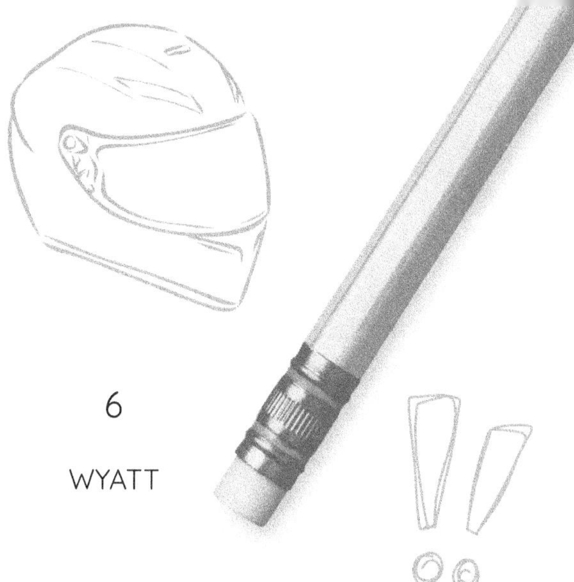

6

WYATT

September, Week 4

THE LAST THING I ever want to do on a Wednesday night is sit around the cramped dining room table and watch my mom's gluttonous husband stuff his face. But here I am as Graham shovels another bite of Mom's pot roast down his gullet without chewing. Then again, the guy has all the table manners of a barnyard animal. The mental image of seeing partially chewed roast and potatoes icks me out more than the bottomless pit act he's got going on.

A hand settles on top of mine, soft and familiar. *My mom's.* She settles into her seat at the left of the table while Graham lounges across from her, placing me square in the middle.

"Will it just be the three of us tonight? I thought it would be the whole family," Mom asks. The yellowing light shining from the kitchen's worn lightbulbs washes over her skin, smoothing out the few smile lines gathering around the corners of her mouth. Under the yellowed tint, her naturally rosy cheeks glow with a soft, pink hue. In the light, her eyes shimmer like honey rather than their usual quiet brown.

Everyone believes I'm the spitting image of my dad, but I can pinpoint the few features I share with Mom without trying hard—the same shade of dark brown hair, bordering on black, the prominence of our cheekbones, and the dimple on the left side of our faces. More importantly, Mom is the closest thing to a best friend I have in this world.

And, like some people hate their best friend's significant other, I *loathe* Graham. Graham, who, at his big age, wears backward snapbacks and a never-ending rotation of cargo shorts older than me. That alone should be an indicator of his status as a member of the "peaked in high school and unable to shut up about it" club, but the vibe radiates off him the same way smoke lingers in a room, clinging to every crevice.

Graham shrugs his shoulders, "No. It's just us tonight. Trav said he's meeting with his tutor for an extra hour. Something about an essay." With every bob and shift of his head, Graham's worn snapback and his greasy, dirty blond mullet snags my attention. Grungy seems polite to describe this forty-year-old man-child, who ambled off the couch smelling of sweaty gym socks for dinner. He didn't bother to shave his three-day-old stubble either, scraggly and patchy in some places.

What Mom sees in him, I'll never understand.

*Tutoring, right...*The scoff echoing in my thoughts would stir up more drama than ultimately worth it. Anyone with half a working pulse would clock that "an extra hour with the tutor" is a load of bull. Golden boy likely ditched the library hours ago to hang out with his boys on the football team to... do whatever stupid activities they found fun. They could be giving each other concussions or breaking into some unaware parents' alcohol cabinet, and I couldn't care less. What I *do* care about is the principle of the thing, the double standard of it all. *Why* *couldn't I take dinner upstairs in my room? There was no reason to insist and complain about me shirking family dinner when your son runs around town doing god knows what.*

Despite the quiet gurgle of my stomach, I push the nearest piece of pot roast around the plate. My fork drags the bite through a well of mashed potatoes and the simmering, savory gravy, bordering on "playing" with my food. Maybe it has everything to do with Graham chewing with his mouth open, but any semblance of an appetite sinks into my stomach, refusing to return.

Regardless, I force a bite down, chewing on the pot roast a little too long before swallowing. If Mom notices my awkward, wordless sulking, she doesn't say anything or prod. She's always good about her timing.

Instead, she giggles from her end of the table, perching on her elbow and fluttering her lashes. She covers her mouth to speak, but it smudges her soft pink lipstick. "What are you looking at?"

"Oh, only the most beautiful woman in the state," Graham replies. His delivery channels all the charisma of a wet rag when he grins and wiggles his brow. I think he looks lecherous, no better than the desperate red pill losers who troll Reddit forums or Instagram comment sections, but Mom eats it up. "Any chance I could take you out, baby?"

Yeah, I'm going to hurl. Or suggest a national ban on grown men calling their significant others "baby" to Congress.

"Graham!" Mom exclaims. Her whole face flushes a deep, resonant shade of pink, the color seeping down the column of her neck and up to the tips of her ears when she buries her face behind her hands. Underneath the table, someone's foot brushes against mine while stretching out, which extinguishes my interest in even looking at Mom and Graham or their general direction.

I fix my gaze on my plate. The uneaten pot roast—one of my favorite dishes on any other night—stares back, taunting me even. As I take another bite to chew and force down, Graham's boisterous laugh and the smack of his hand on the table yank me back into the conversation.

"What? As long as it doesn't interfere with my football, then we should go. You know a man needs his daily dose of ESPN." This is where I check out for the night: football. Apparently, there is only room for three things in Graham's life: football, football, and did I mention football already? He spends more time huddling around the television to watch grown men tackle each other and yapping about sports highlights than any person I've met.

The last time I commented on his obsession, I received an earful on Super Bowl Sunday about how "real men love football." I never said otherwise, but the overcorrection spoke volumes.

The rest of the flirting becomes one of those Peanuts animated specials where all adult conversation transforms into unintelligible background noise. I call it bliss for my poor, abused ears.

My appetite returns once I rescue myself from the flirting awkwardly lobbed across the table. Soon, the full plate dwindles into a half plate and shrinks further into a quarter of the plate left. An escape plan assembles before my eyes with every additional bite. A clean plate means one less dinner at this table, stuck beside a man whom I would drop kick for a single corn chip, and one day closer to getting some much-needed space across the country.

From the depths of my pocket, a pulse-like vibration buzzes through the thick layer of denim against my skin. I reach for it. Part of me expects to see some unknown spam caller or maybe a DM from a cousin.

Instead, I see a Kiwi link and Beth's name sharing the screen, riding along on a few text notifications. Never have I opened a text message quicker in my life.

> **BETH**
>
> I know we hit our quota for songs today. This one is a personal recommendation freebie from one friend to another.
>
> Noah Kahan- You're Gonna Go Far

Ever since Lane Rogers two weeks ago, Beth and I went from sporadic texts to daily conversations, talking about anything and everything that comes to mind. This month's phone bill might raise a few brows. But with Beth, nothing comes as naturally as talking for hours on end, chasing down every thread of thought and point of interest until nothing remains. She's smart, but her wicked and sharp sense of humor gets me.

Besides our endless conversations about useless trivia that could get us on Jeopardy and our mutual grumbling about living through the worst political timeline, we have a playlist. On the bus ride back from Lane Rogers, Beth revisited the playlist suggestion, only with a twist.

Each day for the past two weeks, Beth and I have sent each other a song to add to our lineup. We make a game out of it: whoever suggests the song must provide an argument for why their suggestion should end up on the "Winning brought to you by Beth and Wy" playlist, subject to veto or approval afterward. Much like our debate style, Beth and I are ruthless and relentless in our questioning and ranking the song on some unwieldy criteria that never repeat twice. At the moment, ten songs have passed the test with flying colors, with another three pending appeal.

Beth mentioned Noah Kahan before, gushing references in

passing. Something itches at the back of my brain as I sift through the things Beth has told me. My finger hovers over the link, but the clatter of forks holds me back. In this limbo, Mom's voice cuts through the final barrier between the rest of the world and me.

"What's got you smiling over there, Wy?" Mom asks from behind her napkin. She pushes her cleared plate further up the table, her eyes never leaving me. The dull ache in my cheeks confirms the presence of a smile.

I flip my phone over, the screen facing the worn table. "My debate partner sent me a text. That's all." Withholding the details isn't usually my speed. Then again, Mom and I's debriefs typically don't include the mouth-breathing and awkward staring of Graham on the other end of the table.

"We've talked about her, right? She's... her name starts with a B? Bailey? Britney?" Instead of skipping the conversation, Mom perks up. She laces her hands together and scoots her chair closer to me. She leans in as if to share a secret, "You'll have to forgive my memory. I'm getting old."

"Aren't you supposed to be twenty-one?" I tease. The laughter from her is immediate, and she shoves my shoulder for good measure. "Her name is Bethany, by the way. She prefers Beth."

"Beth... well, this Beth seems lovely from what you told me. I'm so glad you're making friends. You two clearly have a shared interest in debate. You're always welcome to invite her over for dinner if you two need extra practice for competitions like you and Tanner used to."

"Thanks, Mom. I'll let her know, see what she says." In fact, I could text her now. Tanner, my partner back at Viewbrook, occasionally took me up on the offer to practice outside of school hours. Not often, but enough for him to keep up with me at tournaments. I have no doubts Beth would jump at any possible edge over the competition, whether in practice hours or sheer raw intellectual ammunition. Some might find her borderline ruthless dedication as "overboard" or absurd for a high school extracurricular; it's hard to understand when you're looking in from the outside.

But, like most good moments in this house, a snort from Graham punches through the peace. One sound raises my hackles, bringing a sharp "what?" out of me, and I hear the bell ringing before a fight rattling its shrill cry.

Graham must sense the challenge in the air from how he shifts in his seat. A shadow passes over his features, dimming the last traces of amusement. When our eyes meet for a fleeting breath, it's Graham who breaks the stare first. *Good, he's uncomfortable. He should stay that way.*

He never does. No, instead, he sits taller and snorts again, seemingly remembering that he's a big man with opinions he can unnecessarily share. "Hopefully, this girl knows what she's getting into with you. Debate loves to think it's as serious as something like football or one of the other sports teams on campus. Last year, they asked for letterman jackets to put their own patch onto."

"Considering that the speech and debate team has won more trophies in the last few years than the football team and most of the athletic department combined, they're entitled to some bragging rights... and a letterman jacket since those are for athletics *and* academic activities." Bringing up the football team's lack of accolades might be a one-way ticket to a full-blown argument, but oh, how fast Graham's face twists into a gnarled, ugly sneer might be worth the backlash heading my way. So, I twist the knife and dig it in a little more. "As for my partner, Beth knows what it takes to win. She's the best debater on the team for a reason."

"Is that self-proclaimed? It sounds like a resume padder to

me." Graham scoffs. He dares to turn toward Mom with a raised brow, dripping with expectancy for her to chime in. It's got the "kids these days" vibe all over it.

"No. She is responsible for a good portion of the trophies and wins attributed to the team. Two weeks ago, she was a finalist in her individual event and placed within the top five speakers out of fifty entries. For our team event, she took us to the quarter-finals. If anything, I'm lucky that Beth wants me as her partner for the semester when she could have anyone on the team. So, why don't you keep her out of this? You're talking out of your ass."

"Watch your language!" One foul word, and Graham lurches out of his chair. He leans over the table, red in the face, and stares down at me. Men like Graham loom—try to make themselves feel more important than they are.

"Graham, can we not-" Mom interjects from her end of the table.

"How about you leave the disciplining to Mom? This isn't school." I push the envelope a little more. *What about a teen boy who speaks his mind and doesn't mindlessly follow your opinion gets you so angry, Graham?* For a man who isn't my dad, he sure tries his best to impose his authority.

He's just the loser whom Mom married, nothing more.

My gaze lands on Mom, whose eyes shine under a wall of unshed tears. Guilt sets in as I study that watery shimmer, diluting the soft, caring eyes of the woman who loves me more than life itself. Apologizing to that man will remain the last thing on my list, but I know when to stop pushing.

I ignore Graham when I stand up. Pressing a kiss into Mom's hair, I whisper, "Thanks for dinner. I need to clear my head around the block. I'll be back before dark." Although Mom's hand slides around my wrist in a silent plea to stay, I back out of the dining room without another word.

In any other situation, I'd consider this as running away from my problems. However, as my old therapist once said, not every battle must be fought immediately. As much as I loathe the guy, what good will unloading years of disdain and breaking Mom's heart do? I have one school year left until this won't be an issue, besides the times I come home to visit. Even in that scenario, I'll have every chance to be Graham-free.

I grab a bulky bomber jacket off the hooked shelf by the front door, shrugging it on with one foot on the porch and the other in hot pursuit. *My dad's.* With the sun long gone below the horizon, the last threads of sunset linger in the darkening sky, while streetlamps spaced every few houses cast light across the sidewalk. The block winds through our standard coastal suburban neighborhood, much nicer than the last place Mom and I rented out. I'm talking manicured lawns by HOA standards and cheery, welcoming paint jobs lining the quiet streets where kids play on lawns and in the road under proper supervision.

Once I slide my earbuds in, the already quiet world becomes hollow. No ambient noises pierce through the vacuum of emptiness, not unlike how silent space must be. I can't even hear myself breathe. Maybe that's for the best. It'll keep my thoughts at bay, slamming against the door of the cramped mental closet I shove them into. Out of sight, out of mind.

The last Kiwi playlist I listened to automatically boots up, blaring *Grand Theft Autumn* by Fall Out Boy. Something about the desperate, grungy sound of early 2000s punk nips at my heels until I speed a little faster around the block. At this hour, most people are inside and enjoying their dinners or unwinding after a long day. It gives me the whole space to exist without eyes on me.

From what little I know of our neighbors, they seem polite and friendly people. However, that fact doesn't resolve the glaring awkwardness that has been months in the making. I'm an interloper in this place, out of place and unwelcome within the four walls of Mom and Graham's home.

I get halfway around the first loop of the block when the song ends. Something else queues up, but I remember Beth's last text—the song suggestion idling in my texts, forgotten. From the texts, I find *You're Gonna Go Far.*

The opening of a folksy acoustic guitar and a man's resonant voice, one tinged by the all-too-familiar grit of a northeastern accent, chase one another. Noah's words string together effortlessly, poetry to the ears against an otherwise simple instrumental. The song propels me forward faster than the listless amble down the road of a wayward soul. I don't even think I'm listening to the words deeper than the surface of hearing the song.

Only when the song reaches its chorus do I process exactly what it says. My legs lurch to a stop while turning a corner; thankfully, I don't trip or fall into an undignified heap on the sidewalk. Staring down the road, I can see the house's front lawn glowing in the orange haze of the streetlight. I should go back inside and get away from the open air and the potential of strangers. Yet, something loud and panicked rears its head inside me, searching for the exit on an empty street, to where no one knows.

I stand there on the sidewalk. Tears are hot on my face that I miss until the taste of salt and upending grief slips into my parted lips. And my first thought while watching the rest of the world spin on without care isn't about the emotional aftertaste lingering from Graham and I's spat. No, it's about the man who left a void for him to fill with his regrettable presence.

Dad would've loved this song.

7

BETHANY

I'M GOING to a boy's house tonight.

No, not like *that*. But the sentiment stands. If she were here, Nadia would be over the moon, screeching and slapping my arm in excitement. Every introverted person requires their vibrant extrovert to occasionally force them out of the house. Nadia used to be mine. I'd have to burst her bubble of pride by clarifying that the boy in question is Wyatt, and we're going to his house to practice.

Practicing outside of speech hours is a common occurrence for individual events. Debate, on the other hand, tends to remain a team sport beyond the Lincoln-Douglas kids. Most of the team does well within the constraints of our weekly practice, but none of the coaches discourages additional practices after hours. Nadia and I tried several times, but her social calendar kept her busy outside of debate. We did fine without the extra help anyway.

Usually, this would be a hypothetical discussion—except

practice got canceled this week. Coach Kruger had an unexpected engagement out of town and couldn't get a substitute coach for us. While everyone else relished the chance to go home, Wyatt offered to meet and practice by ourselves.

His timing couldn't be better. Tonight, the Edwards house would be overrun by way too many people to focus on homework or college apps.

As I turn onto Crestview Road, the sky paints its sunset glow over the neighborhood and its still streets. The streetlamps join in a chorus of golden orange, brightening the final moments of the fading sun. Most of the houses look the same, down to the complementary paint colors in a range of neutrals or the occasional muted pastel blue, so I keep my gaze sharp when searching for the number. I had turned down the volume of the radio to focus better on the road as I approached the last two turns in my Google Maps instructions.

I think...There it is! The brassy 752 shines from the doorway so bright that I can see it as clear as day from across the street. There's no parking on the side closer to Wyatt's house, so I drive two houses down to commandeer a wide-open space. No sooner than I cut the engine, I have one foot out the door, and my backpack hoisted over my shoulder, darting for Wyatt's house to the scuffle of my Mary Janes.

I reach the porch, quick to ring the doorbell before checking if anyone's home. But I have nothing to worry about when the door swings open, revealing Wyatt leaning in the doorway. The sight of him radiates comfort, something I hadn't noticed was missing in him before; his dark hair flops into his eyes, not damp like fresh out of the shower, but close enough. The cozy, navy-colored sweats and the faded Boston Bruins t-shirt two sizes too big swamp his lean frame. I don't ever think I've seen him without a bomber or leather jacket or in anything more casual than a pair of jeans.

"Hey! Sorry I'm a little late." My hands find their way into the slim pockets of the skater skirt, brushing off the thin layer of sweat coating my palms. Straight away, Wyatt's entire posture shifts. At first, his shoulders hunched over, and a quiet crease in his brow telegraphed something close to annoyance. But now, any tension in his face and shoulders vanishes, giving the floor to a friendly, toothy smile. "I ran a couple of errands before this and didn't expect to hit traffic. I should know that road work is bound to pop up at the worst times."

Wyatt, for his part, laughs in a full, bursting sound that warms me from the top of my ponytail to the tips of the Mary Janes I wear. He steps out of the door frame but holds the door open, "Don't worry about it. Come inside." He waves me inside. "We should be left undisturbed for however long we need."

"Oh yeah? Nice place you've got here." I spin to capture a snippet of Wyatt's home, and what I see isn't far-fetched from the guy I know. The place looks well-loved and lived-in, with the slightly sagging couches and stacks of small clutter spread throughout the living room. Cream-colored walls, butter yellow, medium browns, and the occasional hint of blue blend together in a masterful interior palette, brightening every crevice of the space. Most of all, our words echo off the walls from the sheer lack of noise elsewhere.

It's perfect for a night of news collection and debriefing ballots. My house is currently overrun by a gaggle of sixth-grade girls for a playdate, plied with a stream of pizza and sugar. Knowing how vile middle school girls are, let alone when on a sugar and carb high, Kelsie and her friends might either roast the living crap out of Wyatt or make heart eyes at him for simply breathing.

"Eh, it's fine. But yes, we have the house to ourselves. My mom, her husband, and his son should be out for a while, meaning no distractions." Wyatt steps ahead of me, so I fall in line with him. *Ah, so he has a stepdad and stepbrother...he's probably not close to them, or it's new.* "Anyway, we can get set up in the kitchen. Can I get you something to eat or drink?"

I snort, "You gonna cook for me?" I try to envision Wyatt behind the kitchen counter, wielding some serious knife skills and sporting a colorful apron tied around his neck. *I don't know. He seems like he would have a few surprises up his sleeve. One of those might be baking or becoming the next Gordon Ramsey.*

The subtle arch of Wyatt's brows responds plenty when he abstains from a snarky joke or a quick-witted comment, which seems to be his modus operandi. I've barely known Wyatt for a month, yet his little quirks pop out in everything he does.

Instead, Wyatt wordlessly gestures for me to follow him. We pass through an open archway and enter a cozy kitchen and dining room. A six-seater table and kitchen island occupy most of the room's open space, which fades away from the living room's array of colors for some simple cream walls and medium brown wooden accents.

Wyatt heads over to the ancient-looking Crockpot tucked into the corner of the counter and lifts the lid off it. Smoke billows out from the move, but the mouth-watering, savory scent of something home-cooked explodes across the tight space. He turns over his shoulder to look my way. "Can I interest you in slow-cooked Italian meatballs and angel hair spaghetti?"

"I'd eat that entire Crockpot of them without hesitation." The words fall out, lacking all grace or sense of manners. Wyatt, however, pays no mind to the delivery while he grabs bowls for the pasta. "Thank you."

"No problem. If this wasn't your speed, I would've offered you some snacks from the fridge. One of my mom's favorite hobbies is to restock and rearrange the fridge like those TikTok ASMR videos." To prove his point, Wyatt cracks open one of the fridge doors long enough to grab a container of ground parmesan cheese, but I see shelves of perfect color arrangements and dedicated food groups. A twitch of glee rushes through me. *I might need to ask Mrs. Keene where she gets her organizers.*

"Those videos are so addicting!" I accept the bowl of pasta that Wyatt spoons out for me, complete with two massive meatballs the size of my closed fist. "For a solid three months, I watched them to fall asleep when my insomnia acted up."

"I should try that. I usually fight crime in a spandex bat suit by moonlight," Wyatt remarks. His smirk widens when a rogue snort of laughter escapes from me. He fills his plate to the brim with pasta and slides into one side of the table.

Of course, I join him. We sit side-by-side, brushing shoulders on occasion while we set everything up. Besides pasta, a pile of ballots with handwritten comments end up scattered across the open table, and our laptops crowd the only wall outlet nearby.

I clasp my hands together. "Alright, these are the ballots from Lane Rogers. Do you want to sift through these or handle the article collection?"

Wyatt lifts his head, sauce smeared across his mouth until his tongue swipes over the stains. "I can handle the ballots. I started the folder for today but didn't get around to sorting anything." He picks up a ballot from the stack and shakes it to a crisp snap.

"Fine with me!" I'm not the type to shy away from ballot comments. They can sometimes be insightful in how an outside viewer perceives a team and how well they gel together. At other times, however, you might receive the most asinine comments. That or critique bordering on more hurtful than helpful, I always find the pointless critiques more irritating.

If Wyatt wants to read about our strengths and weaknesses as a team and solo speakers, he can be my guest. I'll be more than happy with articles and putting documents in their proper folders.

Silence falls over the room, or as silent as it can get beyond the clacking of keyboard keys or the occasional scrape of a fork against the ceramic bowls of spaghetti Wyatt and I indulge in. As much as I love Nadia, she wasn't the type of who could leave a conversation alone for more than a few minutes. Her mind always raced, turning over a million different thoughts at any given moment, and she never failed to share those random thoughts with me. "What would you do if you met your clone?" still lives rent-free in my brain.

On the other hand, Wyatt moves through the lack of conversation without so much as a bristle or the awkwardness of trying to contain himself. His eyes glaze over in the intense focus I recognize all too well—I've seen it plenty of times in the reflection of my laptop or a mirror. For now, I appreciate the quiet while opening a dozen new tabs in my browser, joining the prestigious ranks of the pinned ones for half-finished college essays.

Neither of us speaks or breaches the bubble, filling the kitchen with studious, comfortable silence. It's nice, you know? *Cozy, even.*

Wyatt reads the ballots, brows furrowing, while I download enough research papers and news articles to induce a migraine. After twenty minutes, the scrape of Wyatt's chair turns my focus toward him.

Wyatt's lips purse as if he measures his words carefully, "So, most of the feedback is on the positive side. Almost every judge complimented our preparation and use of sources. Also, many said you're a strong speaker with a good eye for spotting weaknesses in arguments."

Then, he pauses, reeking of hesitation. His eyes flit between my face and the paper ballots wrinkling in his hands from how rough he grips the flimsy edges. I put him out of his misery with a dry "Alright, and what negative comments did some of them leave behind? I'm no stranger to unfair critiques."

Wyatt sighs, "They said that you're intense, and that one judge—who was a total prick, by the way—said you should smile more to be less 'intimidating.' Their words, not mine." He tosses the offending ballot onto the table, which I quickly snatch up and read for myself.

Wyatt softened the blow. Apparently, I need to smile more to be less 'off-putting'—direct quote from that absolute loser of a man. I read it twice before tossing it on the pile.

"The opinion of one man who doesn't know a damn thing about debate means nothing. Two years ago, Nadia and I received a comment from an older judge—a woman, if you could believe it—who had a whole conniption about us wearing suits instead of skirts. She wrote across the back of the ballot with her commentary on how young ladies should dress appropriately," I say. It comes out more as an undignified snort. The greater point is that I know how to roll with the punches when this sport throws them my way.

"Wow," Wyatt whistles, slumping into his chair. "Where do people get the audacity to say stuff like that?"

"Welcome to being a teenage girl. Everyone and their mother has an opinion on how we should conduct ourselves, so I don't let it get to me anymore."

"It used to bother you, though?"

I shrug, "It would bother anyone at first. Recognizing it for what it is helps soften the blow. I don't let those comments define me or the perception of myself." I spent too much time during my freshman year trying to hack away at pieces of myself to fit into a more pleasing shape for others. So what if I don't smile while arguing or have an intense stare when dissecting opposing arguments in a round? As long as I stay in the confines of the rules and proper sportsmanship, then the judges can deal with my resting scowl.

"Right…" Wyatt trails off at the sudden creak from the other room—the front door—and rises from his chair. "I didn't think you'd be back so…oh." A single word flips Wyatt's polite tone into something irate. *Oh?*

Wyatt stations himself in the doorway to block whoever entered the house from joining us in the kitchen. But I only catch a glimpse of a bulky figure before he shoves past Wyatt, knocking him onto his heels. And with panic firing through my chest at full velocity, Travis Maynard looms in the doorway.

He freezes when he spots me at the dinner table, eyes bursting wide and mouth parted. *This is the first and last time I'd ever agree with Travis. Same.* Travis' shoulders snap back, and the fool actually puffs his chest out. "Hey, Beth."

If he's trying to seem nonchalant, then he's failing.

"Travis," I reply. No force on the face of the planet could hold back the disdain coating the edge of my greeting. It drips off Travis' name in spades, locked and loaded with intent. *More importantly, what's he doing here?*

I eye Wyatt, ready to demand an explanation from him, when the door creaks once again. This time, a dark-haired woman and Coach Maynard, Travis' dad, enter the kitchen, carrying reusable grocery bags in their arms.

Okay. Things are getting weirder by the second.

"I didn't realize we had guests tonight." Coach Maynard breaks through the five-way staring contest and awkward gawks with his gruff, oh-so-personable demeanor. I've had limited interactions with him, but he feels like the human equivalent of a half-used can of discount body spray.

Do I have any evidence to support this assertion? No. God forbid a girl catches a vibe. I'm sure that, with little effort, I could find empirical evidence to support my argument like any debater worth their salt. But for now, I choose to keep my distance from his kind. *Jocks*.

"I told Mom that my debate partner was coming to study," Wyatt replies. Okay, "reply" might be underselling the curt edge of how he addresses Coach Maynard. "This is Beth."

Coach Maynard's eyes sweep over me, head to toe, narrowing as he takes me in. Mine probably narrow too—enough to make him bristle. However, Wyatt's mom pushes past whatever Coach Maynard is to her, to hug me. This woman wraps her arms around me, squeezing until I let out a hiccupy gasp.

"It's so lovely to finally meet you! Goodness, Wyatt's had nothing but the highest praises," Mrs. Keene grasps me by the shoulder. She holds me at arm's length and examines me. The universe must've had my back because I came *this* close to showing up in sweats and a worn-out debate hoodie. "I hope he offered you something to eat or drink. We have spaghetti-"

"Mom." Wyatt coughs. Our plates of spaghetti sit on the table and cool with each passing moment we leave them alone. He lingers in the doorway, leaving his chair open. His gaze jumps toward Travis, who appears to notice the empty chair beside me.

Right as he surges toward Wyatt's seat, the one holding all his stuff and dinner, I slam my backpack onto the chair before Travis can slide in. My mouth pulls together a smile and a soft "Wyatt's been a perfect gentleman."

This becomes Wyatt's cue to retake his seat at my side. He nudges past Travis with the barest of shoulder checks, sets my backpack between our chairs, and lounges back. "Beth and I are still working on ballots. We can move, though, if you want a clear table for dinner."

Coach Maynard crosses his arms, "Yeah—"

"That's not necessary!" Mrs. Keene interjects. "You and Beth can continue to work in here. Graham and I've been meaning to catch up on Yellowstone episodes. Just leave room for Travis if he needs the table for homework, too. And if Beth needs anything, you've got it handled?"

"More than handled." Wyatt's assurance releases Mrs. Keene from the table. She grabs plates of spaghetti, and Coach Maynard hovers behind her, matching her every step. He reminds me of a lost puppy underfoot. Wyatt's gaze chases the two out of the room, taking a good chunk of the conversation and some of the air with them.

Now, only three remain.

For his part, Travis stands on the opposite side of the table, having moved after I blocked his path to Wyatt's chair. His hand curls around the curved top of another chair. If he squeezes any harder, he might snap the chair's top off. His knuckles gleam a ghastly white, even under the yellowing lights of Keene's dining room.

Travis stares. So does Wyatt. I avoid eye contact with either of them, witnessing how the unsettling ambiance filling this room prods at my half-empty stomach until it gurgles in warning. Wyatt's mom is dating Coach Maynard, which is the last thing I'd ever expect. I swear he was married just last year.

Did he have a ring on still? Awkward if so.

"Can I help you?" Travis snaps, the first to break out of the three of us. His lips twist up into a scowl, sour and strikingly upset. *Poor Wyatt has to see this guy daily? I'd rip my hair out after a day.*

Wyatt rolls his eyes, "I don't know. You're the one who's

annoyingly hovering while Beth and I are trying to work." He glances at me, brow arching like he senses the thoughts running amok in my head.

All the remaining air rushes out of the room, leaving only the suffocating tension pressing against my chest. Under its full weight, the low, persistent buzz of anxiety spreads across my skin, no different than a blush or a nasty rash. I go numb the further it branches out, reaching up the column of my neck and down past my ribs. Lost in the sensation. I don't realize what's happening until my arm tucks right underneath Wyatt's shoulder blades.

The press of my forearm into his back elicits a slight jolt from Wyatt, who stays completely still. The move dragged our chairs closer together where our thighs brush over the edges, much to the thickening of the tension in the air. Travis's eyes narrow, but he slinks away without another word spat at Wyatt or me.

He doesn't go far, opting to linger around the Crockpot and the empty bowl Mrs. Keene left for him on the counter. Now, the most interesting sight appears to be his phone, as Travis glues his gaze onto the screen.

Beside me, Wyatt squirms in his seat, which squishes our thighs together even more. His head tilts toward me, but his eyes never leave Travis, watching him the way a fox outwits its hunter. He whispers, "What's that about?"

"Elaborate?" I mumble back.

"You and Travis? Your arm around my back?" Wyatt's words remind me that I'm gripping Wyatt's body with a firm hold. My arm drops in an instant, slapping against my chest with a sharp *thwack*.

"Sorry. Um, the first part is a little complicated..." This sends Wyatt's face into a dizzying array of emotions, with his brows, mouth, nose, and eyes pulling vastly different expressions. Curiosity, disdain, awkwardness, and something unread-able all vie for control of his features, which helps me find the rest of the words. "Travis and his buddies used to harass my old debate partner since sophomore year. That's the short and sweet of it."

"I wish I could say I'm surprised. The guy's a tool," Wyatt replies after a moment of processing. His face relaxes into a neutral expression, if not one tinted by a mild thread of disgust.

"You can say that again. During those years, he treated me like I didn't exist, even when I cussed him out. Suddenly, at the start of the semester, he tried talking to me and getting my attention. It's weird."

"As if my mom marrying Graham couldn't be more annoy-ing." Wyatt stabs one of his meatballs with his fork. Thank goodness that I wasn't mid-bite, or I would've choked. *Wyatt and Travis are stepbrothers? You've got to be kidding me.* Wyatt hardly lets me savor that realization before speaking again. "If he tries bothering you again, tell me. I'm not above intervening."

"You being a human shield is working so far. Maybe we should try that first." I tilt my head just enough to catch Wyatt's eyes, but the moment our gazes meet, a laugh tacks itself onto the tail end of the joke. Wyatt—maybe to humor me, or maybe out of genuine amusement—breaks into a beaming, ear-to-ear smile.

"Consider me your human shield, then. Happy to be of service." Those words shouldn't fill me with such instantaneous relief. But they do. *They really do.*

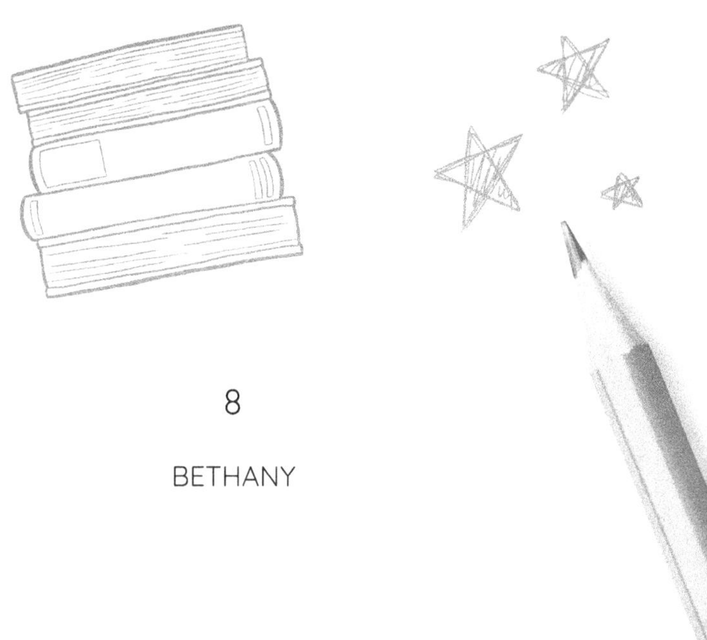

8

BETHANY

I'VE MADE A GRAVE MISCALCULATION.

Practice at Wyatt's house last week went without any other hiccups or hitches after the grand reveal that my new debate partner's stepbrother is none other than the insufferable Travis Maynard. Although unplanned, I thought that would be the end, and the whole show of clinging to Wyatt's body might deter Travis from interacting with me. If he ignored me when with Nadia, maybe the stepbrother he dislikes would act like *ultra-strength* repellent, right?

Wrong. *So, so wrong.*

Ever since that night, Travis has become seemingly dead-set on demanding my attention. At first, he tried the Instagram route again, friend-requesting me, and sent a DM after an hour of no response. When his virtual attempts failed, Travis took his mission offline, approaching me before AP Gov and Econ class during A Schedule.

Thankfully, each attempt ended before it began, thwarted

by Mr. Alvarez or the morning announcements. By the time class ends, I'd be gone faster than anyone else could blink. The strategy has worked thus far, allowing me to dodge Travis's attention. He seems allergic to the words 'no' or 'not interested.'

I can't understand what keeps Travis coming back when my disinterest should be clear. Wyatt is also baffled.

I keep him in the loop whenever something happens, shooting him a text or two throughout the day. Even though tone gets lost over text, part of me wonders if Wyatt knows more than he lets on due to his and Travis' relationship, or lack thereof. Not that it's hard to fathom, but they must have reasons to dislike one another.

Regardless of the why, I can only hope that Travis bores of this cat-and-mouse dynamic and settles for chasing after someone who wants his attention. Or, he can continue ignoring me like he has for the past three years. This isn't some cheesy, feel-good rom-com plot where the nerdy girl trips right into the quarterback's arms and falls in love. He'd need to be more than a pathetic, empty-headed bully to be in the running for even my friendship, let alone for me to want him.

The stone-cold silence of the school's library wavers when the shrill lunch bell barrels through the worn book stacks. The collective shuffle of students, accompanied by the scraping of backpacks and chairs against the ancient carpet flooring, fills the air. I glance up from the weathered copy of Shirley Jackson's *We Have Always Lived in the Castle* to observe the mass exodus of my AP English classmates. The near stampede startles the poor librarian, Ms. Rowland, out of her midday staring contest with the circulation desk's computer. Her weak pleas to 'shhh' fall on unwilling ears as the room steadily empties.

I shuffle toward Ms. Rowland and hand over *We Have Always Lived in the Castle* with what I hope looks like a polite smile. The dead-eyed stare I receive in return shoves the smile back where it came from for the rest of the wordless exchange. Once the receipt slides under the cover, I'm striding across the room to leave.

I am considering staying behind for the lunch period to get a head start on the reading report paper. But the harsh, demanding growl of hunger tearing through my stomach has other plans, gurgling for something sweet to wake me up for an hour or so behind the potter's wheel. One might assume that ending the week with ceramics would be a treat, certainly better than math or an AP course.

Then, there are those of us who are not *artistically inclined*, for whom the mandatory fine arts requirement feels akin to pulling teeth. Almost crying over a stubborn mug handle that is not shaping evenly is somehow the most embarrassing thing I've experienced this semester, and that's saying a lot considering the Travis debacle.

The full force of the sweltering October afternoon hits me as I step through the library's double doors. Being the stubborn girl I am, I ignored this morning's weather report of overcast skies and lingering marine layer for the brand new plaid skirt I thrifted over the summer. It's supposed to be part of my Boston wardrobe, but I can't resist a cute fit. *I always love being right. The weather turned out perfect.*

Through the throng of students heading toward the cafeteria or the front gates for those with senior off-campus lunch passes, I weave and duck into pockets of space, fighting against the current pushing me in the direction of everyone else. Like a fish swimming upstream, I march to my locker. I've been dreaming of the chicken salad wrap and homemade white chocolate macadamia nut cookies in my lunch since first period.

Most of the crowd thins as I reach the base floor of the Hawkins building, where my locker is. All thoughts of that chicken wrap and cookie waiting for me screech to a grinding halt at the sight of Travis. He leans against my locker, talking to two guys in matching letterman jackets, laughing loud enough to echo off the walls in a warning to me. *Looks like my luck just ran out.*

Without a beat, I spin around and walk the other way. *Guess I'll buy lunch off-campus today.* I don't get far before I hear "Beth" from behind me. *Travis.*

I groan, but the speed of my strides increases gradually, spurred by each time Travis calls after me. The sound follows me, growing louder like Travis matches my set pace. I try to shake him, ducking behind people and carving an inconvenient path for him to follow. The disgruntled noises from fellow students become the encouragement I need to jog. Speed walking isn't cutting it anymore.

Travis finally catches up to me just short of the gate. He lands in my peripheral vision, adjusting his letterman jacket and slicking back his hair. His grin, though? He looks smug but probably thinks he's charming. *Ugh gross.*

He chuckles, "I didn't think you'd be such a fast walker with those short legs of yours. Academic and athletic, what a combo."

No response is the best response, even if part of me fights the urge to sneer at him. He followed me halfway across campus, and *that's* his grand opening line? The countdown clock to graduation flashes up in my mind, reminding me I have about seven and a half months until people like Travis Maynard will be nothing more than a footnote in my life story.

My silence appears not to deter him because Travis stands beside me, mouth breathing in full effect, waiting for me to fall into his arms. I slip my hand into the frontmost pocket of my backpack, and my eyes never leave the dwindling distance between the security guards and me.

I count the seconds, tuning out whatever Travis says when he begins talking at me. Then, when the person in front of us steps through the gate, I immediately whip out my student ID.

"Go ahead, miss." Frank, one of the security guards, remarks, waving me through at the flash of the senior sticker on the card. I don't need to be told twice. I surge forward, catching sight of Travis being stopped by Frank and Leon until he produces his ID card before I break into a full sprint.

I have so little time to clear the parking lot and such a little head-start to reach my car before Travis finds his ID. I scan the parking lot, searching for either a group to tag onto or some-where to wait Travis out. But then, a familiar glint of dark metal strikes the light, and I find Wyatt's helmet-clad figure standing at his bike.

Unlike me, whose assigned parking spot is on the far end of the lot, Wyatt's motorcycle requires a specific spot closer to the front. And that just might be my out.

I borderline sprint toward Wyatt, never shooting a back-ward glance to track Travis' location. In a single, strong breath, I shout above the noise, "Wyatt! Hey!"

Wyatt's leg stops midway into his mount, bent at an awkward angle, when his head snaps up. Even through the helmet, the shift in his posture when he spots me barreling toward him has him shuffling back from his bike. He flips the visor up on his helmet. "Beth!"

"Just the man I didn't know I needed!" I scamper to his side, shouldering my bag. Shudders tear through my chest as I hunch forward, heaving, hands braced on my bare knees. "Are you heading off campus?"

"Yeah? Are you okay?" Wyatt's brows furrow, looking me over. The concern is audible, visual—*palpable* even. He reaches his hand out and helps me stand up.

"Travis decided to stake out at my locker and follow me

across campus. What do you think?" I pant, still out of breath. Jeez, I need to get into better shape if a short sprint winds me this bad.

"He what?" Despite the brightness of the afternoon, a shadow slips across his features, darkening them in its wake. Most of his face is hidden beneath the bulky fit of his riding helmet, but the hardened glint in his eyes speaks volumes.

Wyatt steps to the side, spotting something over my shoulder that pulls a furious scowl out of him. *Or maybe, some-one...Travis?* My arm loops through his to hold him back.

"Which is why you're going to plop me on the back of your shiny motorcycle and whisk me away like a modern-day knight in shining armor."

Nothing could've prepared me for how fast Wyatt's head snaps toward me, or for the shock that drains him paler than a ghost. His mouth falls open, speechless as he stammers for a start, then shuts again—just to breathe.

Eventually, he reins himself in enough to ask, "Oh, is that so?"

"Yes. Is there a problem?" My hands find their spot on my hips while I stare down at the burgeoning amusement from Wyatt. He looks me over, turning his shock into a faint smirk.

"Have you ever ridden one of these before?" His hand pats the seat of his motorcycle to the slap of leather.

"I haven't. But I'm sure you can give me a quick tutorial," I reply. *How hard can riding a motorcycle be as a passenger?* "This can carry two people, right?"

Wyatt leans against the motorcycle, arms crossing over his chest, "Yes, my bike is suitable for a two-up. I'm more concerned about the clothing situation." He reaches one of his hands to brush against his thigh, pulling and snapping at the pair of pants he wears—however, his line of sight lands where the hemline of my skirt rests right above my kneecaps.

I scoff, "This is a skort! I'll be more than fine." To prove the point, I lift the skirt a little to reveal the pair of skin-tight shorts underneath. Besides that, I doubt my beat-up sneakers or the balloon-sleeved navy polka dot blouse I wear pose any issue to being a good passenger.

"I also didn't bring an extra helmet today. I wasn't expecting any passengers, and for riding with me, no helmet, no entry."

At this, the fleeting hope that once nipped at my heels to push me toward Wyatt deflates. The sensation isn't purely metaphorical either. My shoulders slump. I drop my gaze to the pavement, which I scuff the tip of my sneakers against.

"Woah. Hey," Wyatt's hands grasp my shoulders until I meet his eyes again. His lips stretch into a smile, a cautious one you'd give to a startled deer. "That doesn't mean I won't be your human shield for lunch today. I made you a promise, didn't I?"

"You're willing to walk down the street for me? You sure know how to make a girl feel special," I tease. The relief coursing through me can't be understated or defined by the thousands of words in the English dictionary. *Better luck next time, Travis.* "For your generous efforts, let me buy you lunch."

Wyatt snickers. He snaps open the strap tucked underneath his chin and lifts the helmet off with ease. Within seconds, he removes the black balaclava from his face, showing off his messy hair with a simple rake of his fingers. He sets his helmet onto the somewhat curved seat of his motorcycle but keeps one of his hands splayed over the raised visor to hold it steady.

"I don't think I could refuse such an offer." He grins.

"Then don't," I scoot closer, grinning too. "Come have lunch with me. My treat. We should head over there so we can grab something and enjoy the nice weather."

"Alright. But first," Wyatt plops his helmet straight onto my head. The low ponytail I chose this morning doesn't fight against the helmet as it slides right on, loose on me. "I need to see something."

"I can't take your helmet, even if the drive is short—" Wyatt's fingers brush underneath my chin. The unexpected touch silences the thoughts going mile-a-minute in my head. Wyatt adjusts the strap around my jaw and chin as tight as it can be. The helmet tilts to the left, a little lopsided.

Wyatt sighs, "As I suspected, this will be a little too big on you. You're going to need a smaller one for future rides...maybe a size down. Two sizes at most." His hands cup opposite sides of the helmet and rattle it. "I could see if my mom still has her old helmet. She should be around your size. She hasn't ridden in years and might appreciate the free space in her closet."

Wyatt's hands linger around the helmet's strap, but his eyes jump over my shoulder. "Is he still there?" The question bubbles out of me when I try to turn my head, and the strap catches on his fingers.

"He's gone," Wyatt confirms. His attention returns to me while he undoes the helmet before sliding it off. "I'm sure this is the hardest he's ever had to work to ruin something for me."

"He's done this before? I know he's a prick, but I didn't expect him to be that awful."

"Oh, him *and* his dad. Neither of them likes me very much, despite us being a 'blended family.' They seem to derive some twisted joy in making my life harder than it needs to be," Wyatt says, like it's nothing. *It's not.* Leave it to the Maynard men— and their insistence on always getting their way—to ruin someone else's blessings.

An involuntary scrunch of my nose elicits a tiny chuckle from Wyatt. I watch him stuff his helmet into his backpack. "Well, if it's any comfort, I'm on Team Wyatt. The day I willingly side with a Maynard, just know I've lost all common sense."

Wyatt says nothing. Instead, he clasps my hand, squeezing our fingers together like a firm handshake. But his smile—bright as the sun overhead—slips something unspoken into the touch. Maybe it's a secret. Or perhaps it's a promise to stand in my corner too. "I'm starving. All this friendship stuff has worked up quite an appetite."

"Try out-running a football player without making it obvious on top of all the friendship. Then get back to me." I elbow him. Neither of our grins seem to vanish as we join the slowing stream of students headed off-campus for lunch.

9

WYATT

October, Week 4

THE EXCITEMENT of young trick-or-treaters floats through the crack in my bedroom window, perfectly embodying the spirit of the cold, dusky Halloween night. Besides the newly alive streetlamps, the white-hot glow of the bedside lamp lightens the midnight blue of the walls. This space is the closest place in the house to being "mine," which isn't saying a lot from how sparsely I decorate it. Besides the textbooks stacked across the desk and the shelf of vinyl records and band posters on the opposite end of the room, these four walls scream "guest room." Granted, that's what it was before I showed up with my boxes of stuff, designed for a transient, temporary energy that leaves after a week of overstaying its welcome.

Graham and Travis would love that, wouldn't they?

The room brightens slightly when my phone screen flashes awake with a new text notification to join the others. Halloween has become one of those holidays that puts me in a weird spot. I'm way too old to dress up and go trick-or-treating among the kids, likely to be turned away or stared at by whoever answers the door. Then, there are Halloween parties hosted by other students. I wasn't invited to any other group activities, like watching horror movies or something, which felt wrong as a solo endeavor.

Snatching my phone off the bed, I roll out of the messy grey comforter to the creaking of my bones. Guess tonight will be me, a snack, and my third attempt to rewatch *Umbrella Academy* beyond the first season. *Dad loved that show.*

The rest of the house falls into an eerie quiet as I step into the hallway, or at least the bottom floor seems abandoned. I pass the stairs and head into the dining room, where someone left the overhead light on. A traffic cone orange plastic bowl sits on the counter, brimming with king-size candy bars and other sweet treats for the eager kids gathering around the block. Some traditions never change; Mom never skimps on the good stuff for the trick-or-treaters.

If my hand dipped into the bowl to steal a Twix bar from the top, no one would be any wiser. The candy finds a new home in the pocket of my baggy sweats, partially forgotten when my phone buzzes with a new text message. Some of my friends from the Viewbrook debate team, including Tanner, my old partner, sent check-in texts and their Halloween plans. Thus far, everyone either has a date planned or will be attending the costume party at one of the football players' mega-mansions.

I must sound bitter about it. Senior year is a busy time for everyone, especially in the thick of college app season. I don't expect my friends and former classmates to drop everything to tend to my every whim. However, it would be nice to receive more than a once-a-month "hey" text after years of daily conversation, memes, and general closeness.

I shove my phone into my pocket to join the Twix at the

latest text. Tanner's out. *Haunted house escape room with his new girlfriend.* I should text him back, promise no hard feelings, and say 'we should try some other time,' which probably won't ever come to pass. We're on separate tracks now, heading toward the rest of our lives

Rifling through the cabinets, rows of powder drink packets and protein bars occupy the shelves, but half of the boxes are empty and left to collect dust on the shelves. *Another instance of Graham and Travis neglecting their chores. Wonderful.* The empty boxes land in the trash with a simple flick of my wrist, opening the space for actual snacks.

After searching high and low, the unopened bag of mild cheddar cheese puffs from the local mom-and-pop deli five blocks from us beckons me like the call of the sea to a sailor. That and a chilled can of ginger ale from the fridge end up on the kitchen counter, ready to be whisked away to my room. It should hold me over for the first hour or two until I decide what to order for dinner. We don't have any leftovers in the fridge, and I have no energy to cook tonight.

I prep my things to go, but everything stops at the clack of heels coming down the staircase. Only when they stop in the kitchen doorway do I turn around, coming face-to-face with Mom. Tonight, she's nothing short of radiant; the intricate finger waves, feather headband, and shimmery red flapper dress paint her in the visage of a bygone era—long live the Roaring 20s.

Her ruby-red lips quirk upward at the corners, breaking into a beaming smile. Mom shuffles in a tight circle, "Be honest: how do I look?" She asks.

"You always look amazing, Mom." I don't need to reach for some honesty. "I know it's Halloween, but I didn't think you'd get so dressed up to pass out candy." In years past, whenever Mom or I had no Halloween plans, she'd pull out an old witch's hat or a pair of cat ears to answer the door and pass out candy. The last time she repped a full costume was when she, Dad, and I all went as the Ghostbusters.

"Oh. Actually, Graham and I are attending a costume party with some of our friends." Mom's fingers pinch at the end of her black elbow-length gloves, stretching the fabric to cover the crook of her elbow. Her eyes flit toward me, "I hope it's okay that we're heading out tonight?"

"Yeah, that's fine. Spending Halloween alone isn't a big deal for me." I shrug. Them heading out for the night doesn't change much. I might just relocate my *Umbrella Academy* watch party to the living room sectional—it makes it easier to pass out candy to the brave kids who show up

"Travis will be staying in with you tonight," Mom corrects.

"Huh?" One tight grip on the bag of cheese puffs pops it open, sending them cascading in the air. Travis and I alone in the house? What a recipe for disaster. "Didn't he spend all week yapping about some party?"

"Yes, but he's been grounded, remember?" The furrow of Mom's brows mars her once-glowing expression. At this, the semi-hazy memory of a blow-up argument between Graham and Travis—one partially obscured by a closed bedroom door— steps forward in my memory. Ah, right.

"I thought his daddy would've bailed him out by now." Mom's face flashes with a glare, demanding me to *'be nice, Wyatt Andrew Keene.'* The full name doesn't need to be said for the emphasis to jump out at me.

However, the comedy writes itself, beginning with the immediate slam of a door from upstairs, followed by a pair of footsteps racing down the stairs. Travis's whining rattles the walls: "Dad, you're being unfair!"

He and Graham enter the kitchen, both dressed in costumes. Graham's charcoal gray pinstripe suit and worn fedora would already look cheap and cartoonish, but the ill fit and endless wrinkles trash any potential saving effort for the 1920s gangster look. Dad's old Peaky Blinders costume when I was eleven blows this poor display out of the water. As for Travis, his generic scary clown mask hangs limp in his hand when he races after Graham's angered strides. Beyond the mask, nothing he wears appears to be any discernible costume. *Imaginative.*

"I don't want to hear it! You've got a C in AP Government and Econ, a C- in chemistry, and you're failing Intro to Graphic Design. How do you fail that class in the first month of school?" Graham snaps with a hand slapping against the countertop.

I, for once, agree with Graham. However, it should be evident to anyone with a lick of common sense how Travis, a chronic underachiever who prioritizes his unlikely football career and social standing over any academic success, might be on the verge of flunking half of his classes. But hey, what do I know?

Travis throws his hands into the air, emphasizing the exasperation thrumming between him and Graham. He scoffs, "So?"

"You know damn well what will happen if your GPA doesn't get back into the clear. I've spoken to Principal Cardenas and the athletics department, but they won't budge. They will bench you for the rest of the season if you slip below the required grade threshold. You can say goodbye to any sort of scouting or championship titles to boost your profile." Graham spits out his ire through a clenched jaw. His eyes snap toward Mom and me, which tosses his entire scowling demeanor into full throttle.

Yeah, shrugging probably doesn't help de-escalate the tension, especially if the pulsing vein in Graham's forehead is any indicator.

"Graham, honey," Mom reaches for his shoulders, eyes softened, pleading for some peace. Although he remains tense, visibly ready to blow, he pulls Mom to his side. I avert my eyes when his hand dips south of her waist, less hungry now. *Gross.* "Maybe we can find some proactive solutions to help Travis, hmm? Does he have a tutor for these classes already?"

"Yes, one I pay good money for." Graham's voice threatens to dip into a hiss, treading above it instead. Mom's presence dulls the edges of his anger like smoothing over jagged shards of glass, only that it should never be her job to placate his rage. "She clearly isn't doing her job right..."

"Or maybe she and Travis aren't a good fit, and that's neither of their faults. I know the school offers free tutoring during lunch hours, but maybe we can see if another student from his class can tutor him instead. They'll better understand the nuances of the teacher's style and expectations. Wyatt has done that once or twice," Mom suggests, echoing the energy of a prim and proper pageant queen offering a shiny new plan for world peace. She is the balm to soothe the ache, the input to stop the ticking time bomb that's Graham Maynard.

The mere mention of me apparently reminds everyone that I, too, am standing in the room. Their attention prods me for a moment before cutting me out of the moment. Graham, now calmed enough to look Travis in the eye. "Well, is there someone in your class you can call and ask for help?"

Back in the spotlight, Travis lapses into silence—almost pensive, maybe for the first time in his life. His eyes glaze over, distant and unfocused, and he stuffs his hands into the pockets of his baggy sweats. Which only makes it more obvious when the lightbulb goes off, especially in the way he turns his head toward me. A smirk pulls across his face, "Beth... Wyatt's partner is one of the top students in our grade. She's in the class. Wyatt can give me her number."

Absolutely not. No way in this lifetime or the next, knowing what I do about his history with Beth.

"Great. Wyatt, you can send me her number-"

"No," I cut off Graham before he has a chance to finish his demand. Not even a request or something with a "please" and "thank you" in it. *He's not my dad.* "I'm not asking Beth to tutor Travis. She's above charity work and lost causes."

"What did you say?" Graham's anger flares back to life, reinvigorated into more than a flicker. As much as he gets mad at Travis, this man holds an endless supply for when I step on his dominance.

"Wyatt, please. That wasn't very kind," Mom says, or rather, scolds. Even when her voice rises in pitch, scraping against the edge of something harsh and disappointed, she can never fully mask the softness.

But I push on, "You know why Beth is the top student and probably valedictorian, right? It's because she dedicates most of her time to studying and debate instead of a social life. She doesn't have the time to salvage Travis's grades. Maybe if he spent less time with football and breaking curfew with his friends, he might not be failing half of his class schedule. Don't shoot the messenger. I'm just being honest."

"Talk like that again, and you'll be grounded for the next two weeks. No debate, no phone." Graham pushes past Mom. His shoulder nudges her out of the way, clipping hers. While it looks accidental, any indication otherwise, and he wouldn't be standing.

"Graham," Mom protests.

"Last I checked, the arrangement of this family unit is that Mom handles me and you handle Travis... in the name of fairness," I reply. Thus begins the high noon-esque stare-down between Graham and me, riding along a knife's edge. Someone must've plugged the room into a supercharged amp from how the tension shoves against every wall.

Eventually, Mom steps forward. This time, she nudges Graham with a twinkling rustle of her dress when she moves. She sighs. "Honey, I know that Travis not playing this season would be hard on you and him. Wyatt, however, does have a point about involving his friend. The school has a list of available tutors, and one is bound to be in Travis's class. We shouldn't burden another student with extra work, especially one as busy as Beth."

Graham doesn't dignify Mom choosing my side with a response. Instead, he mutters something under his breath and reaches for his coat. "We need to go."

"Right," Mom rubs her hands together. Our eyes meet, which is when I send my apology. She nods, understanding without needing it spelled out. That's why I love her most—no one in the world understands me better than her. "Wy, are you staying home for sure?"

"Let me try one more person before I confirm that," I say, phone in hand. Opening my text conversations, I find Bethany toward the top.

ME

got any Halloween plans?

No more than thirty seconds pass before a response comes through.

BETH

my family and I are at the Fangtastic Festival
set up at Lashmer Park. more so for Kelsie
and Sawyer but it's kinda cute this year.

LASHMER PARK IS the only public park on the Hill. I've passed it a few times on rides through Searidge to clear my head. Several of those came after Graham and I wasted another evening at one another's throats.

ME

is that like one of those fall carnival things for Halloween?

BETH

hay mazes, bobbing for apples, and games galore! You should come. I'm dying for more people our age.

My head snaps up, and I find Mom waiting and Graham lurking by the kitchen doorway. I hold up my phone, "Change of plans. I'll be at Lashmer Park for the Fangtastic Festival. Beth invited me."

"That sounds like a wonderful time. Be safe. Text me when you get there and when you get home." Mom reaches across the counter. I meet her halfway, falling straight into her bone-crushing hug.

"Will do. Same for you?" I ask. When she nods, I let her go. I race past Travis and Graham, forgetting all about the unopened ginger ale and the popped bag of cheese puffs on the kitchen floor. Instead, I speed into my bedroom and fling open the closet.

A worn, partially dilapidated cardboard box on the floor gathers dust in the corner of the cramped closet. I drag it from the shadowy depths to plop onto my lap. Fingers trace over the dents and tears in the cardboard, all its rougher edges existing as a perfect metaphor for the state of things, before slicing through the flimsy packing tape. For tonight, I'll bring out the big guns... with a little help from Dad.

XOXO

I HEAR laughter before reaching Lashmer Park. Even through my helmet, the lively spirit of the night sings over the purr of my motorcycle and the distance of several streets. Pedestrian traffic slowed my initial ETA by ten minutes, turning the fifteen-minute drive closer to half an hour. In my defense, I'm not interested in catching a vehicular manslaughter charge because I decided to rush.

Sorry, Beth.

Soon after the influx of noise washes over the remaining stretch of road between the Fangtastic Festival and me, strings of orange and purple lights illuminate the path crowded with families in costumes. Weaving through the chaos as carefully as I can is the easy part. Finding parking, on the other hand, might be borderline impossible.

The long, dark sky paints a perfect backdrop for the explosion of color when the festival comes into view. Carnival rides and orange and black striped booths appear through windows in the tree line, filling the wide-open clearing and the grungy baseball diamond with plenty to do. As I suspected, rows of vans and trucks are crammed into the chalk-drawn parking spaces, packed tighter than comfortable to avoid spilling into the overflow lot.

Maneuvering with a motorcycle instead of a car has its perks—one of which is the speed and size to steal the nearest available parking spot right as it opens up. In the second row from the sidewalk leading into the park, a banged-up Beetle rumbles out of its parking spot, carving out a sliver of room for me to slip through.

A swift dismount plants my boots on the ground, to the rumpling of my black billowy pants. The rest of the costume—

including one ankle-length leather coat—flutters down once I no longer straddle the motorcycle. Practiced fingers switch out my helmet for the top hat, the ivory bird mask, its curved beak and hollow eye sockets, and the accompanying top hat.

I blend right in with the rest of the festival-goers in their costumes, ranging from the cheesy Halloween store costumes to the intricate, made-with-love cosplays.

I scour the crowd, my line of sight jumping over heads, looking for Beth. Per her last text, she promised to wait for me outside the entrance to the festival, and that her costume should make her stand out.

"Oh, Beth...where are you...Wait, is that?" While the crowd funnels into the festival at a steady pace, the sight of a sparkly white dress standing off to the side of the entrance catches my eye once or twice. But after the second time, I look for longer than a cursory glance and find Beth. *Or should I say, Princess Bethany?*

I stride across the parking lot, staying far away from the streamlined direction of the crowd. Beth taps at her phone, unaware of my approach and the rest of the world around us. The blueish tint of the light illuminates her grimace, harshening the subtle wrinkles of her nose and downcast eyes. She doesn't notice me when I step right in front of her, not until I lean in, "Boo."

It comes out in a chuckle, but the way Beth drops her phone and wobbles as her head lurches back. She clutches her chest, "Wyatt!"

"Sorry, I couldn't resist." I pick her phone off the ground since I'm the reason it lies there. She accepts it from me, quick to dust off the screen. "You look. . . sparkly."

Beth's costume comprises pristine white elbow gloves and a dress to match. The full skirt brushes against her kneecaps, poofing out from the waist in a blend of crisp white and silver glittery flecks embedded into the fabric. The silver platform heels gleaming against the pavement match, and so does the sparkly silver tiara on her head. She has a pair of mini sunglasses perched on her nose and the retro headset sharing space with her crown.

"Thanks... and you're... Are you a plague doctor?" Beth skims her fingers over the mask's beak. The subtle push moves the mask away from my face to hang around my neck. One move opens up the world and the airflow I can reach.

"Yeah. My dad made this a few years back. Halloween used to be a huge event in the Keene household." I readjust the mask over my face. Something hot stings against the back of my eyes at the mention of Dad. "And you're supposed to be-"

If Beth notices how I choke on the past tense, she abstains from commenting on it. Instead, she stands there, hands on her hips, duly unimpressed. "Mia? The Princess of Genovia? From *The Princess Diaries?*"

"Ah, I vaguely remember that one. Mom has a soft spot for romance movies," I tease. Now, I might watch bits and pieces of those movies from the living room doorway without Mom ever noticing my presence. But Beth doesn't need that tidbit to hold over my head. Somehow, I suspect she's not above a dose of playful blackmail.

Beth rolls her eyes but loops her arm in mine. "Come on, loser. Let's get in line for the greasy fair food before the lines get too long." She tugs me as she bounds off the curb, so I follow her lead. Our strides are quick to even out, pushing us down the crowded aisles between the booths and games. Joyful screams fill the air alongside the mouth-watering, greasy aroma of fairground food, tied together by an overwhelming amount of noise flooding into my head.

Beth's arm slips further through mine whenever the crowd jostles us around. She guides me to the side, and we disappear into the striped flaps between two stalls, one selling fresh kettle corn and the other hosting a ring toss. But when we emerge on the other side, we stand outside a food tent.

Within seconds, I have my wallet in my hand, stepping up to the register before Beth. "Snacks are on me tonight. Order what you want."

"I'll pay you back-"

"Nope. It's on me. No repayment necessary." The freckled cashier accepts the credit card from my gloved hand, not even batting an eye at my get-up. "Let me get a turkey leg and two churros. And for Beth. . ."

"Turkey leg as well, please. Oh, and a mini strawberry funnel cake with two forks." Beth's eyes sparkle, taking a devious turn when she adds the fork request. She accepts the ticket from the cashier. "I bet you one of your churros that I can beat you in Skee Ball."

Beth points to the stall behind us, which hosts a ten-lane Skee Ball booth. A few kids take up some of the lanes, but six appear free to use.

"And if I win? Do I get half of that funnel cake?" I ask. Never in my life have I been above a friendly wager. Heat and adrenaline rush down my neck and chest, splintering off and branching out.

"Deal," Beth grasps our hands together in a firm handshake before she drags me across the road. We dodge around people and post up at the Skee Ball lanes. "You're so going down!"

"Bring it on!" The attendant starts up our lanes, letting the balls roll down. Beth and I shoot each other one last look before throwing out the first rolls.

And when my first attempt sinks into the 200-hole, I know I'll be enjoying crispy, sweet funnel cake soon enough.

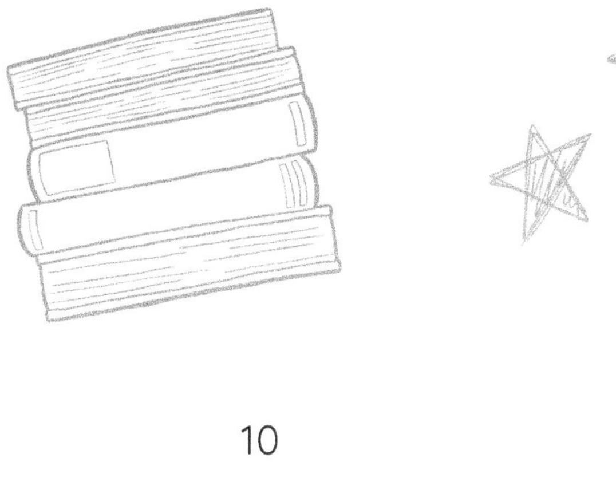

10

BETHANY

"STILL WITH US, BETH?" The garbled cough from my laptop's speaker snaps me out of the daze so fast that my knee slams into the underside of my desk. Pain lances in both directions, crashing and careening under the skin, leaving a trail of pins and needles in its wake. *I'll feel that tomorrow.*

Swallowing the pained yelp puffing in the back of my throat, I play off the tears watering along my lash line with a tiny yawn, "Yes."

In the tiny video call boxes scattered across my screen, Rohan, Fallon, Andrea, and Devon stare at me. Yet, no one comments on the loud 'thump' or the wobbly grimace plastered on my face.

Devon claps his hands, which crackles when coming out of my second-hand laptop's speakers, "Great. Ms. Goodwin sent me the bunking assignments for Wildwood, so we need to approve or modify those before the hour's up." He grins.

The immediate reaction is a collection of whoops, cheering,

and clapping, including from me. Windwood is *the* tournament of the debate season, the one everyone on the team looks forward to. We spend three days out of town—in Palm Springs, to be exact—competing against teams from across the state and neighboring ones at Golden Palms High School. East Shores makes a massive deal of the event; we rent a giant party bus for the nearly three-hour drive, and our numbers require us to book every room in this quaint, family-owned hotel close to downtown Palm Springs.

The screen shifts as Devon shares the list, pushing all our heads to one side of the display. "Alright, Andrea and Beth, you two share a double. Is that okay with you?"

"Finally, I'll get a good night's sleep," Andrea giggles from her corner of the screen. In years past, she shared a room with August, while Nadia and I split a room, either with just each other or, occasionally, a third girl on the team. "If August says I snore, he's a liar."

I shrug, "Hey, I can handle a little snoring, so long as you don't mind the light from the Kindle screen when I can't sleep."

"Deal. It's better than August, who doomscrolls for at least two hours." Andrea and I shake on it through the screen. "Consider our room assignment *approved*."

Devon nods, scrolling further down the list of names until the next member of the board shows up, "Okay, we have Rohan, who's paired with Zion..." And this is where I clock back out, especially when I catch sight of the four pinned tabs on my browser—*college applications*. One is for the UCs, one is for the CSUs, another is for the Common App, and the last one is for all the miscellaneous supplemental essays for the colleges not included in those three forms.

I jump between the tabs, playing a game of leapfrog with the limited amount of motivation I have to crank out the next lucky essay. *Someone's still dragging her feet, huh?* The end of the month might seem far out of reach, but it always sneaks up on me after Windwood. The sooner I get the essays done, the sooner I can throw the applications into the void and have a meltdown about it later.

I land on the lucky winner—the UC applications—while Devon scrolls further down the list. Wyatt's name flashes over the screen, next to August and Josh's.

A thin sheen of sweat slicks over my palms while my fingers hover over the keyboard. The cursor blinks from the nearly empty page, swaying back and forth whenever I delete the first few words I've attached to a star-shaped bullet point. When faced with the prompts about overcoming adversity and the strength of oneself, not a single idea rises to the occasion. I can't even muster up some platitude-laced, fake-it-till-you-make-it fluff to stuff the word count. I need something thought-provoking, *life-changing,* even. Instead, a profound emptiness greets me at the door, familiar like a worn winter coat hanging off the rack.

What can I say that hasn't already been written by much better writers from much worse circumstances? *Being diagnosed with anxiety doesn't make me special, or stand out among thousands of other applicants. Try harder.*

A sigh hangs on the edge of my lips as I leave the essay behind for a new tab—a spreadsheet. Always the meticulous, chronic planner, a spreadsheet is a must for one of the biggest decisions of my life. The college calculus of where I eventually will end up runs a complex set of facts—the benefits of the major I applied to, professional and personal growth opportunities, financial aid, location, if I visited the campus, and the student social culture. I put a lot of stock in a well-rounded experience, especially if I need to take out loans that cost an arm and a leg on top of whatever financial aid and college fund money I can scrounge together. Everything is color-coded, complete with a customized legend in the corner, and ranked in order from "dream school" to "safety net." I even saved an honorable mention slot or two for the local community colleges, where I will go if none of the other options pan out.

Fifteen universities, but *only one* needs to change my life.

I'm sure that years down the line, when this decision doesn't seem so consequential, I'll find it in me to laugh. For now, though? Everything might shove me over the breaking point of stress.

"-and do we want to book that Mexican place for after the award ceremony like last year, or should we pick something different?" Devon's face returns to the center screen, yanking me back into the conversation.

"God, yes!" Fallon's face brightens. "That place has a pozole bowl the size of my head for fifteen bucks!"

"Not to mention, the post-tournament dinner is a time-honored tradition, and we need a restaurant big enough to accommodate everyone. Doesn't Flor do reservations in advance?" Rohan chimes in.

"They do. Ms. Goodwin wanted our input before she put in the official call, so I'll send her the approval with the rooming assignments. If no one has any objections, then we've locked in for Wildwood." No one interjects, not even with a cough or the rogue creak from their chairs. Devon raises his hands and claps them together, "... and sold! Thank you all for attending. I will see the rest of you later this week."

"Bye, everyone!"

"See ya!"

"Bye," I wave to the others. The screen flickers to black before closing in on itself. It leaves me at the mercy of my college application spreadsheet and the unfinished essays haunting the front of my brain. Thankfully, the softest pressure of two front paws dig into the flimsy cotton shorts I wear and the bare skin of my thighs. I glance down, "Looks like the people's princess has awoken from her slumber."

Ziti opens her jaw for the most enormous yawn and stretches, tremors rocking her tiny, fluffy frame. She crawls further onto my lap, pushing onto the tips of her toes until her head bumps into my chin. Ziti's claws might scrape against bare skin, but the gentle kiss I press to the top of her head forces them to retract. She snuggles into my lap, curled up in a comfortable loaf position.

When I run fingers along Ziti's arched spine, her purrs intensify. She rattles like a chatterbox as I repeat the motion. It soothes her; it soothes me *too*.

Too focused on Ziti's pleased purring, I miss the door creaking open and someone entering. They enter my peripheral vision, sitting on the edge of my bed. Ziti and I turn at the same time to face—Mom. She cocks her head, leaning to the side to read my screen.

"College essays coming along?" She asks. "Kelsie said you left for some more quiet, so we all assumed you were working on applications." Kelsie has some friends over for a school project, but that leaves the kitchen a little too chaotic for my focus hence, why I sought refuge upstairs.

"They're... coming," I say, more like a lie. Out of all the essays, I think I've written one in its entirety, not counting the dozens of rewrites since August—*the Wellesley one.* "The prompts require me to stand out from the rest of the applicant body, so I need something bold yet authentic.

"Well, not to be biased, or anything, but I think any school would be lucky to have you." Mom shifts further onto the bed, leaning back on her hands for support. When our eyes meet, her lips curl into a tight, closed-lipped smile—like she already senses the knee-jerk denial rising in me. "Beth..."

"What if they don't want me?" I whisper, careful not to

squish Ziti when I slump forward. "There's a very real possibility that I might not get into any of the schools on my list. Not that community college is something to be ashamed of, but I never envisioned that path for myself."

"I know how much Boston means to you," says Mom, all furrowed brows. She taps her socked foot against my ankle, as close to a reassuring shoulder pat as possible.

Boston means *the world* to me. Searidge Hills is a wonderful place, but everything here moves at a glacial pace. Things are familiar, maybe a little too much. Perhaps I'm suffering from the delusions of grandeur only a young mind can summon, idolizing the idea of being anywhere but the place I've called home. If I'm ever meant to grow, I need challenges and things best found outside the insular little community by the sea.

"There are a lot of what-ifs that keep me up. Like, if I apply to all of these schools, what if I don't get into any of them? If I get into something like Wellesley, what if we can't afford it and the loans will be too much? Even when I find a rational answer, more of them pop up. It's like a never-ending game of Whac-a-Mole."

A tingling, freezing sensation spikes through my chest, leaving goosebumps in its wake, while the numbness seeps into my hips. With it, the rest of the room grows colder around me. Ziti's little body works overtime to keep the warmth alive within me, a small burst of heat on top of my thighs as the rest of my body succumbs to numbness. Twitching under my skin, the feeling takes on a life of its own.

"Beth, honey, you'll only rile yourself up if you focus on things you can't control," Mom hums. I know that sound as a warning bell ringing, promising a nugget of sage wisdom tumbling through Mom's impeccable filter, polished and perfectly digestible to an otherwise obstinate mind. "Yes, it would suck if those colleges overlook what you bring to their student body, and it would be disappointing for you to give up on your dream school over finances. But what can you control about the situation?"

"My feelings? My reactions?" I mumble. This isn't the first time we've broached this discussion before. Mom would've been a frighteningly good therapist in another lifetime, from how seamlessly she can dissect through the shield I form with my words. That, or my therapist, snitched about how I intellectualize my feelings instead of letting them be felt. Either way, she has me pinned down, nowhere to hide, even in the comfort of my room.

"That's right. So, underneath all the what-ifs, what's truly bothering you, honey?" When her hand slides over mine, the walls within me crumble down. Who can I confide in if I can't talk to Mom?

"Colleges are expensive. Boston isn't a sure thing compared to the in-state school options. Am I selfish for still wanting to run away from California and start over somewhere new? For leaving you, Dad, Kels, and Sawyer behind?"

The hand that once sat over mine lifts to cup my face. Mom's thumb traces over the swell of my cheek, quickly brushing away a stray hair or two lingering like whisps of smoke from my face. "There comes a day when you'll spread your wings and leave this place for less than thirty miles or around a couple thousand. Dad and I have braced for that day since we held you in our arms, barely a few hours old, yet so curious about the world. No one would be upset if you go to Boston, not when you're choosing bravery and the unknown. You and Ziti will always have a home here. There's no need to center our feelings over yours; Dad and I miss you when you leave for a tournament. That's inevitable as a parent."

The lump of words pools at the base of my throat. "Any

chance you could write my essay for me?" Although the words struggle to break past the watery laugh, they spring forward with enough levity to push the conversation into calmer waters.

"I've read your speeches, honey. You've got a gift, but, more importantly, you write when you've got something weighing on your soul. I have no doubt that it'll come." Mom shakes her head, winking at me. "You want some pizza? I can bring it to you as long as you work on one of those essays."

"Sounds good. Thanks."

I watch Mom rise onto her feet, whose movement snaps Ziti's eyes wide open. She missed all the good parts of the conversation while catching some extra shut-eye. *Oh, to be a cat whose only worries include mealtime and sleep.* Mom heads for the door, which I follow with the spin of my desk chair.

However, she pauses in the open doorway, glancing over her shoulder at me. Her mouth quirks into the ghost of a smile, "One more thing—you deserve to be happy, no matter what that pesky voice in your head screams at you. You've taken the last few months like a trooper; Nadia leaving and a stronger Buspirone dosage are not easy things to shrug off. It's okay to want things."

With that, Mom excuses herself from the room, heading down into the den of high-pitched shrieking and random snippets of trending videos that have Ziti's ears flattening. She closes the door behind her, but not before silence returns to its vigil by my side.

Regardless of whatever my mind says or what the anxiety whispers in the dead of night to keep me awake, I have time to figure it out.

XOXO

"—JUDGE, who should win this debate should be undoubtedly clear. Only one side solves the harms created by the status quo. You've heard from the other side, who paints us as 'idealistic,' to suggest that our continued practice of solitary confinement in our prisons should cease. This practice is torture, plain and simple, according to the United Nations. We have gone far beyond our burden to offer reasonable alternatives, which have been tested in different institutions nationwide. Therefore, the affirmation maintains that the current use of solitary confinement is inhumane. Thank you."

I hold eye contact with the elderly judge, whose mustache twitches instead of his mouth when he offers a polite smile, and I can tell the win belongs to me. *That's how you stick the landing.* I put everything left in me into that rebuttal speech; it needs to be enough.

When I take my seat, Wyatt leans over, shoulder brushing mine. He passes a bottle of water across the two desks we've shoved together to form our little table, the cap already open for me. I nod, thanking him, and catch the bottle from its side.

In several greedy gulps, half the water disappears down my throat. Crisp and cold, it soothes over any itch leftover after the last five minutes of uninterrupted talking.

Wyatt's shoulder stays close, occasionally bumping into mine whenever he shifts in his seat. Exhaustion crests off him in waves, seeping through every slow blink he directs toward the wall ahead of us. Today, Friday, we drove straight from campus around lunchtime, skipping the day's last class for the first day of the Wildwood Invitational. We arrived at Golden Palms High School's sprawling campus right as students departed for the day, which made for a fun experience to find parking and disembark with all the other buses.

Debate came up first on the docket. Wyatt and I hauled ourselves across campus for our first round—the affirmative team on "The United States Government should lessen its use of solitary confinement in prisons." It's an unpopular position, but boy, does it have a good chunk of articles and statistical evidence to reference.

"Hey." From our right, the opposition team peers at Wyatt and me. Either sophomores or juniors, the two seem relatively new to parliamentary debate. They dropped way too many arguments between each speech and left themselves with the bare bones of a case, relying on the status quo like a crutch. "May the best man win."

The speaker—blond and face dotted with acne—leans around his partner with his hand outstretched toward us. He's not smiling, but the hand promises a gesture of goodwill. So, I reach forward to meet his hand halfway—only for him to curve me. No, he scoots even further over the edge of his seat to grasp Wyatt's hand. He makes a show of it, too.

Wyatt stiffens beyond the awkward flex of his finger. His eyes narrow into thin slits, yet it's nothing compared to the sharp curl of his lip. "Aren't you going to shake my partner's hand?" he asks.

The blonde appears taken aback by Wyatt's sudden, downright harsh reaction. He eyes me, whose hand curls against the buttoned blazer I wear, and still hesitates before offering his hand. I have every right to turn him down, to shun him for his vile attitude. Unlike him, I'm better than that, *most of the time.* So, I give him a handshake, perfunctory and as unenthused as his effort.

His partner—a shaggy-haired guy in a suit with shoulder pads clearly from the 80s, probably from his grandpa's closet—abstains from shaking anyone else's hand. I'm not sure which reaction is worse.

"Good luck. May the best *man* win," I parrot back to the opposition. Their faces twisting up stokes a sick sort of glee in me. Perhaps, next time, they'll think twice about disrespecting their opponents. Beside me, Wyatt's shoulder nudges mine, pulling my focus away from the boys.

At first, I look at him. But when the judge shuffles his papers, glancing up from the ballots to adjust his tortoise-shell glasses, the world narrows into tunnel vision. He grunts, interspersed with a few coughs to clear his throat, while sifting through the ballots, scribbling down comments. I can see a good stretch of writing bleeding past the margins of the ballot, but the specifics aren't clear.

The judge looks up from the ballots and says, "Alright, I can disclose who I've voted for if both sides are comfortable. Otherwise, all feedback will be contained in these ballots."

"Yes." Our opponents jump at the chance, eager and sounding as though they're on the verge of scrambling out of their chairs. *So sure they've won, huh? Oh, to be that confident.*

"We'd appreciate that. Thank you." I vouch for Wyatt and myself. He nods, whether to confirm our acceptance or encourage me to go on. Our shoulders and knees press together while our hands hover a breath's width apart, a natural consequence of the closeness of our desks. The closeness brings comfort as we dance along the silence's edge.

"I will be siding with the affirmation in today's debate. I've been judging for at least ten years, as noted in my paradigm*. A good chunk of my personal philosophy focuses on the strength of arguments, which includes not dropping them. For that reason alone, I rule in favor of the affirmative. I found their arguments compelling, backed by a good blend of statistics and case law, and they didn't make the mistake of forgetting their arguments for low-hanging fruit," the judge remarks.

The other side can't hide the sourness in their reaction, not when their faces scrunch like someone shoved a lemon down their throat. We hold the line on our side, except for Wyatt's barely-there chuckle. He reserves that for me, a secret between partners.

"Thank you for judging." Wyatt is the first among us competitors to break the silence. The judge nods; that's our cue that the round is over. Both sides gather our respective bags and head for the door. Wyatt and I hang back while our opponents blow past us, thundering off into the evening with a rousing "What a load of bull—"

I stare after them, eyes following their angered march down the winding walkways of this massive school campus. If East Shores used to be a community college, then Golden Palms has that 'private university' vibe. Its modern architecture and endless display of palm trees splash against Mount San Jacinto and the dusk-touched desert in the distance. Other debaters move past us and down those same roads, either on their way to rounds or leaving the first of hopefully many in the tournament.

When Wyatt steps next to me, I hum, "Thanks for defending my honor back there." I catch how his head whips toward me—*poor guy*. I might've given him whiplash.

"No need to thank me," he replies. His hands sink into the pockets of his suit trousers. "We're off to a good start. One win in our pocket and more to come."

"Definitely." I grin as we begin our trek across campus. During the debate, Deanna sent me my room assignment for the first speech round—I only saw it when I reached into my purse for an extra pen. I'm probably walking in mid-round, but the tournament gods were kind: I drew the last speaker slot. I glance at Wyatt, who measures his longer strides to match mine, shouldering his messenger bag higher whenever it slides further down his arm. The arid desert night follows us as we walk past the streetlamps, casting patches of the campus in a yellowing glow. "Thanks for being my partner this season. You're making it better than I ever thought it would be."

"Aww," Wyatt teases. His arm slings over my shoulder, drawing me into his side. "Okay. Don't tell Tanner, but you've been my favorite debate partner."

"You're not so bad yourself," a snort escapes me. I would've shrugged off anyone else's touch, but Wyatt's arm shocks warmth into me against the dropping temperatures of the desert evening. Besides, Wyatt always has this sixth sense of when to pull his touch back without the words ever leaving me. "It's different with you than Nadia, my old partner."

"Good different?" Wyatt asks.

"Yes," I reply. I mean it, too. The kind of debater I was with Nadia hardly resembles who I am with Wyatt. Dare I say, I've become better and more well-rounded because of how Wyatt pushes me, providing a level of *friction* that Nadia and I never had. She and I are too similar, a sharp-tongued extrovert-introvert duo whose ideals align in every conceivable way. Wyatt, on the other hand, opens a whole new avenue of perspectives with the experience to boot.

Wyatt says nothing to that. Yet, I catch his quiet grin, one he savors for a moment before it slips away, fleeing into the night. His eyes, however, never seem to lose the slight twinkle in them. It accompanies us across campus until we reach the room assignment for my next round—*Monstrous, Take 1*.

I face Wyatt, "This is me. Thanks for the escort."

He nods, eyes locking with mine. "Good luck..." His hands lift, almost to draw me into a brief embrace like a hug. Instead, he pats my shoulder with the faintest twitch of his lips.

"I don't bite." I grin, even though the clock ticks, telling me I should head inside. Wyatt's brows raise. So do mine, mirroring him until he chuckles.

"Maybe not me. But you look at Travis like you want to tear

him apart with your teeth," Wyatt hums. He's not wrong; Travis's persistence continues, but Wyatt's committed to his role as my debate partner and human shield.

Applause echoing through the closed door interrupts our conversation before it goes anywhere else. *That's my cue to enter the ring.* I snatch my binder from my purse and down the last bit of water. Winking, I laugh, "I should channel that energy while I'm in there. See you on the other side."

Wyatt and I go our separate ways as the applause swallows me whole and envelops me in its adrenaline-soaked embrace. *It's showtime.*

11

WYATT

November, Week 2

A CAR WHIZZES past the crosswalk at the corner and honks its horn loud enough to drop-kick the exhaustion straight out of me. My eyes snap wide open, and my hand curls tighter around a plastic bag of Chinese take-out. The crinkling and rustling of the stacked paper boxes within the bag join the streetlight symphony, driven by the rush of cars roaring by.

Tonight's warmer than last night, but the otherwise blistering temperatures become tolerable once the sun goes down in Palm Springs. I've always been more at home in the cold anyway.

"Walk sign." Beth's elbow grazes against my waist, touch as soft as the beat of a butterfly's wings or a tepid ocean breeze. She hovers next to me, carrying her own bag of takeout, then shuffles forward to step off the crosswalk and into the street.

I glance up, and sure enough, the crosswalk is flashing the little walking sign as the intersection lights gleam red. Beth doesn't glance over her shoulder when she declares, "We have an 8 p.m. check-in deadline!"

I bridge the gap between us in two bold strides, quick to match her brisk pace. "I'm coming. I'm coming. We're going to be on time, if not a few minutes early," I assure her. I don't think Beth notices how the weight of her nerves is pressing down on us. The crosswalk sign hasn't changed to the flashing red hand, yet Beth appears on the verge of sprinting the rest of the way. Her voice strains— maybe that's her poor voice box giving up after the day we've had.

Day 2 of Wildwood ran Beth *and* me into the ground. The day began bright and early with a 6:45 a.m. breakfast and a 7:30 a.m. registration time on campus. For me, I didn't have much to do in terms of 'getting ready' for competition; Beth, on the other hand, said nothing when she slid in the chair next to me at breakfast, except that her day started at 5:30 AM.

The worst part about tournaments is the wait. Even when double-entered, like Beth, tournaments drag on for what seems like an eternity. Time always moves slower than usual, with the monotony of the wait interrupted by the rush of competition. It's not a strange sight to see competitors catching naps in corners or people cracking open textbooks to catch up on missed classes once they finish their run-throughs or warm-ups.

The campus had been empty since Saturday, adding to the eerie quiet that stretched out every excruciating moment.

Beth and I scramble onto the curb right as the light changes and the stream of cars surges ahead. However, we stand at the edge of the motel parking lot. *Someone said this place is a family-owned, independent lodging... I think.*

Wordlessly, we head across the lot for the automatic doors, passing a family of four dripping wet and still in their swim gear. They gawk at us when we pass, which might be funnier any other day. I'm sure that, to the outside observer, Beth and

I's mismatched appearances and dead-eyed expressions paint a rather unfortunate visual.

Beth's last speech round had run late with a rule dispute while the rest of the team waited on the bus. Most of us changed during the wait, myself included. So while Beth rocks her sensible charcoal-colored dress and her worn flats after hours of kitten pump heels, I go whole athleisure in my baggy shorts and a long-sleeved shirt.

It's all about balance, right?

A blast of tepid air from the air conditioning hits our faces when the front doors to the motel slide open, rushing into the night we leave behind. Maybe fifteen feet to the left of us, Ms. Goodwin glances up from her clipboard, in the middle of clicking her pen when she sees us.

"Ah, and that's everyone," Ms. Goodwin checks us off her list, not moving from her post at the doors. No one had dinner since the tournament provided only a hot lunch, and the debate rounds ran late. So she let us go in pairs to the shopping center across the intersection from the motel to buy ourselves whatever we wanted, as long as we returned by a specific check-in time. "Just remember that you two can explore the motel and hang out with the other students, but be in your assigned rooms by 10 for bed checks."

"Yes, ma'am," Beth and I chorus while we shuffle past her. The motel's lobby should qualify as a time capsule because of how perfectly it encapsulates the '60s. Coral wallpaper assaults visitors' eyes as they enter the room, full of odd shapes, chartreuse, and daffodil-colored furniture to accent the already eclectic space. The outside isn't any calmer; someone painted different segments of the buildings in vibrant pinks, blues, and oranges to break up the monotony of faded white paint. I'm still unsure if Beth and I stumbled through a time machine or a gap in the timeline to end up at some point in the distant past.

Beth's arm reaches out, looping through mine. "We should eat outside," she says. I follow her line of sight to the gaggle of some of our teammates overflowing onto a few lumpy couches across the room. Just past them, however, the double glass doors lead to the fenced-in tables and pool. "As much as I like our friends, I need some quiet time."

I don't miss the rasp grating against the edge of her words, rougher than sandpaper on the ears. Her throat can't be much better, either. From what someone mentioned, Beth's speech this year requires a lot of screaming and strain on her voice. Somehow, she's avoided going hoarse despite the extent to which she used her voice today.

"Lead the way, boss." My tongue-in-cheek nickname choice earns me a pointed eye roll from Beth. But I swear there's a tiny smile she allows when her face turns away from my view. Together, we leave the lobby for the ambient noises of the desert evening, which include the stray hum of passing cars or people's conversations when moving around the outer areas of the motel. Still, the outside proves far more peaceful than inside.

I eye the placid, turquoise-blue waters of the empty pool. "Care for a dip?"

"Huh?" Beth coughs, taken aback. Our arms break apart when I stride ahead, approaching the edge of the deep end, and Beth hangs back. She watches me kick off the slides I wear toward a lounge chair. "You're not actually about to jump-"

"Whoa, who says anything about jumping? I'm dipping my toes in!" Grinning, I set my takeout a little further from the edge before sitting on the ledge. My legs sink into the pool as the immediate cold rushes up the rest of my body. The pool water rests right below my kneecap, no longer still after my subtle intrusion.

Seconds later, Beth's legs enter the edge of my peripheral

vision. Her plastic bag crinkles when she places it on the opposite side of her. But she joins me, kicking off her flats to rest by my slides before her feet dip into the pool.

Neither of us utter a single word. Instead, we break into our bags of takeout. Beth wanted Italian, and I couldn't shake the craving for Chinese food. We ended up getting our own dishes, but also bought a slice of tiramisu to share for dessert.

So, a symphony of plastic and to-go boxes cracking open fills the air, followed by the mouth-watering smell of dinner. Hunger rumbles from deep within me, so far down that I forget about its sharpened teeth piercing through my skin. A rogue car horn howls in the distance, here one moment and gone the next, but that barely rattles the comfort settling over the abandoned pool.

Beth's legs drag through the pool waters, moving slowly from all the resistance. She scrapes her fork against the aluminum tin for more cheese in her bite of lasagna. Beth hesitates as the fork hovers in front of her lips.

She sighs, "As bad as today was, we have another long one tomorrow. I swear the promise of a slice of Flor's famous tres leches might be the only thing getting me through the day."

"Not even a finals trophy?" I snort.

"Well... that too," Beth amends. She leans over to examine the kung pao chicken I stuck my chopsticks in, humming in approval.

"Remind me how far you've gotten again? I just need to know how much of our continental breakfast I need to smuggle for a snack later on." I say.

"For me?" Beth asks. When I nod, she puts her lasagna to the side. "Since I got top-three placements in every prelim round and the first spot in the elimination round, I'll be in the quarter-finals. As long as I get within the top half of the room, I should advance to the semis."

I push around some of the chicken with the sauce-stained end of my chopstick. "And if you get the top scores, then the final?"

"You've got it," When Beth's legs kick faster, small waves slosh against the tiled walls behind our knees. Some water kisses the curved edge of the ledge but never reaches high enough to douse our dinner in chlorine. "This might sound bad, but I deserve to be in the finals. I'm performing *Monstrous* the best it's been all competition season. I'm sure there are other deserving competitors, but some of them will have another year or two to prove themselves. I have one shot left."

"Is it bad to want to be recognized for being at the top of your game?" I ask.

Beth pauses. When her body shifts, turning away from me, I follow. She doesn't look at me when she speaks, "I don't know. Some people probably see me and write me off as arrogant, self-absorbed, or desperately needing a lesson in humility. But I can't tell you how many guys I've met who speak without thinking, and no one bats an eye. Nadia and I had a lot of conversations about being confident and being a woman and how we need to tread a fine line for the comfort of others."

"Well, I might not be a woman-" The words fumble out of me, riding in on a half-formed stutter. I don't realize where I'm going with this until mid-sentence, which earns me a befuddled look from Beth. "But you don't need to feign humbleness or anything with me. You deserve to feel proud about your achievements, to shout them from the rooftops or through a megaphone pointed at your opponents' faces."

A grin cracks through the confusion, straining Beth's face. She even laughs, head rolling back, chest stuttering and heaving underneath the sheer weight of her cackling. Her laughter is infectious, neither shy nor feigned for an audience, just *like her*.

The same Beth who unapologetically marches to the beat

of her own drum and kicks down every door standing in between her and her way. If nothing else, no one can accuse Beth of putting on a performance or exaggerating herself. She wears her heart on her sleeve.

"Thanks, Wyatt," Beth's shoulder bumps against mine, her smile going strong. The fading light of the day meets the glow of the pool, illuminating her face in a spectrum of colors, refracting like a rainbow over her skin. She leans back on her hands, eyes closing.

"At least we have a later registration time tomorrow. We get to sleep in for an extra hour," I reply. One of Beth's eyes cracks open but shuts just as quickly. She hums in acknowledgment. "You have all your speech stuff. Then, we have the quarter-finals round for debate. All these top placements are exhausting to maintain!"

"Hah, I know other teams who would do heinous things for a flawless 4-0 run. 'Edwards and Keene, Top 16 debaters' sounds too right, though." Beth glances my way, finally slowing her kicking legs to a standstill. Our eyes meet in the middle, soaking in the saturated blend of color from all around us.

I nod, "Of course it does. We earned those wins." If we push ourselves tomorrow, Beth and I have a solid chance of taking home an award. First place isn't necessarily off the table, but I shouldn't bank on an unsure thing without the confidence to back me up. And, yes, the point of debate will always be to strive for your best and continue growing as a young academic. But nothing feels quite as good as bringing home a physical representation of greatness to show everyone the blood, sweat, and tears poured into each argument.

Beth and I agree there. We love to win.

"We earned those wins..." Beth parrots back to me. She reaches back for her food, reminding me of my own discarded dinner. Between bites of lasagna, a quiet puff of breath passes through her lips. "And to think I planned to return after the competition today and work on college apps. I doubt I could barely string together a coherent sentence at this hour." She tsks.

"Where are you applying to?" Curiosity wells within me, burning white hot and insistent. Some of the other debaters and I discussed our top choices while waiting for postings; Beth had been at her final prelim round, probably delivering the performance of a lifetime, from how she skipped over to the lunch table where the rest of us sat when she finished.

"I have a comprehensive list of fifteen schools, five of which are in-state. Those are typically better for tuition costs and housing since I'd commute for most of them. Then, we have five others out of state in Washington, DC, New York, and Pennsylvania. The final five are all in the greater Boston region."

I perk up, "Boston?"

"Yeah. My dream school is out there, and I've been in love with the place since I was a kid. All it took was one family vacation during the winter months; I refused to stop talking about snow for a solid two weeks afterward."

"Small world," I spear a chopstick through a particularly stubborn piece of chicken. "I'm from Boston. My dad grew up there, and we lived there until I was four. He and Mom moved us to California for a promotion at his job. The rest is history."

"Do you miss Boston?" Beth sets aside her dinner for the second time in this conversation. She looks at me, eyes as earnest as the sky is blue, hanging onto my every word. Even now, I see the wheels spinning in her head, calculating her next question in the minefield of things left unspoken. I know part of her wants to ask more than if I miss *Boston*—everyone does.

I shrug, "Sometimes. Don't get me wrong—California has become a special place to me with a lot of good memories. But whenever Mom and I go out there to visit my dad's side of the family, I often wish I didn't have to leave. It's nice to be close to him again."

Beth nods at this. Yet, she doesn't pry into all the past tense I use whenever my dad's mentioned. This isn't the first time a conversation has steered toward him, but Beth avoids all the pitfalls of the other curious people who came before her. She never pushes, never acknowledges it, despite how obviously she connects the dots internally.

So, I jump the gun, setting aside my dinner with a cough. "You've probably figured out why I only talk about my dad in the past tense..."

"It's not my place to demand answers, Wyatt. If you want to tell me, then I'm here to listen. But you don't need to spell it out for me or explain anything you don't want me to know. Our partnership doesn't hinge on me knowing your secrets." Beth interjects. She's not forceful, but her firmness draws a line in the sand.

It's *my* choice. It's nice to have an option to leave that door closed, even if I won't.

"You're right. It's my choice, but that's why I want to talk about it," I reply. This elicits a nod from Beth, who goes silent. Her eyes, however, never break from mine, softer than I've ever seen them. The light and color around us ease the sharp edges of her stare. It helps me find the words a little faster. "This past summer marked four years since my dad passed away. It still feels like yesterday for me, even though I no longer fit into the suit I wore to his funeral, and I've run out of his favorite discontinued cologne."

Beth moves all our dinner dishes to rest on the nearest lounge chair. She scoots closer to me until our thighs press together. We face the pool's glassy, glowing surface, watching the waves die down.

"I can't imagine how hard it's been on you," Beth murmurs. For once, the news of my dead dad doesn't invoke some stumbling over awkward condolences and the ever-present twinge of regret about asking.

"When people talk about grief, they always focus on the after. No one told me about anticipatory grief. My dad had been sick for a long time; he had a lot of issues with his kidneys, like repeated cases of kidney stones, but we didn't catch the early signs of kidney failure after one illness too many, missing a pivotal opportunity to get him care. Mom got tested to see if she could give him one of her kidneys, but she wasn't a match. I was too young to get tested, so we'll never know if I could've—prevented his slow death. No one we knew could give a kidney, so we waited on the transplant list for close to a year. He passed away before a kidney ever freed up."

I speak through measured breaths. Otherwise, the half-eaten Chinese takeout might decide to crawl back up the way it came. Mom and I don't talk about Dad as much as we should, never as much as I want to. If I broach the subject, the glistening pain in her eyes severs the conversation before it begins. I lost my dad, but she lost her other half and her perfect partner. Her soulmate.

Something warm presses over my hands, loosening them from their death grip on my shorts. *Beth's hand.* She says nothing while flipping my hand over, palm to face the sky, and clasping hers on top. When she squeezes our interlaced hands, I match her grip.

Oh. That's nice.

"What was he like? Your dad?" Beth asks. She still looks ahead, but as if she hears the small voice pointing out that little fact, she turns her head to face me again.

"He was my best friend. He loved motorcycle rides and the smell of pine tar. He loved pickles an unhealthy amount, so much so that my mom always fed him hers whenever restaurants forgot to remove them from her burger. He spoke in 70s movie references and sarcasm. He'd always get up an hour earlier to enjoy a cup of coffee, the birds chirping, and a crossword puzzle." A watery laugh falls out of me. Four years later, none of the details have faded at the edges. He lives in my memory like I might open the door to Graham's place and find him perched at the kitchen table, a crossword in his hand and thick-rimmed glasses perched on his head.

Beth's lips quiver, pulling into a faint smile, "Hmmm, some of that sounds familiar. I'm sure he was an amazing guy."

"The best. He loved us, my mom and I. Years ago, she told me that she'd never find another guy like my dad in this lifetime." I remember that statement as clear as day, despite the dark shroud of the funeral draping its unwanted weight over the memory. "So, I have no clue what she sees in Graham. The two of them met in this grief counseling support group and hit it off almost two years ago. They married about nine months ago."

"Let me guess: that's what brought you to East Shores for your senior year?" Beth's hand releasing mine shocks me back into the present moment. I hadn't noticed I trailed off, nor the heavy, prolonged silence that trudged in behind me.

"Bingo," I sigh. "The conversation came down to the fact that Graham teaches there, and Travis's football prospects are too great to jeopardize in a move. I would've been fine riding out my last year with my mom in separate residences, but she really likes Graham. For the life of me, I can't understand why-"

Beth snorts. "I wish I could offer my sage insight, but I have no clue why any woman would put up with that man or his offspring." That draws a laugh out of me, which has me doubled over and wheezing into the pool. It's the crass delivery of it—coupled with Beth's nonchalant shrug and the smirk like she knows she's right—that makes it funny.

"It won't matter in a few months anyway. My mom deserves happiness, so I'll put up with Travis and Graham. They can hate me and keep me outside of their perfect little family act because, by graduation, I'll have my one-way ticket back to Boston. I'll get into a school out there, pick up a part-time job between classes, and see if anyone in the family has a room they're willing to let me use for discounted rent." I straighten up to the snapping cracks along the length of my spine. Wincing, I run a hand over the tension coiling around the lower half of my back.

Beth's eyes rake over my face. "Any chance you could smuggle me in your suitcase and take me with you?" She jests, but part of me isn't sure she's totally joking. Something treacherously hopeful brings out the green in her eyes.

"Tell you what," I hum. "You get yourself an acceptance letter to a school in the area, and we can take this partnership on the road." I raise my hand, offering Beth my pinky finger. Pinky promises are legally binding commitments in the Keene house.

"Deal," Beth locks her pinky around mine without hesitation. When she grins, I feel the matching one appear on my face. Well, if nothing else, fleeing to Boston come summertime includes a partner in crime.

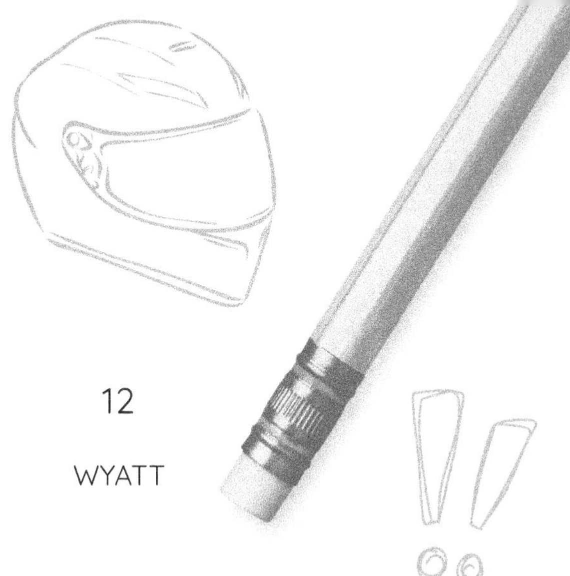

12

WYATT

BEFORE CLOSING my eyes last night, I drifted off to the hope that, despite the potential of reaching the final round of competition, things might go smoothly today. Yeah, I basically jinxed myself. That's on me.

Even with the extra hour of sleep and fewer competitors in rounds, Wildwood puts Beth and me through our paces. Nevertheless, considering she and I reached the finals in our respective events, it paid off. We might've discussed it last night, but I still float through the surreal feeling of exiting that final round with Beth at my side. Neither of us said a single word until our teammates, who came to spectate, surrounded us, shouting and jumping.

I can't imagine how fast the thoughts run through Beth's head, though. She reached the finals in not one, but two events. A final spot is no small feat, not in a million years. Yet, Beth makes the rest of us look like slackers. Her back must hurt from carrying the team's reputation on it.

Now, we wait, sitting in the auditorium beside one another, silent while the rest of the gathered students, coaches, and Wildwood volunteers cram into every available seat. Chatter floats over the room while the tournament organizers roll out the table carrying the awards to the center stage. The screech of microphone feedback disrupts the thrilling energy bouncing off the walls until the room falls silent.

Beth leans toward me to the swish of her ponytail brushing against my cheek, "Let's hope this ceremony doesn't take too long. I'm already at risk of falling asleep in my chili relleno before someone places a slice of tres leche in front of me." She rasps.

When I say "rasp," I mean it. Beth went hoarse sometime between her final speech performance and now, which shouldn't come as a surprise after the strain she puts on it for competition. To start, our semi-final round included an indignant opponent who refused to let Beth speak until she raised her voice to drown hers out. Then, the repeated performance of her speech added more grit to an already exhausted tone, especially with the blood-curdling scream she gives toward the end of the piece. Devon, Andrea, August, and I attended her final speech round as spectators.

I doubt any of us left that room unimpressed by Beth's performance. From Clytemnestra to Carrie White, Beth's performance is nothing short of legendary, channeling the rage and wrath of wronged women across literature and film. The wild look in her eyes when she surveyed the crowd...she looked ready to leap across the judge's table and tear into them with her bare teeth. Chill-inducing, to say the least.

I can see why she's the speaker to beat.

The furrowing of my brows tightens the faint pain banding around the circumference of my head. "You didn't manage to get any sleep during the day?"

Beth shakes her head. I study her, ignoring the preamble and opening remarks from the tournament organizer, barring the few moments where I clap in sync with the audience. Beth's eyes droop despite matching the audience's applause at the right times, never too long or too short.

I recall Beth mentioning that she had a rough night, getting somewhere around four hours of sleep on and off. The nerves got her during the night, whereas mine sank its claws into me right before our first round, threatening to leave my breakfast on the lawn. Finding somewhere to sleep during tournaments can be hit or miss, depending on the noise level, size of the campus, and other factors.

I guess she never found the chance to close her eyes between all the running across campus.

"-And now we begin with the award distribution! Starting with our speech awards, may all the finalists from dramatic interpretation please come to the stage?" More applause snaps Beth's heavy eyelids wide open, much to the scowl on her face. It deepens each time the slightest noise provokes her awake.

I nudge her, "Hey. Use my shoulder as a pillow for the next few minutes. They're likely saving debate for the second half, and your speech event might be held toward the end of the procession. I'll make sure you don't miss it."

Beth's face scrunches, expression conflicted. Mostly her eyes, which flicker between the stage and me. She debates the offer, clear from the tiny shifts in her expression that fluctuate between acceptance and polite refusal. In the end, she whispers, "Okay. If you're sure."

"I'm positive," I promise. Beth, without a fuss, closes her eyes. Her head slumps against my shoulder as the audience applauds the speakers on stage. I watch them pass out smaller trophies to everyone who misses the top three spots. The bulk of the applause remains for the top finalists and signals the passing of time. Most award ceremonies at these tournaments drag on for far too long; today's isn't an exception.

The tournament organizers try to streamline the process through the "one clap" rule, except for the top three finalists. However, that gets forgotten during each event by a few students screeching for their teammates. Not to mention, the awkward shuffle of students on and off the stage slows things down to a grinding halt. Glaciers move faster than this.

Beth might actually get an hour of rest at this rate.

So engrossed in watching the stage for Beth's turn, I miss the presence of Ms. Goodwin kneeling next to me in the aisle. Thankfully, I don't jolt when she taps my arm.

"Once you two head off stage with your trophies, go straight to the back of the auditorium. We're leaving for dinner since no one else made it to the finals," she instructs in a hushed whisper. When a parent across the aisle, filming their kid on a digital camera, glares at us for talking during the ceremony, Ms. Goodwin levels the nastiest smile at her until the woman looks away. *Note to self: stay on Ms. Goodwin's good side.* "We have a long ride and Flor reservations to celebrate the big wins."

"Yes, ma'am." I nod, tearing my eyes away from Ms. Goodwin at the sudden onset of extended applause. Ms. Goodwin uses that as her cue to leave and hustles down the aisle toward the back of the auditorium exit.

They're switching events now.

"For our last individual event, may we have the finalists from Program Oral Interpretation come to the stage?" The organizer, who is way too chipper after the long day, calls out. The shuffle of students out of their chairs has me reaching for Beth.

"Hey," I whisper. A gentle shake or two to her shoulder snaps Beth out of a light rest. Her eyes flutter open, still laced with drowsiness. Some of her eyeliner appears smeared along her lower lid, but it looks tasteful, as if she smudged it intentionally. "You're up, superstar."

"Think I can ask for five more minutes?" Beth grumbles while stretching out of her chair. She yawns hard, drawing a few wayward stares from the people around us. But their attention flits away to the echoing cheers for other students.

"Probably not," I snicker. I step out of my chair and into the aisle, offering a hand to Beth, who slips back into her sensible heels. She takes my hand and trudges into the aisle with me. Each step further knocks off the sleep, dusting her features, becoming more alert and poised. "I don't think you need an escort to the stage. Knock 'em dead."

Beth wiggles her brows, her grin still on the tired side, "Yeah, yeah." She arches her shoulders to a loud 'crack' before striding toward the stage. She jogs onto the stage behind the gaggle of finalists she competed against a mere hour before, carrying herself as the best of them. Atta girl... *that's* the Beth I know.

In the up line-up, Beth slots herself into the center—foreshadowing or perhaps pure instinct—as the organizer's pawn off the trophies. Under the hot spotlights, Beth stands and holds her composure as the line-up thins out with every "next we have..." from the organizers on the microphone.

If I look close enough, the ghost of a smile emerges in the hazel of her eyes. Places seven through three pass without Beth's name being announced in the blink of an eye, abandoning the glacial pace from before.

She stands next to another girl, whose program I vaguely recall from bits and pieces of slam poetry and songs. Her piece on "creating joy" had been great, on par with the rest of the finalists in the round. But Beth should win, all bias aside. In a week's time, I know whose speech will linger in the back of my mind, whose blood-curdling screams and the haunted, tearless stare will shape what fear means moving forward in my life.

On stage, the other girl whispers something to Beth and nudges her with her shoulder. Beth's eyes flicker to a sharp and uncomfortable gaze, even when she plasters a polite smile—a *fake one.*

I wonder what that's about.

"... now, the moment you've all been waiting for. In first place, our Wildwood Speech and Debate 2025 champion is..." The organizer flips open her sealed envelope. She reads over the card and gasps, "... with a near-tie and a one-point difference, from The Millenium Institute, Paityn Faulkner—"

A round of screams and chants of Paityn's name from her teammates pierces straight through my skull. Shrieks sharpened into brittle sounds for maximum hearing damage. But I focus on Beth, standing at the receiving end of all the applause for someone else.

Her hands clasp together at the front of her pressed blazer—matching the muted burgundy of her billowing pants—tighter than the smile she wears. Without a hair out of place, she radiates power and poise, the perfect paragon of manners. She doesn't grimace or pull a face when one of the organizers approaches her with the second-place trophy, a smaller, silver-tinged silhouette of a woman holding a laurel wreath over her head.

Beth cradles the trophy into the crook of her arm, waiting for Paityn to finish her final bows for the adoring audience. She waves, mustering the shy blush and broad smile of a pageant queen, which welcomes another wave of applause. Behind her, Beth stands in her shadow, politeness wavering ever so slightly.

Once Paityn strides out of center stage, only after the organizer shoos her with a pointed cough does the microphone screech, "Let's give a well-deserved round of applause for our second-place speaker, from East Shores High School, Bethany Edwards!" They clap.

The audience's applause repeats, bolstered by the screams and cheers of "Bethany!" and "Yeah, Beth!" For a second, our cheering sounds louder than the previous round of applause, giving Beth her moment to shine.

Beth steps into the spotlight, hoisting her trophy into the air above her head, prompting more roars from the crowd. From the ashes of her disappointment, a fiery, undeniable smirk turns her silver into spun gold. She stands on that stage, carrying herself with the confidence of a champion.

She is a champion—second place or not.

"Thank you to everyone who participated in an individual event in this tournament. We had record numbers of entries, which include over thirty double-entered speakers," the organizer shuffles through her envelopes, handing off the ones with broken seals or open flaps to one of her assistants. At this, Beth inches out of the spotlight, heading for the nearest staircase. "Now, we begin the debate awards, starting with Parliamentary... Can the final four teams come to the stage?"

Beth stops halfway to the staircase in a total record screech moment. She wobbles in her heels but holds steady until her balance returns, gripping onto her trophy for dear life if her white knuckles are any indication. She lets Paityn pass her without making a move to step aside.

I'm out of my seat and halfway down the aisle to the stage when I catch the icy look Paityn shoots Beth's way.

So much for choosing joy and the power of being positive.

Somehow, I don't think Paityn is as sunshine and rainbows as her speech claims.

I bound up the stairs, taking two at a time, to reach Beth quickly. My presence seems to snap Paityn back to reality, judging by how quickly she scrambles to rejoin the audience.

She leaves behind a heavy mouthful of powdery floral perfume in her wake, like the kind borrowed from an old lady's vanity.

"Look at you. Silver looks good on you." I whisper to her when some of the other teams reach the stage. We scrunch close together, and my hand hovers over the small of her back.

"I'd prefer gold, but this won't look too shabby in my trophy case," Beth mumbles. I lean closer to her, all the better to hear her when she says, "I've competed against Paityn a few times. Never like losing to her."

"Why's that? Besides the fact that you don't like to lose?" I ask, softening the approach with a joke.

Beth rolls her eyes while the rest of the teams shuffle around us. Their awkwardness pushes us closer to the center, "She's a sore winner. This time, she told me she hopes I enjoy second place."

"You've gotta be kidding." Oh, I know I sensed mean girl energy on her for a reason. She reminds me of Travis, made up of superficial charm and showboating for the audience. Hell, they even have a close enough resemblance that they could be distant cousins.

"Every time, without fail, I swear," Beth laughs. I might, too, from how incredulous it sounds. Beth and I take our craft seriously, but not to the extent that we need to be jerks to strangers. "Some speech kids are wonderful. In fact, most of them are. But, sometimes, you have a rotten one to spoil the bunch. Paityn allegedly loves punching down on everyone who isn't in first place. We're simply *not good enough*."

"Somehow, winning second place out of dozens of entries makes you one of the best. Paityn and her superiority complex can't take that from you." Something about Beth internalizing Paityn's words turns my stomach. So, she lost the age-old battle of choosing a serious topic and losing to something fluffy and less confronting?

In the grand scope of things, her speech will be the one that leaves a lasting impression, even though she walks away with second place instead of the gold she probably deserved. I stand by that.

"Maybe, but it also means I can be better. These rounds were my personal best, and I won't settle for that being good enough." Beth replies with this air of finality, like she won't stop until she gets the last word.

Before I can rebut, not one to roll over and accept something patently false, the organizer taps on their microphone, "Let's begin with our fourth-place finalist, from The Millennium Institute, the team of Hall and Harding."

The team in question steps forward to accept their miniature trophies, basking in the applause for a moment. With four teams, we seemingly forego the one-clap rule to give everyone their moment to shine.

Beside me, Beth's hands flex and grasp at the air. I only catch the strangled twitching of her fingers when my eyes drop to the stage floor. In silence, the hand I hover over the small of her back snaps up her hand instead, lacing our fingers.

Beth's eyes meet mine just as they announce to the audience, "And in third place... from Charles Darwin High, the team of Esparza and White."

These two were the teams we faced off against in the semi-finals round. They accept their trophies, but neither appears to be smiling when cradling their bronze statuettes to their chests. Their demeanor remains the same despite the audience's warm greeting. Third and fourth place shuffle further down the stage, where shadows eclipse them in their heavy shrouds.

Only Beth, our opponents, and I take up center stage in the finale. Neither she nor I loosen our grip on each other. The faint yet undeniably warm slick of sweat stains our skin from the heat of the stage lights, especially against the ridges of our palms pressed together. I genuinely forget to breathe once or twice until a dizzying buzz crawls across my face to remind me that I need air.

When Beth squeezes our interlaced hands, I glance her way. But I find her staring at me already, those hazel eyes wider than the full moon. We lock eyes, neither of us pulling away at the rogue drum roll from some of the audience members.

"Now, the moment we've been waiting for. First place and the champions of this year's Wildwood Invitational Parliamentary Debate division." Beth winces at the swift tear of paper when the organizer opens the envelope. No matter what happens, we gave our all in this tournament. We'll do the same for the next one, too.

"... from East Shores High School—" The name of our school is the last thing I hear before the world goes so loud that the sound blends into one massive wall of noise. Nothing gets past the jackhammering in my ear... my pulse. That's my pulse roaring out of my chest, probably loud enough for everyone else to hear.

Without thinking about it, I'm hoisting Beth into a crushing hug. The feel of two arms and the light thud of a trophy against my shoulder blades tells me she reciprocates the embrace, kicking her feet no longer on the ground. We sway side to side, or rather, I sway, and Beth comes along for the ride.

"We did it!" Beth's breathless exclamation tears down the wall between me and the audience's reaction. The chants of "Go Wyatt!" and "We love you, Wyatt and Beth!" barely rise above the downright earth-shaking response from the audience.

The approach of one of the assistants with our shiny, golden trophies breaks the moment, leaving Beth to respond with dignity on the stage floor. I set her down to accept our trophies, and we, just as quickly, step back so the second-place team has their moment. The kids from Westwood Academy—

Manning and Cisneros—had been super respectful after the round ended, shaking our hands and complimenting our strategy. Second place couldn't have gone to anyone more deserving.

Beth and I juggle the three trophies between us once we receive the cue to leave the stage at the announcement of the following category. Remembering Ms. Goodwin's instructions, I link Beth's arm around mine and stride toward the back of the auditorium. Beth follows, not questioning why we head for the doors instead of our seats.

Waiting for us outside the auditorium, Ms. Goodwin lifts one of the trophies from Beth's hands. "Everyone's heading for the bus. We can catch up quickly and head straight to our dinner reservations. Great job, you two."

"Thank you," Beth, now one hand free, reaches for the crook of my elbow instead of our linked arms. As Ms. Goodwin leads us to the bus, Beth and I stay a few paces behind, strolling across the darkened campus with our trophies in hand. They catch on some moonlight, glittering brighter than the faint splatter of stars above us.

Yet those trophies glint cheaply compared to the way Beth radiates joy—pure, genuine joy. First place looks good on her, too.

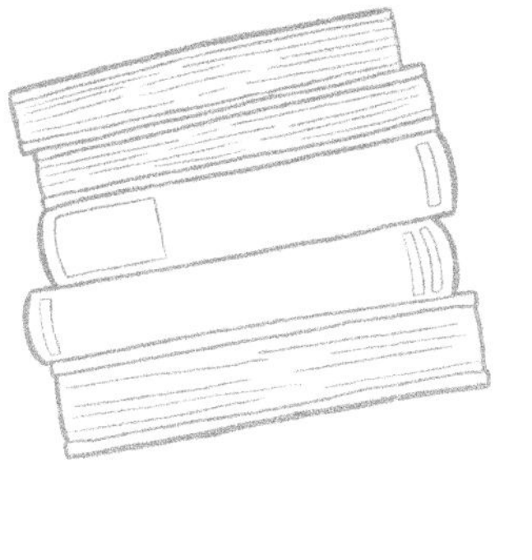

13

BETHANY

December, Week 1

"ONE OF THESE YEARS, all this Christmas cheer will cause a city-wide blackout." I say while staring at the *monstrosity* of Christmas lights and the hollow eyes of the inflatable Frosty the Snowman stationed across the street from where I sit at the hot cocoa stand.

Good grief, that thing never gets less creepy.

If the lights aren't any indication, the holidays are right around the corner, including a blissful three weeks off from school into the new year: that, and less than six months until graduation. The weeks between Wildwood and Thanksgiving break always pass in a haze of nothingness, bombarded with pre-finals chaos and last-minute debate tournaments. Ms. Goodwin requires every student to attend two tournaments per semester, one of which is a local league tournament. It's necessary to qualify for the state competition in April.

This year, however, brings new meaning to the holiday haze. The amount of hardware I brought home from Wildwood, and then Wyatt and I's subsequent reign at another local invitational in Fullerton, marks a record-breaking season in terms of awards. Coach Kruger tries not to show it, but she looks at Wyatt and me like we're the best investment she's ever made.

My stare-down with the freaky Frosty ends abruptly when two eager kids, bundled up in winter coats and trailed by their exhausted parents, approach the hot cocoa stand. Their wide eyes and ruddy cheeks fit right in with the seasonal decor of Snowflake Village, Searidge's annual holiday tradition. Much like the Fangtastic Festival for Halloween night, some locals band together yearly to put on a walkable winter wonderland called Snowflake Village. It's our spin on the iconic Candy Cane Lane in Torrance; the neighborhood volunteers deck their homes out in strings of lights and gaudy displays of Christmas decor. The electric bill for the entire neighborhood must be outrageous.

"Hi there," I greet the kids as they peer at the assortment of sweet treats and hot chocolate jugs on the table. "How can I help you two?"

"I want a donut! Can I please have a donut?" The little girl bats her lashes at her parents, bouncing up and down to the rustling of her winter coat. From the high neckline, a pair of braided pigtails flop in unison with her eager hops.

"Me too! Me too!" Her brother, who looks around the same age as her and has the same light hair, rattles the table under his hands. His mom quickly lifts his hands off the table, flashing me an apologetic grimace. The kids can't be more than six, so a little chaos is to be expected.

"We have several plain glazes, chocolate glazes, two Christmas sprinkles, three snowflakes, and one sugar twist left. Which would you like?" I aim my question at the kids, even though the parents reach for their wallets.

"Snowflake!"

"Chocolate!"

"That'll be $6 for just the donuts. But each hot cocoa is only two dollars extra," I offer. I'm not usually this pushy, but all the money goes to fundraising. Snowflake Village allows vendors to sell at the light show entrance, and East Shores clubs take turns running the booth. The proceeds fund travel, equipment, and other club expenses.

"We'll take four of those," the dad says, handing over his card, which I take. I ring them up for drinks and donuts. Despite some fumbling on my part, the family leaves with their sweet treats, heading for the marvel of lights.

I dig my hand into the pocket of my jeans, checking for my phone. As my co-president, Devon should be here by now since all shifts at the booth are a two-man job. However, his mom still insists on driving him everywhere until he gets his license, which means the two of them find themselves stuck in traffic and the subsequent hunt for nearby parking.

ME

ETA?

DEV

like 10 more minutes. Maybe.

Groaning, I tuck the phone into its pocket again. *Great.* By the time Devon arrives, our hour-long shift will be over. Devon's covered for me plenty of times—I don't hold it against him. I know friendship isn't about keeping score or trading favors.

Guess I'll be pulling a solo shift. Let me amp up the charm real quick.

I settle into the folding chair, uncomfortable as the cold plastic of the seat shoves into my back through the fleece inside the team crewneck. People pass by the stand, sometimes sparing a second glance or hesitating before moving on. Others eye me from their place in line at the other vendors, those peddling hot food and small, hand-designed trinkets, gauging the risk of jumping from their line to my nonexistent one.

Laughter swirls around me on the evening breeze rustling through the thick canopy of leaves. Everything about the evening feels soft—the twinkling of bells, fake snow, an overwhelming amount of white lights, and the palpable cheer in the air. I'd argue the joy makes the holidays worth celebrating, even without all the gimmicks and the showstopping house designs.

My people-watching proves to be somewhat entertaining, mostly for the little stories I conjure up at the sight of strangers or people I vaguely recognize. But all the fun escapes out the window faster than a winter's whistling wind when I see a group of four students in varsity jackets led by a familiar face.

Travis.

Immediately, I try to look busy, hoping the universe won't throw him into my path. As it turns out, that plan crumbles the second that one of Travis's friends tugs at his sleeve and points in the booth's direction. I have no time to gather composure before Travis marches over, chest puffed. He looks like a bird with all his bravado leading the way. If I didn't know any better, I would guess that he enjoys being humiliated and rejected.

Despite the annoyance sizzling on my tongue, red-hot and poisoning my words as they cobble into a polite greeting, I smile at them. Not an open or teeth-baring grin, but the closed customer service grin I learned from Nadia, "Welcome to Snowflake Village. Is there anything I can get you?"

Behind Travis, his two friends peer over his shoulder to see the bakery and donut options. I've seen them trailing after Travis this whole semester like a pair of lost puppies, which makes me assume they're underclassmen trying to suck up to the quarterback for some extra perks and social clout. I never learned their names since everything seems to be the Travis Maynard show 24/7.

However, I know the girl on Travis's arm—Maritza, captain of the co-ed dance team. Her glossy black hair curls around her face, which brightens with a polite smile. "Hey, Beth!"

"Hi Mari," What a nice girl like Mari wants with a wet rag like Travis will never cease to astound me. In the last year alone, Travis went through at least five different girlfriends. Those are the ones I was forced to hear about during competitions by some of the debate kids, the *public* ones. "Can I get you some hot cocoa?"

"I'd love to, but I've reached my limit." With the subtle shift of her loose cardigan, I catch sight of a glucose monitor sticking out of her bicep. "Travis insisted we come over and support the school." She says, yet it feels more akin to an accusation from how her eyes narrow at him.

Welcome to the Travis Maynard Show, everyone.

"I'm being generous," Travis corrects Mari. His short, snippy tone at her curdles the last of my pre-shift snack left in my stomach. The way Mari's eyes dim slightly, and her hand on his arm relaxes, makes me ready to stand up and tear Travis a new one. He could consider it an early Christmas present. But when he turns to me, disgust keeps me planted in my chair. "Hi, Beth."

"Travis—what would you like to order?" I ask, holding onto that composure with my nails digging into its sensitive flesh. Behind him, a line of people forms. I need to get him out of here fast.

"Hmmm, I don't know. What would you suggest?" At this, Travis fully shrugs off Mari, whose crestfallen face punches me straight in the gut, to lean on the table, bringing us to eye level. He grins, which might be charming to *literally* anyone else on the planet. To me, though, it screams nothing short of lecherous.

He knows I can't leave. For all intents and purposes, I'm his captive audience, unable to run away or hide behind Wyatt. He doesn't care about the line of people behind him who might leave instead of spending their money on the school. To Travis Maynard and his golden boy complex, it's a small price to pay to get his way.

I feel my composure slipping as the urge to glare at him grows louder in the back of my head. *I hate Travis and his stupid fu-*

"Hey! Sorry, I'm late!" Four breathless words throttle me directly out of my anger, dispelling the tunnel vision narrowing in on Travis. For his part, Travis snaps to attention like one of the JROTC kids, almost stumbling into his lackeys in letterman jackets behind him. A presence slumps into the chair beside me, but Devon doesn't wear a leather jacket or carry a motorcycle helmet underneath his arm.

Lo and behold, I face Wyatt's flushed cheeks. Underneath his riding jacket, his chest heaves, gulping down air with such greediness as if he ran to the table. He slides his helmet into his backpack, which goes underneath the Christmas tree-patterned tablecloth.

"It's all good—" I start.

"You told your mom that you didn't have plans tonight," Travis sneers at Wyatt, almost calling his bluff. I doubt the growing line behind him appreciates the extended chit-chat—or the brawl on the horizon if Travis keeps at it.

I watch Wyatt for his response, unsure where he plans to go. My heartbeat screams in protest when it beats a little faster, a little more irregularly with its rhythm. At the edges of my vision, tingling blurs the colors and many sights of Snowflake Village. I fixate on freaky Frosty for something solid, something familiar to anchor me before breathing becomes too difficult to manage. *Thanks a lot, anxiety.*

Unlike the chaotic swirl of thoughts inside my head, Wyatt leans back in the folding chairs, unfazed by Travis's interrogation. His hands tuck behind his head while staring at his stepbrother. Then, his brow quirks, preceding the tiniest smirk.

"You must've misheard me. I never said that," Wyatt remarks. Travis's posse and I observe from the sidelines of the brewing argument, fixated on the tense glares and every ounce of tension coursing through the vein pulsing out from Travis's neck. Red splotches scatter across his face and neck quicker than a nasty rash, while he glares at Wyatt, who chooses to double down. "Now, are you going to order something? You're holding up the line."

Travis says nothing as he storms off in a huff, without a warning to Mari or his shadows. The three gawk at one another but chase after Travis. The shaky exhale pushing out of my chest takes all the tension with it.

Wyatt's hand reaches and clamps down on my shoulder. "You okay?"

"I'm fine now that you're here," I promise. When I smile, Wyatt does too. His hand lingers, but drops when the next customer approaches. "Thanks for swooping in."

"Of course. Can't leave you without your favorite human shield." Wyatt replies, dropping his voice to a whisper for only he and I to hear. Heat blossoms across my cheeks, probably turning me red like Rudolph's nose. My only saving grace might be the amount of distractions in the lights and Christmas displays, ranging from a seasonal sensation to a holly jolly eyesore.

"Hey! You're the one who offered. I'm merely appreciating the resources I've been given." I protest, matching his volume, and elbow him between the ribs. Wyatt chuckles and swats my hand away.

We drop the conversation in unison and focus on the sizable line waiting for hot cocoa and baked goods. Wyatt and I fall into a seamless routine; I speak with customers while he packs the orders in silence, ready to hand them off. Together, we make quick work of the decent line, sending each customer on their way with a healthy dose of evening sweets. I'm sure the triple digits on the nifty little card reader will make some school administrator jump for joy.

Once the line dwindles into nothing, I face Wyatt. "So, you want to tell me how you knew I needed a rescue?"

"Devon texted me. He said something about running behind and other texts from others who saw Travis heading your direction," Wyatt doesn't fight the conversation. The admission comes out casually as if dropping your free evening to rescue someone from being bothered by an unwanted suitor is a normal thing between friends. "I happened to be driving by and redirected to the parking lot, which was a labyrinth to navigate by the way. I had no idea Searidge Hills goes all out for every holiday on the calendar."

I snicker, "Yeah, this place loves its holiday celebrations. The money from visitors and locals seems to pay for the maintenance of the festivities each year, but thank you for braving the horrendous traffic. I owe you."

Maybe all the silvery and white lights around us play a trick on my already tired eyes, but Wyatt's face appears to soften. At least, his eyes lose some of their sharpness, the ever-present intellect radiating off him in spades.

Wyatt's head tilts. "You owe me nothing. It's my legal obligation to be a royal pain in Travis's behind. He doesn't get to mess with my partner." He says so confidently that I fight the urge to parrot back something stupid like "yeah."

Instead, I nod and stuff my hands underneath my jean-clad thighs for warmth. Gradual warmth sinks into my skin, racing up the length of my forearm in tiny pinpricks. The awkward angle forces me to shuffle around on the plastic folding chair for some comfort.

"Cold?" Wyatt asks.

"Just my hands. It's not normally this cold, even in December, to need gloves. So, I didn't bring any. I'd like to be able to feel my fingers." I wiggle my fingers some more, seeking more heat faster.

The next thing I know, Wyatt pulls off his riding gloves finger by finger and coaxes my hands from under my thighs. Then, he slips his gloves over my freezing hands, sandwiching them between his own. This time, warmth envelops my fingers, defrosting them faster than my thigh heater.

"That better?" Wyatt's eyes find mine. He looks concerned as he kneads my newly gloved hands between his, manually ousting the cold from me. With no line, no one pays attention to either of us.

"Very," I swallow down a million different, arguably more cringy responses within a split second of opening my mouth to speak. Wyatt's acknowledging nod nudges us into another lapse in conversation until I leap across the gap. "So, what are your holiday plans? Anything exciting?"

"Yeah, Mom and I will drive to Boston for the holidays. We have Christmas out there every year with my dad's side of the family." Wyatt's cheeks fluster. Looks like the cold finally caught him.

"Lucky! I'm sticking around the Hill for the next three weeks." My groan elicits a laugh from Wyatt.

"Didn't we say something about smuggling you via suitcase?" The motel pool flashes before my eyes, recalling the sunset backdrop behind Wyatt's head as we talked well into the night. "I'm sure your family won't mind if I borrow you for a few weeks."

"As much as I appreciate the offer, just focus on having a safe trip. I like having a competent debate partner." I wink. *And a friend.*

Wyatt will be enjoying the East Coast, and I love that for him. Would it be too ridiculous to ask for a souvenir?

"Ahem," A voice interjects, insistent and pointed. Wyatt and I face the newcomer, revealed to be none other than Mr. Alvarez. I almost didn't recognize him from the patchwork scarf he wears and two-day-old stubble along his chin. "Nice to see you, Beth."

"Mr. Alvarez! Could we interest you in hot cocoa? It's for charity." I lay the charm on thick with a smile.

"As delightful as that sounds, I'm here to report that I'm relieving you and Mr.—I don't believe I've met your friend here," says Mr. Alvarez when his eyes land on Wyatt beside me.

His gaze jumps to the middle, followed by mine. Wyatt's hands still cup mine while I wear gloves that are too big for me. Oh, I know how this looks—

Wyatt and I let go almost at the same exact time. If he glances my way, I miss it from how fast I lock eyes with freaky Frosty for the third time tonight.

Wyatt offers his hand. "Wyatt Keene, sir."

"Wyatt's my partner—my debate partner." I must've lost my brain in the last minute and a half, from how I've become a stuttering mess. The weight of Wyatt's eyes on me burns into my skin, but I hold steady in my staring contest with freaky Frosty.

Mr. Alvarez shakes Wyatt's hand, "Nice to meet you, Wyatt. I'm here to relieve you and Beth for the next shift. You two have a good night now." He shoos us away from the booth, grinning wide when shouldering his favorite bag.

"Thanks, Mr. Alvarez," I beam and snatch up my tote bag. Wyatt mimics me with his bag. "Any plans for after this?"

"You know, I'm kind of in the mood for a stroll. Care to join?" Wyatt's eyes flit toward the trickle of people walking down the neighborhood of Snowflake Village.

I loop our arms together, "Lead the way."

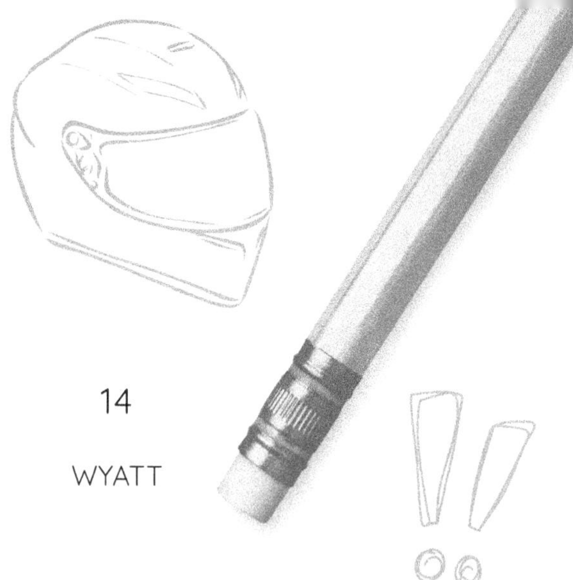

14

WYATT

December, Week 3

THERE NEEDS to be a word or a combination of them in the English language to describe the devastating food coma I'm about to enter once dinner concludes. Somewhere between the buttery mashed potatoes and the tender, cooked-to-perfection Christmas ham, drowsiness worms underneath my skin.

I hear the conversation churning around me, words flying every which way in voices I recognize. Aunt Jenny, Uncle Owen, Grandma, my cousins, Lindsey and Val, and my mom—everyone who matters sits around this table, making merry in the spirit of the holiday season.

Then, something pokes my cheek. Hard.

I blink and swat it—a finger—away from my face to a round of snickering—Val's.

"Didn't you learn to keep your hands to yourself in Kindergarten?" I glare at them beside me.

However, Val shrugs off my question, too preoccupied with the mountain of mashed potatoes they've turned into a malformed sculpture of—something. They carve more of a shape with their knife; if I could be more specific, I would.

"You were so out of it that you didn't hear Mom talking to you," Lindsey chimes in, glancing up from her smartphone. Her bubblegum pink hair sits atop her head in twin buns, including a few wispy strands framing her face.

"Sorry. I'm still shaking off the travel exhaustion," I say, mostly for Aunt Jenny's sake.

In the spirit of old times' sake, Mom and I loaded our bags into the car as soon as winter break began for a cross-country road trip. Road trips used to be Dad's favorite way to vacation; the journey felt like carrying a tiny piece of him back home, back to Boston. From Searidge Hills, we visited Zion National Park for the first time in years, spent a night in Denver to see the Air & Space Museum, enjoyed Chicago, and even caught a show on Broadway. If anyone asks, I will deny crying during the second act of Wicked until I go blue in the face.

"Don't apologize, Wy. We're just glad you and your mom came to see us!" Aunt Jenny squeezes my hand in hers. When I look at her, I see Dad. Despite Aunt Jenny being at least three years older, they could've been twins—same dark hair, mischievous eyes, and the lopsided grin the Keenes are known for. "We're sorry that Grant and Travis couldn't join us-"

Grandma coughs on the opposite end of the table, but it covers something that sounds suspiciously like "No, we're not." No one else reacts to it, so I keep my evil smile to myself. *Love you, Grammy. Never change.*

Mom dabs at her mouth, "Don't worry about it, Jen. *Graham* and Travis are visiting their family for the holidays. Christmas in Boston is our thing." Mom shoots me a look as comforting as her bear hugs and her cooking.

"It will always be. You two have a place here with us." Uncle Owen chimes in. He is normally a man of few words, but he and Mom always shared this special kinship; they both married into the family, the other halves of the inseparable Jennifer and Justin Keene.

Aunt Jenny clasps her hands together, "-but we're so grateful for social media. That way, we can keep up with everything, like Wyatt's debate stuff. He's been rocking it this year!"

"Hasn't he? He comes home from nearly every competition with some kind of certificate or medal. Enrolling him at East Shores has proven itself a fantastic decision." Mom agrees. All the gushing and fawning over me might inflate my ego to the size of Jupiter. Beth would be teasing me right about now.

Lindsey waves her phone in her hand, mid-chew, when she snorts, "Instagram sends us notifications about whenever he decides to grace us with a new photo or something. Somehow, in the span of months, he's doubled his social media feed. Where did the camera-shy Wyatt go?" she asks.

"More importantly, who is the girl with you in almost all of them?" Val asks, despite their mouth being full of half-chewed food. They slap a hand over their mouth no sooner than they find themselves on the receiving end of several pointed stares. A full mouth doesn't derail their inquiry, though. "About this tall, dark hair, smile a mile wide as you grip below her waist and hold up a trophy."

I know exactly who she means. But I swallow back the jolt of nerves buzzing in the back of my throat, washing it down with the flattening sparkling cider Grandma requested for dinner. "You mean Beth?"

"Beth," Lindsey and Val repeat, although their version of Beth sounds all lilted and singsong like they know something I don't. "So, who is she? Is she your girlfriend?"

"My debate partner." Shortness undercuts my otherwise flat reply. The first thing to know about Lindsey and Val—those two are nosy. Search for nosy in the dictionary, and there they'll be, grinning underneath the definition. I suspect they picked up their gossip habit from Grandma, a known gossip by everyone who attends her church and the little old ladies who comprise her weekly bridge club. No secret escapes Grandma's knowledge.

I eye them when neither says anything after a few moments. Lindsey and Val shoot glances each other's way before giggling.

Val fans at their face, "Wy, you can't be serious. Dude, look at your hand placement in almost every photo of you and her. You're either gripping onto her harder than the literal trophy in your hands or holding her below the waist. That hardly says 'just friends,' okay?"

"To you." I scoff.

"To anyone with functioning eyes!" Val retorts.

Thus begins the stare-down between Val and me, uninterrupted by the clinking of silverware or the shuffle of Christmas dinner around the table. Neither of us moves or tears our eyes away, intending to be the last one standing. Maybe it won't change anyone's mind, but it'll show I hold firm to my truth. Beth and I *aren't* dating.

So focused on Val, I miss Lindsey handing her phone across the table to Aunt Jenny, who gasps. Val smirks right as I break, unable to stop myself from losing.

"Woah! This girl is beautiful!" She says, passing the phone to Uncle Owen, who grunts in agreement. He passes the phone to my mom, who passes it to Grandma. Within seconds, Val and Lindsey gave the entire table a crash course in Beth Edwards despite me being the only one here who knows how she drinks taro boba like she needs it to live or that Phoebe Bridgers is her top-streamed artist on Kiwi. Nothing in the photos of her captures the depths of what makes Beth...*Beth.*

Grandma fumbles for her glasses, clutching the phone close

to her chest. Once she pops them on, her eyes go wide. "My goodness! Such a beautiful young lady, indeed. I'll try to live long enough to see you two get married," she cackles.

By now, the burning sensation that started at the tips of my ears travels along the length of my spine, racing through me faster than a high-speed train across rickety tracks. I set my fork down on the half-eaten plate of seconds in front of me. I guess I'm not hungry anymore, not while on the defense.

"Has everyone forgotten what the words 'just friends' mean? Beth and I aren't dating, nor will we be. *Ever*. So, please don't start with the 'for now' comments. I know you're chomping at the bit to use them, but spare us all the misery of an argument for Christmas." I announce, rising from my seat at the table. That should be the final word.

But as I reach for my plate, ready to discard the scraps for Millie—Grandma's ancient papillon dog—Lindsey snickers, "Do you really think anyone buys that?"

My hands freeze. "What's that supposed to mean?" I ask.

"When someone mentions her name, you look more excited than Millie when we feed her bacon bits underneath the table. Sorry if I don't believe that you, the lord of scowls and sarcasm, don't have any interest in Beth beyond friendship. You practically light up brighter than the Christmas tree in the next room over her. You're so red right now. I'd think someone suggested you should pull her under the mistletoe."

Lindsey doesn't mince her words, making them the verbal equivalent of taking a sucker punch straight to the jaw. Denial sits on the tip of my tongue, but a rogue thought crosses my mind, threatening to derail everything else behind it. I see the vision of Beth in Boston so clearly, walking down the snow-covered streets in a ruby-colored turtleneck, beckoning me to follow. We'd weave down the roads as she let me show her all my favorite places in the city. Then, the next thing I see is Beth peering up at me, unable to hide her grin at the bushel of mistletoe hanging over our heads. She glows, all pink cheeks and nose from the cold, waiting for the next move with the same look she gives me during competition.

I know the dead silence speaks volumes. But my tongue feels heavier than lead, too thick to form words or anything close to coherent. Even a grunt and leaving the table would do right now. Lindsey's smug expression and the rogue buzz of a phone seem to lift the spell from me.

"Guys and girls can be friends without some ulterior motive. Anyone would be lucky to have a friend as funny and smart as Beth." My reply lacks the usual bite, the sarcasm everyone seems to expect from me, but I couldn't care less. The words are out, forced into existence by sheer will.

"Wyatt's breaking out the fancy words... that's how we know he's scrambling." Val jumps back into the conversation. Lindsey reaches out and the two high-five, taking this as a win.

I let them; I dismiss myself from the table with an eye roll, snatching up my plate before I head for the kitchen. I spot Millie lying by her bowl, head halfway into the kibble bits Grandma's been feeding her since before I was born. But her ears perk up before I approach with a small chunk of ham and mashed potatoes. She scrambles onto her feet, spinning around until I drop the plate into her bowl.

"There you go," I sigh. Millie thanks me with the sounds of ravenous chewing. "You're the one person who isn't trying to set me up with my friend—so you're my new favorite."

I slip my plate into the otherwise empty sink, barring all the dishes leftover from Uncle Owen's cooking. Snippets of dining room conversation fall short of the kitchen door, muffled by the paisley-patterned walls. I've stepped into a time capsule, one shrouded in nostalgia and hinting at something a little burnt.

I glance toward the kitchen door. I should sit with the

others, bask in the banter and good vibes of the family I rarely see. It's not their fault that a tiny piece of me waits for my dad to take his rightful seat at the table, the one I know Grandma leaves open for him all these years later.

My hand finds my phone from deep within my pocket. Texts from Beth are the first things on the screen, sitting at the top of the notification mountain. The twist of something shameful bears down on my full stomach, stinging and burning. But I shake it off; the opinions of others shouldn't change how Beth and I are now. We work well together. Who cares how everyone else perceives us?

BETH

attached one photo

we miss you! hope you're having fun in Boston!

A photo of the parliamentary debate team, along with Devon in festive attire, fills the screen. I spot Beth in the middle of the group, rocking a pair of reindeer antlers and an oversized snowflake sweater. Her attention appears fixated on something off-camera, but her grin stretches from ear to ear.

ME

You've got the whole gang there. Tell them I send my holiday greetings.

BETH

I'll do that between all the rounds of bad Christmas caroling that August keeps starting.

how's Boston? How's your family?

ME

I'm enjoying the snow and having more leg room than the front seat of my Mom's Honda.

"Is that Beth?" Leaning in the doorway, Mom carries a small stack of empty dishes. Knowing her, she offered to clean the table, ignoring the protests of Aunt Jenny and Grandma. Some things never change. "Tell her happy holidays for me."

"I'll send her your regards. Don't tell Lindsey and Val I'm hiding in the kitchen and texting her. They'll never let the crush allegations go." I mumble.

Mom shakes her head, "Ignore them. They like getting a rise out of you. That's what cousins do." She pinches my cheek.

I swat her hand away, no matter if I secretly love it when she dotes on me. "Yeah, yeah. . . I know."

Mom sits at the island across from where I rest my elbows against the counter. She picked one of Dad's favorite ugly Christmas sweaters tonight. He's still with us in small ways—in what we wear, in the places we stop. I miss him all the time, but I know she does too. Maybe even more.

Mom exhales audibly as she perches her chin on her hands. "This trip has been the best yet. I think we should return to road trips; flights are faster, but they don't have as many opportunities to make memories."

"We should do one before college. We'll hit all the old haunts Dad adored in his honor. You know, since he had to be all rude and die on us." Mom and I meet eyes, but the taste of dark humor sends us into a fit of laughter. She wipes at her eyes, catching the few tears before they stain her cheeks. Whether from laughter or the sudden reminders of the man she loved, whom she buried far too soon, her eyes glisten in the kitchen's ambient lights.

Mom reaches across the counter, grasping one of my hands in hers. Her smile teeters on the edge of watery, "Goodness, don't remind me how fast you're growing up. We have a few months before you'll be spreading your wings, and I must... let you go." She fans at her face, fighting the onset of more tears.

I watch her fight the grief, different from the one she and I share. A tiny part of me considers the consequences of telling her to ditch California with me and forget about Graham and Travis. It could be her and I against the world forever with a support system that genuinely loves us instead of tolerating us for the sake of their wretched progeny. But I hold it in.

"We still have time. Besides, even in college, I'll always be a plane trip away." I promise. Our fingers lock together, guiding me around the counter to crush my mom into a bear hug. The last thing I ever want is to make her cry. She deserves better—deserves the world. I'd put up with anything just to keep that sadness off her face. That's the love she taught me, burning bright with nowhere to go but out.

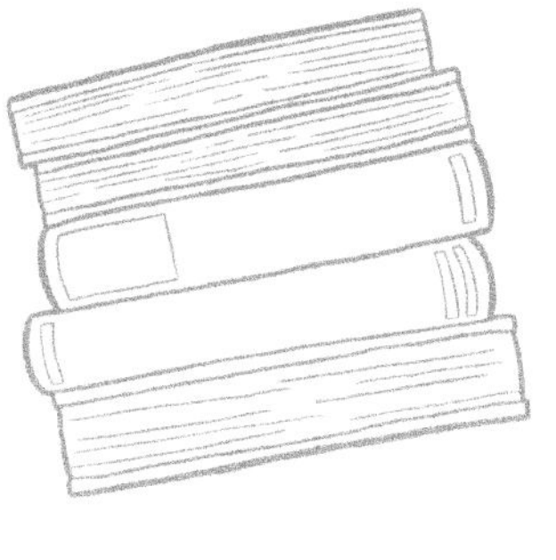

15

BETHANY

January, Week 1

"-REMIND me why I chose to major in bioengineering again?" Nadia's self-pitying groan hooks my attention back into the video call. I glance up from the AP government textbook, cracked open against my desk, and all its clear sticky notes, to see my best friend. Nadia admires her reflection on the screen, a make-up wipe ready to adjust her berry-colored lipstick. Talking coherently while applying lipstick has never been a skill either of us possesses. I learned that from all the time we used to spend getting ready while waiting for the bus.

I press a sky-blue sticky tab onto the top edge of my current textbook page, marking it for eventual return. I should've known I would get little to no work done once Nadia and I sat for a video chat. The two of us could spend hours talking about nothing, giggling about the dumbest things known to man, and feel like no time had passed.

Given our out-of-sync schedules, text conversations have been the most frequent form of communication between Nadia and me. I'm so used to talking in person on a daily basis that the shift in our friendship still shocks me. I've mostly adjusted and able to enjoy the texts and infrequent calls. Like the gem she's always been, Nadia carves out enough time for me once a month so we can see each other's faces.

"I believe your rationale was that you need enough money to survive living in California, and you liked biology and math most in school." I snort. She and I had plenty of conversations about what our futures looked like.

Nadia slumps into her chair, flinging herself dramatically. Now, I see more of her dorm through the tiny square frame. Either she or her roommate added more decorations since our last video chat, including a wall of Polaroids hanging on rows of sparkly string and a Progress Pride Flag hanging over the entryway to the door. Nadia's comfortable there, ready to be herself as unapologetically as possible.

"Four years or more of torture will be worth it for living in comfort for the rest of my life. Or, maybe I can find a rich wife to take care of me. Nonna has a few recipes that'll score me a ring!" Nadia mumbles, still slumped over the school-issued dorm desk chair.

"I'm sure Nonna will be thrilled," I giggle. "Cooking those recipes for anyone will mean you've graduated past burning marinara sauce."

"That was one time!" Nadia slams her closed fist against the desk, spluttering and gasping. With all her flailing around, she's got a perfect fish-out-of-water impression. "No one lets me live that down!"

"Either that, or I tease you about hitching yourself to a grueling degree for the next four to five years. Your choice." I shrug, but my cheeks hurt from the wolfish smile I catch myself wearing on the screen.

Nadia sighs, "I'll take terrible cooking skills for four

hundred, Alex." She waves her hand as if encouraging me to continue teasing her, then ducks away from the camera for a second, returning with a turquoise blue eyeliner pencil. She drags her lower eyelid down to expose her waterline more, tracing blue in a slightly messy line over it. Bold, but it complements her dark brown eyes nicely.

She does the other eye, pausing long enough for me to appraise, "Alright, how does this look? Good? Even lines on both sides?"

"Might need to extend the wing a little on the left, but you look great otherwise. This is pretty fancy for studying and some coffee." I flash her a thumbs-up. At this point, I shut the textbook and toss it onto the bed. I'm ahead of the syllabus anyway —I can afford to spend half an hour with my best friend.

"Study *date*. Andie specifically called it a study date. I like them a lot, and I can't make it seem like I'm not interested," Nadia fluffs her hair out from around her face. "Stanford is a big place, but the openly sapphic dating pool is still so small. They're in my major and absolutely stunning. She could be a model, Beth!"

I say nothing, watching my friend fawn over a crush. When Nadia crushes, she falls head over heels for the object of her affection. Her feelings can never be defined as superficial or fleeting, even if they might appear so on the surface.

"Well, I wish you luck. The only date I have in the future is for the upcoming government unit exam that I should be studying for." The quip rolls off my tongue, free of any possible bitterness. In the early days, at the start of the semester, I felt Nadia's missing presence like a gaping wound someone punched through my chest. Over time, though, the pain muted into something manageable, something that lives in the back of my mind until she texted me. I guess Wyatt plays some role in that; we work together so seamlessly that I forget someone else used to be there before him, as bad as that sounds.

Nadia leans out of frame again but returns with her favorite necklace dangling between her curled fingers. She hums, "Funny you should mention that. I heard some rumors from some of our friends on the debate team."

"About me? Look, if this is about the Travis thing—" I cough. I'd rather not waste my limited time with Nadia talking about Travis, even if it devolves into us laughing about his loser behavior. I did share a little about his sudden interest in me on the first day back, but not much else. Talking about Travis' continued interest would require me to delve into the complicated Wyatt-Travis mess, which seems like something Wyatt keeps hidden from our classmates. I don't blame him. I wouldn't claim Travis, either.

"What Travis thing? I was talking about whatever's going on between you and Mr. Wyatt Keene." Nadia trails off, leaving us in awkward silence.

I squirm in my chair. "Oh." I can't wait to see how I talk myself out of this mess, if I can. Once you give her gossip, Nadia becomes a bloodhound for information. She'd be an astonishing lawyer if she weren't so against the idea.

"Is there something I should know about you and Travis?" Nadia's grimace speaks volumes. She waits in bated breath, chewing on her cheek hard enough for me to notice it.

"I feel like I should start with the whole Wyatt thing, but no. Travis being a jerk? That's nothing new." I want to laugh, to shake off the awkwardness still clinging to the air. "And when I say 'Wyatt thing,' I mean nothing—because nothing is happening between Wyatt and me," I add. Denial comes first, the knee-jerk response to the confusion turning my skin hot. Anyone with eyes could acknowledge Wyatt's objectively cute; Nadia might even argue that Wyatt would fall into my type of guy. *Dark-haired, witty, and fluent in sarcasm. Usually fictional, too.* But Wyatt and I have a good thing going, so letting myself have feelings for him would derail my plan.

Nadia's face shifts, trading discomfort for disbelief. Her sleek, perfectly done brows crinkle with the scrunch of her nose. "Is that your final answer?" she hums.

"...Yes?" In one single word, I forget the cardinal rule of the Nadia Inquisition—Nadia never asks a question that she doesn't already know the answer to—her words, not mine.

Nadia reveals her phone. She wordlessly opens it, unable to curb the disappointment in her sigh, and spins the phone around. "Is this you and Wyatt?" She points to the screen and holds it close to the camera.

Shock swells into a lump in my throat as I stare at the photo she shows me. It's one of Wyatt and me; we're on a bus at night, clear from the dark skies and the shine of passing cars or nearby stoplights. My head rests on Wyatt's shoulder, and my eyes appear closed. Wyatt stares out of the window, holding our trophy from Wildwood. Neither of us acknowledges the cameras at all.

"Where did—" My voice falters when Nadia swipes to reveal another angle of the scene. She swipes again, showing off a third perspective of the scene. "—You've got to be kidding me."

"Oh, we're far from done," Nadia responds. Five words flip my stomach over, tying it into knots when she pulls up a new photo. This one has me reading from my POI binder, and Wyatt standing together. His elbow rests atop my head, to my scowl and his teasing grin. "Exhibit four, and then our final show of evidence."

Nadia reaches the final photo, which shows Wyatt and me sharing a basket of fries at The Stack after a tournament. We're in matching black blazers and deep green accents in his tie and my turtleneck. None of the photos identify who took them or how Nadia got hold of them, either.

My voice eeks out in a tiny, nervous whisper, "Okay, I'm scared. Where did you get these photos?"

"I'd joke that I have my ways and several photographers on my payroll, but I'm not the mastermind behind this operation. Allegedly—and you didn't hear this from me- there might be a photo album exclusively for photos of you and Wyatt. The number of photos in it isn't merely a handful either." Nadia sets her phone aside for a tube of clear lip gloss.

"Great, now I have people assuming I'm in a relationship with Wyatt or something? And *that* hasn't stopped Travis from chasing me?" I meant to keep that thought to myself, but the quiet "oop" and Nadia's dropped jaw tell me my mouth beat me to it. Her lip gloss slips from her fingers and clatters to the floor.

"Okay, you need to tell me everything. Now." Nadia demands, borderline rattling her desk from how fast she scrambles out of her seat. I watch her pace around the tiny sliver between her desk and her roommate's bed.

So, I spill. Everything from first meeting Wyatt, to learning about the Travis-Wyatt stepbrother relationship, and Travis's obsession, flies out of my mouth in the most undignified case of word vomit. No filter, niceties, or polishing precedes my explanation of the last few months to Nadia. She stares at me, slack-jawed and unresponsive, until I finish my ramble with "...That's everything, I think."

"First of all, this is the greatest drama to happen to East Shores since that guy ate a whole edible and stole a chicken suit to crash the homecoming game two years ago," Nadia, standing in the middle of her dorm room with her hands behind her head, giggles. She hunches over, hands sliding down her thighs to rest on her knees, but the laughter never stops. "Second, I can't believe you didn't tell me until right this moment."

"It was never the right time! You're telling me about all the serious college stuff. I wasn't sure where to interject with a 'By the way, your former bully keeps following me around campus like a dog who wants to hump my leg. xoxo' in our chats. I have limited time to hear about Stanford instead of witnessing your life through your social media feed." I protest.

In the universal sign of surrender, Nadia holds her hands, "Fair enough. But we're talking about it now." She ambles back to her chair and snatches her lip gloss up. She applies a generous helping of her base lipstick, giving her lips an almost blinding glossy layer. She smiles at herself for a moment, fluffing out her dark waves to reach a beachy and effortless look.

"You sure we can't save it for next month? You have a very special study date to get to." The look Nadia shoots me causes an eruption of laughter from both of us. As good a debater as I am, Nadia remains one of two people who will never allow me to worm my way out of a conversation.

"So, what are you going to do about Travis? I assume you already pestered the school for help, and they've refused to do anything about it," says Nadia.

"As always, they take his side, or at least the side of inaction. I believe Principal Cardenas's advice ran along the lines of —ignore him." My involuntary eye roll earns a sympathetic groan from Nadia. She's heard it all—useless advice, the same brush-offs. Except when Travis messed with her, she also got the classic "he-said, she-said" treatment.

"Wyatt thinks he just likes the chase," I say. "But he has to get bored eventually. Graduation's around the corner—he should worry about making the cut instead of bothering me and Wyatt."

"Ah, and then we have the other player in this game.

Unlike Travis, whose sole qualities seem to be annoying and repelling women with high self-esteem, Wyatt and you have something there. I don't need to set foot on East Shores's campus to prove it; the photos do it for me."

"No, we're friends. *Just* friends. That's okay with me, and I'm sure he feels the same way." I shake my head as if my denial might make a difference this time. When people get stuck on an idea, they refuse to budge.

Yes, he's attractive by an objective metric. And yes, I enjoy spending time with him in and out of debate because of common interests. However, those two things don't automatically make it a love story.

Nadia frowns at me, "Okay, what if he did feel differently? Hypothetically."

"Hypothetically, it's a bad idea. High school relationships rarely work once the couple heads to college. We're running against bad statistical odds. Wyatt's the first friend I've made in years. If we date and then break up, that throws a wrench into our friendship, and depending on when this imagined split happens, could destroy our chemistry as debate partners. It's not worth pursuing on the off chance that it might work out and last for a long time. I know I can't demand a sure thing—no matter how badly my anxiety needs it—from anyone besides myself."

The line goes quiet. So does my heart in my throat, waiting for Nadia to tell me I've said too much or sound stupid. *She never has before, but there's a first time for everything.* I sit still, ignoring how my chest aches from the wait.

Nadia scoots closer to her camera until her face takes up the entire screen, "Bethany Madison Edwards, I'm going to throttle you the next time I see you. I love you, but you can't let your anxiety dictate your love life forever. You deserve to live life to the fullest, and having what-ifs won't guarantee happiness in the long run. Boston isn't a sure thing either, but you're chasing it anyway. Do the same for the rest; there's more to life than school, hon." She wags her finger at me, a move she picked up from her Nonna.

"I'll think about it," I lie through a tiny smile. If Nadia knows, she says nothing about it. Instead, she ducks out of frame for another moment and leaves me alone with my thoughts. Ones that will *not* be considering what it would be like dating Wyatt Keene.

"Fine by me. Now, which one of these dresses screams 'I want to drop the study from our study date' to you?" Nadia holds up two dresses. I, for one, embrace the change in conversation. Let the thought of Wyatt and I die in the back of my mind. Nadia must have love on the brain with her new Stanford sweetheart. That's all... *right?*

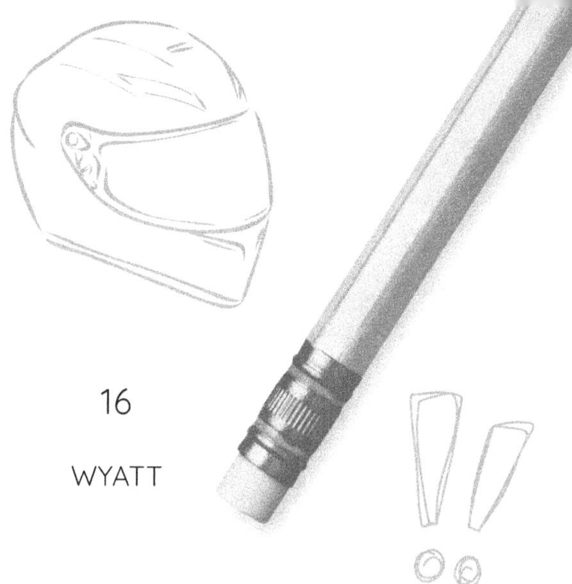

16

WYATT

SOMETHING'S WRONG WITH BETH.

This thought echoes in my head for the millionth time as I search for her among the other competitors at this invitational we signed up for last-minute. No one else at the table notices her missing presence, gone for over twenty minutes. She hasn't been herself today, which doesn't bode well for us advancing past prelims.

Maybe it's *my* fault. Right behind the never-ending worry, even the most rational parts of my brain point the finger back at me. It could be anything I did today. I drove us to Anaheim on my motorcycle because Beth's car wouldn't start, cramming our bodies close on the narrow seat of my Kawasaki. I spent all day rambling to hold her attention about the most ridiculous things. I thought about how perfectly she wears green in the middle of the round, but swallowed the fleeting thought down faster than a mouthful of bile.

Ever since Christmas in Boston, everything I do regarding

Beth and me runs through an extra filter, scrutinized down to its core. No matter how hard I try, Lindsey and Val's words surface from the depths of my mind at the worst times. Now, I overthink and calculate every step with Beth so I don't cross an imaginary boundary.

But after hours of silence from Beth, who's spoken maybe five sentences to anyone outside of rounds, I reach an undeniable conclusion. She's hiding from me and I can't figure out why.

"Do you think the elimination rounds will be posted tonight?" I pose a question to the other parliamentary kids. We huddle together in a tight cluster at the table our team claimed at the start of the tournament. My voice pulls a few heads from the ongoing conversation—something about college acceptances and early decision letters.

"They should be," Josh drums his fingers along the edge of the faded blue lunch table, lips pursing when he glances toward the wall. Despite the frequent use of Tabroom notifications, some tournaments still adhere to the old-school method of posting physical notifications on a designated wall. Part of me thinks they do it to watch a miniature brawl erupt between eager competitors—anything to make a debate more entertaining for the admins, I guess.

I grab my phone and not much else, leaving our bags behind. "Text me if the postings drop? I'm going on a walk."

When I receive a few nods, I pull an about-face and march out the cafeteria's open doors. Those JROTC kids are starting to rub off on me with their after-school drill practices. But my marching eases into a stroll when I exit the double doors, abandoning the urgency for everything but finding Beth. Even if the postings drop right now, Beth will stay my priority.

It turns out that I don't need to search too hard. The cafeteria exit spits me out into an elongated hallway, newer compared to the rest of the campus, or maybe that's the fresh paint job talking. Rows of lockers blur together while I look for Beth. The rest of the world becomes background noise, including the people I pass by, until I reach the end of the hallway.

A glance to my right reveals a tiny outdoor garden full of vegetables and fruits, and Beth sits among the dark green foliage. Her back faces me and the rest of the world, seemingly lost in thought, while our team waits for the news of who advances to the next round. But the slump of Beth's shoulders shouts resignation to me. *She's given up.*

I push into the garden, quiet when I close the door behind me so as not to startle Beth. I don't get very far before the crunch of gravel underneath my dress shoes causes Beth's head to snap up. She glances over her shoulder, and her eyes soften. "Wyatt! Sorry, I was worried it was someone else."

That elicits a smile out of me. A tiny one. "Good to know you still like me," I murmur while walking closer to the bench where Beth lounges.

Beth cocks her head to the side, eyes still on me. Confusion plasters her face. "Why wouldn't I?" She asks.

When she asks, though, I don't miss the strain on her voice or the way her leg starts bouncing. Beth's nervous. I made her nervous.

"Well, you've been quieter than usual today, and you vanished from the cafeteria about twenty minutes ago when you said you'd be gone for five." My eyes take in the wide open space on the bench next to Beth, waiting for an invitation.

Beth notices. She scoots over and pats the bench in a silent offering. I take a seat, leaving space between us so she can breathe.

Neither of us speaks for a moment, content to bask in the silence of the night. In the distance, cars speed along the streets, and the rest of the night's mellow song plays out unobstructed. I cling to stillness as a lifeline while Beth can't seem to find a comfortable seated position in my presence. Guilt breathes down my neck, ready to sink its sharp-edged teeth through a skin I thought was tougher than this.

"Do you want to talk about it? Whatever's upsetting you?" I offer. I already know Beth's answer, even before she shakes her head. It's time to switch tactics. "Okay, how about we start packing up our stuff to head home a little early? I doubt either of us will be coming back tomorrow, so let's go home and get a head start against any traffic."

"You're driving. It's up to you," Beth brushes off her wide-legged dress pants before rising. We'd need to grab our things from inside and convince the chaperone to let us leave before the official announcement of tomorrow's competitors. Andrea, August, or one of the others can text me the results if Tabroom faces a delay in notification.

Standing up, I smooth out the creases in the sleeves of my blazer, despite knowing the ride back home would press new ones back into the fabric. Then, I offer my arm to Beth.

"I say let's leave. I'll make up some excuse for Coach Andrew. There's no need for us to sit around and wait for an announcement, especially since we're down 1-2." I wrap my arm around Beth, staying above her waist, and guide her out of the garden. We stumble down the hallway together, with Beth's strides trying to match mine, yet dragging behind slightly.

We enter the cafeteria, not slowing down, when one of us almost trips over the raised flooring. Beth pulls ahead of me as we skid to a stop at the table, but I haul her back to my side.

"Uh, Andrew?" At my call, Andrew—the coach for East Shores's policy debate squad—spins around on the bench, ending up in an awkward straddle. He hardly looks out of place from any of us competitors, beyond wearing an oversized

UCLA hoodie and jeans. Plus, the dead-eyed expression he focuses on me could only be that of an overworked college student. "Beth here isn't feeling too well. We're likely not advancing to tomorrow's rounds, so can I take her home? I'm her ride."

Andrew rakes his gaze over us. Out of the corner of my eye, I notice Beth grimacing and hunching over. Somehow, she loses all the color in her cheeks, bordering on an ashy pallor. Andrew sighs, "Sure. If you advance, show up tomorrow before eight for registration."

"Thanks, man." I escort Beth to the nearby bench where our bags lie. I put on a whole show of gathering our bags, slinging them over my shoulder, and checking that Beth's ready to ride. She feeds our friends the same easy lie for our quick getaway.

I hand Beth her gloves and the helmet my mom had gifted to her to hold. Besides that, she wore long enough pants and thick-heeled boots, which will work for a short ride.

"Thanks," Beth whispers, and I understand its true meaning. *Thanks for being here for me. Thank you for taking me home.* She tightens the wrist strap around her glove before offering me her helmet. "Give me a hand?"

"Always. Let's grab the bike first." Our arms loop together again as I escort her and our bags from the cafeteria for the final time. Some of the others wave and wish us goodnight, which we return in polite smiles until they are out of view. Then, Beth hip-checks me into racing with her down the hallway.

She giggles for the first time all day.

I do, too.

Beth follows me out to the parking lot, weaving with me between cars and empty parking spots for the far-off spot where I parked my motorcycle. The sleek black body of my Kawasaki gleams underneath the sickly yellow flickering of the closest streetlight, sandwiched between two vacant parking spots.

As promised, I turn Beth's helmet over, running my gloved fingers against the familiar ridges and worn straps. Before me, my dad used to whisk mom away on romantic motorcycle rides. When we moved to California, he traded in his woodsy views for a sea breeze and loads of sunshine while revving his engine down PCH. Mom doesn't ride anymore; that adventure belonged to her and my dad.

"Here we go," I say as I slip the helmet onto Beth, who takes her hair down from its signature high ponytail. Like an expert, I glide through all the straps and secure the helmet onto her head as tight as possible. Beth's face vanishes behind the red plastic and dark-tinted fiberglass. "How does that feel? Make sure it's nice and snug. We wouldn't want it to fly off mid-ride!"

My instructions accompany my hands gripping both sides of the helmet. I rattle, shake, and knock my hands against the curved edge of Beth's helmet to test the fit. Through the helmet, I hear a muffled laugh from Beth. Her hand taps over the front of the helmet until she finds the ledge to lift the visor.

"Can confirm: not an inch of space." Beth flashes me a thumbs-up, but, more importantly, her eyes are sparkling again. Ah, there she is.

I chuckle as I shut her visor over her face. "Good. Now, wear your backpack on your back. Get ready to climb on, short stack. You remember how to climb on like I showed you this morning, right?"

I offer my hand to Beth, who throws her leg over the motorcycle as effortlessly as an experienced rider. With a little boost from me, Beth mounts the back half of my motorcycle's seat on her first try. She's a quick learner, already better than her first few attempts this morning. Color me impressed.

Before I mount, I check all the final details, such as loading my backpack on my front versus my back. I take control of the motorcycle from the kickstand, propping it up on the asphalt; a sense of familiarity, with its dual undertone of complete control, curls around my fingers when I grasp the handlebars.

Without me reminding her, Beth's arms loop around my waist and clinch her grip on me. Her fingers curl hard into the fabric of my blazer, and our bodies scoot together to close the gap. No need to be shy, we're both friends here. *Good friends.*

The engine revs to life underneath the practiced check-list I run through without devoting a single thought toward it. My motorcycle and I run on a mutual muscle memory, in perfect sync. I tap Beth's hands as we take off into the night, running on the wind and away from whatever negative emotions had their hold on us.

XOXO

THE RIDE to Searidge Hills flew by faster than expected, even when Beth and I hit half a dozen red lights and opted for a drive-thru pit stop. Normally, we'd hit The Stack for a post-competition meal. Today, on the other hand, we needed a change, something to shake off the funk that Beth and I landed ourselves in.

Chicken, rice, and cheesy bean burritos, along with a side of churros, from a drive-thru Mexican place should do the trick.

I drive down the darkened street to Beth's house, half-expecting the lights of the houses we pass to switch back on. I can't imagine a motorcycle in an otherwise bike-free street jiving well with the quiet of the sleeping neighborhood. But no one appears disturbed enough to switch their lights back on.

Thus, the last leg of the ride to Beth's house ends in a hoarse purr as I roll up to her packed driveway.

Beth waits for me to park us along the curb, engine off and kickstand holding the motorcycle up before she relinquishes her hold on me. I dismount first and give her a hand off the back of my bike. Beth's boots thud against the driveway and she hoists off her helmet. The speed with which she unbuckles the straps threatens to drop my jaw to the ground. Oh yeah. She's a *fast* learner.

Beth shakes out her hair with the biggest grin, "If I go out and get a motorcycle license, I'll tell my parents it's your fault. I've never liked driving this much in my life." She says.

I flip up my visor. "To be fair, you weren't the one driving," I remind her, but the tone stays light, all in good fun. Beth rolls her eyes but doesn't interject with a snarky retort; I'll say this: Beth knows how to pick and choose her battles, at least with me. "But I'm happy to add chauffeur to my growing list of duties."

"Wyatt Keene, human shield and chauffeur, I don't know. That sounds fitting to me." Beth remarks, pretending to give it thought. Did I walk into that one? Yes. Do I regret it? Not in a million years. After the day we've had, I want us to be back on track as partners—as friends.

I let Beth laugh at her little quip. She keeps it cute and short, smothering her amusement behind a gloved hand. Eventually, when her chest stops shuddering, she catches my eyes with hers. "Thanks for the early escape, Wy. You're the best partner a girl could ask for."

"It's no problem-" I pat her shoulder. However, as I prepare to venture toward the 'you know you can talk to me about anything' spiel I brainstormed on the ride over, the lights over Beth's front porch snap on. The door flies open to reveal a woman who stares at us while holding a cat in her arms.

A loud yowl erupts from the fluffy cat's mouth before it wiggles and attempts to jailbreak from the woman's arms. That must be Beth's mom and Beth's cat.

"Beth, who's your friend?" she questions from the doorway while handling the fussy creature. "And why do you have this nice young man standing outside when he could be inside?"

Beth turns to me, face redder than the helmet. "Any chance you'd like to escape now? My mom will only take no for an answer if it comes from you."

"Well, my mom won't be expecting me home for a bit, and I don't want the food to go cold. I wouldn't be opposed to hanging out for a little while," I shrug. Beth assesses me for a moment. But she beckons me to follow her to the door, where her mom still waits. I offer my hand to her. "Good evening, ma'am. I'm Wyatt."

"Wyatt? Oh, we've heard a lot about you. Please come inside," Beth's mom gestures to enter after shaking my hand. In one fell swoop, Beth scoops her cat off the floor and grabs my wrist to drag me inside. I barely manage to examine my surroundings before Beth brings me to the stairs. "Keep the door open, Beth!"

"I know!" Beth replies, not missing a beat.

As Beth and I race up the stairs, two male voices float from the other room. I have no clue where to go, so I follow behind Beth and the wide-eyed cat peeking over her shoulder. Beth leads me down a narrow hallway until a door on the far right end, cracked open—*her room.*

Beth holds the door open with her foot, letting me in before her, and sets her cat down with a kiss on its white and gray forehead. The door, as promised, stays wide open.

"Well, this is my room, not much to see," Beth gives half-hearted jazz hands while gesturing to the room around her. This time, my survey of the room enjoys no restraints. Most of the room slots into a palette of neutrals, with black and white walls or a gray bed, but then pops of color emerge more expressively. If bedrooms could stand as a metaphor for the inside of someone's mind, Beth's room would perfectly parallel her contradictory nature. *Loves structure and order yet explodes off the wall with such creativity, not defined by the rigid box she shoves herself into.*

The nudge of something against my leg draws my attention away from the rest of the room. I gaze down to see Beth's cat standing on its hind legs and stretching its little claws into my slacks. When I graze my fingers over the cat's head, its purrs roar louder than my motorcycle's engine. The cat even chomps its little teeth around a finger that ventures too close to its wet nose.

"Ziti, don't bite." Beth chastises her cat, who has the sense to appear apologetic. Who could be mad at such a cutie? For their part, Ziti continues to purr and rub against my leg. "Sorry, she's not usually this social with strangers."

"I probably smell like food. She's a smart business woman." Grinning, I scrunch my nose at Ziti as she flops over on the floor, even when Beth lifts her off the ground. I know a grift when I see one. *Well played, Ziti.* "Speaking of—why Ziti?"

"My dad found her as a kitten in a dumpster outside an Italian restaurant. She was about this big, chewing through a box of ziti. The name kind of stuck," Beth kisses Ziti's head. "Besides, her scrappy nature and willingness to thrive inspire me."

"Because of your anxiety?" My voice drops lower than a whisper. Beth hears me anyway.

"Yeah. Ziti helps where she can as my emotional support animal. Nine times out of ten, though, I try to lean on the coping skills I've developed over time and hope for the best. I take my medicines and see my therapist, who specializes in anxiety disorders. Today was one of the bad days when things weren't working."

Beth doesn't meet my eyes when she speaks. I don't perceive any shame there, just exhaustion. She sighs, "I really appreciate how patient you are with me. I know sometimes I act out and panic over things that seem so stupid, it means a lot to me that you never freak out when I do. You're steady, holding me down and anchoring me to reality until I can push forward."

"Of course. If there's more I can do when you're having a bad anxiety day or a moment, I want to know. Being partners means I'm here for every moment, good or bad." I don't know what compels me to tip Beth's chin up so she can see the truth pouring out of me, but my hands find themselves on opposite sides of her chin. The gentle nudge pushes Beth's gaze off the floor, showing the wall of unshed tears building around her eyes.

However, Beth swipes a hand over her eyes, smudging her make-up a little. But the tears stop. She hums, "Sorry to go all sappy on you. We should eat before the food gets cold, and maybe we can watch something too."

"I like the sound of that," I concede. I've gained enough ground on the enigma that is Beth Edwards tonight. A push too far might slam the door back in my face after she wedged it open. "Maybe you can indoctrinate me into that D&D show you like so much."

Beth scoffs, giving my chest a harmless shove, "It's a good show!"

17

BETHANY

February, Week 1

"BETH! You have to try these pears!" At the sound of Mom's voice, the rather lovely daydream I had been concocting in my head vanishes into the exhaustingly sunny February weekend.. *It was nice while it lasted.*

A slight twinge of irritation rears its ugly head. The worst part of me—the anxious, chronic overthinker who needs everything to go according to plan—twitches with the urge to say something out of pocket. After all, what's more important: strategizing how Wyatt and I could win a spot in the state championship or a pear?

Instead, I shut down whatever angered instinct arises and silently turn to Mom. She holds a cubed chunk of pear out to me, wearing the biggest smile. She has no clue about the saliva dribbling from the corner of her mouth, too enraptured with the fruit she offers me. I'll admit, the sight softens my knee-jerk reaction of annoyance.

So, I slip off my headphones and accept the pear. I inhale it in one go; a mild sweetness and crisp aftertaste hit me. It's quite a nice pair.

"That's good," I hum. Mom hustles to grab some pears and add them to the massive haul of produce in her rolling cart. And when we head for the register, I leave the bitter animosity in the discarded fruit bin.

Once a month, Mom typically takes Kelsie with her to survey the new goods and favorite vendors at the East Shores Farmers market. Without fail, she comes home with a massive haul, full of bread, produce, and sometimes even flowers to spruce up the kitchen.

This time, however, she asked me to come along since Kelsie would be on an overnight field trip for the entire sixth grade. Mom knows where my soft underbelly is from how fast she brought up the "since you'll be heading to college soon" defense when I groaned and moaned about spending my weekend morning looking at the fruit. She played me like a fiddle.

"Come on, Beth! We have more stands to hit before the market closes." Mom loops our arms together, borderline dragging me along. At this point, everything before us blurs together until I can't remember which stands we've visited versus those we merely passed by. It doesn't help that all of them look the same.

Or maybe that's my cranky brain talking. I will never be an early bird gets the worm type of girl. So, being out in public for anything but school sounds like my personal definition of torture.

If I'm lucky, I'll be able to avoid early morning classes in college.

I trail behind Mom, always two paces behind her chipper speed, walking through the cramped, packed walkways of the market. From looks alone, half the town peruses the wares of local California farmers and small businesses, enjoying the sunshine and clear skies.

The market teems with so much life, wrapped up in a million different conversations. Threads of people's lives intersect over the simplest interaction, tied up in a friendly greeting or the simple act of sharing space. Something tugs on my arm as I observe the microcosm of humanity laid out before me.

I bite back a wince when I face Mom, whose nails scraped a little too hard down my bicep. She cocks her head, gesturing across the walkway, "Isn't that your friend? Wyatt?"

My head snaps in the direction she's pointing. Lo and behold, none other than a tired-looking Wyatt and Mrs. Keene hover by an orange stand. Wyatt becomes his mom's shadow, lingering behind her every step with his hands jammed into his pockets and his eyes downcast.

Hah, we do the same thing.

"Yeah, it is. I didn't know he'd be here today." My eyes follow Wyatt's movements around the orange stand as if he might sense me telepathically reaching for his attention

Things have been much better since he and I talked about the elephant in the room—anxiety. Wyatt handled the information with grace and a ton of kindness. Even before he knew, frustration never seemed the first instinct for a response. I'm lucky to have Wyatt.

Without him, I wouldn't still be debating or having the best season of my four-year career.

"We should go over and say hello!" Before I can process the suggestion, Mom drags me clear across the walkway, unfazed by the foot traffic heading our direction. She strides with enviable confidence through disgruntled shoppers, who receive an apologetic smile from me, myself, and I. She walks straight up to Wyatt and his mom, beaming. "Wyatt! Thought that was you."

Wyatt's eyes widen. "Good morning, Mrs. Edwards!" His gaze travels over her shoulder until he finds me. I watch how quickly his startled expression eases into the laidback smirk I know all too well. "Hey."

"Hi," I stammer around the lump in my throat. Suddenly, the light blue sundress I wear itches around the shoulder straps, feeling out of place on my body. Wyatt dresses like his usual self, sans the riding gear. "First time at the farmer's market?"

"Yeah, it is. Mom heard about it, so she suggested we check out some of the booths." Wyatt tips his head toward his mom, who watches the exchange with a polite smile.

However, my mom never hesitates to strike up a conversation; it's the businesswoman in her. Her hand reaches for Mrs. Keene. "I'm Francesca. It's so nice to meet you. Your son was an absolute delight to have over. Beth adores him, but our other kids think he and that motorcycle of his are the coolest thing since sliced bread," she remarks.

The gushing compliment turns Wyatt's neck as red as I feel, running hotter than before. After Wyatt hung out a few weeks ago, Kelsie and Sawyer haven't stopped talking about Wyatt and his cool leather jacket and even cooler motorcycle. In fact, I suspect Kelsie harbors a fat crush on Wyatt since now he's her new favorite topic of conversation with me.

Mrs. Keene glows with pride at that little tidbit. She shakes my mom's hand in return, "Alyssa Keene. I could say the same about your lovely daughter. She's always been such a delight when she comes to study with Wyatt. We've raised quite the pair of debaters, haven't we?"

"Oh, we have." My mom steps around me to continue the conversation, leaving Wyatt and me on the sidelines while she and Mrs. Keene chatter away. Well, my mom always complains that she wants more mom friends. No harm to Wyatt and me if our moms get along. "Does yours whip out statistics in daily conversation like they're preparing to win an argument, too?"

"Oh my god! Yes! Finally, someone understands my plight!" Mrs. Keene exclaims. She damn near jumps for joy at the thought of someone else's kid being our special brand of weird. She and my mom grasp onto each other, full of laughter and amusement. Wyatt and I lock eyes while the two launch into a whole tangent about the little quirks he and I picked up from years in debate and how winning a simple argument has become a herculean endeavor. When the debate terminology begins to leave their lips, I sidle up to Wyatt.

"I'm not sure if I rescued you from a boring morning of shopping or made everything infinitely worse," I joke.

Wyatt lets out a huff, one sounding suspiciously close to a laugh, and jams his hands back into the pockets of his basketball shorts. "We could classify it as a rescue. Mom wanted to shop for more high-end ingredients because the in-laws are visiting for dinner."

His grimace and the strain on 'in-laws' tell me everything I need to know. Wyatt must not like Graham and Travis's family; if they're anything like those two pinheads, I'm in Wyatt's corner. How he manages to endure them daily never ceases to amaze me.

But, as I stand next to him, a devious thought flickers to life. *This could be more of a rescue.* Next thing I know, all eyes are on me from how fast my hand shoots into the air.

"A couple of our friends are meeting over at Fresh & Frosted in a little bit. Any chance Wyatt and I can go? Everyone's excited about the acceptance letters rolling in." I ask. The lie appears on my tongue without much effort, with a story not terribly inconceivable for two high school seniors. What neither Mrs. Keene nor my mom needs to know is that our friend group already did that two weeks ago.

And what an experience that had been. Not the good kind, either.

While I focus on our moms' pensive looks, I glance at Wyatt. If he's shocked, his face adopts an emotionless expression, revealing nothing about whether he knew my plan in advance.

When our moms look at him, he contributes a wordless nod. The silent defense works well for the moment.

After a pause, Wyatt's mom shoulders her bag higher, "That's alright with me. I'm just glad Wyatt is making more friends," she says, ignoring Wyatt's scowl. "You can either meet me back here, or maybe Beth's mom could lend you a ride?"

"Absolutely! I'd be happy to drive him home afterward. You two be safe and text me if you finish early." Mom chimes in. "Since our kids are too cool for us, maybe we should hang out. I'll show you where all the good deals are." She pats Mrs. Keene on the shoulder, who brightens.

"That sounds amazing! I need more friends who like to cook. I used to do recipe swaps all the time." Mrs. Keene loops her arm with my mom's, and the two stroll away from Wyatt and me.

The Keenes must have this natural knack for making friends effortlessly. Wyatt might be on the quieter side, but people listen whenever he talks, and eyes follow him when he struts into a room. The charisma skyrockets off the charts. And don't even get me started about when he adds his favorite riding jacket or any of his biker gear. He becomes magnetic, the immediate subject of conversation.

Wyatt and I don't talk as we depart from the farmer's market. Our steps fall in sync in a scuffle of sneakers against the sidewalk. As we walk, our knuckles continue to brush with every other stride down the street. The silence carries us past the intersection, along the crosswalk, and right to the edge of

Fresh & Frosted's outdoor dining deck when Wyatt snags my elbow to stop us.

We pause, stepping to the side to let other kids pass us. Wyatt slumps onto the closest surface, burying his face into his hands.

I slide across the bench until our thighs bump together. Wyatt's head snaps back up, but he manages a smile.

"I'll say this now—Graham's family isn't outwardly hostile or anything. They treat me differently, like they don't know what to do with me. The wedding was a prime example of that." Wyatt explains. He wrings his hands.

"You'd think they'd be more welcoming for their new daughter-in-law and her family." I chew down on my cheek, choosing my words as cautiously as possible. These are uncharted waters for me; everyone in my extended family married the same person and stayed together, usually for the better. It's a privilege, I know that.

"You'd think. But at every gathering we attend, the questions always stick to the superficial, always the same exact ones. They never remember previous conversations, some don't remember my name, no matter how many gentle corrections my mom offers. I've stopped trying."

Oh. I can't imagine how frustrating, how isolating that must be.

In my head, I imagine Wyatt sitting alone with only his mom paying attention to him. He lost his dad; now, he needs to play nice with someone else's family, who can't be bothered to learn his name correctly or anything meaningful about him. No one deserves that. The more I think about it, the worse the weight in my stomach becomes.

"My house is always open to you," I blurt out. The subtle furrow of Wyatt's brows as he studies me worsens the flush of heat beneath my skin. "I've always considered my house my safe place, and I want it to be a safe place for you. We're part-ners, but you're one of the best friends I've ever had."

"Beth. . ." Wyatt whispers. However, my hand flies up, beckoning him to wait until I get everything out. I need to purge this from my system, or I might explode.

"You've been nothing short of good to me. You know all the right things to say when I'm so caught up in the details or the negatives that I fail to see the forest from the trees. Like a few weeks ago, when we talked about college with everyone, I hadn't heard anything back from colleges but a handful of denials and one waitlist. And when everyone else gushed about their acceptances, you climbed into the mess I made by being too honest and ruining the good mood. . ."

"You didn't ruin the good mood, Beth. Sorry, but I'm not going to co-sign that idea. That might be your anxiety talking because no one in the group thought any less of you for being honest about receiving denials instead of faking a smile for our sake." Wyatt interjects.

My lip trembles. *There he goes, knowing how to walk the line between patronizing and handling me with such care.* I don't need kid gloves, but the gentleness touches me like salve rubbed on still-aching wounds. "Okay."

"You need to be nicer to yourself. That includes giving yourself and others the benefit of the doubt sometimes, okay?" Wyatt points at me. How did this conversation become about me? "Do you know how thankful I am that I asked you to be my debate partner? Words don't begin to cover it."

When I gaze into his eyes, I find nothing but an open book. No voice inside my head defeats the one that believes every word coming out of Wyatt's mouth. I stifle a laugh as Wyatt's arm slings around my shoulders, "Aww, you like me?"

"Says the girl who's gone all soft. I know you've quite the

reputation for scaring half the guys in our grade." He says, "Joke's on them: I like you when you're sweet and scary. Guess I'm built differently." Wyatt fires back, even throwing in a wink. "Come on, let's stop the sappy stuff. I've got drinks to buy for us."

"Want the usual?" I ask. *One taro milk tea and one classic house milk tea, extra boba in both.* "Oh, and can I trouble you for one of those strawberry custard croissants, too? I didn't eat anything besides the free samples at the farmer's market."

"As you wish, so long as you catch me up on what I missed from last week's episode of Dimension 20." Wyatt's arm never drops from the cozy rest around my shoulders. Not when we get off the bench or when Wyatt guides us to the door to Fresh & Frosted.

"I knew you'd like it!" I exclaim.

Wyatt doesn't dignify me with a response, but the wide grin on his face tells me I was indeed right, *as per usual.*

The shop door swings open before Wyatt can grab the handle, and he instinctively pulls me back. I scrunch harder into his side to leave enough room for the departing customers to pass. Except none other than Travis and a new girl step into view, holding what appears to be two smoothies. I don't recognize this girl; things between him and Mari must've fizzled out. Nadia's chant of "rotating door of girls" grows truer with each passing day.

"Dude, can you move out of the way?" Wyatt remarks without missing a beat or hiding the annoyance in his voice. Somehow, he and I can never escape Travis as long as we live in this town.

"Sorry about that-" Travis's new date stammers and attempts to move from the doorway. But Travis nudges her back. His eyes rake over Wyatt and I, narrowing into heated slits. At first, I sneer back until the weight of Wyatt's arm around my shoulder reminds me of its presence. *Does that upset him? Good.*

"Beth, I've been meaning to talk to you," Travis ignores the quiet protests of his date to step forward. With the height difference, he looms over me and uses it to his full advantage. Real charming, I'm sure. "So, Valentine's Day is next week-"

"Don't even think about it-" I interrupt him before he finishes a complete sentence.

"She already has plans. With me," Wyatt, speaking at the same time as me, remarks. Neither of us looks at the other. This is the second major lie of the morning, and yet it's somehow crazier than the last one.

"Oh yeah? What's that?" Much to my shock, Travis sounds —in disbelief. Unlike everyone else in our lives, he's the only one who can't believe Wyatt and I would have Valentine's plans together. Somehow, I suspect it has everything to do with his weird fascination with my attention.

"Beth and I will be attending a debate tournament together. What's a better gift than winning first place to share?" Wyatt replies. He grabs the door from Travis, opening it nice and wide as a sign for him and his date to depart.

Travis catches the hint, leaving with his very confused date. I don't see them lasting long before Travis hunts for a new girl willing to jump into his arms. But I wait for them to vanish before looking at Wyatt.

I snort, "We didn't sign up for that tournament. Registration is due in two days." Wyatt holds the door open for me, and we duck inside to the instant relief of A/C and the smell of sweet treats.

"Well then, I can email Ms. Goodwin and expedite our registration check as long as you say yes to being my date for a local league tournament this Valentine's Day," Wyatt replies. We step into line together, never breaking eye contact.

"I thought you'd never ask. I'm yours this February 14th."

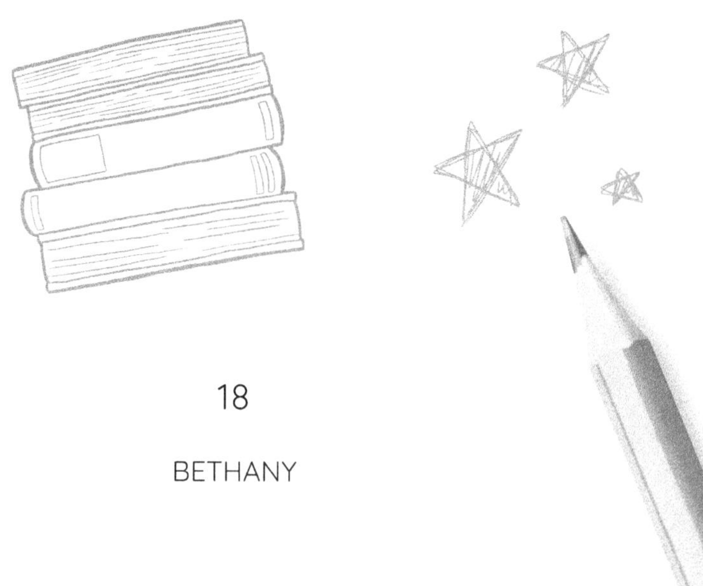

18

BETHANY

LOVE MIGHT BE in the air today, but I can't find it anywhere in a semi-packed high school cafeteria. Not to play into stereotypes, but debate kids are one of the few extracurriculars where a good chunk of their membership would willingly sign up for a tournament instead of scheduling plans with a special someone on Valentine's Day.

Pink and red papier mâché hearts line the walls, and streamers hang from the ceiling above us, creating the ambiance of a long-abandoned party instead of a competition. The nearby snack shack offering discounted heart sugar cookies and themed candy bars really sells the vision, but all the pink threatens to make me dizzy—whatever floats everyone else's boat.

As I shuffle back to my seat, Wyatt's and the other speech kids' heads snap up from their various means of passing the time. Some finish homework, others run through their speeches. Wyatt, on the other hand, is on his third crossword puzzle of the afternoon. The rest of the table barely reacts to my return—only a cluster of debate kids I don't really know, lost in their own conversations, do. Even as co-president with Devon, the size of the team means some people slip through the cracks. Devon's the extrovert, so he handles getting to know people and making everyone feel included. I focus on the competition to bring us trophies—mine and those from the other speech kids. Together, we create one functioning leader.

"Hungry?" Wyatt asks, his gaze already returned to his crossword. His fingers fly across the keyboard while he fills in the clues. He doesn't glance up or slow his roll when he passes me a plate of greasy, cheesy pizza with the crispest pepperoni I've ever seen. The aroma of hot, mouth-watering grease and melted cheese awakens an otherwise dormant hunger. Practicing *Monstrous* always leaves me hungry—for a win *and* a snack.

"What would I do without you?" I groan, throwing myself onto the bench next to him. With everyone packing into a single table, Wyatt and I's shoulders stay pressed together, but he doesn't seem to mind my presence all up in his space. I'd mind if it were anyone else.

"May we never find out." Wyatt teases. I ignore him and sink my teeth into my first bite of still-hot pizza instead. Cheese and grease melt on my tongue, a truly unbeatable combo after a long day of performing, especially when double-entered. Wyatt has seemingly taken it upon himself to wait on my needs. His attentiveness isn't necessarily random, but after Travis sent me an obnoxious valogram this past week in a big display, a long overdue perspective shift hit me over the head. Wyatt cares about the little things, the unspoken needs I never let myself utter into existence, and provides without so much as a complaint or stipulation.

I sink my teeth into another bite and watch Wyatt

complete his crossword from over his shoulder. Through bites, I fumble through my bag for my water bottle, which seems to be nowhere to be found. "Wy, have you seen my-?"

Before I finish my sentence, Wyatt sets my newly refilled water bottle on the table. Its slender neck glistens with recent condensation and is cold to the touch when I wrap my hand around it. *He refilled it for me?*

"I managed to charm some workers into giving me some ice from the cafeteria freezer. That way, it's as close to ice cold as we'll get." Wyatt remarks. The words roll off his tongue like such a gesture is insignificant—case in point.

"Thank you," I mumble around the stubby straw of my water bottle, to which Wyatt shrugs. "Are you going to start another crossword?"

"Maybe. I also brought earbuds and have access to the home Netflix account on this laptop. Or YouTube, where I'll watch more of Dimension 20 without you." Wyatt smirks.

He dodges around my playful elbow aimed at his ribs, "Evil!" I shriek, nose and mouth scrunching with my displeasure. "E tu, Brutus?"

"You're the one who got me hooked on D&D shows. I almost want to buy myself a guidebook and a pair of dice now." Wyatt retorts, throwing the blame into my lap. Yes, I'm the one who showed him the wonderful world of the Dungeons & Dragons web series. Throughout the past week, he's been sending me live texts of his reactions to D20's Fantasy High saga, one of my favorites.

Still, I pretend to faint, only after tearing off another bite of pizza. "Yes, but I won't get to savor your reactions if I'm in round, performing for my life." I protest through the pizza.

"Consider it your motivation to crush everyone in that room who has the misfortune to cross your path," Wyatt replies as nonchalantly as possible. Yet, his eyes twinkle when the light hits them just right, darkening those brown irises with mischief's presence. As he says that, someone enters the room with papers above their head. *Postings for the next round are here.*

"No!" I face the remaining few bites of my pizza left on the plate. By the time I return, the pizza will have gone cold, and half a slice probably won't hold me over through the hour I'm gone. "Impeccable timing, Wyatt. The dodgeball of prophecy has hit you."

"Huh?" Wyatt's brow crinkles. Right, I forgot that he has little to no current meme literacy. One of us needs to stay chronically offline to maintain some level of sanity, and I'm willing to let him make the sacrifice. He glances between the crowd surrounding the postings like sharks circling the smell of blood and me. "Finish your pizza. I'll check what room assignment you're in."

"Ugh, you're the best. My code is E07." I don't need to be told twice by Wyatt to eat. Without a shred of dignity left in me, I scarf down the last few bites of pizza, not sparing a single bit of cheese or crispy crust. Pizza makes me crave Italian food, specifically this little fancy Italian place back in Searidge: cuore del mare. I get the same dish each time I go—which isn't often, mostly for special occasions—in their signature chicken pesto pasta.

I prepare my purse and meet Wyatt in the middle of the cafeteria. He shows me a photo on his phone, "Looks like you're in Room A30. Good luck."

"Thanks. Save the luck for everyone else," I toss my hair over my shoulder to Wyatt's proud grin. I pat his chest when ducking past him and joining the back of a group of competitors heading to their rooms. Five of the large group—including maybe fifteen speakers—head toward the A building. So, I follow them, staying a pace or two behind to preserve some distance.

At first, none of their conversations pique my interest in eavesdropping. I focus on myself, getting into the zone with my binder in hand and a tube of tinted lip gloss in the other. I need a touch-up before the round starts. And, as I blindly fumble for the compact I know I packed this morning, I hear one of the girls in front of me giggle. "-God, he's so cute."

"Wait, who are we talking about?" One of her friends whispers. I use the term 'whisper' loosely; her voice carries down the hall in an echo, nowhere close to a whisper or the semblance of hiding the conversation.

"The debater from East Shores. The tall one, dark hair, navy blue suit." The way I almost trip over my feet and fall face-first onto the concrete walkway. *They're talking about Wyatt!* A tight plume of heat starts in the center of my chest.

If I didn't have a round right now, the sensation might pin my feet to the floor and keep me hostage. The feeling evades me. Too wily for me to attach a name to it. So, it remains nameless as it wreaks havoc on the tentative calm I reserve for pre-round jitters.

Wyatt's a handsome guy—I know this. I admitted this to Nadia in one of our many chats about "her replacement," as she teasingly calls him. But I shouldn't be hearing this conversation. *I don't want to hear it.* I won't be able to unhear what these strangers say while fawning over my Wyatt.

Wait, he's not *my* Wyatt; that sounds way too possessive on my part.

"Oh, yeah! Girl, you should ask him out. He's your type."

"She would, but allegedly, he's preoccupied with his debate partner all the time. The girl attached to his hip," A third girl chimes in with her input. Now, I get dragged into the conversation by these strangers, who remain blissfully unaware of who lurks behind them. "Pete and Joey had a round against them this morning. Apparently, those two finished each other's sentences two separate times and exchange looks like they're communicating telepathically."

The others hum. What started as a red-hot pain begins to blister and push hard against my stomach. *Annoyance? Ire? Pride? Something more sinister?*

Regardless of how I feel, my petty side grabs my lip gloss and the compact mirror, trading my binder for the latter. I unscrew the tube and squeeze a sizable portion of gloss onto the tip. Then, I speed up, turning a casual stroll into a brisk pace to pass these girls by.

I swipe the lip gloss over my mouth and use the mirror to check its spread. Without glancing over my shoulder to see their shocked faces, I say. "His name is Wyatt, by the way."

XOXO

AFTERNOON MELTS into the evening without much excitement. After the accidental eavesdropping earlier, I need uneventful. One of the girls had been in my round—the one with the alleged crush on Wyatt—and couldn't stop glaring my way as I performed. Good thing I pretend to be going insane throughout my performance, so the dirty looks provided the perfect energy to channel into rage. Whatever emotions left my stomach unsettled and hot were expelled the moment I stepped onto the stage, gripping my binder like a lifeline.

But I, maybe for the better, chose to keep the exchange from Wyatt. If the girl wants to confess, she'll find her courage. I won't interfere with her chance by giving him the heads up.

I can't stop thinking about it, especially with Wyatt sitting beside me. Whenever our shoulders brush, or I glimpse him in my peripheral vision, the conversation rushes back to the forefront, including the discomfort. Well, if the girl wants him, I'm sure she'll make her move before we leave.

"How long does it take to calculate scores?" One of the new speech kids, Katrina, grumbles across the table from me. She sheds her oversized, plum-colored blazer to drape over her backpack, which she uses as the world's most uncomfortable pillow. She shuts her eyes and groans while searching for a suitable nap position. It takes time to master the tournament nap without incurring neck and back soreness.

"You'd be surprised," I respond before anyone else takes a stab at it. All the speech kids perk up, some of them physically shifting in their seats to face me. I catch a few rogue debaters further down the table, who glance up from their conversations, and Wyatt with a single sentence. "For speech, plenty of judging relies on subjective opinions and interpretations of a piece, which reflect in the scoring. As much as the rules and regulations can help, ties happen organically. So, organizers comb through all the scores to ensure no ties, apply tiebreakers where possible, and process any challenges to judge or competitor conduct. It's a lot."

"Got it. Any idea of when they might have that figured out?" Katrina rubs her eyes. A quick check of the time reads 7:30 PM, and I know we could be here for a while. League tournaments often run over time and can end as late as nine, making for a twelve-hour day of mostly waiting around and fighting off abject boredom.

"Nope," That ends the conversation, and everyone else returns to their preferred method of passing the time. I spot cards, books, homework, people conversing amongst themselves, and a million other things to burn through the downtime. So, I reach for my phone to clear out all my outstanding notifications, unread texts, and emails. Something about the glaring red number on my screen causes an itch to fester underneath my skin until I handle them all, whether they get read in full or marked read without a glance.

As I open my email, the page refreshes with several new emails on the top, including a notification from Stanford labeled "admissions" in the subject line. I rush to click it, too curious to worry about concealing my disappointment from the table if I receive another denial.

Nadia suggested I apply so we can reunite at Stanford, even in different departments. She would be a STEM queen, and I'd be on an international law or political science track. Stanford would keep me in California; I ranked it number six on my list behind all of the Boston colleges. In no world would I be disappointed to attend THE Stanford University.

My finger misses the email, hits the wrong button, and backs me out of my inbox. Right underneath the inbox, my spam folder flashes five unread emails for my consideration as well. I should handle those first and let myself steep in the anticipation a bit longer.

But the moment I open my junk mail, I see it. There, at the bottom of the unread pile, with a timestamp of two weeks ago, Wellesley College sent an update on my application status.

The impact hits me with an immediate sucker punch straight to the throat from how a painful cough tears through me. I gasp, choking on nothing but air and surprise. One leg flings over the bench, and the other trails right behind, propelling me out of my seat and the cafeteria. Panic drives me now, its familiar hands pulling a sharp left turn at the wheel.

Heels can't stop me from jogging out of the room. Someone shouts my name, but I scramble ahead, looking for somewhere private to shut myself in for the inevitable fallout. The thunder of footsteps echoes in my wake, growing closer and closer until the person jumps in front of me. *Wyatt.*

"Is everything okay?" Wyatt pants from the unexpected sprint I put him through on a Saturday evening. His gaze rakes over me, searching for signs of distress or a clue as to what sent me fleeing into the night. I, on the other hand, grasp his wrist and proceed to drag Wyatt into the nearest quiet space—the girls' bathroom.

He splutters, still out of breath, "Beth? What-?"

"Wellesley!" I hiss, pushing on every stall door to check for anyone else in the bathroom. I shut the bathroom door once all the stalls turn up empty. The nearby trash can becomes a makeshift door jam. "Wellesley emailed me their decision two weeks ago! It ended up in my junk mail."

"Oh! Did you read it yet?" Wyatt beckons me over. He flicks on the light and banishes the shadows shrouding us for the sickly, flickering fluorescent ceiling lights.

I shake my head. I'll be the first to admit that opening the admissions letter for my dream college in a dingy bathroom on Valentine's Day hardly resembles the vision I've spent the last few months painting in my head before I went to sleep or while I wrote my application. Yet, life never comes out perfect anyway. The moment is here, waiting for me to take the leap of faith.

This is it.

"Stay with me?" I beg. Never in my life have I desperately wanted company, not when the chance of disappointment looms so tall over me. But if I do it alone, I might puke on the floor and never get back up. "Just for this letter and Stanford's?"

"Always," Wyatt steps forward, opening his arm for me. I tuck into his side and let him hold me up just in case my knees buckle. "Start with Stanford?"

Upon such wise advice, I find the Stanford letter first. Trembling fingers punch in my log-in details to reach the portal and open the new status of my application. Through a shaking inhale, I read, "... it's a waitlist. I can live with that."

"Okay. The waitlist at Stanford is still pretty big. But we're here for Wellesley." Wyatt murmurs. His arm squeezes tighter around my waist as if he senses how the nerves threaten to reach their fever pitch. Shaking hands might be the least of our problems, with my whole future on the line.

Unlike Stanford, whose letter I grabbed with such efficiency, returning to the junk folder and retrieving the log-in information for Wellesley sees me dragging my feet. Silence beyond the heavy breaths I force so I don't pass out amps the anxiety up ten notches; with my shaking hands, I'm likely to collapse on this bathroom floor before I read out the results of this letter. Wyatt's arms around me remain the sole thing keeping me upright.

Eventually, I log into the Wellesley portal to stare at the letter. All I'd need to do is click the link to know whether Boston will be my home for the next four years, whether years of hard work were enough to take me where I want to be. But no matter how much I might want that yes, the fear of the no leaves me paralyzed.

"I can't do it." My eyes shut tight, and the phone almost slips through my unsteady hands. "Wyatt. . ."

Without a word, Wyatt's hand lifts the phone out of mine. My eyes fly open to watch him, with resolve painted across his face, as he clicks the link on my behalf. His arm around me squeezes harder, ready to support my weight come what may. He clears his throat.

"Dear Bethany...Congratulations," Those three words are the only thing I need to hear before the first tear falls, splattering against my cheek. The rest follow behind it as the dam holding every single fear and hope back shatters. Sobbing, I bury my face into Wyatt's chest; he keeps me upright to shed my messy, happy tears. Through the noise, I can hear the smile in his voice. "The Board of Admissions is delighted to offer you admission to the Wellesley College Class of 2029."

I reach out to take my phone and double-check with my own two eyes. I probably read the first paragraph of the letter at least ten times until the realization sinks in. *Boston, here I come!* Tears continue to fall, but a thrilled shriek escapes me.

Wyatt's one-armed embrace morphs into a full-on bear hug. He cradles me against his chest, rocking us side to side. "You did it," he whispers. "Tell your anxiety that it lost this battle."

"Take a hike, anxiety!" I exclaim. My head rolls back to see Wyatt's grin. "I won."

"And the next time it tries to say you're not enough, just remember that you're more than enough. Wellesley thinks so." Wyatt whispers, which feels so much bigger in the hollow bathroom acoustics. I almost forgot where we are from the sheer joy filling this space. My joy.

I nod fervently, too happy to consider debating Wyatt's points on the merits. I need to call my mom and the rest of my family. I should text Nadia. I want to run down the hallways and scream at the top of my lungs that I'm going to Wellesley College, and literally nothing could ruin this for me. I squeeze Wyatt in one last hug before I let go.

I can stand on my own now, thanks to him.

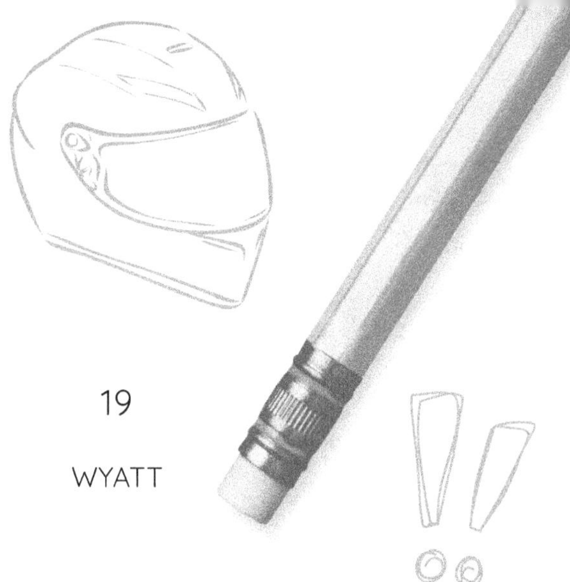

19

WYATT

February, Week 3

I HAVE Boston on the brain.

Opening Beth's Wellesley letter in an abandoned girl's bathroom last week reminded me of the stack of letters piling up in the top kitchen drawer. I came home from that tournament with a first-place trophy—Beth and I took the top spots in our respective events—and a bright, burning desire to know where I might end up by the end of summer.

"Wyatt? Can you go grab the mail?" Mom's voice floats down the stairs, pulling me out of my reminiscing.

"Sure! Be right back!" I shut my laptop closed as I slink from my chair. The screen goes dark on the email folder with every college admissions letter I've received in the last few months. There are a few physical letters in the bureau's top drawer by the front door for me.

Mom and I came to a mutual decision to gather as many letters as possible before opening any of them. We figured opening them at the same time would prevent me from growing attached to one specific school. Sure, there's a top five favorites which will be hard for other schools to beat. But, I'm willing to make a practical choice over one for purely sentimental reasons. The cost of college alone worries me.

I snatch the mailbox key from its drawer in the kitchen. The keys hang off my finger, jingling with every step. I jog into the colder evening to the edge of the driveway, where the mailbox rests.

A small pile of mail fills the hollow interior of the box, which I collect to take inside. Most of it appears to be bills addressed to Mom or Graham, but I sift through the pile anyway, searching for anything with my name on it.

The first thing belonging to me turns up in the middle of the pile—a letter from Babson College in Massachusetts. Great, that's another one to add to the stack. A few more letters down, I shuffle past two letters from East Shores. But, right as I step into the house, I hit the bottom of the pile and see it: a second college letter, one from Boston College.

Boston College, *my* dream school and my mom *and* dad's alma mater.

Mom and I stipulated our "wait until most of the letters come in" policy around the promise that we'd only begin opening letters once Boston College arrived. It's my top choice, the one that could demolish all the other options, even if they offer the best possible financial aid or some perks for my chosen major. What Wellesley is to Beth, Boston College is for me.

I almost drop the rest of the mail onto the entryway floor when I sprint for the kitchen—instead, the mail lands on the table in a haphazard splatter of paper. But bills and other miscellaneous things become the least of my concerns. I flip open my laptop, re-opening the acceptance letter folder before I sprint out of the room.

Taking two stairs at a time, I rocket toward Mom and

Graham's room, ready to grab her for our promised letter opening. Reaching the top step and hearing angry, hushed voices, however, stops me in my tracks. The door to Mom and Graham's room appears ajar at the opposite end of the hall from my room. Voices slip through the crack, loud enough to sneak down the hallway but not further than the stairs.

". . . We're supposed to be a family, Graham," Mom's voice shakes as she stands on the verge of tears. "You and Travis being there while Wyatt opens college letters would be a great showing that we're united."

Disgust flares in me at the idea. Family unity sounds idealistic for our blended nightmare, even without the never-ending annoyance living inside of me toward Graham and Travis. Besides, why should my college admission letters be the occasion for three out of four members of our family to pretend to tolerate one another? No one suggests ruining Travis's big moments to fulfill some futile semblance of familial love.

From the scoff Graham lets out, he and I appear on the same side—*a resounding "fat chance in hell" on all accounts.* But ire joins forces with disgust; his acting dismissive toward my mom might ignite the tinder box of emotions within my chest. I've been waiting for him to mess up, to cross the line.

"That is the worst idea, Lyss." Graham snaps. His raised voice sends a shockwave down my spine. My hackles rise at the undercurrent of aggression in there, the kind he reserves for when his favorite football team seems to be throwing the match or when I step on his toes in our scuffles.

"Why? Sometimes, I feel like I'm the only one of us trying to help the boys become closer. I know being a teenager is an angst-ridden time in anyone's life, let alone two boys who've lost a parent. But what I can't understand is why I'm doing the hard work by myself."

I wince. Sorry, Mom, but you're alone on this for a reason.

Graham's voice grows louder and closer to the door. "Travis has been upset with his prospects. He's gotten several rejections from his top schools, and the football offers aren't rolling in the way they should. My boy deserves to go pro more than anyone else on the team, but they refuse to see his talents. So, I refuse to make him stand there and pretend to be happy for someone like Wyatt while he gets his pick of the litter." He barks.

The Boston College letter in my hand crumples in my fists. The thought of marching into the bedroom and socking Graham clean across the face plays out with such sickening satisfaction. Maybe he should re-evaluate why Mr. Slipping Grades isn't earning many college offers. Not to mention, his son being one of the better players on the East Shores team doesn't absolve him of his mediocrity either.

Mom, however, goes a little cold when she asks, "Someone like Wyatt? What's that supposed to mean?"

"Travis is having a tough time adjusting to all of this. Wyatt's attitude doesn't make our family better. He could stand to be more humble and considerate of Travis' and I's feelings." Graham defends himself, armed with a sanctimonious attitude.

He says I'm the one with an attitude problem, and yet... here we are.

"Have you considered extending him some empathy? I lost Justin, but Wyatt lost his dad at fourteen. You, of all people, should understand how that impacts someone." Mom argues back.

"He needs an attitude adjustment." Graham hisses.

Somehow, that becomes the lit match hovering above the gasoline-soaked emotions. Within seconds, anger envelops my chest with its raging inferno. Despite Graham's view, I've shown immense restraint when dealing with his and Travis's snide remarks and attempts to isolate me from Mom. For her peace and happiness, I bite my tongue and choke on the urge to lash out at them. If they want a fight, I can bring them an ugly one.

I don't want to listen to this.

I hear Mom inhale sharply, which she does whenever she prepares to argue some more, but I dismiss myself from the hallway. No more eavesdropping tonight.

The Boston College letter uncrunches in my hand once my grip loosens, now all crumpled. I try to smooth over the creases in the envelope, but the damage is done. August can't come soon enough, so I can leave this house for Boston, where I'm wanted.

I make a beeline for the kitchen, knowing I won't run into Graham as long as he continues arguing with Mom, or Travis, since he's no longer grounded for his persistently bad grades. No one will notice when I slip out for a while and clear my head. Tonight might worsen if I stick around long enough for Graham and I to come to blows.

I stuff my bag nice and tight, including the Boston College letter. I move as stealthily as possible to pack my things for a ride. I know where I can go to breathe a little easier.

I shoot two texts, one to Mom and one to Beth, before I walk out the front door. My motorcycle waits for me in the driveway, letting me be my own getaway driver. Green Day blares into the built-in speakers with the heavy punk and undertones of anger. The white-hot lump of rage cements its place in my chest along with the thrum of the bass. The world passes by in a blur of light from the fading pink sky, and every intersection I speed through when the light flashes yellow.

Vibrations from the engine roaring beneath me keep me grounded when all other rationality abandons me. The sensation courses through my veins, reminding me that I have more in me than anger to give. For the twenty-minute drive to Beth's place, I remember the small things that keep life in Searidge Hills tolerable. *Debate. Motorcycle rides along the coast. Fresh & Frosted boba runs. The random assortment of memes the debate guys send me at 3 AM when I'm sleeping. Taking photos of the sunrises and sunsets over the water.*

As I roll up to the curb outside Beth's house, I find her standing on the porch in a pair of flannel PJs and an oversized Wellesley hoodie. I know she's on that list, too, at *the very top*.

Beth waits for me to dismount and climb the stairs of her porch. She gestures to the worn, wicker couch beside the front door, and we sit together. With the sky darkening, the distant streetlights at every third house and the outdoor lamp attached to her house illuminate us with their amber-tinted glow.

Beth stares at me, unable to hide a single iota of concern from her hazel eyes when they look me over. She grips her phone in her hand, knuckles white and pronounced. She nudges the wooden porch flooring with the tip of her fuzzy slippers, which happen to be shaped like the yellow Care Bear. Yet, she never prompts conversation, waiting on me.

"I hate Graham," I sigh while easing my helmet off. "Apparently, I'm in desperate need of some humility. He managed to turn Travis's lack of college and football offers into my fault while arguing with my mom."

"Are you serious?" Beth's face twists up, punctuated by her disgusted scowl. *Exactly how I feel after hearing Graham's words.* Her hands flex into fists but release as quickly. Her energy redirects into a nervous bounce of her leg. "What a d–"

She catches herself before calling Graham any number of names that could rightfully describe him. Instead, she offers her hand to me and laces our fingers together. She tilts her head toward the door, "Do you want to come inside? I'll warn you in advance: Ziti might glue herself to your lap and refuse to leave until you feel better."

"Maybe later." Despite the hot, lingering embers of anger, Beth's mental image elicits a small laugh from me. Instantly, the tightness in my chest lessens. "I was supposed to open college letters with my mom tonight."

"I thought you were waiting? You got your Boston College letter?" Beth's eyes blow as wide as fine china dinner plates.

I pull the letter from the backpack and hand it to her to examine. She runs her hand over the crinkled, damaged envelope with such reverence. Her thumb traces over the sealed flap for a second longer before returning the envelope to me. Beth hums, "What do you want to do?"

"Would you open it with me? Yeah, it should be a moment with Mom, considering this is hers *and* my dad's alma mater, but I don't want that house to spoil whatever celebration I might have. I know Graham will make a huge problem out of it because he already has." I toy with the letter between my gloved hands.

"Absolutely!" Beth scoots closer to me. She beckons for the letter again, which I hand over without hesitation. I watch how she stares at the face of the letter. "Before we do, I need to say something. Promise you won't be mad at me-"

"Why would I be mad?" The anger becomes a burning lump of nerves in my throat. Beth's eyes focus on the street, avoiding me.

"Because you're close to your mom. It's obvious how much love you have for her, how you sacrifice a lot of your well-being to keep her happy and her marriage stress-free," Beth remarks. She tucks her knees to her chest, resting her chin on her knees. "She should be defending you at all costs. That man put a ring on her finger, but you're her flesh and blood. You're the last piece she has left of your dad and the love they shared. In no universe should she stay with a man who disrespects you, who acts like you're a burden when you're nowhere close to it."

At first, Beth started meek, hesitant to criticize the one person she knows I adore in this world. Yet, with each word, Beth latches onto the undertone of anger that seems to be in the air tonight, raising her voice and becoming more impassioned. Her expression, however, channels a thunderous rage, the kind she only lets out when she steps up to a captive audience with her binder clutched in her hands.

"Beth—"

Beth barrels past me, still riding the heat of her emotion, "No, what angers me more is that Graham should be thankful he has a stepson like you, but that would require him to yank his massive head out of his ass. Okay, you're one of the funniest people I know, even if it's the trauma talking. You're brilliant in the book-smart sense, but also so intuitive emotionally. But, most of all, you're kind—genuinely and unforgettably kind. Every day teaches me why I'm glad I said yes to being your debate partner. So, your housemates should act right." She declares.

I can't say a thing after that. The words refuse to budge or come out of me while Beth pants a little, coming down from her tangent.

Beth finally glances at me for the first time since I told her about the letter, meeting my eyes. Any worry or sheepishness melts back into her features when I tap the letter. *Open it.* Regardless of this decision, I'll be in Massachusetts again before the end of the summer. She'll be there too. Maybe we'll see one another, grab lunch or coffee, and talk about the life we left behind in California. She'll understand me in a way no one else will, maybe for the rest of my life.

Beth digs her nail underneath the sealed flap, careful as she tears open the envelope without touching the letter waiting inside. She takes out the letter, pinching it between two fingers. Then faces me, a question in her eyes, while she holds the letter between us.

"I can read it," I assure her. Beth doesn't question me or insist on taking more space in the moment. She hands me the letter and tosses the envelope onto the table at the end of the couch. "Here goes nothing?"

"Regardless, you're still the coolest person ever, according to my siblings." Beth jokes to lighten the atmosphere. Usually, I'm the one with the quick-witted commentary or a comforting word, but not tonight. For now, I'm the one searching for his way back home, however possible.

I unfold the letter without looking at it. Sucking in a breath, I glance down at the letter, roaming over the official Boston College seal and its greeting to me. "Dear Wyatt Keene…I am delighted to offer you admission to the Morrissey College of Arts and Sciences…" I can't read the rest.

No, I fixate on that first line, reading it over and over. *Accepted.* They've accepted me. Boston College is a go. Someone needs to pinch me because nothing about it feels real yet.

Something wet and hot splatters onto my cheeks, falling onto the letter. I'm crying. The rollercoaster of the evening leaves me stranded in an emotional wasteland, unsure how to throw myself headfirst into joy the way Beth did. The tears stream down my face, singing their promise of catharsis as the weight lifts off my shoulders. I no longer carry the world upon my back like Atlas; I have my way out, typed and contained on the four corners of this letter.

Beth's fingers brush underneath my chin and tilt my face toward hers. The yellowing artificial light replaces the twilight skies to encase her in an aura of amber, faint but still visible through my tear-stained vision. When her thumb swipes over my damp cheek, I fall forward into her. Our arms end in a tangle as I hug her, but Beth always gives as good as she gets.

"Your dad would be so proud of you." She whispers into my temple. The words pierce straight through my chest and come out clean on the other side, as precise and devastating as a bullet. My dad, who couldn't be here through no fault of his, would be proud to see the little boy he used to carry on his shoulders follow in his footsteps.

"Yeah, he would be," I agree. Beth's hands rub soothing circles into my back; I'm sure she feels the tears dripping onto her shirt. "He'd also like you a lot. I can already hear his dozens of jokes about how we're taking our debate duo act on a one-way trip to Boston."

Beth laughs, and so do I. Our arms disentangle from the hug, but Beth grasps me by the wrists. "We should celebrate. We can seal the envelope so you and your mom can have your moment if you want?"

"It's okay. I'll re-do it with the portal," I tuck the torn envelope and the letter into my backpack. The do-over will come with the conversation about the logistics, such as calculating financial aid from the college and confirming where I intend to live in Massachusetts. "How exactly are we celebrating at 6 p.m. on a Wednesday night?"

"We're going to The Stack for some burgers and milkshakes!" Beth scrambles to her feet. She throws open her front door and shouts something inside to her family. She ducks inside for a few more seconds, only to re-emerge with her car keys. "Bye, Mom! Wyatt and I will be back before 8!"

"Have fun! Congrats on the admission, Wyatt!" Mrs. Edwards exclaims from inside before Beth shuts the door.

She grins at me, beckoning me to follow her with the curl of her finger. I don't argue with Beth, choosing to sling my backpack over my shoulder and head for the passenger side of her pristine white Solara.

"Hey, what are you doing for spring break?" Beth asks while unlocking the car. Spring Break is two weeks from now—the third week of March—and right before the state qualifying tournament. The next few months promise a series of back-to-back events, starting with Spring Break and culminating in prom and graduation. Don't even get me started on the stretch of state testing in April and AP seasons in May.

"Not sure yet," I admit, between buckling myself in and Beth turning the ignition to her car's polite purr. "Travis and Graham keep talking about a camping trip, but those plans don't sound concrete."

"Well, considering that you just got into your dream school, I think the house might be tense for the next few weeks. You should come with me and my family on our trip to Bass Lake. We do it every year with another family, but they pulled out due to personal circumstances." Beth offers, holding my gaze until she pulls out of the driveway, headlights on full.

Now, *that* sounds like an idea. The less time I spend at home, the better.

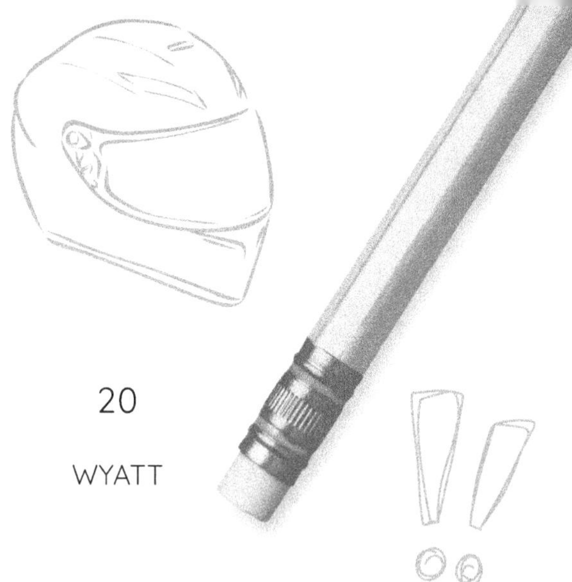

20

WYATT

THE LYRICAL GROOVES and steady melodies of the Arctic Monkeys' *Favourite Worst Nightmare* light a fire underneath me to cross off every item on my spring break packing list. I woke up from the best sleep of my life, despite the nightmare of a family dinner that had taken place the night before. Once again, I caused trouble.

This time, though, I never uttered a single word yet still managed to ruin dinner.

I had approached Mom with Beth's proposition for me to join her family for spring break. I figured she might go on the trip with Graham and Travis for the sake of "family bonding" while I headed north with Beth's family. She and Mrs. Edwards, who exchanged numbers that day at the farmer's market, began sorting out the details. Beth and I let them do their Mom thing and kept out of their hair beyond the occasional request for updates.

However, last night, my mom decided to drop the bomb

that she would be accompanying Beth's family and me upstate. Apparently, the cabin rental has a guest house, and the owner confirmed that no one else booked it. So, the original plan of me crashing on the pull-out couch in the living room went into the trash without Beth or me knowing.

I have no qualms about Mom joining me on vacation. Graham, on the other hand, lost his ever-loving mind. I recall smoke billowing out of his ears when Mom informed him about her new plans. He protested until he went red in the face, ranting about her choosing some strangers over their family. *Yeah, real rich on his part to use "family" as a means of winning an argument.*

However, Mom reminded him that his trip had been designated as a bonding trip for him and Travis. In their planning, they had forgotten all about her and me when scheduling activities. From her understanding, she and I would've spent the spring break in Searidge while they galivanted off to their camping trip. Besides, according to her, married couples having separate hobbies or activities is healthy for them in the long run; she didn't need to be attached to his hip every day.

I had almost shed a tear of joy and stood up to applaud her. I might be the debater, but Mom had put Graham in his place. Watching him sulk around the house all last night fueled a tiny, evil part of me, one that hungers for Graham to choke on a slice or two of humble pie. He loves being the "big man" but only seems to exercise his authority over people he considers smaller than him.

No matter how hard Graham pouts or tries a subtle dose of guilt-tripping, Mom is settled on joining Beth, me, and her family at Bass Lake. We're going where I'm welcome, and I know it kills Graham to be thwarted by a seventeen-year-old boy and his secret accomplice.

But now, I need to get my bags packed before we leave in

two days. Mom hates the last-minute scramble to pack before any big trip or debate event in the last few years. Hence, she gave me a list this time, expecting it to be done early. I won't even argue with her on this one, I'm too ready to be out of this house.

"Alright. Toothbrushes, beach towels, a laundry bag, a spare tube of large toothpaste, extra deodorant and sunscreen." I read a whole line of items aloud. All of these should be in the hallway cabinets or the shared bathroom space, along with half of the list. Frankly, the convenience of it all works out in my favor, so there are no complaints on my end.

Trudging out of my room, me and Mom's packing list go on the hunt for the first set of items. With Mom and Graham out of the house, I don't worry about missing anything important as I make Arctic Monkeys and maybe some Queen the sound-track of my morning. Perhaps I'll borrow the "Winning Brought to you by Beth and Wy" playlist for some extra inspira-tion; the playlist never fails to amp me up before tournaments.

I start in the bathroom first, which means less crouching and crawling halfway into cramped cabinets to find items involved.

No one else in the house also means a few off-key rendi-tions of whatever song plays might escape me. I stay away from karaoke bars for a good reason, but sometimes, I can't help a song or two.

With the laundry basket I've collected on my way to the bathroom, I start dropping the items into the basket. It works better than trying to carry everything in tiny trips to the bedroom.

I lose myself in the music, letting time slip past me without a care in the world. Only when the basket grows heavy do I turn around and find a figure lurking in the bathroom door.

In the crustiest "East Shores Athletics" shirt known to

mankind, Travis hovers in the door. His frame blocks the upper half of the doorway, leaving a small sliver of space on either side of his legs. He says nothing; his lips stretch into a thin, "menacing" scowl. Such a look might scare the freshman he lords over on the football team, but nothing about him screams "frightening" to me.

I wait for him to enter the bathroom, to shoulder me out of his way, and grab whatever he came here for. Instead, we eye one another in an unexpected, wordless impasse until I remove my headphones—the heavy bass lines of *AM* scratch against the otherwise grating silence.

"Can I help you?" I snap at Travis, whose presence irritates me beyond the pale. I'm sure the feeling's mutual.

"Do you ever get tired of ruining everything?" Travis sneers in return. His lip curls at the corner to bare teeth like he's some threatening predator. His ire deepens into his expression when I quirk a brow. *Go on, Travis. Elaborate on your position with some evidence. Arguing is my forte.* "I know you convinced your mom to go on that trip with you so she'd ditch my dad and me. We were going to have a good time until you swooped in and stole her away like you always do."

Oh, that's hilarious. I'm stealing *my mom* from some kid she barely met under two years ago. I have at least fifteen years of a leg up on him in the relationship department.

Scoffing, I step closer, "You can't stand not being the center of attention, can you? You and your dad want to ice me out so your little family feels complete, but that'll never work. You can use my mom as a replacement for yours. I won't be playing nice with people who haven't earned an iota of respect from me." I enunciate every word so Travis doesn't get it twisted. He and his dad need to learn that no 2-v-1 will ever back me into a corner.

Using the laundry basket, I leverage some room to slip

through the door. Travis stumbles back as if I used the force of an entire linebacker to manhandle him out of my way—*drama king behavior*. I walk away from the bathroom, making a beeline for the cabinets, when Travis speaks up again.

"Life will be so much better when you're gone," he says. The smugness around his words tells me he expects the words to hurt. They don't. Life will be better for everyone, including me, once I leave this place.

"Then maybe your dad should've married a single woman if another child threatens your perfect little family," I fire back. "Oh, and back to that stealing comment of yours? People aren't things to be stolen, but of course, you believe that. With your entitlement, you think everyone should bow at your feet and kiss the ground you walk on—my mom, the freshman you torment, every girl you date and drop, your football teammates, Beth."

The mention of Beth shifts the air in the hallway. Travis's expression flips on a dime, turning into something *unhinged*. He inches toward me, "Beth. See, I know her type. They play all tough and hard to get, but girls like her always have a weak spot. I'll wear her down eventually, get her to see that I'm the better pick between you and I. Maybe I'll apply some public pressure. Prom season's coming up. Girls love that stupid stuff."

"That'll never happen." At the clench of my jaw, shockwaves reverberate through the rest of my body in a warning plea. *Put the laundry basket down. Be on the defensive.* The voice in my head screams; it almost sounds like Beth's strained whisper she reserves for strategizing during our competition rounds.

I set the laundry basket down by the door and face Travis, who stalks closer. He squares his shoulders. Nothing else precedes his hands grabbing my shoulders like one of the grapplers on the wrestling team. But I don't wait for him to throw the first punch or jostle me around.

I might not be a football player, but I know my strengths.

I drop my weight toward the floor to loosen Travis's grip and ram my body into his torso. The shock factor knocks him off balance, giving me enough leverage to slam him into the nearest wall. A wedding photo falls from its precarious position on the wall.

Travis gasps when his back hits the wall, mouth flapping wide open like a fish stranded on land. Our eyes meet perfectly level as we stand at the same height. Good. Maybe he'll listen clearly to what I say from here on out.

"I've let this go on long enough because I didn't want to overstep. But that ends today. Stay away from Beth," I might whisper, but there's a threat lying in wait for the day Travis messes up again. "She may not need my protection, but just know that I'm not above settling this in the only way a meathead like you comprehends."

I release Travis and step out of his space. I pick up the fallen picture from the floor and set it somewhere safe, ridding myself of its cursed touch. Travis stays pressed against the wall, breathing heavily.

He can run and tell his daddy about what happened. All I care about is that he stays away from Beth—for good. She deserves to be free of him before I am.

XOXO

THE WARM SPRINGTIME air hangs around the lake in thick pockets of sunshine, amid a partially cloudy sky. As promised, Mom and I are in the middle of our spring break vacation with the Edwards.

Graham continued to be mad, and Travis learned how to shut his trap for the remainder of the time before the trip. It's too soon to tell whether my intervention worked, but here's to hoping.

Glistening blue waves lap at the rocky, dirt-lined shores of Lake Bass. At this hour of the afternoon, other visitors must be enjoying their lunches, given how sparsely populated the lake appears. The tall, lush green trees create a wall of foliage as far as the eye can see. The faint aroma of pine carries on a phantom breeze. Limber branches reach toward the skies, which gleam in the same breathtaking hue of blue as the lake. Sunlight skips over the ripples and waves of the water, bathing everything in its subtle golden shimmer.

Views like these will be missed once I'm across the country, back in Boston. California and Massachusetts are two different places, one no less breathtaking than the other.

"Looking a little lonely here, stranger. Mind if I join you?" Beth asks from behind me.

Lifting my sunglasses, I glance over my shoulder. Beth stands there, hands tucked into the front pockets of her light blue denim shorts. She opted for sneakers and a navy blue polka dot swimsuit underneath her shorts and the thin, cream-colored shawl to protect her shoulders from too much sun exposure. Our entire group has gone through an exorbitant amount of sunscreen in the last few days.

"Eh, I don't know," I hum while patting the open spot next to me on the dock. Beth takes the spot, joining me at the edge of the wooden planks where our legs hang over the lake. "Where's our moms?"

"They're still enjoying the wares of that little gift shack. I swear my mom plans to leave with a dozen knick-knacks she doesn't need, despite the fact that we come here almost every year. She keeps them all in this little drawer in her office at work," says Beth.

"And your dad and the kids?"

"Oh, they're checking out some of the activities for the lake. I told Kelsie that you like adventurous girls, and she's spent the entire morning trying to convince my dad to take her white water rafting."

Beth snorts, but I'm not much better. Poor Kelsie. I can already see her little pigtails struggling to stay above the water in still lake water, let alone the rapids.

"That's evil." I nudge Beth with my shoulder. It seems Kelsie has a huge crush on me, and Beth never lets her live it down. Crushes happen to kids all the time, so I ignore it. Besides, Beth and I often split off from the family to do our own thing, limiting my interactions with sweet but obvious Kelsie. Sawyer, though? I like him; he's a cool kid.

"Eh, she'll get over it. She crushes on anyone cute or a boy who breathes in her general direction. As soon as the next cutie comes along, she'll forget all about you and your motorcycle." Beth waves her hand in the air. She, with such nonchalance, pushes her sunglasses onto her head.

"Oh yeah?" I chuckle. "So, which am I? Cute or a boy who breathes in her general direction?"

"You're annoying," Beth retorts. She shoves me with barely any force as I chuckle some more. "I should've left you at the cabin with Ziti. She's also obsessed with you and would be all over your lap while she naps."

"Guess I have that effect on all the Edward ladies." I lean onto my hands behind me, propping myself up from the otherwise warm deck. Sneaking a glance toward Beth, I spot nothing but flushed cheeks.

Then again, that could be sunburn in the making.

Almost as if she reads my mind, Beth's fingers trace over

her cheeks, dancing along the reddening skin. "I need more sunscreen. Don't want to burn because I take too long to recover." She hauls her shoulder bag around to grab some much-needed SPF.

Beth rubs a small dollop around her face and neck until the whiteish cast disappears. She offers me the bottle wordlessly, never taking her gaze off the lake.

"Thanks," I squeeze some sunscreen onto my hands and work it all over. The skin around my shoulders shows signs of a slight flush, so I get more sunscreen. "We can't be burned and peeling at the state quals."

I wait for Beth to laugh, maybe crack a smile at that. But she doesn't. Her legs swing over the ledge in an aimless rhythm while she stares out at the water. Then, the fidgeting begins, restless and a surefire sign that something weighs heavily on Beth's mind.

"Beth? You okay?" I angle myself into her line of sight, catching how her eyes dart away.

"I—I'm nervous," she rubs at her arms to soothe herself. "The state qualifier tournament has one of two major consequences. Either we secure one of the three debate slots or nab an alternate slot, or we lose big and end our otherwise massive win streak with a pathetic crash and burn."

"Considering our track record, why wouldn't we qualify for the first option?" I prod a little further.

Beth hesitates, biting on her lip with a pensive sigh. "Because of me. Last year, Nadia and I almost didn't make the state tournament because I made a mistake mid-round. I spiraled. I panicked. I crashed and burned in a spectacular ball of flames, which Nadia had to salvage. We only went due to being alternates and another team dropping out with a severe case of the flu three days before."

Oh, well, that definitely would impact me, too. But Beth, as great as she is, lets anxiety get in her head and rewrite the story. Maybe she messed up that round, but it could've been a non-issue. She wanted something to blame, and she was her favorite target.

"At the end of the day, I can't let myself believe that we're 'the team to beat' or whatever our teammates say. I need to prove it first." Beth adds before she reaches forward to run her fingers through the lake's water.

"I get that. But, I want you to know right now—I won't be upset if we don't make State. Everyone will be bringing their top game to the tournament next week. I know you, Beth. You're a force of nature. Regardless of the end result, you will bring the roof down." I say.

We have two choices: either give it our all or roll over and quit before we get started. Somehow, I suspect Beth will always choose to fight, even if the end result turns out to be the end of our high school debate careers. However, I have enough faith in this duo to see our path to State. *Oh, and it's bright.*

Beth faces me, pushing her hair away, revealing her face. She offers a tiny smile. "I'm glad I get to do this with you. We've said it a million times, but-"

"I never get tired of hearing it," I promise.

"Me either." Beth and I sit by the lake as the birds cry in the distance and the waters beneath us churn sunlight into its soft waves.

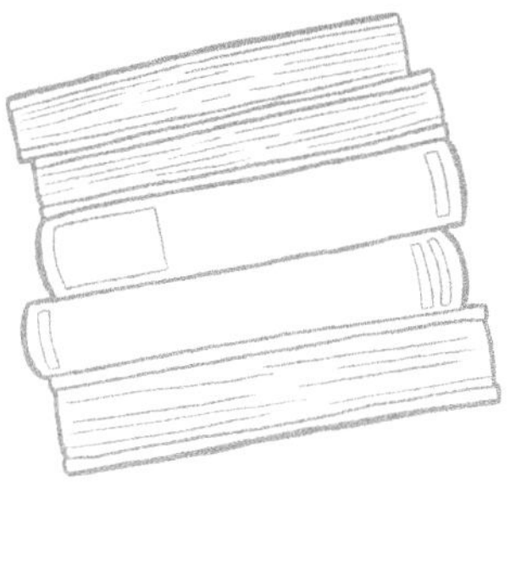

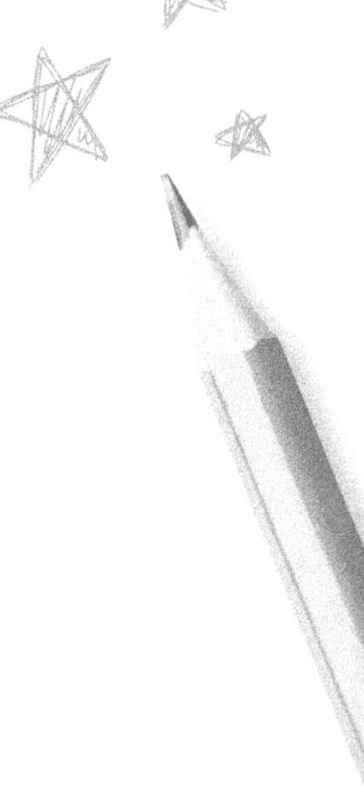

21

BETHANY

March, Week 4

"OKAY, I know you don't have all morning to sit with me and yap about how bioengineering is actually stealing years off my life, so let me make this edition of the Nadia Inquisition a fast one. How are you feeling?"

Nadia's voice—rather perky for 7 a.m.—blares through the speakers of my car's radio. Flecks of static chew at the edge of the conversation, even when I crank the volume up.

"If I said I felt great, would you believe me?" I chew the tip of the straw in my hibiscus iced tea, almost inhaling a mouthful of the mildly tart drink by accident.

"Not in a million years. That would worry me more than telling me you're nervous," Nadia snorts. I adjust my phone from behind the steering wheel to get a better view of Nadia. She sits on the lawn of her school, soaking in the sunshine in a crop top. She hides behind sunglasses and sips an iced glass of milk with a side of coffee through a lipstick-stained straw. "Last I heard, you and Wyatt are a debater's dream team. Allegedly, whenever you two come back from competitions, Coach Kruger does backflips for joy at the sight of your gold medals."

"No—I mean, yes—It's complicated! Yes, Wyatt and I have done great this season. Coach Krueger most definitely thanks her lucky stars that she let me negotiate Wyatt's spot on the team during tryouts. But I can't let myself head into today with the expectation that every round will go smoothly and we'll waltz onto the qualifiers for State..." More of a ramble than a coherent explanation, the taste of frustration sours in my mouth. Its aftertaste extinguishes my appetite for iced tea and the smell of freshly baked bread from the backseat.

Nadia pauses, "You're worried about repeating last year, aren't you?" She asks. She even lifts the sunglasses away from her eyes and scoots away from some of the louder conversations in the background.

I hate to monopolize her sun and fun time with all her college friends, but I can't bring myself to lie. So, I nod, pursing my lips into a tight line. "A little. But can you blame me? We had such a good season, too, and I almost jeopardized every-thing by getting in my own head."

"Beth, honey, you had a panic attack mid-round," Nadia corrects gently. "Your sister accidentally texted you about Ziti having some stomach issues when your mom had it under control, and it caused you to spiral. There was nothing you did wrong in that situation. Besides, we ended up going anyway."

"On a technicality. I can't ruin this for a second time with a whole new partner!" As I feel myself getting riled up, I loosen my grip on the steering wheel to flex my hands. Talking about it doesn't help much except to stir up every instinct to fight and latch onto loopholes in logic. This is the energy I should be saving for the next three rounds of debate today.

"Okay, I can see I'm not being very helpful right now. I'm not sure what else I can do, and I don't want to upset you,"

Nadia drops out of frame as the phone tumbles into the soft blue gingham picnic blanket and meticulously trimmed grass. She snatches the phone up, chest heaving. "Sorry, didn't mean to drop you. But how can I help?"

"A simple 'good luck' will suffice. That's all I need." I assure Nadia. But a tiny, guilty part of me stuffs down the harsh thought sprouting among the fertile anxiety. *Nadia has never been the best at comforting me when anxiety had me in its claws. But she always hypes me up.*

"That I *can* do. Good luck. You're going to be amazing," Nadia grins before she pans the camera toward the gaggle of other college students on her blanket. These must be her friends from classes and clubs. "Everyone, wish my little rockstar, Beth, good luck! She's heading to the state qualifier for speech and debate without me!"

The group devolves into an assortment of cheers and applause at Nadia's prompting. Total strangers seeing my face for the first time and wishing me well does a bang-up job at erasing the worries I started the conversation with. I wave to the smiling, friendly faces, unable to hold back the fizzy sensation spreading under my skin. Yeah, this is a Nadia special.

A gentle knock on my window jolts me into the real world. Only one person would be here an hour in advance and know where to find me in the parking lot. *Wyatt.*

I gesture for him to hop in the passenger side–the door is already unlocked for him—off-camera. "I've got to go, but I'll call you soon! Enjoy the sunshine for me." I smile at Nadia, who grins back.

"Sure thing! You're my rockstar!" Nadia waves before ending the call right as the passenger door flings open. Wyatt fidgets with his helmet, loosening it to reveal his scraggly tufts of hair. He tries hair gel once in a blue moon, but he looks much better without it slicking down his fluffy hair.

"Morning, stranger," I greet Wyatt as he slides into the seat, one leg hanging out of the car while he maneuvers his backpack and helmet into the limited legroom in the front. "Are you ready for today?"

"Of course. Did you get the goods?" Wyatt flips down the visor and fixes his hair in the mirror, fixated on his reflection. I observe the small things—like how his tongue pokes against his cheek while he struggles with a stubborn strand—with total amusement. I'd jokingly say he's emerging as a full-on passenger princess, but I'd probably scar him. The aghast expression he made when I called him that during our late-night burger run will forever live in my brain.

I nod. Without unbuckling, I lean around my seat to grab the collection of bags and the paper drink tray. I pass the drink tray to Wyatt first and then hand him the paper bags. "We have one iced coffee and two New York-style bagel breakfast sandwiches. An asiago with egg, spinach, bacon, and cheese for you. Then, a plain with egg, chicken sausage, and cheese for me. We can also split the hashbrowns I got."

Wyatt nods, impressed, while our hands divide our spoils. Yesterday, we arranged to have breakfast together before the competition because I promised to get plenty of fuel for today. Can't have me running around and performing at the top of my game without food, now can we? I picked the place, Wyatt supplied the cash; that's good teamwork.

I reach for the volume knob to turn the radio louder. My phone connects to our shared playlist, kicking off with Queen's *Don't Stop Me Now*. From how many times I've listened to this on a loop, I know we're in for some Green Day and Michael Jackson within the next few songs. We need all the energy and focused vibes heading into this tournament.

"I raise a toast to us. Three rounds stand between us and the State championship. We've got this—" My voice trails off as I face Wyatt, finding him already looking at me. All intensity or sarcasm appears nowhere in his dark eyes when they lock my gaze onto him. His inexplicable tenderness steals the rest of the words from my tongue, which ties itself into knots when I think about saying anything and disrupting the moment.

Then, Wyatt breaks the spell enveloping us when he clears his throat. "Cheers to that." He says, without the toast being finished. I drop my eyes from his face, and the crinkling of parchment bridges the gap.

XOXO

"—FOR these reasons, you must vote for the affirmation. Thank you, judge." The voice of one of our opponents stammers to a clunky closing, finishing with a whole two minutes to spare. *Leaving time left on the table. Rookie mistake.* I can hear Coach Kruger's disapproving tongue click loudly in my head.

I set my pink glitter pen down in the middle of my flow, which straddles the line between incomprehensible and a perfect demonstration of the old saying, "method to my madness." All the shorthand and never-ending arrows might confuse the onlooker, but it makes perfect sense to me. It'll deter cheating from the other side and keep the runaway thoughts organized as I chase the thread of logic woven by my opponents.

As the opposing speaker takes her seat, brushing off her sports jacket, which is two sizes too small, I push out of my chair. My absent-minded fingers skim over the lapels of my blazer to tuck the button into its rightful slot and brush off any lint. I'd already spent plenty of time obsessively ironing and removing any visible cat hair or dust this morning. Still, that fact lapses from my memory occasionally, usually when the nerves nip at my heels.

My movement catches the attention of the judge, who stares at me like a deer in headlights. The poor woman adjusts her aggressively floral patterned cardigan and knocks a few pens off her borrowed desk. She staggers to pick them up but bumps against the chair beside her. *Yikes.*

"I need another minute or two," the judge pleads. She must be new, much like the speakers on the affirmative case, still green around the gills. "Is that alright?"

"Please take your time. Let me know when you're ready for the Leader of the Opposition speech,* ma'am." I could press the issue, cite the rulebook, and be a stickler. However, kindness never hurts the scorecard. Nadia taught me *that*. And, from the relief seeping through the judge's expression, I've made the right call.

I sink back into my chair. Wyatt's head stays buried in his flow, which looks radically different from mine in its shorthand and charting of the different arguments, as well as the separate notes with our incoming rebuttals. The latter grows longer by the second. Any moment now, I expect a sticky note or two stuffed into my hand with suggestions for what to address.

My eyes flicker toward the nearby clock, content to watch the little hand in its stillness. No one speaks or breathes out of turn, yet that silence cracks open the door for an uninvited guest to enter. Anxiety lurks behind me, its hands clamping down on my shoulder, skipping straight past the gradual onset for an instant buzz. My breath shudders in my throat, uneven and heavier than it should be.

This exact moment was where I faltered last year, down to being the first speaker. How will you mess it up this time? Thinking this way never bodes well, but the thoughts spiral out of my hands, slipping through my fingers too slowly to salvage my confidence. Something unsure, unstable, and uncomfortable slithers along my spine, branching out until the rest of my body feels its presence. *Even if Wyatt and I qualify, the self-fulfilling prophecy promises a pathetic end. Everyone will see that your wins are nothing more than a fluke, a stroke of luck never to be replicated.*

Anxiety moves the goalposts out of reach. I let it.

Heat envelopes my hand, stealing my attention away from the brewing storm alive in my head. Wyatt's eyes pin me down with his knowing stare; he must see the panic on my face. He sees right *through* me.

"Do you need a second to breathe?" He murmurs while beckoning me closer to shut out the rest of the world from our conversation. It ends with our cheeks nearly pressed together and him gripping my hand as my anchor.

I swallow back the urge to tear up, to shut down, "No, I've got this." I remark, borderline snapping from how I force the words out.

"And it's okay if you don't. Remember what we talked about on the dock? We win no matter what happens." Wyatt squeezes my hand twice before relinquishing me to the world. Anxiety lingers in this room, still waiting for my downfall. Guess it'll be disappointed today.

When the judge glances up from her papers, everyone in the room faces me expectantly. They all want different things, but I usher those expectations to sit down and wait for their moment. Right now, this is my moment.

I rise from my chair, barely avoiding the urge to fix my outfit or some other nervous fidget. My eyes find a point behind the judge's head as my horizon before I begin to speak. "Good afternoon, Judge. As the leader of the opposition, we reject the argument that countries should adopt sunset clauses that legally force them to review and either re-authorize or revise their constitutions every generation. For this speech, we shall take a two-pronged approach in presenting our prima facie case and rebutting the incorrect presumptions of the government."

No stutter, no stumble. I speak as if last year never happened. And, for now, it never did. See you later, anxiety. You can torment me another time when I don't have a state qualifier slot to nab.

XOXO

APPLAUSE RATTLES off the walls of the shiny new auditorium as the qualifiers for Lincoln-Douglas bask in their hard-won victory. I cup my hands around my mouth, whooping, "Go, Devon! That's my co-president!"

Devon, who secured a shiny second place and a qualifying spot at the State Championship, locks eyes with us at the East Shores table. He gives us his best pageant wave, complete with kisses blown our way, causing even more boisterous cheers. I'm sure the other schools in the league find us obnoxious for our excitement.

They also probably despise us for sweeping many of the categories. In every individual speech event, someone from East Shores qualified, including me. I'd argue that my leadership by example set the standard for excellence, but I had the easiest qualifier in my event. When only three competitors enroll, and the league can send three, we all advance to the State Championship.

The organizers still made us compete for placements, though. So, the shimmering golden "League Champion 2025" trophy nestled in my arms right now? I earned it.

"One last round of applause for the qualifying students before we turn to our final event of the night," the League President summons a new wave of cheers. The debaters on stage walk off with their trophies and smiles. "It's time to announce the Parliamentary debate qualifiers. We had quite the turnout in this event; the competition was fierce. But we only have four slots."

A hush falls over the room. Four slots and at least a dozen teams mean we wait for a blood bath. It's enough to make me sick to my stomach, abandoning the small drops of joy I got from watching my teammates succeed.

From beside me, Wyatt sets his phone down. His whole posture screams "alert" while the League President accepts the envelope with the scores. She tears the flap and pulls out the card, taking time to read it as if the room isn't on the edge of their chairs, salivating in anticipation.

Someone behind me pats my back in a fleeting gesture of comfort. The touch, however, has the opposite effect, like dropping a toaster into the bathtub. Bumps rise across my skin where they touch me, and I lurch forward to lean against my thighs. My elbows hold me up from slumping completely over. I breathe in and out through my nose, counting the seconds between each inhale and exhale until the discomfort disperses.

"In fourth and the first pair of debaters heading to State, we have... from Pacific Grove High, the team of Shaw and Bailey!" The team in question rushes up to the front, ecstatic if their faces are any indication. The two girls jump on their heels, shaking one another by the shoulders, while their classmates cheer them on. The rest of the competitors offer tepid applause.

Wyatt's body shifts closer to mine, starting with the shy bump of his knee against mine. Unlike before, his touch doesn't inspire a flush of hives to break out. But Wyatt doesn't push, either. He merely sets his hand on his knee, leaving his palm up to the ceiling with an invitation for me to link our fingers.

He must sense my nerves again, too good at reading me for a guy I met at the start of the semester. Mere months shared between us, yet he understands what makes me tick. I'd never admit this to anyone, but especially Nadia herself.

Wyatt *is* my best friend. He's the one person in the world who, I swear, gets me to my core. He's the partner I needed to be *great*, not just good or passable.

"In third place and our second pair of debaters heading to State, we have... from East Shores High, the team of Torres and Torres!" Screaming erupts from either side of me as August and Andrea's names are called. I braced as soon as I heard East Shores, so sure Wyatt and I did just enough to clinch a spot. But the Torres twins swooped in and grabbed their hard-earned spot.

I clap as the rest of our teammates do while the twins run up to collect their trophies. They shove and laugh in one another's faces, on the verge of playfully wrestling one another in front of the audience.

I'm happy for them, even when my heart tumbled through the floor at the call of their names instead of ours. Each round, Andrea and August had come back to the table with the utmost confidence in their performances, in stark contrast to Wyatt and I, who couldn't decide where we felt on the spectrum. And if the pattern holds that no school secures two entries in a given event, then Wyatt and I have already figured out we won't make it to State.

I'll let myself be disappointed in due time, away from the prying eyes of my team. *You'll always skate by on a technicality, huh? Not good enough to crack it on your own?*

As much as those words strike me through the gut, their

honesty cauterizes my pride's gaping, bleeding wounds. My therapist might strangle me for intellectualizing and dismissing my feelings instead of feeling them, but the last thing I need to do right now is cry.

More applause snaps me back to the moment. I spot a new duo sauntering toward the front to grab their trophies—silver ones for second place.

This time, I throw my hand on top of Wyatt's, sucking in a sharp inhale loud enough for him to hear. Wyatt laces our fingers together. Maybe I imagine it, but I swear Wyatt's thumb traces along one of my knuckles. The touch happens too fast for me to tell.

Murmurs stir around us at the abrupt pause in the announcements, the drawn-out silence drumming up more suspense. *Let's rip the band-aid off, shall we? Get it over with.* I focus on my lap and watch my knee bounce, occasionally knocking into Wyatt's. He never interjects or tells me to calm down or to mind his personal space. Wordlessly, he steps into the mess with me.

"In first place, the League Champions for the Western Bay Forensics League, and the final pair representing us at State, we have..." the League President's voice hushes all conversation once more. I tuck my tongue between my teeth, ready to bite down on the disappointment inching its way up my throat. "...from East Shores High, the team of Edwards and Keene!"

For the second time today, my heart stops. Only this time, the world goes mute from the sudden crush of Wyatt's arms around me, turning the volume down on the screams and cheers from our teammates around us. Hands jostle us in their excitement, yet Wyatt never lets go of me.

I bury my face into his shoulder and squeeze, channeling every ounce of energy left in me not to cry in front of these friends and strangers. The rush of emotions might force my dinner to crawl back up my throat, but I choke it down in the safety of Wyatt's shoulder before stepping up to take our trophies.

State better get ready for us. Wyatt and I might be unstoppable.

22

WYATT

April, Week 2

"—I'M just saying: I'm one minor inconvenience away from vanishing into the woods never to be seen again. Call me Bigfoot."

This line yanks me straight out of whatever tentative focus I cultivated despite the endless chatter around me.

"What are we talking about?" I cough on the unfortunate sip of water I took when August recited that gem of a line. I manage to turn over my shoulder and let the water splatter onto the uneven, cracked ground instead of covering everyone in my spit.

To my right, Beth snorts, "August here is complaining about the trials and tribulations of applying through the FAFSA. Try to keep up, or at least get your head out of the clouds." She crunches a ranch-dipped carrot in half to an audible 'crack' before nudging the homemade veggie and fruit platter toward me. I also spot some sliced deli meat, crackers, and cheese cubes in there, forming a lunch-sized charcuterie snack box.

I accept the offer when I scoop a cracker and some deli meat from the box. Beth preens as if satisfied with my choice and places the box in the center of our corner of the lunch table. For once, we're eating lunch on campus with some of the other debate kids; the school stated today would be a rare no-off-campus day due to safety concerns with ongoing construction nearby.

"Right," I drawl. Beth smirks at me while she crunches on another carrot, saying nothing else. She turns back to her laptop, as do I. "You guys are weird."

We lurk in the article archive for our weekly headline collection while everyone else chats about colleges. By now, the bulk of acceptances and rejections have come in for East Shores's seniors. Unless people intend to hold off for a spot on the waitlist, most people have some idea of where they plan to go come fall.

I do. Mom and I talked about it extensively, and when most of my letters for colleges out there yielded yeses, we made a few calls to the family out in Boston. We sorted through all the financial aid offers and the college money left behind by Dad since I was born. Having the logistics sorted out before the acceptance deadline and all the end-of-the-year hecticness bodes well for focusing my efforts on debate, APs, and graduating.

A pad of pale blue sticky notes lands in the center of my keyboard, with the top one scribbled all over in Beth's pristine handwriting. I pull the note off the stack to read when someone from the group groans. "They're passing notes again."

"Are you two allergic to not being obnoxiously cute?" Mai jokes. A few snickers escape the others around the table, but Beth ignores them. I follow her lead and hand her the sticky pad back, writing something of my own onto the top note.

Beth reads my note, laughs, and tucks it into her bag. The

rest of the table peers at us, waiting for more. Neither Beth nor I spill the beans; we write in code, speaking in a shorthand we've developed during parliamentary prep. It's our personal language, one meant for two pairs of ears and eyes, no more.

Beth twirls her pen between her fingers, huffing, "I could say the same about all of you being nosy. Can we please get back to the college conversation?" She never lifts her eyes from the screen. I notice the dozens of open tabs to different news outlets and the poor, buffering download button in the corner.

"If you insist," Devon speaks up from the head of the table, where he dragged over a spare chair. "You've been keeping hush-hush about where you committed. Everyone assumed you'd be shouting from the rooftops about your decision."

"Well, that's because I hadn't decided until a few days ago. I needed to get more letters back before making my decision." Beth hums, which causes everyone's head to snap up, including mine. She drops the pen onto her laptop and lowers the screen a little. "I wanted to be sure I had everything in order before confirming. That's all."

"You're committed now?" Andrea's eyebrows shoot into her new blunt bangs. "Are we looking at a Wellesley girl? Or somewhere in Boston?"

"She has been more smiley lately..." August agrees, but his comment elicits a few rogue stares in my direction. *I am not the reason Beth's been smiling more. She's excited about Wellesley.*

I shoo them away with a subtle shake of my hand. Beth, however, doesn't seem to notice. She clasps her hands together, all while smiling like she won the lottery.

"My family and I discussed all the options, making the best decision for me and our finances. We had to compare financial aid packages since a good chunk of the schools offered some degree of help through scholarships and work-study opportunities." Beth's words drum up anticipation for everyone else around the table, who lean closer for when the announcement comes.

But all the preamble gives me pause where it didn't exist before. I thought Wellesley was a done deal; she called it her dream school and cried tears of relief when the acceptance came in. Is the tuition too much for her family to afford? Will she choose another school to pursue her Boston ambitions? Did she decide to stay close instead, backing out of Boston to keep her familial support close?

We haven't talked much about college since before the State Qualifier. State kind of took over every conversation from the excitement. Beth will return to State for the second time, whereas I've never been.

But, before Beth can end the suspense and tell us what school she chose, an especially loud clamoring erupts from somewhere around the gate leading to the student parking lot. Everyone at the table looks over their shoulders to see a group of onlookers gathering around the entrance. They hold their phones out, recording whatever has their attention.

Then, emerging from the sea of students, Travis marches out in a baggy, powder blue suit straight out of the 80s with aggressive shoulder pads. Behind him, several of his football teammates carry different items in their hands—bouquets of flowers, a speaker blasting the opening instrumental of *Can't Take My Eyes Off You* by Frankie Valli with a microphone attached, and a rolled-up banner. Oh, I know a prom-posal when I see one.

"I need Witness Protection," Beth mumbles, her hands ghosting over my riding jacket as she scrunches behind me. Once again, I've become a human shield between her and Travis. As she ducks, I slip off my jacket over her shoulders to block her from view. "Please tell me he isn't heading this way."

"Tough luck." Devon's voice hardens because, much to

everyone's dismay, Travis heads in our direction. His eyes lock with mine, but, for once, I can't get a proper read on him. The rest of the table pushes away their lunches and clears their laps, prepared to stand and guard Beth.

I, on the other hand, might follow up on my promise to Travis and settle this with fists. He wants to mess with Beth to get to me. How about we cut out the middleman and address the root of the problem? I'd happily go home and earn a scolding from Graham after I knock his son's front teeth in.

"Beth, if he keeps coming over, do you want me to handle him?" I ask her, never taking my eyes off Travis as he inches closer. He still gives no indication of his intentions despite the shrinking distance between our table and his procession of absolute buffoonery. He even whips out the microphone to sing the song lyrics as he approaches.

Not well, but the sentiment evokes a well-known image—*10 Things I Hate About You*. Beth loves the film as a connoisseur of romances or romcom movies. The thought of Travis weaponizing something Beth loves threatens to unseat every shred of dignity I hold. Red-hot ire drips down my throat, preparing to say something vile, and my fists clench.

Climbing off the bench, I square my shoulders. *Round two, Travis?* And as he reaches the point of no return, our eyes lock, giving me a front-row seat to how fast his once cocky grin drops into a scowl. Those eyes scream a thousand hateful, spiteful curses without a single word exchanged, and then he walks past us.

Someone at the table gasps in shock, doing it for me as I stand too stunned to comprehend. *Had my intervention actually worked?* Travis marches past us and his procession never glances our way either, too focused on his new target—Tate, the captain of the girls' soccer team.

He croons to her with his mediocre vocal range while his

lackeys roll out the banner, which reads '*No one will take their eyes off us at prom*' in block lettering. The impromptu audience screams and gossips when Travis tosses one of the several bouquets toward Tate upon finishing his serenade. Tate considers it for all about five seconds before nodding, resulting in a win for Travis.

He needs one.

While everyone observes the scene, I sit with the other debate kids. Beth pokes her head from behind my jacket, quick to hand it back to me.

"That's Travis's seventh girlfriend this semester." If I had been drinking, water would've shot out of my nose in a demonstration that would put Niagara Falls to shame. *How does he continually get these girls to date him with a reputation like his and a personality worse than his dad's?* "I don't know if I should be impressed or worried for some of these girls."

At Mai's comment, Beth rolls her eyes, "I'm shocked he had time for other women, considering how he made bothering me his second favorite pastime this year." Her comment earns a rumble of laughter from the others. Apparently, Beth wasn't shy about the details when the speech kids asked what the deal was, and the story spread like wildfire across the team.

"Not to be too on the nose, but who among us has prom plans?" Devon clears his throat. The question manages to sweep everyone back in. The group rattles off their plans for the seniors or juniors to enjoy their differing proms. The few underclassmen stay quiet on this one, but so does Beth, who slips her laptop into her bag and picks at her lunch without so much as meeting anyone's eyes.

"Wyatt? Are you going to prom?" Andrea's voice snaps me out of my absent-minded stare toward Beth. I find the entire table, sans Beth, focused on me, but their expressions run the gamut of emotions.

I shrug, "It's never been something I considered or felt strongly about, one way or another. However, if anyone needs a date, I wouldn't say no." This answer appears to please the group, who nod and mumble their agreement. All except for Beth. "What about you, Ms. Romcom? Are you going to prom?"

Beth's eyes flicker between me and the others, who aren't subtle about their piqued interest, before she hums. "As a kid, I expected I would go and had a specific vision of prom night, down to the dress. But as of now, I don't foresee that magical prom fantasy coming to life any time soon. So, I might get a group together and go."

"Someone got too attached to being a champion debater to find a date." Andrea sighs, sounding more sympathetic than teasing. Yet, Beth's mouth twists into a tight smile, one not quite reaching her eyes.

XOXO

A WEEK LATER, I see myself up at the crack of dawn, halfway drowning in a bowl of cornflakes in my mostly dark kitchen. My suitcase and spare duffle rest at my feet, ready to be tossed onto a bus headed for San Francisco, where the State Championship Tournament will take place starting tomorrow.

With the number of competitors East Shores has in the tournament—somewhere between twenty-five and thirty because the speech team scored nominations in every possible category—we need a large enough bus for all of us, our luggage for a three-day trip, and the few judges we need to provide to the tournament like a tribute. We have a long travel day ahead of us, even before the competition begins, a boring one with too much free time.

"Wy, did you want any other snacks for the ride? I don't know how many stops the bus will make to San Fran. It seems like a long ride." Mom holds a brand new lunch bag stuffed to the brim, so bulky it can barely zip up.

I would've driven myself to school to not disturb her rest on a Thursday morning, but she insisted. My motorcycle can't stay at school for three days. But once I agreed to the ride, she went full steam ahead with helping me pack and prepare a fridge's worth of meals.

"I should be good with all of that." I scrape the edge of the bowl down to my last few bites of semi-soggy cereal and milk.

"And how about Beth? Is there anything she likes that we can pack for her?" Mom asks without skipping a beat. She dangles the lunch bag from her fingers on the thick, sturdy shoulder strap.

I slink out of my chair for the pantry to grab a few snacks I know Beth enjoys. Within seconds, I add five new items to the lunch bag, on the verge of bursting at the seams, and ease it from Mom's hands. *Now* it's ready to go.

"What's going on?" Graham's gruff, sleep-ridden voice announces his arrival in the kitchen, but the creak from the stairs signals Travis isn't far behind him. The latter emerges from behind his dad. Both hover in the doorway, wearing their PJs; neither attempts to hide their clear displeasure at the noise in the kitchen so early.

"Morning, honey!" Mom beams at their presence as the only one of us who is happy to be here. She rounds the island to stand beside me, arm curling over my shoulder in a laid-back one-armed hug. "Wyatt's got his big tournament tomorrow, so I'm driving him to the bus. I told you yesterday, remember?"

By the look on Graham's face, I can tell he tuned out of the conversation the moment Mom brought me up. But he covers his tracks with an "Oh, yeah." *Smooth. Give this man the nuclear launch codes next.*

"We should be heading out shortly, so you two go back to sleep. Hand me your luggage, Wy." Mom doesn't wait for me to comply before she hauls my three bags into her arms. She wheels the suitcase past Graham, stopping to kiss his cheek, and Travis for the car. Neither of the Maynards leave the kitchen despite their obvious exhaustion and irritation of being up at such an hour.

No, they linger, blocking the doorway. Travis scrolls on his phone, looking bored, when he snorts, "Good luck at your nerd convention." He says like he rattles off some sick burn and not a half-baked comment that sounds straight out of the mouth of a cheesy 8os bully.

Graham truly has done his spawn a disservice by feeding him an exclusive media diet of campy 8os films and little else.

"I'd say the same about the football team, but they've never won more than a season, let alone any championship titles." I reply, avoiding a smirk when Graham and Travis get the sleep knocked off. Unlike them, I'm in the perfect headspace for an argument.

"Watch your tone, you little—" Graham steps forward, but I meet him halfway. We almost stand at the same height, close enough to be at eye level. Suddenly, whatever colorful name Graham had ready for me dies on his tongue when I laugh in his face.

"I already handled your dimwit of a son, but maybe I should address the source of the problem: you. You're a grown man beefing with a seventeen-year-old boy when you should be worrying about your impending mid-life crisis and your subpar football team." I keep my voice low; there's no need to yell when I can play my cards right, and the same effect lands.

"You think you're tough, kid?" Graham bares his teeth,

aiming for a wolfish grin but falling short. He walked head-first into the point with this one.

"No. I think you're pathetic," I correct him. "There will come a day when I no longer live under this roof, but don't mistake that as anything but a win for me. If I wanted you out of my mom's life for good, I'd find a way. Step over the line more, and that day will arrive quickly."

Without much else to add, I scoop up the cereal bowl and drain it of the last few bites, never backing down on the eye contact. Graham and Travis stare at me, jaws slack and faces painted in unspoken discomfort. The days they walk around with impunity are over.

"Wyatt! Let's go! We'll be late!" Mom shouts from the other room, timed perfectly to break the silence I leave. As I pass him, I drop the empty cereal bowl into Graham's hands, knowing I toe the line of being just as much of a jerk as these two. They'll learn how much it sucks to receive a taste of their attitude on a near-daily basis.

I could be the bigger person. But not today. Now, I've got a bus to catch and a State tournament to reach; my partner needs me there, and I'd hate to disappoint her.

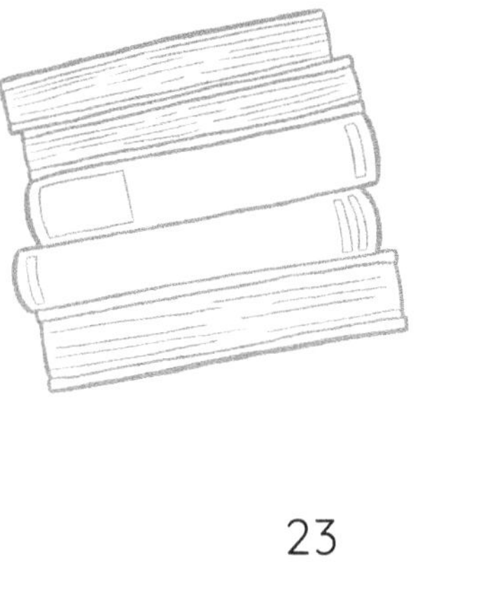

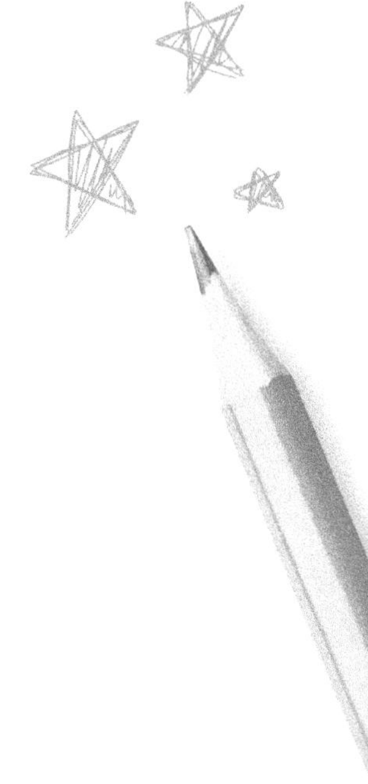

23

BETHANY

April, Week 3

SOMEONE GET me off this bus.

Twelve hours crosses the line of how much I can tolerate the same metal walls, the same faint odor of worn bus seats, and the same ebbs and flows of bored conversations. I can't remember last year's trip or if the drive there was this boring.

Then again, last year's championship took place in San Diego, which is never more than four hours from Los Angeles.

This year? Our allegedly simple six-to-seven-hour trip extends over twice the length due to the bathroom breaks, stops for gas, bouts of rush hour traffic, and the brief stint of over-heating on the side of the road. Beyond that, most of our on-the-road scenery for the past few hours has been empty. After three hours, the sight of rolling fields and flat farmlands lost its charm, no matter how many times someone pointed out cows on the side of the road.

With so little to do, people retreat into themselves. The initial burst of energy wore off somewhere around hour five of the trip, which had been punctuated by someone blaring throwback songs from the 2010s, a whole lot of hype chanting from three of the guys, and an impromptu hour of off-key karaoke after a snack run.

Now, everyone sleeps, scrolls on their phone, or focuses on other solo activities. Exhaustion begs me to join those napping to pass the time. But I flip the page of the worn, crumbling copy of *Hamlet* for AP Lang, using the natural light from the window to illuminate the words. I read this play for the first time in middle school and several times since then. So, no amount of bouncing along the uneven roads will disrupt me from following the plot for my refresher.

At the next major jostle in the road—likely from some uneven patches or a pothole—Wyatt's sleeping form slumps into my line of sight. He doesn't stir, not with his earbuds in. He curls into himself and uses a hoodie as a makeshift pillow against the window; these bus seats aren't the most comfortable, but everyone makes do.

I lean over just enough to tuck the hoodie further into Wyatt's hands. He nestles into the fabric without so much as a peep. Slowly, I inch away from him without disturbing his sleep. He'll need the rest before tomorrow. *We both do.*

With *Hamlet* in my hands, I dive back into the mercurial angst of the one and only Prince Hamlet of Denmark for another ten pages. Hamlet is perfect for teenagers; the lead character is as dramatic as some of my classmates, but for much more valid reasons, I'll give him that.

Sure, there are better ways to spend my time, more conducive to the upcoming AP season, or drinking in the passing scenery of a whole lot of nothing. But I left all my text-books behind to enjoy the three days in San Francisco. No distractions, no excuses to drag my feet and self-destruct at the championship level.

My knee bounces in time with the bus as it runs along the interstate. Fingers skim over the yellowed pages and walk me straight into Act II. The ambient noises of the bus's engine and the stillness in the air accentuate the agonizing slowness of the plot. Every time I re-read Shakespeare, I remember why I love his work. It's meticulous, stitched together with copious details and a resonating theme that outlasts empires and stands the test of time.

"Good read?" Devon's voice derails my focus. I glance up and find him in the seat across the aisle from me, a seat that was empty maybe five minutes ago. He lounges, leaning forward on his thighs to peer at the cover. "Ah, *Hamlet*. I don't think I got past the first fifty pages before googling SparkNotes and a few Crash Course videos on the plot synopsis."

"It's one of my favorites. I don't want to know how boring you found it." I crinkle my nose at him, nudging him back with a playful swatting motion. I curl my thumb into the last read page to hold my place, knowing full well a bookmark would be better.

Devon raises his hands in the universal motion of surrender, "Okay, okay!" He grins while slouching back into the safety of the otherwise empty bench. "I won't tease you anymore for your love of dusty old books."

Devon's eyes dart around the surrounding seats, with all the others either asleep or preoccupied, before scooting up to the edge of the bench. His legs extend into the aisle, reaching my side of things. He hums, "I'm surprised you haven't noticed any of those sneaky photographers nabbing pictures of you and Wyatt. Bus ride photos are their bread and butter."

"You know about that?" I feel my hackles rise, and I am immediately on the lookout for cameras. Call me Hamlet from how paranoia sinks to the bottom of my stomach, heavy and hardening into a knotted pit. "Who else knows? Who else participates?"

"Everyone with functioning eyes on this team. Last I checked, someone named the photo album 'for when Beth and Wyatt get married.' I'm sure a small chunk of those photos are blurry, taken in a rush. But some are artistic." Devon shrugs.

My expression must telegraph my confusion because Devon crosses his arms over his chest, face fighting to stay neutral. "Let me guess, you think we're all insane and looking for something that isn't there?" He asks.

I nod, which elicits a small chuckle from him, one teetering on the edge of exasperation.

"If Wyatt and I wanted to date each other, don't you think we'd be together already? Everyone needs to accept that they're wrong about us. No big deal-" I counter.

Devon takes this with as much patience as he can muster. He pinches the bridge of his nose, mumbling, "For someone so smart, you're either the most oblivious person I've ever met or stubbornly clinging to denial."

I scoff, "Hey! I'm not oblivious. I can tell when someone likes me and know if I return those feelings." Anxiety twinges in my stomach, dissonant and angered like someone plucked an off-key guitar string. The sensation causes my nails to sink into the thick fabric of my Wellesley hoodie.

"Can you? Because everyone on this team has come to the same conclusion except you and Wyatt," Devon points to Wyatt and me, which feels like an accusation, an insinuation against the intellect he praised moments ago. But he continues, undeterred by the frown I'm likely wearing. "So, maybe it is denial. Maybe you're nervous about introducing romance to a dynamic that already works. Maybe you've been so adamant about dodging advances from his annoying stepbrother that you refuse to see the organic connection forming between you two?

Regardless, turning your head and pretending like nothing exists does a disservice to you, Wyatt, your intellect, and your happiness."

That throws me for a loop. When did happiness become a factor in this conversation? I don't need a relationship to be fulfilled. Yes, the rom-com lover in me always has a soft spot for the concept of a happy ending and the tender, all-encompassing understanding of what it means to be loved. To be loved is to be known. To be loved is to see someone and want them to stay, not because you need them to live, but because you choose them to be yours.

My brain short-circuits. My mouth isn't much better, hanging limp and useless while Devon looks at me with gradually increasing concern creasing into his forehead. I grasp at the air, searching for something coherent to say and convey the chaos erupting inside me—a side effect of the emotional war Devon has unleashed with his words. No magical response comes to my rescue, so I drop my hands into my lap.

"Happy?" I manage to croak out, sounding thoroughly wrecked. "I don't understand-"

"Okay, maybe I came on too strong with the tough love," Devon grimaces. He reaches across the aisle to take one of my hands and force my attention onto him. "Let me tell you what me and the rest of the team see when it comes to you and Wyatt, okay?"

"Yeah, sure," I mumble. What else can I say?

"You and Wyatt are inseparable, often attached at the hip far beyond any regular pair of partners. You two always sit together, no matter how many empty seats remain. You'll rush to him after speech rounds, and he follows behind you when you go anywhere, drawn together like magnets or by some gravitational pull. You walk perfectly in step with one another without fail; Wyatt will slow his strides so you don't need to rush in heels. When you talk, no one seems to be able to steal him away for anything. It's like the sky could come crashing down and kill us all, but he wouldn't give a damn unless you told him to. He stares at you like you hung the sun, the moon, and the stars."

"So, we're physically close. Is that shocking because we're a guy and a girl? If one of us swapped genders, would it be even half as interesting to everyone else?" If physical closeness throws people off, that's an easy fix. Wyatt would understand if I told him to scale it back, given all the silly assumptions our teammates had tossed around about our partnership.

"Beth, that's the tip of the iceberg," Devon stops me before I mount my defense, pulling the fight out of me as easily as someone deflates a helium balloon. "First of all, no. If you were a man or Wyatt were a woman, I doubt anyone would change how they feel. That level of physical closeness reads as far more than platonic."

"I'm resisting the urge to play Devil's Advocate, so you should keep talking." My response feels snarkier than I intend it to be. Devon shoots me a look that demands I listen and not focus on spinning arguments in direct response to what he alleges. It wouldn't be the first time someone's called me out on that; it's a force of habit, and, man, do habits die hard.

"As I was saying, the physical stuff alone is far from the only observation we've made. You two speak in totally separate conversations from the rest of the group, communicating via looks and passing sticky notes. He brings you extra food at tournaments in case you forgot yours. The inside jokes you two share seem like a never-ending list, evident from how often this man makes you giggle. Not laugh. *Giggle.* You've gone from someone who cracked a smile once every three to five business days to constantly smiling when Wyatt's around. He cares for you in his way, and I know you well enough to see how much you reciprocate that care."

Devon lists these instances of "proof" on his fingers, counting down until he runs out of fingers to use. He shakes his head when I stare at him, not giving him a single inch. "Beth, I'm speaking to you as a friend when I say this, one whose interest extends as far as you being your happiest self. Not even Nadia could elicit this much joy and comfort from you after three years. You might need to face that there's something more than strictly "friends" here for you to consider. Maybe it won't happen now, but if both of you end up in Boston-"

The implication doesn't need to be spoken for it to hit me square across the face. *Wyatt and I in Boston means no long-distance, none of the typical hurdles long-distance couples face.* Not that we are a couple—or plan to be.

Devon's mouth twitches, almost as if he senses his point finally latches onto me, sinking its hooks into a brain prone to overthinking. He says nothing else when getting up from his borrowed seat and pats my shoulder before departing for his original spot toward the front of the bus.

In his departure, I sit at a loss for words or any justification for the warm, fuzzy sensation blanketing the upper half of my body. From the top of my neck to the peak of my hips, I feel nothing except the heat beginning to dial up to an eleven. The thought of Wyatt and I leaving this state together, with an emphasis on together, sounds absurd yet too plausible. Devon got into my head; he won.

Or maybe he's right about Wyatt and me. A traitorous voice's singsong rebuttal grips my heart into a firm squeeze, letting its nervous pulse gush through. My eyes wander toward Wyatt, who sleeps soundly against the window. Jealousy flares up in a sickly green flame; he has no idea of the turmoil slipping through my thoughts, how I'm second-guessing everything about us. *Could we stay platonic when the people in our lives think otherwise?*

This line of thought never materializes beyond such grim rhetoric. No, the bus decides to run over another rough patch of the road so hard that it ousts Wyatt's sleeping form away from the window. His body leans toward me, and I brace as his cheek smashes into my collarbone at an awkward angle. Our seatbelt prevents him from a crash landing in my lap, but helps with little else.

I stiffen as Wyatt's warm breath grazes the skin of my collarbone and neck, while the rest of him tangles against my side. Devon called it magnetism, and Wyatt proves his point, even in sleep.

I make no move to ease Wyatt's full weight off me or angle his face out of my collarbone, no matter how awkward the position might be for me. However, the quiet grunt and inhale tell me Wyatt might figure it out soon enough.

Wyatt's voice, sleepy and groggy, rasps into my neck, "Did I fall asleep on you?" Sprinkles of confusion lace around his words, which tighten the tension looping around my stomach. "Sorry-"

"It's not your fault. You shifted with the bus and landed on me. I didn't want to wake you." This is where I make the second mistake of the exchange. The first one was not nudging Wyatt toward the window when he slumped over. This time, I tilt my face when I feel him shift, almost nose-to-nose with Wyatt.

Maybe two inches of space exists between our faces. We breathe in one another so close that our warm exhales merge into one heavy heat. My hands ache from how firmly I clench the copy of *Hamlet*. It's here, in the dying light of day, where I stare into Wyatt's eyes. His eyes lose their dark brown, replaced by a stunning, honey-tinged glow when the sunset casts its light over Wyatt's face. Have his eyes always been like that, or am I discovering these details now?

Wyatt's lips part as he breathes. I wait for him to say something, maybe to apologize, and back out of my space. Instead, one of his hands brushes a thin hair away from my cheek, and he says nothing. Our eyes mutually break the stare when one of our stomachs growls for dinner—it doesn't matter whose.

When Wyatt slips me a package of the strawberry jam fig bars I love, and I hand him a jumbo candy bar from our last rest and bathroom break, Devon's words come back around. *No, he's right. They all are.*

Someone get me off this bus.

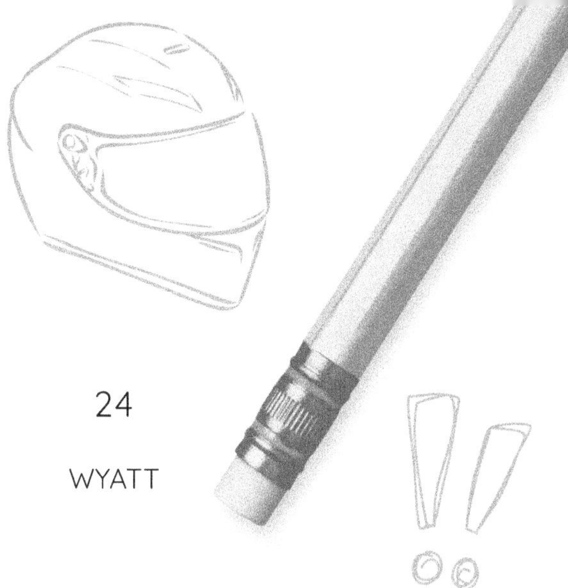

24

WYATT

The State Championship (Day 1)

"IF YOU'RE HERE for parliamentary debate, you should've gotten your side assigned to you already. Please direct yourselves to the correct room. Thank you."

Through a yawn, the volunteer stationed outside the door to the lecture halls where Beth, the other debaters, and I will spend our thirty minutes of prep time points to the signs taped to each open door. They place affirmation on the left and opposition on the right, a simple yet effective approach.

"To the left we go," Beth whispers while we wait in the winding line to get inside. She must've slept well last night because her bright-eyed, go-getting mindset returns in a show-stopping demonstration. "Round one at the State Championship. How do you feel?"

"Honestly, I'm ready for whatever happens. We're still the East Shores Dream Team." I muse, which earns me one of those sparkling, million-dollar Beth smiles. She offers me her fist, and I bump mine against hers.

Whatever happens today, we're among the top debaters in the state. Nothing can take that accomplishment from us. Even if we mess up and fail to bypass the preliminary rounds, the trip isn't a total loss.

Ms. Goodwin planned activities in San Francisco for students who don't advance past the prelims or who get eliminated during the rounds leading to the finals. Chaperones will take students to explore the city's hidden gems, rather than overcrowded tourist traps, and will provide plenty of photographs for the school's newsletter and yearbook. Therefore, Beth and I can drown our sorrows in adventures around the city whenever we get eliminated, unless we reach the finals.

Once we enter the room on the left, Beth and I make a beeline for second-row seats. The people around us might be representing the same side as us in their respective rooms, but we never want to give anyone an advantage. They could become our opponents later down the line.

Beth sits first, grabbing her sparkly glitter gel pens to write down the necessary headings and the notes we take into round. Once prep finishes, the computers go away, and that becomes especially true at the championship level. Everything needs to be analog. Beth and I worked out this system ages ago, considering her handwriting is visually stunning, and mine is deemed "barely legible."

Scooting into the chair next to her, I fish out my laptop. If Beth writes the notes into arguments, then I can handle collecting the research. I know my database the best, and all the shortcuts I've developed come in handy to find those hard-to-reach pieces of information. Together, we'll use those twenty minutes to our advantage.

We wait for each competitor to take their seat. As soon as the last student sits down, the proctor approaches the front of the room and adjusts his glasses. "Good morning. Welcome to the first round of the California High School Speech Association State Championship. You all shall begin your unassisted, offline preparation in one moment."

One of his assistants walks around the room to hand out a little printed card with the rules typed out in the finest print possible. *Was 12-point font not available or something? Good grief!* Beth reads them over my shoulder, even when I offer to pass them to her, before I slip them into her bag.

The proctor waits for everyone to skim over the rules before setting the alarm clock on the front desk. Its letters blink a cool blue, reading twenty minutes for its countdown. He clears his throat and flips through his thick paper packet. "Now, the topic for the first round is as follows: the United States federal government should enact AI regulations equivalent to those of the European Union. I repeat, and I'll write this on the board, the United States government should enact AI regulations equivalent to those of the European Union. You all may begin."

The scribble of pens against paper and the click of keys fill the room with urgency. Beth and I exchange a fleeting glance before running to begin our tasks. We never break, not when our elbows bump together on occasion, or a blue sticky note lands on my keys. I split the computer screen between the archive and an open notes document, where I write in our shorthand for Beth to read and rewrite.

Our flow moves seamlessly. Twenty minutes whittles to nothing in the blink of an eye, under ten sticky notes, and a lot of shorthand erased as soon as I tuck away my laptop. Beth guards the notepad with our case in chief to her chest, as if she carries the nuclear launch codes or some big national security secret instead of the mental ramblings of two opinionated seventeen-year-olds. She always says it adds more fun to the mundane process of preparing debate notes.

When the alarm's horn shouts into the mostly silent space,

Beth and I are among the first debaters out of our seats. We check our room assignment on the paper posted by the door before we head off, marching in step with one another.

"We are so lucky," Beth groans once out of earshot. "How did you know an AI topic would come up? I didn't think CHSSA would be so tech-savvy with their topics this year."

"That's why I suspect they picked it. I heard rumblings from the college debate circuit about it being a hot-button topic last year. So, I started collecting articles that were pro and against AI in different sectors where we might need it. Looks like we got lucky with some of my finds." As soon as the proctor dropped the topic, I could feel Beth's nerves radiating off her in a palpable wave.

However, the energy was muted when I pulled up the folder with the dozens of articles saved up for this moment. If that's a sign, we're off to a good start.

Beth and I wander across the school's campus in matching slate gray outfits—me in a two-piece suit and her in a work dress she brought to Wildwood. We hardly look out of place with the mass flood of students milling around on the sprawling grounds. Beth sticks closer to my side when more people head our way on the narrow path. When I throw my arm over her shoulders, she sinks into my side, and our pace slows to a stroll.

Beth and I arrive at our room before the round's set to begin. Standing outside the door appears none other than the two boys from that round at Wildwood, who refused to shake Beth's hand or pay her any respect. *Fantastic, just what we needed.* I glance Beth's way, but she shows no signs of upset or negative emotions. She doesn't leave my side when she nods to them.

"Is the judge inside?" Beth asks the two boys, who nod almost immediately. What a refreshing change of pace since our last encounter. Perhaps they learned to treat their opponents with respect across the board, not just the male ones.

"We should head inside then," I say, not waiting for them to follow up or say anything before opening the door. The two guys scurry inside, leaving Beth and me to stand in the hallway alone. I tilt my head toward the doorway. "Ready to begin?"

Beth winks at me, "Never been more ready, as long as you're my co-captain." She stretches her hand to me and drags me inside.

XOXO

"—POINT OF INFORMATION!" The voice of the opposition interjects as their hand raises into the air, threatening to derail me mid-sentence. But I hold it together enough to chug along, ignoring the hand.

"—Social media companies are private entities whose terms of service often outline the kind of conduct they deem acceptable and prohibited on their platform. Politicians cannot be exempt from that, nor should they be. It is the opposition's view that the First Amendment does not apply here." Staring down three stone-faced judges, I can only hope confidence projects from every word leaving my mouth.

Beth and I aren't stuck in the preliminary rounds anymore. We flew past those with flying colors yesterday. Now we fight our way through the elimination round trenches, needing to avoid losing more than two rounds.

You'd think we'd avoid any chance of risks in our strategy with such a narrow margin for error. But I'm not stubborn-headed enough to tell Beth no when she asks for a favor, even if it forces me out of my comfort zone.

When she requested that we reverse our usual speaker

order—her as the first speaker and me as the second speaker, where I would go first to lay the groundwork for the arguments —I said yes. I haven't taken the role of first speaker since the start of our season, which meant I needed to knock the rust off. *Leave it to Beth to have my back covered, holding herself back from backseat driving.*

She couldn't have picked a better topic, either. Debates involving anything related to the First Amendment are some of my favorites, and I excel at them no matter what position I take.

The panel of judges writes down copious notes with every argument I lay on the table, able to follow along with a rapid-fire flow. Their focus hops between me and their ballots, but I try to keep their attention on me more often than not. The more I grip them with my arguments, the more likely those points will stick in their mind.

As I flip the page on my notes, ready to move on to the next point, a pointed "ahem" from my left reminds me of the hand still raised in the air. In my peripheral vision, I catch a glimpse of a smirk on one of our opponents. She wiggles her fingers as if it will get my attention faster.

"Would the Leader of the Opposition yield for a point of information?" she asks. In any other circumstance, I would consent to maybe one or two questions. In fact, I already have. But this marks the tenth point of information requested by the other side, and I know a stalling technique when I see one.

Any coach worth their salt would train their debaters out of prioritizing low-hanging fruit arguments and abusing points of information. Those rarely win points, no matter how good the potential 'gotcha!' might be, and run the risk of losing the round for bad sportsmanship.

Apparently, the other side never received that memo, given how frequently they request one. I can barely get out two lines before their hands shoot for the sky, and I hear the dreaded "point of information" being asked.

This time, the judges stop writing their notes to glance between me and the girl, who doesn't try to hide her smug expression. I, however, slam a tight lid on my annoyance and push it far down into my system. Letting the irritation get the better of me is a surefire way to tank our case; it's never a good look for a man to yell at a woman, especially when it will come off as condescending.

As we gradually progress in the tournament, Beth's demeanor backslides, turning her into a walking bundle of nerves. Even routine parts of our process receive more worry and scrutiny. Hence, the request to switch things up completely threw me off guard. Ultimately, the lesson I've learned about myself is that I will do anything Beth asks of me.

I'd do *everything* for Beth.

If it's in my power, I would chew off my tongue before I let my temper get the better of me and ruin this for Beth. That final spot belongs to her, and I'm along for the ride.

"At this time, I won't be taking any further points of information. Should there be time at the end, I will happily address any remaining questions you have. However, I can't promise anything with many substantial arguments to address in our case in chief." I measure out my response, leaving no room for misinterpretation. I aim to be smooth, polite, yet not deferential or skittish.

I want them and everyone else in the room to know I clocked their strategy, but they won't catch me in a bad position.

My opponent's smirk falters, and their hand drops into their lap. I catch how the two scramble and write something down on their shared notepad, borderline frantic. They should've prepared a better strategy than *that*.

I sneak a look at Beth, seated next to me, who follows and tracks what arguments I run and which I save for her to bring to her speech. She never tears her eyes away from the paper to acknowledge the exchange. However, a rapid double click of her pen speaks volumes; it's part of our shorthand, our wordless code.

It says, *"Atta boy, Wyatt,"* without showing our cards to the rest of the room.

I lean down to write on the sticky notes and leave it for Beth. *Go easy on them when it's your turn, okay?* I can't see her reaction to that little poke—too focused on clasping my hands. "Now, where was I?"

XOXO

THE REST of the rounds progress somewhat smoothly after that, despite the mounting difficulty of competing against teams whose skills challenge us. The power matching never works harder than at the state championship level. Here, you truly compete against your accurate matches.

"Pass the lo mein, please?" I mumble, voice somewhat missing after the semi-finals. Devon passes me the plate from several chairs down to serve myself. Once the last of us in the semi-finals finished our rounds, the East Shores's team crammed ourselves into a hole-in-the-wall Chinese restaurant for dinner.

I don't know about anyone else, but I'm eating like a starved hyena, wolfing down plates with little remorse. Those of us who went all day—all ten of us—share the same hunger, pushed to our physical limits. None more so than Beth, who qualified for the semi-finals in both debate *and* speech.

She rests beside me, a steaming cup of tea in one hand and

her chopsticks in the other. She hasn't spoken a single word since we arrived at the restaurant, which I chalk up to her voice being unable to reach above a whisper and her nerves peaking at an all-time high.

Within the next hour, we'll receive confirmation from Ms. Goodwin about who advances to the final rounds, if anyone. Should no one make it past the semi-finals, we head home a day early and count our wins where we find them. But with ten chances to reach the finals, the likelihood of someone qualifying isn't exactly terribly slim.

Beth wants it to be her, I know it. Whether she is a solo speaker or in our debate duo, she needs to be in that final round like we need air to breathe. What better way to cement her senior year *and* the best season of her debate career?

I lean over, tapping her plate. Beth never removes her headphones when she faces me, head cocked to the side. I hold up the platter in a silent offer to add to her plate, which appears empty except for a few specks of rice and a smeared sauce.

Beth nods and lifts her plate to meet the edge of the lo mein platter. I heap more food onto her plate. Seeing her with an appetite to eat, rather than shunning food, equals a positive sign in my mind. Beth snaps up a few pieces of chicken as well.

I'd dig back in, but the universe has other plans. From several tables over, Noemi scrambles out of her chair. "Ms. Goodwin's texting me... final postings are out. She says the following students will be reporting to the championships tomorrow at 11 AM. Other students may come to watch and cheer on their classmates. . ."

Within seconds, all conversations wither into silence. Those of us who reached the semis climb out of our chairs to line up together. Ten students, including Beth and I, stand in front of the faces of our classmates, taking in their bated breath expressions as Noemi waits for the results to come in.

When they do, she inhales, "We have speech first. Our advancing speakers are Mikey, Deanna, and Beth." She announces. Several cries ring out as those named rush to one another, collapsing into a tight hug. Beth throws her arms around her speech friends, and the three jump up and down, celebrating their hard-earned wins.

"That's my partner!" I whoop, clapping along with the others on the team. Beth eventually breaks the hug to give those who didn't qualify a warm hug and some words of comfort. In moments like these, I catch a glimpse of Captain Beth, something I regrettably never get to see.

Beth smiles at me from the opposite end of the line while she pats one of her speech mentees on the shoulder. She stays there when Noemi clears her throat: "We have two finalists for debate. It's Devon for Lincoln-Douglas... and Beth and Wyatt for parliamentary debate."

The room explodes, all clamoring and shouting Beth and I's names. I hear some people hooting for Devon, too, but I can't do much besides breathe out Beth's name. She stands in the same place as before the announcement, mouth parted open. The tiniest tremble of her shoulder precedes the quivering of her lip and the watering of her eyes.

She blinks back any tears before sprinting to me. I brace and catch her as Beth flings herself against my chest. "Are you serious?"

"You and I in the finals, let's go!" I lift her off her feet. "This calls for dessert."

"I like the way you think." Beth giggles as I set her down on her feet. We clasp hands and take our bows for the rest of our classmates. They cheer us on, but we should save all the energy for tomorrow. We're going to need it.

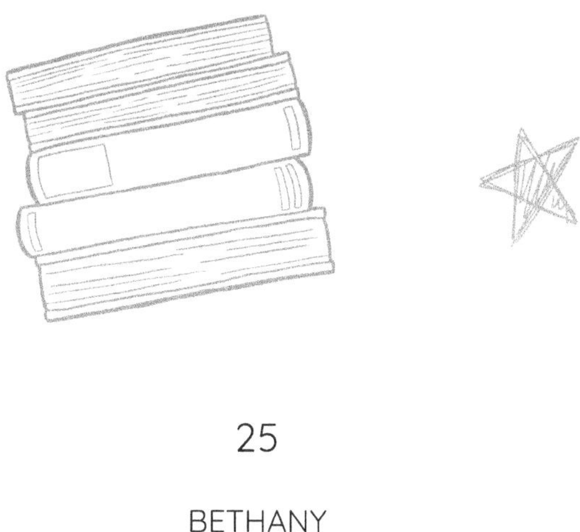

25

BETHANY

"BEGIN WHEN YOU'RE READY," one of the judges says to me, and I smile despite how every word becomes garbled in my ears. My heartbeat roars too loud for anything to feel coherent or reach my brain through all the static and emotions.

Somewhere between our opponents on the opposition team finishing their speech and the judge speaking to me, my mouth turned as rough and dry as sandpaper. We enter the final stretch of the final round—one speech left—and it's all up to me to do something. I feel the power matching* more than ever as I side-eye the opponents sitting across the narrow aisle from Wyatt and me.

Depending on the semi-final performance yesterday, Wyatt and I either stare down the first and second-place trophies, or we fight for the third-place slot, hoping to clinch it by the skin of our teeth. Something in my gut tells me that Wyatt and I fell into the lower bracket, but Wyatt spent all morning joking to aim higher and not doubt myself.

Imagine we're fighting for first place, regardless of where we ultimately place. He had said those very words at breakfast, dropping that kernel of confidence between bites of his toast and jam. Sometimes, I want to strangle Wyatt for how calm he remains under the pressure. Other times, I want to grab him and bury my face into his shoulder with the hopes that he promises everything will be okay.

I eye my flow for the final time before I fold the paper into a little square and lose it somewhere in the depths of my debate stuff. The paper's heading reads *'The United States government should ban the disenfranchisement of felons'* and its body contains endless red ink stains to mark arguments felled by opposition fire or added arguments mid-round written in sparkly blue gel. This provides a roadmap to victory, although an uphill one, for me to chase.

It's time to give this my all.

Hesitation receives its space to breathe as I adjust the rumpled lapels of my blazer. Every piece of fabric weighs on my skin, from the dark green turtleneck inching up my neck to the layers of my pristine pantsuit, which hoards body warmth from the foggy April afternoon. However, there's a time and a place for caution. It won't be here while I lay everything on the classroom floor.

Inhaling, I force the rough taste out of my mouth before speaking, "—Nowhere in the stated goals of incarceration or penological theories exists the idea of continued subjugation to judgment and social ostracization. This arises from our attitudes and misconceptions about why people end up incarcerated, allowing the opportunity for the creation of legal barriers to uphold a de facto second-class citizen—" At this point, the words rush out with little ongoing filtering or overthinking by me.

I black out a little, unable to hear the words when they fly out. I'd panic, but this isn't a new sensation by any means. When I fling myself into the zone, the rest of the world melts into the background. For a brief, shining moment, I pour my heart out to the audience like an actress delivering a monologue, not searching for their reactions as I recite my piece.

I slip through degrees of awareness as easily as one changes the radio station. My voice fights through periodic bits of silence—my version of static. "—When someone has paid their debt to society, as it were, they are no longer in breach of the social contract. Therefore, they should be restored to all the benefits given to citizens of this nation—" In and out, I lose the frequency once more, yet my mouth still moves so the words spur out of me.

I'm merely the conduit for the intellect, the megaphone through which these ideas are broadcast to this room of inquisitive listeners.

Fighting the urge to move around, I grip the edge of the desk to anchor. It has nothing on the grounding effect of Wyatt's warm hands, but it manages in a pinch. Digging my nails into the old, worn wood, I plant my heels in one spot and hold myself there. *No fidgeting. The judges can smell fear.*

"—Disenfranchising a segment of the population from the political process never makes a nation better, especially when those individuals have demonstrated some degree of rehabilitation. We fail to address the root causes of crime and then expect that further exclusion will somehow fix what we slapped a bandage over—" I wager a look at the judges, who have all but stopped writing on their ballots.

Their gazes meet mine, which would typically make me want to curl up on the floor. Not now, though. I ride the high of every bit of this journey. If someone told me at the start of this season that I would find Wyatt and we'd end up in the finals at the State Championship, I might've checked them for signs of a concussion.

But here we are, doing exactly that.

Wyatt kept me calm enough to get us here; the least I can do for him and all he's given me and this partnership is to leave no argument behind. The minutes might slip through my fingers faster than grains of sand swirling into the bottom of an hourglass, but I make each of them count.

"—What this side urges is an appeal to common decency and the recognition of humanity above someone's incarceration status. Formerly incarcerated people deserve to be seen as citizens. The affirmation has met its burden by presenting facts, studies, and an appeal to the humanity that is intrinsic to us all. Only one side provides a better outcome for the greater good, a net benefit. Therefore, you must vote in favor of the affirmation regarding a ban against disenfranchising felons. Thank you." I blurt out as the beep from someone's phone timer ends.

"Thank you, Madam Speaker." One of the judges, the middlemost one, acknowledges the end of my speech and, thus, the end of the round. He glances around the room at his fellow judges. "Let's have a round of applause for these amazing speakers?"

The gathered audience, made up exclusively of disqualified competitors, snaps to their feet to give us a standing ovation. Wyatt joins me in basking in the applause as he stands up from his chair. We throw our arms around each other's shoulders, which forces me to loosen my grip on the desk.

As soon as the judges start packing their things, Wyatt spins me into a crushing hug. His chin settles atop my head. "Thank you for the best season ever. You made everything an experience," he whispers before our friends and teammates surround us.

I can't say anything back, but I hope Wyatt knows he did the same for me. Honestly, he's changed my life.

Wyatt lets go to grab our stuff and pack up. The rest of our friends surround me, shaking my shoulders and passing me through different hugs. These touches are fleeting and quick, so everyone gets a piece of me.

With my purse tucked into his elbow, Wyatt materializes at my side, ready to leave. He and I loop arms and shuffle out of the room behind our friends.

We hang a few steps behind them as we walk toward our tiny encampment in the school's library. Wyatt leans in, never breaking step with me. "So, you've got one final down and one more to go." He sighs.

"Don't remind me. The postings could drop at any moment." I crinkle my nose. The foggy, misty air hanging over our heads caresses my face, gentle and damp.

Wyatt chuckles, "Don't hate me, but I can't wait to sit this next one out and watch you devour the competition."

A palpable warmth stings at whatever exposed skin once touched the foggy San Francisco air, awakened from a single compliment. *Careful, Wyatt—any more flattery and my heart might stutter.*

If it hasn't already.

XOXO

SOMEWHERE CLOSER TO two hours after Wyatt and I walked out of our final round, leaving our fate in the hands of the debate gods, the postings for my final solo round dropped. Along with my stomach. Straight through the floor.

The walk to the room feels less harsh with an entourage of adoring teammates surrounding me, including the one and only

Wyatt. He loosened his tie, one in a dark green to match my turtleneck. It hangs around his neck haphazardly, furthering the disheveled look of his moussed hair after an impromptu nap on a library bean bag.

Besides him, we have the entire speech team, Devon, Andrea, and August, ready to cram themselves into one corner of the room and cheer me on. Unlike debate, the program oral interpretation room will have five speakers and their whole support crews, the judges, and any unaffiliated observers who want to watch the finale.

All of them trail behind me except Wyatt, who escorts me with a hand hovering over the small of my back. He also carries my purse without complaint—truly a multi-purpose man.

"Room 298, right?" Andrea points toward a red brick building ahead of us and a sign stationed right outside it with the assigned room number. I nod; there's the arena for my "final battle," as August and Wyatt keep joking.

As we walk by, we pass two other groups of students following their competing speaker. If they wave or acknowledge me, I return the gesture with a polite wave, not getting too lost in the headspace needed for *Monstrous*. That will come once the door to the room shuts us in.

We proceed into the building and wander down the hall until we reach the room with "298" emblazoned in a gold-laden plaque next to the door. A glance inside reveals a lecture hall set up, meaning plenty of room for my friends to watch.

"Beth," Wyatt's hushed whisper pleads with urgency, not fast enough to alert me to the incoming nuisance until I see her. *Paityn.* She and her tiny posse of teammates, all wearing their mandated uniform, approach the door, comfortable enough to shove past us to get inside first.

Paityn pauses outside the door. "Bethany! Nice to see you here!" She remarks with a tone that can only be described as sickeningly sweet—a saccharine poison she injects through her biting, backhanded compliments.

"Everyone, head inside," I usher my friends inside, not wanting them to observe Paityn and me exchanging barbs in the hallway. Everyone goes inside as directed, save for Wyatt. No, he lingers at my side like a ghost, as silent as one, too. "You as well, Paityn."

Neither of us means it, evident from the edge of her smile. She can never hold the mask long enough before her true colors bleed through.

"Well, good luck today. I must say, silver always suits you best." Paityn can't help herself, can she? The silver jab cuts deep enough to tighten the already sharp pain collecting in the back of my jaw. Every instinct in me screams to say something vile and bitter in response; the energy I want to channel for *Monstrous* seeps out, tainting my good judgment with its petty, vindictive streak.

Instead, I hum, maybe more condescendingly than necessary. "I don't know. Gold suits me just fine. But we'll see that tonight, won't we?" The response has its intended effect without digging back as hard. Paityn's eyes narrow, and her nostrils flare when she excuses herself without a word.

"She's still a piece of work, I see," Wyatt grumbles beneath his breath. I swallow back my agreement, opting to take his wrist and drag him inside.

Our friends were smart and reserved two seats behind the judges for him and I, second row on the right-hand side—a perfect, unobstructed view for my triumph or disappointment.

As Wyatt and I take our chairs, the lead judge spins around in her chair. She can't be more than her mid-20s, but her icy blue eyes scan the crowd, heavy with a cutting familiarity. She clicks her pen and turns toward the front.

"Good evening, everyone. This is the final round of the

program's oral interpretation. I assume you all understand the rules and the associated penalties for violating them. The tournament will institute a thirty-second grace period for any competitor whose speech exceeds the allotted ten minutes. If there are no objections, we can begin—" She pauses for a minute, waiting for the objections to roll in. When none appear, she twirls her pen. "Very well, let's begin with our first speaker: E04. Is E04 here?"

"Present," I snatch my binder from my purse, which Wyatt holds on his lap. While the rest of the room breaks into tepid applause, Wyatt beckons me to lean in so he can murmur something as a parting message.

"This is yours to win. Good luck, and don't let the likes of Paityn get in your head." Wyatt whispers, keeping it light, tongue-in-cheek even. I tuck the binder under the crook of my arm and wink.

Won't need luck. Skill will handle the job.

I stride to the front of the room, tightening my ponytail on the walk there. Within two breaths, I hit my mark on the invisible 'x' in my mind's eye, to stand center stage before the judges. Until their signal, I become like stone, still as can be, and staring past the judge's head for my horizon.

Then, upon the almost imperceptible nod from the lead judge, I open the binder to the front page. My head tilts backward until I glower at the judges through a callous, empty laugh.

"Here you sit, begging for my mercy. You crawl across this blood-soaked floor, as pathetic as a bug I should crush under my heel, hoping a few tears might salvage what *you* broke. Where were those tears when you pillaged and burned villages to the ground, when you killed mothers and daughters with no remorse? You beg for what you could not give others, what peace and dignity in death you denied them. Shed every last tear in your body. It will not save you from reaching the end of Fate's thread, that I *promise* you—" I snap the binder shut in one swift move, causing a few people to jump, including a judge or two.

Now, I like that reaction.

The air evaporates from the room, making breathing a little harder. But as I sink into the character persona I built into this piece, nothing can touch me. Any last scraps of anger or tension arising from Paityn's snide remark dive into the inferno licking at my skin. I *feed* the flames.

"—Is it that time of the month? You're hysterical—a *mad* woman. Women's emotions have been a convenient target for centuries, often demonized and devalued compared to their male counterparts. But when a woman embraces her darkness, she becomes something other than a woman. Monstrous even. With excerpts from Florence + The Machine lyrics, *Carrie* by Stephen King, *Gone Girl* by Gillian Flynn, *Nightbitch* by Rachel Yoder, *Medea* by Euripides, and *Clytemnestra's Grief* by Grace Iris, this is Monstrous: A Parable of Feminine Rage."

I find the point on the horizon as the binder bends open again, hanging onto the last shred of normalcy before I descend into the madness of womanhood. Then, I sink beneath the waters, submerged in the hopes of winning.

26

WYATT

HOT STAGE LIGHTS beam down on me and Beth, blinding us from a clear view of the restless audience. A very exhausted audience. I can't blame them one bit. I intend to crash as soon as we return to the hotel. Three days of competition have finally caught up with me. If it were up to me, I'd sleep for another week straight. Competition demands a lot from me and everyone else on the team, judging by the percentage of the bus that falls asleep after a given tournament.

Hint: it's not a small number by any means.

Beth's quiet yawn draws my attention to her from where she molds against my side. Her eyes droop heavily despite the weight and brightness of the spotlight on us. My hand covers her eyes, for which she hums in appreciation. We need sleep, a hot shower, and something greasy or a sweet until we feel human again; at this point in the semester, I know Beth well, as well as anyone would know the ins and outs of their best friend.

"You doing okay?" I bury the question into Beth's bouncy,

wavy tresses, catching a whiff of her shampoo. She smells of lavender, vanilla, and something cozy like a hot, honeyed mug of tea after a long day. The scent nearly pulls me head-first into the foggy exhaustion clouding around the auditorium, but I fight it. "We're almost done."

"Not soon enough," Beth yawns for the second time. She stretches and arches her shoulders back to the creaking and crackling of bones. She turns her head to gaze down the line of the other parliamentary finalists. "Wanna bet on what position we won?"

I snort, "Okay. But if you say fourth place, I'm going to shake some sense into you. At least aim for third if you're going to be pessimistic." Beth's lips open and close, quickly followed by a scowl. Yeah, she reads like an open book, at least to me. The mortifying ordeal of being known, I suppose.

"Fine," Beth muses while rubbing at her eyes, careful not to smudge her make-up. She sizes up the three other teams on the platform. "We're either third or second place."

"Nuh-uh! You need to pick one and not half the board." I protest. Beth sticks her tongue out at me. But she considers her options and holds up three fingers. *She chose third place. Interesting.* So, I flash two fingers, earning an approving nod from Beth. We either placed as the winners of the "loser" bracket or landed in the runner-up spot instead.

We could also be wrong and end up winning the whole thing. I refuse to believe we would be fourth place. We belong on the podium, not to be egotistical or anything.

"Thank you for your patience," the CHSSA president, the individual responsible for running the tournament to end all tournaments, shouts into the microphone, inducing feedback and waking several segments of the crowd from dozing off. Beth and I are included in that group. We will start with the fourth-place team...Please give a round of applause to the team of Hall and Harding from The Millennium Institute."

Although the name strikes a chord from the Wildwood finals, the team that steps forward to accept their trophies isn't the team we stood against in our last round. And if those two earned fourth place, Beth and I have to be in the "winner's" bracket. We wait for a first or second-place announcement, a heart-stopping outcome either way.

Beth's realization dawns seconds after mine, as she gasps and claps a hand over her mouth. She faces me, craning her neck so our eyes meet.

"Wyatt-" Beth's voice wavers, so close to a strangled cry. Her eyes shine under the sheen of tears gathering on her waterline. I'm not far from tears either, hit by the sudden and overwhelming realization of how victory rests in the grasp of our fingertips.

"I know," I murmur, taking her hands in mine. We lace fingers together as third-place saunters up to grab their trophy; the two girls couldn't look more thrilled with their placement when tapping their trophies together like you'd clink champagne flutes in a toast. "We're so close."

I *knew* it! I knew we set our ambitions for the stars and climbed every painstaking mile to achieve those dreams. What Beth and I have? It's like magic. I can't describe it to someone from the outside, and I'm at a loss for the words to perfectly encapsulate how Beth and I feel like two halves of a whole brain.

Beth and I and the other debaters from earlier shuffle closer together when the previous two teams vacate the stage. These guys, wearing classic black suits with differing tie colors, glance our way.

The blue-tie guy smiles, and his red-tie companion offers his hand, "Congrats to you both! You guys did such a great job in that round. Your arguments about how a lack of political and economic power further fuels the prison-industrial complex were mind-blowing!"

"Thanks man," I grin and shake his hand. Beth does too. "It's a close one—it could go either way."

"Oh yeah. Our mom will be thrilled either way, so the best of luck to you both!" A red-tie guy offers a cheeky salute and gestures to a woman in the front row. She has face paint on, two blue and red streaks slashing across her cheeks while snapping a million photos with the flash on. There are supportive parents, but this takes it to a whole new level.

Beth and I face ahead when the CHSSA president clears his throat, manhandling the microphone to bring it to his face. *Dude, this isn't WWE.* He surveys the crowd before waving the cue card around, "Now, in second place, please give a round of applause for the team of Edwards and Keene from East Shores High School!"

Beth and I are on the move as soon as he says our names. It looks like I was right about second place. We wave to the brothers, who embrace one another while still giving us our moment to shine through as we race forward.

Two volunteers step forward to meet us with our trophies. Beth and I grasp hands and raise our interlaced hands to the sky, taking a stage bow to the wild cheers from the audience.

Second place feels more than alright when I get to share it with Beth.

XOXO

BETH and I get maybe fifteen minutes with our gleaming silver trophies before the ceremony whisks her back on stage for round two. She leaves her trophy on the empty seat beside me, which I guard with my life. No one will come within a foot of us without some major side-eye.

As Beth heads for the stage, I see her swerve away from Paityn sauntering up to the stage. Beth takes the long way, opting for further steps so she can reach the opposite end of the line. She tucks her hands behind her back and squints into the crowd, looking for something.

I lift my hand and wave, knowing she likely won't see me with the lights shining in her eyes. After a moment, Beth's eyes drop to the stage, and she appears to be conversing with the eager, bubbly junior next to her. I analyze every crease and shift in Beth's face, waiting for any inkling of what is running through her head.

I have a good idea of what she's thinking, but nothing on her face reveals the turmoil going through her mind. Anxiety must be having a field day with each person eliminated from the stage. They start with five, but soon enough, that number whittles down to only Beth and Paityn remaining.

It would always be the two in the final stretch.

They couldn't look more opposite of each other. Paityn resumes her beauty queen act with practiced pageant smiles and a flapping finger wave to the crowd, riling them up through the stray whistle and cheer of her name. To an outsider, they might consider her the shoo-in to win, the reigning champion coming for her rightful crown. But no one knows my dark horse, Beth.

Beth's face holds everything close to the vest, which would make her an unbeatable poker player. She stares straight ahead, leaning on the old horizon trick every speaker learns within their first year. The untrained eye couldn't tell the difference between her staring past them or piercing them through the chest with her sharp hazel gaze. Sometimes, when she looks at me mid-round, I wonder if she could see right through me and pluck out the desire from my soul.

Paityn and Beth leave a gap between them as they wait for the CHSSA president to pick up the right card, neither of them glancing the other's way. Beth holds firm to her expressionless mask for dear life, appearing calm, cool, and collected. Paityn, however, falters as her crown slips a little.

"In second place, please give a round of applause for...." He flips open the flap of the card. "Paityn Faulkner from The Millennium Institute!" The crowd cheers for her roar loud, especially those from her teammates, yet no amount of applause can mask the shocked pallor on her face.

Paityn struggles to conceal it from the audience, and her face cycles through several different colors before settling on a blustery, tomato-red hue. She staggers forward to accept the award, devoid of the smiles and pageantry from before. *I guess the judges think Paityn looks better in silver.*

My eyes seek out Beth, who stands in the spotlight with the closest example of shell shock written all over her face. She covers her mouth behind her hands, quickly rolling her head back to hide the tears likely springing from her eyes.

She waits for Paityn to shuffle off the stage with her silver before she surges forward, arms out and open to accept the trophy. The CHSSA president barely announces Beth's name before I rocket onto my feet, applauding louder than the rest of the audience. "Now presenting our new California Program Oral Interpretation Champion, Bethany Edwards of East Shores High School!"

Beth fans at her face, cradling the trophy in her other hand, as the auditorium nearly crumbles under the applause. She doesn't wait for the CHSSA president to finish his pleasantries or waxing poetic about the importance of high school forensics.* Beth rushes off the stage, making a beeline straight for me.

She manages to hand off the trophy to someone seated behind me. Then, her arms curl around my shoulders, and she crushes herself against my chest. "State Champion? They appointed me the best speaker in the event *state-wide*?" Beth can't seem to find her breath, oscillating between hyperventilating and crying.

"The judges merely recognized your talent. You did that; you're the best speaker in your event because of all the hard work *you* put in, no one else. So proud of you, Beth." I cup her face to the soft squish of her cheeks. It forces her to take a few steady breaths, matching the quiet and slow rise and fall of mine.

Beth shakes her head and sinks back into a hug. She burrows into my arms, and we rock as the crowd settles down. I should let her go and give her a moment to sit and breathe before all our teammates swarm her with questions and their congratulations. Before that, I'd like a moment with my partner.

Woah, don't sound so territorial over her. A voice inside me teases, but I let it roll off my back. Maybe it's selfish, but I like having a piece of Beth that belongs exclusively to me. A piece of her that no one else gets to see. It lives in the pool back in Palm Springs, or her darkened bedroom with an episode of Dimension 20 on, or at two desks in the Hawkins building with fresh boba awaiting my arrival.

The exclusivity is woven into the fabric of Beth and my story, keeping it alive and allowing it to thrive.

XOXO

AS I PREDICTED, our teammates surrounded Beth, snapping photos of her with her two trophies, as if she were a local celebrity. Beth played along with their mock interviews and endless paparazzi-style photos, smiling through each one despite her exhaustion.

We don't make it far out of the auditorium before a beaming Ms. Goodwin guides us away. She parks the students in front of a grassy ledge overlooking the city from its higher elevation. We can see all the way to the bay from where we stand, and, for Ms. Goodwin, the twinkling and lively backdrop of the illuminated city will make for perfect pictures.

"Noemi is grabbing the camera from the bus. Everyone, stay right here, and we'll take some team and finalist photos." Ms. Goodwin instructs mid-turn, and she sprints toward the crowded parking lot at a speed that might put Olympic track stars to shame. Someone in the crowd whistles, and several others agree with snaps and hums.

"We should take photos while we wait!" Andrea raises her bag into the air, quick to unearth a pastel blue Polaroid camera. She shakes it. "The overall tournament-winning school should have all the photo keepsakes." We had won a final trophy beyond the ones obtained by the finalists, dedicated to the school whose students won the most trophies during the tournament. The Millennium Institute tried to compete, but we nabbed a solid lead over them with at least three more students in the final rounds.

"Beth should go first! Our first-place speaker!" Devon exclaims to a rousing 'yes!' from the crowd. Beth's cheeks flush a faint pink where the color spills down the side of her neck and disappears into the neckline of her turtleneck. He hauls out his phone, too. "Anyone good at photography?"

A few hands raise, but so does mine. I haven't taken photos in years, not since Dad passed away. But a thumb drive of nature and landscape shots hides in a thrift store tin at the bottom of my desk's topmost drawer.

"Wyatt has to take photos with me!" Beth waves her two trophies in the air and fixes me with an arched brow as if she expects a protest from me. But I shrug off my backpack and put my trophy into the safety of its main pocket. August eases the backpack from my hands, and Andrea replaces it with the Polaroid camera.

"I'm coming." I hustle over to Beth. After adjusting her against the sparkling city backdrop, I station myself at her side, bending my knees to bring us closer to face level. Beth does me the courtesy of burrowing into my side and passing me one of the trophies to hold. "Okay, how many do you want?"

"Three," Beth's words brush against the curve of my jaw from our proximity. Her body leaning against mine welcomes warmth between our intersecting limbs and edges. Even through our thicker clothes, body heat seeps through, striking me to the core. Up close, the overwhelming aroma of her shampoo—or maybe that's *hotel shampoo*—tickles my nose. "Smile, Wy!"

I grin as I'm told. Beth and I grip one another tightly as I snap the first photo—the Polaroid's flash deposits stars in my eyes, which I shoo away after some forceful blinking. As I ready the second shot, I feel Beth shift a little in my arms, but not enough to disrupt the photo when the flash goes off.

However, once the flash vanishes, I tip my head toward Beth, curious about the shot. What I don't expect is Beth's face mere centimeters from mine, too close to move without an accident waiting to happen. Halfway into the turn, I realize the consequences a split second too late. Our lips connect and not in some tiny graze, either. No, we are nose to nose, our lips parted, and the air we breathe mingling into something heavy and unbearably hot.

Beth, of course, has the sense to move backward and out of the awkward tangle we've found ourselves in. Her rush to escape ends in disaster when she stumbles over her heels, losing her balance until my hand with the camera snakes forward to hook behind her hip. The gesture holds her upright but also brings her close again, chest to chest this time.

"Oh!" Someone from the crowd yelps, perfectly describing the feeling sinking to the bottom of my stomach. I don't look at them; I look at Beth, faced with scarlet cheeks. Her eyes avoid mine, and her head fully tilts away.

"Beth-" What should I say? What can I say? *Hey, us accidentally kissing isn't so bad unless I actually have a crush on you like everyone seems to think? What's an accidental kiss between friends?* My tongue refuses to participate, twisting itself up in knots. We kissed. We *kissed.* Yes, by accident, but tell that to the slow-blossoming burn awakening in my stomach.

Beth keeps her face away from me. If she notices me breathing hard or the sweatiness slicking across my palms, she says nothing. Her throat bobs, "Sorry. Didn't mean to do that. You can let go of me now."

"Right. Sorry," I say. Immediate space slots between Beth and me as we disengage from one another. Through it all, Beth refuses to look at me or smile. A cold shoulder douses whatever conflicted feelings fuel the warmth under my skin in an ice-cold reality check. But, despite the reminder, the incident replays in my head ad nauseam. "Are we okay?"

Beth never responds beyond scuffing her heel against the ground. Her lips part after a moment, but Ms. Goodwin's harried return shuts that down before any chance for closure.

I feel like someone punched me through the chest and knocked my heart over the ledge, leaving it to fall somewhere into the busy San Francisco streets. Maybe a streetcar will run over it and spare me the embarrassment. What a mercy that would be.

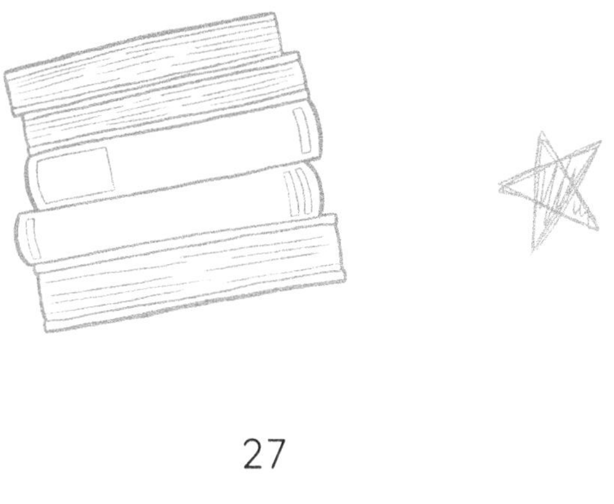

27

BETHANY

May, Week 2

"—SO, YOUR LIFE'S A MESS," Nadia remarks without so much as a shred of hesitation to the distant, disappointed groans of her name off-screen. She throws up her hands, shocked by the unanimous disapproval from her friends, all of whom become the Greek chorus to my tragic decision-making.

"Where's the lie?" I mumble in return and rest my forehead against the cool tiled wall. Even when sitting alone in the single-use bathroom, my voice stays low. I'm borderline whispering into my phone. "Things are weird with Wyatt, and it's my fault. I have no one to blame but myself for dragging my feet for so long."

"Okay, you're being overly harsh on yourself. Beth, you're still seventeen with a complicated school schedule and big feelings. You're bound to make mistakes and act a little silly when you're dealing with love stuff. Trust me, I'm the queen of acting a fool for love." Nadia sighs. I swear she wants to grab me by the shoulders and rattle me until she can confirm the presence of a functioning brain. When a tiny voice snaps at me to give myself the benefit of the doubt, one sounding identical to Wyatt, I consider slamming my head into a nearby trash bin to scream my lungs and throat raw.

With AP exams following in the immediate aftermath of the State Championship, I rode the high of my wins and the confusing lows of the aftermath. *The kiss. What else could I call it but a kiss?*

Wyatt and I should've talked it out by now, about what happened. Beyond my hurried apology in the aftermath, we sat on opposite sides of the bus and pretended nothing had happened. Yet, neither of us forgot. I prefer to address the problem in person. But, with the debate season over, besides the board planning for the banquet, I don't have a built-in excuse to see him. Our text conversations no longer carry the same playful banter, thanks to the elephant lurking in the corner; every extended exchange serves as a reminder of what happened in San Francisco. Worst of all, everyone in the club hasn't stopped talking about it or mentioning it to me, subtly fishing for updates.

No. The worst part of all has nothing to do with anyone else. It has everything to do with how I see the night of the championship so vividly whenever I try to close my eyes at night. No amount of de-escalation techniques can stop the heart palpitations when I recall the full-body chills that broke across my skin the second my lips met Wyatt's. I *liked* it.

Guilt tears me open with a Prometheus level of consistency, yet I can't kick the piece of me that craves to return to the night of the kiss so I can do it all over again.

Sure, an accidental kiss might seem like the kind of thing we should let go. It was an accident, an unintended consequence of getting carried away in the moment, and not knowing how to proceed. I'll admit it—I'm not always the best at communicating my feelings when emotions get involved.

Logic and playing by the rules? No issue.

Explaining any number of the messy, anxiety-riddled emotions taking up space in my head? A nightmare of unreal proportions.

A stray knock against the bathroom door shoots panic straight into my veins, giving me worse jitters than the first time I drank espresso. I almost drop my phone into the toilet I'm perched on, but yank it close to my chest. "Still busy! Sorry!" I lie through my teeth.

Nadia snorts once the footsteps fade away, "Oh, Beth. You're in desperate need of some help. Unfortunately, I'm at least four hours away by car, and I don't have the power to teleport into that bathroom of whatever banquet hall Goodwin rented for the evening." She teases.

"We're at that fancy country club you and I used to make fun of whenever we went on a boba run off the Hill." I pinch the bridge of my nose. I *know* I'm a hot mess right now, I didn't need that pointed out.

Tonight is the annual speech and debate banquet, also known as the first and potentially last time I'll see Wyatt in person until graduation. This marks a 'now-or-never' moment, where the stakes have never felt higher. Somehow, this rivals the Wellesley decision. Note to self: *never develop a crush ever again.*

Catching a glimpse of Nadia's face, her expression shifts into serious mode, which rarely emerged in the four years of our friendship. She frowns, "As much as I'm trying to lighten the mood, I can see you're struggling. Not talking to him has hurt you badly."

"Yeah. It has." The admission drops the temperature in the bathroom by ten degrees. Missing Nadia had been rough on me at first, but I learned to adapt over time and with the introduction of someone new. Missing Wyatt, on the other hand, evokes what I imagine shoving a knife straight into my chest and trying to carve out all my vital organs with less than surgical precision feels like. The pain lurks in the shadows of my mind, keeping me awake at night.

"I'm going to say something slightly cliche, slightly annoying... but you need to hear it," Nadia fixes her frame, cutting into the sound a little. But she waits until she likes her view before she resumes with her proposed advice. "The longer you let this stuff go unspoken between you and Mr. Wyatt, the harder it'll be to come back from it. Your window to address it has become slim as of tonight."

"Yeah, well, I have a bad habit of letting things fester. The last thing Wyatt needs from me tonight is to ruin his dinner." Am I being stubborn? Undoubtedly. But I can't stand the thought of upsetting Wyatt further and becoming a buzzkill for his evening of triumph. I refuse to burden him anymore.

Nadia's brows shoot up. I can't recall the last time I let her hear me talk so bitterly, if ever. She crosses her arms, "Bethany Madison Edwards, you're letting that jerk named Anxiety wrench the wheel out of your control. What's the worst-case scenario here? A guy turns out to be a jerk who can't deal with his emotions or a little awkwardness? Even if you both end up in Massachusetts for college, the likelihood that you'll ever see one another without keeping in contact drops to non-existent." Her rant earns a few snaps from the other side of the screen, to which she takes her bow.

"The worst case scenario is me having to go to Wyatt and apologize for the kiss, but not actually being sorry for it because I liked it. I *like* him, okay?" I hate how I cry out. I hate how Nadia freezes on the other side of the screen, staring at me with wide eyes and a slackened jaw. My lips quiver while the words pour out. "Happy? I hope everyone else who said anything about Wyatt and me harboring these secret feelings is so happy with themselves. They figured me out; they know me better than I know myself."

Silence falls on both sides of the call. Beyond the bathroom door, I overhear the hustle and bustle of the kitchen and the faint conversations from the dining room, where Wyatt and every other debate team member wait for speeches and the slideshow.

"But are you happy?" Nadia's eyes seek out my face. Hurt swirls around her rich brown irises, but I can tell it's not for her. *It's for me.*

"I was happy. I'd be happy if Wyatt and I could return to where we were before that night. I could live with those feelings staying buried and withering away into the dirt. I'd shove this revelation into a box and kick it into the ocean if it means Wyatt and I are okay again." It's honest. Pathetic, too, but ultimately honest.

"Then fix it." Nadia stares me down until I meet her gaze. There's no mistaking the intensity simmering underneath her concern. Nadia was the doer to my thinker; for her, action comes as naturally as breathing. I have the extra roadblock of devastating anxiety to clear before any momentum will ever arise. "Go out there, find a moment to pull Wyatt away, and tell the boy how you feel. I don't know him, but I have the impression he'd appreciate the unfettered truth."

And Nadia would be right.

I nod, unsure how else to convey to Nadia that I'll choose bravery tonight. Anxiety might have the wheel in its grasp, but I stand behind it, ready to lunge and wrench it from its hands.

Nadia winks, catching the message loud and clear. "Go get your man, Beth. If my intuition is right—and it always is—those little flutters in your stomach aren't exclusive to you." She blows me a kiss before hanging up, leaving me with her vote of confidence.

With a sigh, I abandon my bathroom perch only after flushing the flimsy toilet seat cover and cleaning off my hands. All part of the cover for my extended disappearance from the banquet—people would question where one of the stars of the evening wandered off to: a senior *and* the league and state champion in several events.

I sneak down the hallway, passing the kitchen, to the wide, open dining room. The room blossoms with color, mainly teal in the tablecloths and flower centerpieces, while people converse at their respective tables. The families of the team members and a few teachers from the school fill any remaining spaces at the tables. My family is no exception, filling a table toward the front with none other than Mrs. Keene and Coach Maynard.

Allegedly, the latter forced his way into the banquet as a late-minute teacher addition, and Ms. Goodwin obliged his request out of courtesy. I guess he didn't want to claim himself as Wyatt's stepdad, huh?

I search for Wyatt at the table to no avail. Instead, I see an empty seat where he should be, sitting directly across from mine. He probably would've switched tables if the form hadn't closed two months ago. So, he's stuck with me tonight, and we are in perfect eye contact range.

As I reach my chair and join the table with no preamble or apology for my absence, someone taps on the microphone at the makeshift stage a few feet away. All eyes, including mine, glance to the stage as Wyatt approaches the podium.

The sight of him in a crisp white button-down, no suit jacket in sight, and a pair of sleek dark brown slacks inspires an ache from deep within my chest. *He looks great.* The bags under my eyes I hide behind concealer feel ready to bulge out, to tell the world how poorly I'm coping with it all.

Wyatt shuffles a notecard in his hand. I see a hint of his handwriting in the margins of the card, something short and messy scrawled between the lines. He leans into the microphone, "Good evening, everyone. On behalf of the East Shores Speech and Debate Team, thank you for joining us tonight. Tonight's banquet is meant to honor and celebrate our graduating seniors, such as myself, and their successful season. More speakers will come up to give their remarks, but I'm here to kick off the honorary opening toast. My partner, Beth, originally wanted to give this speech, but she generously let me take a crack at it—"

At this, several people's laughter echoes off the walls, and more join in. Kelsie elbows me in the ribs while Sawyer snickers; my siblings love to remind me how bossy I am. For the audience, I throw them a playful wave and soak in their amusement. The team knows who I am and how I want the best for us.

When I glance at the stage, I spot Wyatt's eyes fixated on me. His mouth twitches at the corners like he fights a smile, but the smile eventually wins. Oh, how I miss that smile or the ones he reserves for me and our secrets.

He swallows and drops his eyes to the card, but they return to me when he resumes speaking. "—I joined the team in August after spending three years at a different school. I assumed it would be an adjustment—one I might not be successful at making before the senior year ended. However, this team proved me wrong. From Day One, it wanted me and wasn't shy about it. The team wrapped me in its welcoming embrace and gave me a space to be myself. The team offered me a safe place to land and find the pieces of myself I never knew I lacked. I'm short; this team changed me for the better."

Wyatt speaks about the team, portraying it as a cohesive entity. Humanized. Or perhaps the fact that his eyes never leave me hints that "team" stands as shorthand for something else. Someone else. Me.

Cleave my heart in half, why don't you, Wyatt? He has it in his hands anyway.

"Our seniors, our leaders, will leave the Hill soon, onto the next chapter of their lives. So, I raise a toast to them and everyone else who remains behind to continue the East Shores legacy. Go team." Wyatt holds up the water flute, which he likely snatched from the table.

And I'm the first to join him, raising my glass high into the air. He and I lock eyes when the rest of the room chants their rousing agreement. Wyatt departs from the podium to return to our table. He climbs into his chair and tucks the water glass further into the table before looking up.

"Wy, that was beautiful." Mrs. Keene fans at her face, batting away tears through sheer force of will. She slings her arm over Wyatt's shoulder and brings him close to kiss his forehead. Wyatt doesn't try to fight out of the embrace and shrugs.

"Your mother's right, Wyatt. You carry yourself as a well-spoken young man. This is the kind of masculinity we need more of in this era." My dad chimes in to praise Wyatt, whose rosy flush deepens around his cheeks. The tips of his ears are a dead giveaway when someone's praise hits him in the secret soft spot he hides under all his cool-boy attitude and snark.

However, the good mood can never last when Coach Maynard hangs around. The mere mention of masculinity summons a nasty smirk to his insufferable face, which he attempts to hide behind the rim of his wine glass. Yet, his amused huff rings loud enough for the rest of the table to hear.

Yeah, that's it.

"Did you say something, Coach Maynard?" I question and

observe how quickly his face changes when more eyes land on him. If he wants to play games, he stepped into the wrong arena. Unlike Wyatt, I don't need to take anything from him.

"No. Nothing." He replies, you know, like a liar. He scrapes together a smile to appease the newfound attention on him, yet I see nothing but a lecherous piece of garbage.

I smirk and huff just like he had, "Okay. That's what I thought." Without fail, anger flares in Coach Maynard's eyes. The rest of the table tunes into what I say now because I don't intend to be a coward tonight.

"Beth!" Mom exclaims, ready to apologize on my behalf to Coach Maynard. The adults at the table appear aghast by my sudden turn from a respectable young woman, well-mannered and the "pleasure to have in class" on every report card type, into a mouthy, rude woman. Hey, the Maynards bring out the worst in me.

"Don't apologize for me. I'm not sorry for what I'm about to say. Coach Maynard reminds me of his son, Travis. I mean that as an insult," Mid-sentence, I pluck my fork from the rolled silverware to stab a Brussel sprout on my plate. I sink a bite into it. "Neither of you have much respect for anyone but your-selves. The apple never falls far from the tree."

"Is that any way to talk to a teacher?" Coach Maynard grunts. He's never beating the Neanderthal allegations, huh? He laces his hands on top of the table as if the gesture could intimidate me.

"I doubt anyone could call what you do in your government classes 'teaching' in good faith. But I would willingly wager my valedictorian status and diploma on what I'm about to tell you. Your black-and-white view of masculinity might be limited to big, sweaty men tackling one another for a ball, but that doesn't give you the right to undermine Wyatt. He's an amazing man, a testament to the way his late father and mother has raised him.

So, if you have a snarky comment about debate, you should leave. You disrespect not only Wyatt but also every student here who works hard to become a champion debater. You don't understand how much we sacrifice to be great because of your narrow-mindedness."

I'd argue that the best reaction from the table is from Kelsie and Sawyer, who conceal their phones, which are likely recording the entire exchange. However, a single glance toward Wyatt shreds that theory into ribbons.

Wyatt looks at me, visibly breathless. His eyes sparkle brighter than any of the shimmery streamers attached to the ceiling while raking over me. The old Wyatt emerges from the guy sitting across from me, bringing hope neatly wrapped in a little bow.

My chest heaves from the emotion I've expelled toward Coach Maynard. After weeks of walking a tightrope, I feel lighter. But the unfinished business with Wyatt lies at the bottom of my stomach, heavy even as the water around it recedes.

My lips part, ready to ask Wyatt for a moment to speak, when a hand lands on my shoulder. I turn to find Ms. Goodwin hovering behind my chair. "It's your turn to speak, dear," she remarks.

Ah, right. Within seconds, the momentum crumbles underneath my feet, and I fall, spiraling down and smiling for the sake of my company. Wyatt's eyes follow me to the front of the room as I stand at the podium. I watch him straighten in his seat, and the light vanishes from his eyes.

The dull 'thud' of my heart dropping through my stomach signals the window closing in my face. The universe hand-delivers the verdict with a punch to the ribs. *Now-or-never? Looks like we're squarely in the camp of never.*

28

WYATT

OUT OF THE horror show of Beth and I's awkward fallout, watching her serve Graham the verbal equivalent of a knuckle sandwich and then proceed to shove the whole humble pie down his throat without breaking a sweat felt like a light at the end of the tunnel. But, no matter how often we spent the night searching for each other in the crowd, the universe refused to give us a moment to breathe.

She'll never know how many times I type out a text to reignite the dead conversation and delete it before I can hit send. Past attempts to broach the topic have felt more like text tag with large gaps between messages and the conversation falling apart before we reach the necessary point.

Besides, how am I supposed to phrase "Hey, sorry we kissed in front of all our teammates and haven't cleared the air yet" and "By the way, I can't stop thinking about you as more than a friend since before the kiss" in a way that won't complicate things further? Don't even get me started on the fact that

I've confronted the possibility of more since winter break in Boston.

"If you stare at your phone any harder, you might set it on fire." Mom's voice from behind me snaps me out of a staring contest with my phone. It rests screen-up on the table untouched, for ten minutes.

Or maybe, if I watch it closely, I'll figure out how to text Beth and breach the gap one more time. Maybe this time, it *will* stick.

"Guess so," is my reply when Mom drags out the chair closest to me and joins me at the table. We haven't said much about Beth teeing off on Graham; truthfully, I dread the conversation. I won't hold back if asked directly about him or Travis's treatment of me.

Mom leans forward on her elbows, saying nothing while she studies me before humming. "We need to talk about Beth."

"I don't think that's a good idea—" I scoot backward in my chair. Beth isn't here to defend herself, which means it's up to me. Nothing Beth said at the banquet last week was untrue or uncharitable. Graham thought he'd get away with acting like a catty teenage girl after forcing his way onto the banquet guest list. Mom hadn't asked him to come, but he loathed the thought of being home alone and handling his own dinner.

Mom's hand grabs the back of my chair to hold it in place, much to my shock and the acidic burn at the base of my throat. She swallows hard, but nothing could prepare me for what comes out of her mouth next: "How long have you had feelings for her, Wy?"

"What?" Of all the responses to leave my mouth, that has to be one of the dumbest ones possible. I heard what she said perfectly. My brain must've short-circuited. "Mom—"

"Before you deny it, I want you to look at something." Mom pulls her wallet from her purse hanging off the back of the chair. She eases out a photograph from the tiny plastic photo slip at the front and sets it on the table. The photo captures the smiling, tender-eyed expression of my Dad, looking at my unsuspecting Mom in a conversation with someone else.

They can't be more than college-age, closer to their sophomore year, when they met for the first time. Right now, I realize how much of Dad lives on in me. We're identical, save for the loose curls falling onto his forehead and the thick glasses he wore back then.

Mom pushes the photo toward me before she sets down her phone, which shows its own photo. At first, my eyes gravitate toward Beth in that sage green cocktail dress she wore for the banquet, remembering the fluttering sound her skirt made whenever she walked. But my eyes skim over the rest of the photo until I see me, and the puzzle pieces slot together with a resounding 'click.'

When I compare the photos side by side, it becomes unmistakable that I am my dad's kid. I stare at Beth with the same yearning expression as him in the photo of my parents; thirty years later, we draw a perfect parallel, a visual double with too many similarities to unsee.

"Beth's little sister took this photo at the banquet the other night, one of many. You can imagine why this one caught my eye," Mom rubs at her misting eyes and traces a finger over the photo of her and Dad. "Wy, I think we both know the evidence speaks volumes here."

It does.

So, I crack, not sure what else to do besides shut down, "I don't know when it changed. It could've been after Lindsey and Val ambushed me during Christmas dinner. It could've been after we sort of kissed in San Francisco. Beth has intrigued me since we first met, but I don't know where the shift happened.

Mom's eyes widen, but she grasps my hands in hers. "I don't know the circumstances of this kiss, but I'd argue the awkwardness between you and Beth right now means it should've gone differently. You can do something about that... find a chance for a do-over," She advises with all the motherly wisdom she can muster. "I can't promise it will last forever, but running away from something good because it might not work out will never be the way of us Keenes. I never shied away from loving your dad, even when death decided to close the curtains on our life together far too early."

"Any suggestions on how?" At that, Mom laughs. She shakes her head and picks the photos off the table, handling the one of her and Dad with great care as she slides it into her wallet.

"That's up to you. You're the one who knows Beth the best." She says, leaving the room after a parting kiss on my hair. But those words turn over in my head a little. *I know Beth the best?* The light bulb in my head flickers to life, gleaming bright.

I snatch my phone and run straight for Beth's Instagram, specifically her tagged photos. I don't need to scroll far before I see an older photo from last season of Beth and another girl, who I assume is the one and only Nadia. If anyone knows how to win Beth over, it should be Miss Stanford herself.

When I click the 'follow' button, I expect a few hours to gather my thoughts and some ideas to bounce off Nadia's expertise in all things Beth. However, when I go to tuck my phone away, the notification that she followed me back pings within literal seconds of me following her first. My stomach twists into knots at the sudden flash of new DMs waiting for me.

What have I gotten myself into?

NADIA

Are you and my best friend together yet, or
do I need to fly down to Searidge and shake
some sense in her?

Woah, way to get to the point. I can't say I don't respect it, though. After the back and forth, maybe Beth and I need some bluntness to put things into perspective for us.

ME

that's why I'm reaching out to you. Is there
any chance you know what Beth's ideal prom
night looks like?

NADIA

you've come to the right place. Let's get your
girl so she'll stop moping in our text chat and
sending me sad cat videos.

For the first time in days, laughter ditches the bitter after-taste or the heavy guilt weighing it down. I have a week to turn things around for Beth and me, a week to give these feelings a fair shot at becoming something more. But first, Beth and I need to be on equal footing again.

I need my partner back. I'm going to get her back.

XOXO

WIND RIPS against the sides of my helmet as I ride down the abandoned streets. Tonight, I skip the music; my mind feels like a chaotic mess without it. Besides, I should prepare for the night ahead so that every step of Nadia's and my strategy goes according to plan.

Otherwise, the sheer amount of times the term "Wybeth" appeared on my screen will haunt me. Nadia said I lack whimsy and a sense of imagination if I can't handle a ship name, which then devolved into a mini-lesson in "shipping" and fandom. Nadia reminds me of Beth, but the extroverted, more expressive version who will say just about anything to your face.

The steady purr of my motorcycle's engine buzzes through my bloodstream, supplying a helpful dose of adrenaline straight to the chest. My heart hasn't stopped pounding since I left home. In the hour it took to get ready—suit, hair, grabbing the bouquet of flowers I pre-ordered—I questioned whether this was the right way to go about it.

If Beth hates me co-opting her dream night for my plea to be something more than friends, I doubt any number of little things could smooth over such a mistake. Nadia, however, has enough confidence for us both and sent me on my way with a "Good luck, kid."

That helped about as much as a pat on the back before throwing me into a lion's den.

All I need to do is give Beth a good night and find time to talk about everything that happened. *We should at least clear the air.* The distance between Beth's house and mine whittles down to less than a mile, less than a block, less than a street, and right around the corner. As I round the corner, the sight of something sparkly and midnight blue on Beth's porch raises my hopes from zero to at least fifty-fifty.

I don't waste time rolling to the curb outside her house and parking there. The kickstand pops out without a fuss before I dismount, standing in the road. My helmet peels off under the work of practiced fingers, no stumbles in sight.

Beth perks up from her spot on the couch at the rev of my motorcycle, scrambling onto her feet. She trades heels for a pair of sensible flats and keeps her dark hair pinned back in an intricate braid. Yet, her dress steals the show. The top part clings to her torso with a heart-like neckline. The soft, bouncy skirt poofs out, reminding me of a fairytale princess, and brushes against her ankles. One strap slips down the curve of her shoulder when Beth scurries onto her feet. She pushes it up to no avail, and it immediately slides back down.

"Wyatt? What are you doing here?" Beth jogs down the porch stairs but never strays more than a foot from them. She crosses her arms over her chest and rocks on her feet, swaying side to side. Her eyes gleam brighter than the dress's sparkles, thanks to her eyeliner, which emphasizes the depth but also the liveliness of her hazel irises.

"Well, I heard you were supposed to be going to prom with some of the debate kids, but they figured you could use an escort. So, here I am, a knight in shining riding gear." Nadia and I couldn't pull off a magical prom night without a bit of help. She reached out to old friends, some of whom Beth was supposed to ride with, and they were open to staging a "delay" for me to swoop in.

Finding out most of the debate team seriously wants Beth and I together was a humbling experience.

Beth bites her lip, "You want to spend prom with me? I thought it wasn't your cup of tea." She asks, hesitant for good reason. But when she walks over to me, crossing the lawn to stand at the edge of the curb, the fifty-fifty hope rockets toward seventy-five now. *C'mon Beth.*

"For you, absolutely. I've missed my partner," I offer my hand to her in a gesture for her to take however she sees fit. If I expected a handshake, that dives into the bushes when Beth nudges my hand away to almost jump on me in a hug. "Hey there."

"I hated not talking to you. I just didn't know what to say —" Beth stammers, but the press of my gloved thumb against her cheek shushes her.

I shake my head. "We can talk about it later, I promise.

Right now, I only need to know if you'll be my date to prom... and the dinner reservation we have at cuore del mare in under half an hour?" In the grand scheme of things, missing dinner wouldn't be the end of the world if something needs to happen to let us have the conversation we've been planning for several weeks. But tonight should be Beth's night.

Beth's hand settles on my hand, cupping her face, lips twitching into a smile, "Yes. To all the above." She takes in my outfit with an unabashed, slow rove of her eyes. "As much as I love the bike, I don't think I'm wearing the right equipment for a ride tonight."

She gestures to her dress, flats, and pristine braid. Nothing says prom night like showing up to the dance with a bad case of helmet hair and wind-rumpled clothes.

"Good thing we've got your car. Your parents would let me keep my bike here until we get back, right?" I ask. Beth doesn't need to know I've already cleared it with her parents, down to the last detail of when I'd bring her home. It takes a village for a lot of things in life—including planning a dreamy prom night.

"I can do that. I'll grab my keys," Beth stops mid-turn to glance at me. Something mischievous tinges her eyes, more green than brown, while she examines me again. "Before we go, I have one thing to do." Beth inches to the edge of the curb, drops my hand from her face, and pushes onto her tiptoes. When her lip grazes against my cheek, opportunity taps me on the shoulder with a knowing look.

If I want a do-over, no moment like the present. Let's do it right this time.

I wait for Beth to pull back, to leave a little distance between us, before whispering, "Hmm, you missed a spot." Beth lifts a brow at my little comment, observing the smirk I wear with a matching one.

She reaches forward to curl her arms over my shoulders as

we sway in a songless, slow dance. My hands migrate to rest on the curve of her waist, visible from the design of her dress, holding her closer with a simple flex of my fingers. Our eyes never abandon one another, facing the possibility with them wide open, unflinching.

"Did I now?" Beth questions, head tilting to the bounce of the tiny curls framing her face. Up close, her eyes become impossible to ignore, lined in sparkly blue and fluttering her dark lashes in such a distracting way.

"Yeah," I chuckle. "See, last time was an accident, but I haven't stopped thinking about it. So, we should try it again and see if it goes better. Trial and error, you know?" If I sound hopeful, Beth must find it endearing, considering how her cheeks tinge red.

"You make a compelling argument. How could I ever rebut that?" Beth murmurs as the tip of her nose brushes against mine. The closeness draws me in until our lips hover mere centimeters apart. But when Beth's eyes flutter and she sucks in a sharp breath, I lean in and close the gap between our lips. Intentionally, this time.

Beth tastes sweet from whatever lip gloss she wears tonight and cool, reminding me of the strawberry-flavored mints Dad used to slip me before our bike rides. She kisses me back, not holding back or shy. We move together in sync, not unlike how we operate on the debate floor, reading each other's moves without words needing to be said. We're partners through and through.

When Beth's arms tighten around my shoulders, I tug her closer. When my fingers run along the fabric of her dress, she cards hers through the hair at the nape of my neck. It's a back-and-forth exchange, a give-and-take, a perfect example of how she ends where I begin.

The rest of the world fades into the background, which

offers us silence to relish this moment. Kissing Beth on the curb outside her house feels second nature to me, as effortless as riding my motorcycle. And I'm sure I could exist in this moment for the rest of time, but the soft shudder of a camera reminds me of the time-sensitive arrangement I spent the last week crafting.

"Mom!" Beth exclaims when pulling out of the kiss. She touches her fingers to my lips, where some of her lip gloss has likely smeared onto me. Beth's mom stands on the porch, holding up a phone without a hint of shame.

"You'll thank me later," she cackles while snapping another photo of us. "Wyatt, my husband, will open the garage for your bike. Wheel it in there, and you can leave your helmet and anything else there, too."

"Thank you, ma'am." I shoot Beth a wink before letting her go. Beth waits at the curb while I park in the Edwards' garage. She and I have a long night ahead of us, so I'd like to get on the road even if I'd like nothing more than to kiss her again.

If our first second kiss is anything to go by, we'd forget all about prom. I didn't put on this silly bowtie for nothing, and it would be a shame no one saw how stunning Beth looks tonight.

When I return, now motorcycle-free, Beth's hand latches onto mine, and we head for her car, racing to get to our dinner reservations. Things might be out of order, but Beth seems okay with the unconventional for tonight. *I'll take the wheel tonight, anxiety. Step aside and stay there.*

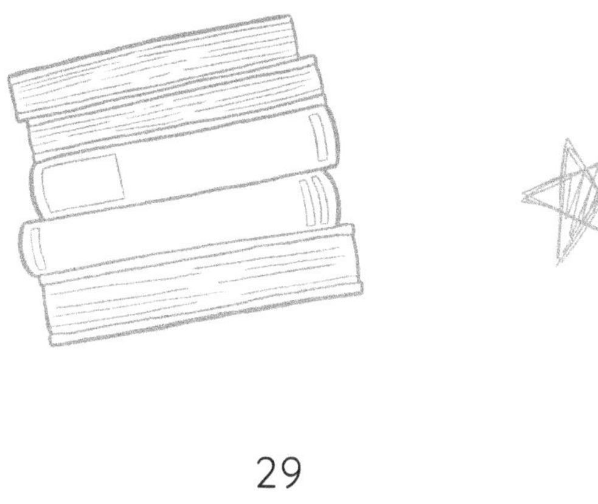

29

BETHANY

May, Week 4

WYATT KEENE IS A MASTERMIND—*AND* a good kisser. Being both should constitute an unfair advantage in life, but I'll allow it. Unlike debate, there's no perfect rulebook regarding matters of the heart, no guidelines for how to proceed.

It's the first time in a long time that I'm forced to let go of my control, only for a night. I can handle one night of spontaneity and fun.

As the driver's side door to my car opens, Wyatt's hand reaches in and guides me from my seat. Even when I step out of the car, neither of us lets go of the other. Our status sits somewhere between friends and something romantic, but I'd argue we belong in both. People always say you should fall in love with your best friend, right?

So far, the night has blown me away. Our reservation at cuore del mare was nothing short of romantic; Wyatt snagged us an outdoor deck table, where we shared plenty of laughter over giant plates of pasta and an evening sea breeze. We tabled the eventual relationship talk after we got our fill of dinner and dancing. Dinner is done, but prom awaits us inside the gorgeous set-up of Primrose Point.

When Searidge Hills was founded decades ago, the town's founder lived in a lavish, mansion-like residence. He called the place "Primrose Point" for his beloved wife, Primrose, and the lands served as their home and gardens. Searidge transformed the property into a historical landmark, one rentable for certain gatherings by locals—like this year's prom.

"Ready to head inside?" Wyatt asks. His hand reaches forward to adjust a particularly stubborn curl sticking to my cheek since dinner. And when his fingertips ghost over my bare cheek for an extra second or two, I don't complain. *Goodness, he still looks so dapper in his suit.*

I lace our fingers, extending beyond palm to palm, "Let's do it! I'm sure our friends await our presence."

"Oh, you have no idea," Wyatt chuckles while escorting us toward the front door, where students in suits and dresses move freely. His confident strides stay slow so I can keep up, exactly like Devon described on the bus ride to State, but his hand abandons mine to rest against the small of my back inside. It is a small change, yet the increase of fluttering palpitations against my rib cage doesn't feel small in the slightest. "Half of them were in on it."

"Which ones?" I gasp. Within the first ten minutes of driving, Wyatt had admitted to soliciting help with his plan. Nadia earned half a dozen exclamations in the nearly twenty texts I sent her, half of which were emoji chains and indecipherable keyboard smashes. Now, knowing several more of our friends offered their assistance, it puts the whole speech and debate team's investment in our relationship into perspective again.

"You'll be able to tell. Look for the ones who can't stop

giggling when they see us reach the ballroom," Wyatt remarks, playing so coy while he dodges my answers. Even if I try to coax the answer out of it, it'll be too late. He knows all my tricks and intellectual traps; Wyatt could evade my questions without breaking a sweat, knowing me all too well.

When we reach the doors, he hands Frank and Leon, who guard the entrance, our tickets. Security wraps two golden wristbands around our right wrists before allowing us entry.

Wyatt and I walk through the hallowed halls of Primrose Point, past roped-off doors and the vintage portraits of the family who lived in these four walls. We can't explore much else before the path spits us out into the sprawling backyard, complete with a DJ booth, tables for people to sit with their punch, and a wide dance-floor. The upbeat mix of the newest Lady Gaga and Chappell Roan incites a few dance circles to form across the floor. Other students with dates dance on their own, spinning and shaking under the supervision of teacher chaperones.

The night appears cloudless for a faint sprinkling of stars across the darkened blue and purple skies, so worn they dip into black. I add a few more glittering things to the evening, which catch the gentle luminance of the lengthy strings of old-timey light bulbs.

Wyatt leads me down the stairs, and we slot ourselves into a tiny opening on the dance floor. When Wyatt faces me, he poses his hands in a standard waltz hold; I remember five things from middle school cotillion, and this happens to be one of them. I clasp our hands together, and Wyatt takes the lead again to spin us around the floor.

Dancing may not be one of his strengths, or at least not off the bat, but Wyatt gives it his full effort. We sway more than we move our feet, save for the occasional spin where I duck under his arm or a surprise dip that steals a laugh out of me. Does our dancing match the upbeat energy of the DJ's music choices? Absolutely not.

But the sight of Wyatt smiling wide like the Cheshire Cat while he twirls me around him makes it worth it. *Has anyone told him how beautiful his smile is?*

"Thank you," Wyatt remarks. The tips of my ears burn so hot they must be ruby red. He wasn't supposed to hear that, but oh well. His ego deserves a little pick-me-up after the last few weeks. We maintain our quiet sway amidst the high energy of the dance-floor, bodies close and taking up our little slice of peace without much interference from the outside world.

Eventually, Wyatt's head perks up, and he snickers, "Don't look now, but our friends found us." He nods, and I fight the urge to look over my shoulder. As if Wyatt senses my curiosity, he rotates us around until I spot some of the debate kids—Devon, Andrea, and August.

The three make eye contact with me, throwing thumbs-ups into the air. August pretends to make out with someone, which I assume represents Wyatt and me. Is it obvious to everyone that Wyatt and I kissed... again? I need to work on my tells more.

"We'll link up with them in a bit," I shimmy closer to Wyatt until I can tuck my head against his chest. His arms slip further down, dropping below my waist. He slows our pace to a practical standstill beyond a tiny sway. "Before we get too carried away, I want to apologize for the radio silence the last few weeks. I had been mortified about the kiss, and it forced me to re-evaluate how I felt about you. Nadia and Devon had talked with me before San Fran about my pathetically obvious feelings, which I didn't believe. In hindsight, the signs seem obvious that you and I would be something special from the first day we met."

All of this streams out of me in a polite word vomit, less

anxious than I initially thought I would be. I guess the anxiety doesn't stick when I know Wyatt likes me enough to kiss me back.

"You too, huh? My cousins clocked me first over winter break," Wyatt murmurs. Somehow, *that* becomes the most relieving thing about the entire experience. He *and* I walked through our crushes with blindfolds on, while literally everyone else screamed at us to pay attention. "Glad to see we were equally clueless—or stubborn."

"Or some mixture of both," I add, rather helpfully from the quiet snort Wyatt chokes on. A small inkling of pride flares up to warm the expanse of my chest and knock off any cold from the evening.

"Yeah. And, for the record, I'm sorry too. I know you have your struggles with anxiety, and I should've made more of an effort to reach out to you. I'll admit that I struggled with what to say about how I felt and realized that I'd been denying feelings for a long time. Honestly, I think I fell the first time I saw you glare at Travis." Wyatt's hands hold me steady despite the realization bursting through my thoughts like the old Kool-Aid man commercials.

"He's going to be mad when he finds out I chose the better brother." The mood around us switches when the DJ slows the music down, playing Laufey. Her jazzy serenade brings more couples onto the dance-floor, boxing Wyatt and I closer to the center.

"Eh, he'll get over it," Wyatt jokes. No love lost between us and Travis, who kept his distance these last few weeks, even with Wyatt's presence notably missing. *I hope he forgets all about me before I move to Massachusetts.* "But, back to us, we really dropped the ball in expressing our feelings and talking through things. We're so good at that with debate."

"Unfortunately, we failed to develop shorthand to tell one

another that we've got feelings for one another and don't know how to handle it. The silver lining is that we learned from this experience, and I'm committed to practicing being better at talking about feelings. Would you try with me?"

Wyatt's face brightens at the suggestion. Instead of a nod or some form of "okay," he leans forward until our mouths brush together, savoring the breaths we share before he kisses me in full. *Yeah, still not used to that... like it a lot.*

I grip either side of his face when he adds more depth, angling his mouth over mine. Wyatt hums against my lips, and I swear my legs turn jelly. The rest of the world disappears into nothing as Wyatt's mouth moves with mine. *Careful, he might get me hooked on him before graduation rolls around.*

The kiss lasts for an eternity, or maybe I hope it does. Wyatt kisses me in a secret language, one he mastered in a million different touches throughout the school year, and a gentleness he must've learned from his parents' once-in-a-lifetime love. He somehow unlocked the secret to thawing the walls around my heart.

"Ahem." A pointed voice next to us startles me out of the kiss. Wyatt pulls back, fingers pressed to his mouth, staring to our right. Standing there, Mr. Alvarez adjusts the sleeves of his mauve-colored suit. "Miss Edwards, Mister Keene, please keep all PDA appropriate for a school function."

In our defense, Wyatt and I didn't intend to start making out on the dance-floor. We just... got carried away.

"Yes, sir!" I squeak out. By now, my face must be several shades of red and pink from the number of surprises tonight has in store for me. Wyatt nods, mustering a solemn expression that drops once Mr. Alvarez departs.

Then, he doubles over, chest heaving under his howls of laughter. I don't last long, covering my mouth to muffle the heaving cackles. The moment of sweet, slow music heads out for the night as the DJ throws *Let's Groove* by Earth, Wind & Fire onto the turntable—one of our *favorite* songs from the playlist. More bodies rush to pack the dance-floor, cramming past us and rushing to enjoy the vibe.

"Come on," I roll my eyes at Wyatt. "Let's go find our friends and tell them how their meddling worked." Wyatt follows when I grab his wrist and drag him to search for our friend. He catches up to me within seconds, back in sync at my side where *he belongs.*

XOXO

WALKING along the path to the cliff edge outside Primrose Point, I listen to the distant cheering and screaming of lyrics from off-key students. Prom rages on without us, but Wyatt and I hardly mind. We got our fill of dancing and rightfully earned teasing from the debate team.

Allegedly, someone proposed a betting pool for when Wyatt and I would "figure our stuff out," but too many people vetoed the idea. And get this—they only worried about us finding out about the money before we confessed, *not* about the ethics regarding betting on your peers' love lives.

Any other night, and I might've strangled someone. Wyatt's presence and the otherwise magical night he planned for us smoothed over any annoyance within me. Look at him being a good influence on me. He's the kind of guy you bring home to meet your parents, motorcycle included.

Wyatt veers toward the railing a few inches from the cliff-side, bringing me along with him. We stand among the dark-ened trees where the moon's silvery touch becomes our only light source. He leans against the railing, so I join him, matching his posture and far-away look directed to the sea. He sighs, "I think it's time we talk."

"Yeah. Tonight can't end before that," I agree. "Do you want to take the lead?"

"I want this to be a back-and-forth between us. We like one another, that much is obvious. But I don't want us to be something for the summer, and then, by the time fall rolls around, we will stop being. . . us. What I guess I'm saying—*asking,* actually—is that I want this to be something real. I want you to be my girlfriend." The Wyatt standing before me, delivering the most endearingly awkward love confession possible, shows me a totally different side of him. Vulnerable, unsure, but so eager to be met halfway. Our pool conversation at Wildwood only showed me a fragment of how much hides behind his effortlessly calm demeanor.

Wyatt spent so much time this year as my rock, the anchor holding me down. Now, I get the chance to be the same for him.

"Beth Edwards, girlfriend. Sounds like perfection to me." Although I open with something teasing, I step closer to him until he wraps an arm around me. "I've never been the girl who looks for a summer fling. You have me for as long as you want me. College won't change that."

Wyatt grimaces in time with the crash of the nearby waves. "Many people struggle with long-distance relationships, even strong couples. So, we should figure out how that won't happen to us—"

"—I don't think that'll be an issue. You're at Boston College, and I'm only going to be under an hour away from you at Wellesley." Within seconds, I watch Wyatt's face cycle through several emotions. *Confusion. Shock. Joy.* Nothing prepares me for Wyatt sweeping me clean off my feet into a hug, coaxing his warmth into every pore.

"You're coming with me? To Massachusetts?" He whispers into my hair, sounding like he'll ask me to pinch him so he knows he isn't dreaming—*Wyatt's such a dork.* My face might hurt tomorrow from how much smiling I've done tonight.

"It's you and I, partner. No matter what happens now, this summer, or beyond, you're in my life forever. That's what happens when you become my best friend." I trace a finger over the curve of his jaw. The moonlight bathes his skin in an ethereal glow, softening Wyatt more than I have. His eyes gleam when studying my face, and when the feeling sinks in, he catches my hand.

He grazes his lips over my fingers, then my knuckles. He murmurs something low and unintelligible against the skin. But he winks. "Well, my mom always says that the best kind of love starts with your best friend. Guess we're on the right foot."

"Guess we are. But I think we're friends and so much more." I lace our fingers together for Wyatt to keep kissing. He has no other objection, no rebuttal of "what-if this" or "what happens if that," but neither do I.

Forever doesn't need to be figured out tonight. It's enough to be here with Wyatt—the greatest possible surprise and the best friend I never knew I needed—and open to love. All the arguments in my head quiet when his lips find mine again, pulling me into his orbit until space becomes a foreign concept to me.

Romance wins this round. *I yield.*

Bethany, it was wonderful to have you in my class over the years. You are an immensely talented and brilliant young woman. Your future is so bright. Don't limit yourself to what you think is possible. You should always reach for the impossible. Thank you for being a hopeful sign of what the future holds.
-Mr. Alvarez

WYATT, SENDING YOU ALL THE WELL WISHES ON YOUR ADVENTURES IN BOSTON. DON'T BE A STRANGER! MAKE SURE TO TAKE CARE OF OUR GIRL, OR SHE MIGHT DECIDE TO FINALLY TRY HER HAND AT WORLD DOMINATION!
-DEVON

Wyatt, we only had you for a year and you became one of my favorite people on the team. It was great to get to know you. Good luck with everything and may your life be full of successes.
-August

BETH!
It's going to be so weird next year not seeing you around my campus ;—; It's been great being your teammate on debate for the last four years. You're going to crush it at college- Andrea

The Romance Rebuttal began in 2023 as a true passion project. Ever since I was a teenager myself, I loved young adult books, especially YA romances and romcoms. I'm what people would call a "late bloomer" when it comes to love. While most people had their first romantic experiences in high school, I spent my time focusing on my academics and extracurriculars. The extent of my romantic interest stayed purely in the realm of fiction, explored between the pages of books and extremely long fanfictions I binged at ungodly hours of the night.

Such an academic-heavy focus kept me too busy to feel like I missed out on the quintessential teenager experience. I was the type of student who traded prom and homecoming for staying in at home to read. Thus, the limited scope of my social life revolved around one thing—speech and debate.

Speech and debate changed my life for the better. I had always been an eager, talkative child, the "pleasure to have in class" and "mature for her age" archetype. Bookish with a strong sense of opinions and viciously articulate, I received the expected "you should be a lawyer" comment from every single authority figure I met—which I took seriously. High school rolled around, and I joined the debate team before the school year even started, ready to embrace my "destiny" as a future lawyer.

I wasn't shy or afraid to stand in front of a group of strangers and spout off my opinions. It made me a natural fit for the debate team. Beth and Wyatt represent the type of students who gravitate toward the debate team—strong-willed, intelligent, ambitious. If you asked people on my old debate team, they'd immediately flag me as a "Beth" type. It's a badge of honor I wear because Beth's journey as a character reminds me of my personal growth.

Consequently, all resources and references to debate in this book come from two sources 1) experiences from my debate years and 2) the rule book of the California High School Speech Association. These sources of first-hand knowledge and cold hard rules are the debate I'm the most familiar with, even with other additional governing bodies for the "sport," such as the National Speech and Debate Association. Since the book takes place within California, I focused on California's rules. Therefore, any discrepancies or differences from other states, the national high school debate circuit, or the collegiate debate circuit are accounted for by the virtue of such a narrow lens.

At 24, I realize I'm slipping further away from my high school years. Hell, I'm closer to 30 than I am to 18 these days. I say this to underscore how much time has passed since my teenage years. That daunted me when approaching this project for the first time.

However, I worked overtime to capture the frantic, somewhat dramatic energy that defined my teenage years and distilled it into the story. I sought common experiences—dating, trying to fit in, the whole college acceptance process—as the stage to showcase the heightened emotions of the average teen. At that age, I remember every decision feeling heavy, like disastrous, end-of-the-world consequences might ensue for making the wrong decision. Throw in big things like anxiety and grief, and the average teen would struggle to wrap their head around impending adulthood.

Ultimately, I hope this book's message finds its readers. This book is made for the anxious go-getters who set their sights on big things. This book is for those stuck in the heavy fog of grief and finding their way out. This book is for people who feel out of place in their own families. If you're one of those people reading this very note, then please know you aren't alone.

I see you. I did this for us.

ACKNOWLEDGMENTS

This book marks the start of many new 'firsts' for my writing career—the first YA book I've written, the first "double digit" book, etc. I know such exciting milestones wouldn't be possible without the support of some truly incredible people. I'd like to thank them in no particular order:

A huge shoutout to the newest member of the team: Bobby Jackson, my editor. Bobby and I connected this year while I went on the hunt for a new editor. Immediately, Bobby's style as an editor added a certain *sparkle* into my manuscript, finding how to tread that delicate balance between preserving an author's voice and improving the flow of the manuscript. Her changes managed to better showcase my voice. She provided great feedback and support. I can't emphasize enough how her presence on this story made it the best version of itself—the version you've just read.

Thank you to my amazing alpha/beta reader, Olive, for joining me on another project. She was there for my first book and every subsequent novel since then. She knows me well enough to trek through the scatterbrained first draft I dropped into her lap and found some enjoyment from the story. Her endless squealing about Wyatt and Bethany helped me focus on the endgame of making sure this book made it to publication. Her commentary always made my day whenever I went in to edit the document.

While I designed the cover, I owe a huge shout of appreciation to @agusballester and VP Creative Shop, who designed the front cover art of Beth and Wyatt and the fonts used respectively. All these moving parts came together beautifully in a Canva browser. Not bad for my first time at designing my own cover, huh? Indie authors are super resourceful!

Thank you to my friends and family. Evelyn (who did the interior formatting), LV, Estelle, Aubrey and Hannah. Shanti, my angel baby, and her younger siblings in Salem and Luna also helped tremendously. However, the biggest show of appreciation goes to my mother—who enrolled me in debate back in high school. She paid for every tournament, the nice professional clothes, and plenty of lunches during long tournament hours. I tell her how that investment paid off in my legal career, but it's opening doorways in my creative ventures. This book is a perfect example of that.

Finally, I must acknowledge the final piece that brought all the moving parts into one cohesive novel. Me. I wrote this book from February to late May of this year but outlined it maybe six months beforehand. I had such high hopes for a smooth process, even though I walked head-first into a new genre. Life, however, had other plans for me—throwing curveball after twist after me. Law school and personal commitments took a lot of my time and attention, pushing this onto the back burner for me. I fell a whole month behind schedule and wanted to give up on myself. Instead, I showed up every damn day and wrote until I finished the manuscript, relentless and creatively pushed to the max.

I wrote this book *for me*, the high school version of me who would've rolled her eyes at the cheese but secretly climbed under the covers and devoured every page of Beth and Wyatt's story. This was her story, her moment to savor. And I sure did.

ABOUT THE AUTHOR

Cass Rougeau has lived many lives. Grad student. Author. Cat mom. She relishes all her hats; it must be the Gemini in her that loves being a jack of all trades. When she's not penning her next novel, she can be found either at home with her three cats or enjoying life as a SoCal resident.

She loves bookstore visits and hotpot dinners, crime drama television, FaceTime calls with friends, spending hours scrolling through TikTok edits, and researching niche concepts for academic papers.

Under Cassandra Diviak, Cass has written a total of 10 books (and 1 forthcoming). All these can be found on her Instagram page (@author.cassandradiviak), in major retailers such as Amazon, Barnes and Noble, Kobo, Ingram, or SoCal indie owned bookstores + her personal shop.